P9-DYJ-371

Praise for *Strong Justice*

"Intense, skillfully plotted . . . Events hurtle to an explosively satisfying finale." —*Publishers Weekly* (starred review)

"Readers who enjoy action, gunplay, violence, arch dialogue, and imaginative plotting will thoroughly enjoy Caitlin's adventures. . . . The pages flip swiftly as readers careen toward a satisfying conclusion."
—*Booklist*

"I've always wondered why there isn't an estrogen-driven, sometimes skirt-wearing female competitor to James Bond, Jack Reacher, Mike Hammer, Spenser. . . . Well, now there is, and her name is Caitlin Strong."
—*San Jose Mercury News*

"A fantastic, riveting read. Historical lore and contemporary terrorism are interwoven into this gripping story, but the underlying themes are timeless: honor, valor, and justice." —Sandra Brown,
#1 New York Times bestselling author of
Smash Cut

"Land delivers one of the toughest heroines around, fighting to hold some of the roughest real estate around. Throw in a serial killer, a couple of drug lords, and a handful of deep, dark family secrets, and it'll take some *Strong Justice* indeed." —Lisa Gardner,
#1 New York Times bestselling author of
Love You More

"Land is a pro. He delivers exactly what readers want. *Strong Justice* kicks butt and takes names. Long live Caitlin Strong." —Steve Berry,
New York Times bestselling author of
The Paris Vendetta

"Merges the old and new Wests in an action thriller that hits the bull's-eye dead center. If you like Stephen Hunter's gunfighter books, this one's for you."

—David Morrell,
New York Times bestselling author of
The Shimmer

"From the gripping first page to the pulse-pounding climax, I didn't want to put it down. Texas Ranger Caitlin Strong is a compelling heroine."

—Carla Neggers,
New York Times bestselling author of
The Mist

"Dark and ornery and moody in all the right places. Doing a series is hard. But in *Strong Justice*, Jon Land shows exactly why to do it, digging deeper and deeper into his delicious characters."

—Brad Meltzer,
#1 New York Times bestselling author of
The Book of Lies

"The book is a page-turner, the pace blistering, the characters well-drawn, and the action hot. The plot is timely, exploiting fears of border smuggling, torture, high-tech snooping into private lives, and out-of-control private security companies. Land, a better writer than most who work in the genre, lays the story down in a tight, vivid prose style."

—Associated Press
on *Strong Enough to Die*

OTHER BOOKS BY JON LAND

The Alpha Deception
*Blood Diamonds
*The Blue Widows
The Council of Ten
*Day of the Delphi
*Dead Simple
*Dolphin Key
The Doomsday Spiral
The Eighth Trumpet
*The Fires of Midnight
The Gamma Option
*Hope Mountain
*Keepers of the Gate
*Kingdom of the Seven
Labyrinth
The Last Prophecy
The Lucifer Directive
The Ninth Dominion
The Omega Command
The Omicron Legion
*The Pillars of Solomon
*The Seven Sins: The Tyrant Ascending
*†Strong at the Break
*Strong Enough to Die
The Valhalla Testament
The Vengeance of the Tau
Vortex
*A Walk in the Darkness
*The Walls of Jericho

*Published by Forge Books
†Forthcoming

STRONG JUSTICE

A CAITLIN STRONG NOVEL

Jon Land

A TOM DOHERTY ASSOCIATES BOOK • NEW YORK

NOTE: If you purchased this book without a cover, you should be aware that this book is stolen property. It was reported as "unsold and destroyed" to the publisher, and neither the author nor the publisher has received any payment for this "stripped book."

This is a work of fiction. All of the characters, organizations, and events portrayed in this novel are either products of the author's imagination or are used fictitiously.

STRONG JUSTICE

Copyright © 2010 by Jon Land

All rights reserved.

A Forge Book
Published by Tom Doherty Associates, LLC
175 Fifth Avenue
New York, NY 10010

www.tor-forge.com

Forge® is a registered trademark of Tom Doherty Associates, LLC.

ISBN 978-0-7653-6317-6

First Edition: June 2010
First Mass Market Edition: June 2011

Printed in the United States of America

0 9 8 7 6 5 4 3 2 1

For the Texas Rangers.
"One Riot, One Ranger."
True then. True now.

**Mercy Ridge
Library**

ACKNOWLEDGMENTS

Those who've been with me through the long string of tales that cover twenty-seven years now are used to me using this page to thank those who've either helped me tell them better or made it possible for me to tell them at all. Lots of the usual suspects here, my appreciation stronger with each book for the names you've seen before and will see again.

These aren't great times for the publishing business, but that hasn't slowed the support of the Tor/Forge Books family headed by Tom Doherty and Linda Quinton, dear friends who publish books "the way they should be published," to quote my late agent, the legendary Toni Mendez. Paul Stevens, Patty Garcia, Karen Lovell, Phyllis Azar, and especially Natalia Aponte are there for me at every turn. Natalia's a brilliant editor and friend who outdid herself on this one. Publishing a book is definitely a team sport, and I've certainly got a great one behind me.

An answer to any question, meanwhile, remains only a phone call away thanks to the now retired Emery Pineo, my former junior high science teacher and still the smartest man I know. Thanks also to Mike Blakely, a terrific musician and writer in his own right, for help with all things Texas. Dylan Gregory helped out with some of the gun stuff, and Laura

Aames provided terrific insight into Kilgore, Texas—the model for the town of Sweetwater you're about to encounter.

Speaking of Kilgore, it was the wondrous Sandra Brown who gave birth to that entire subplot featuring Caitlin Strong's grandfather Earl in an e-mail to me a couple years back about the legendary Ranger, Manuel "Lone Wolf" Gonzaullas. Many of you will wonder if the Texas Rangers really did go to war with Al Capone's Outfit out of Chicago in the 1930s. Well, truth be told there's no evidence to say they did, but none to say they didn't either. And since The Outfit never did take up roots in Texas during the oil boom years . . .

Well, you be the judge. But first you'll have to turn the page, prepared to meet some old friends and some new ones as we begin.

P.S. For those interested in more information about the history of the Texas Rangers, and to see where a lot of my info comes from, I recommend *The Texas Rangers* and *Time of the Rangers,* a pair of superb books by a great writer named Mike Cox, also published by Forge.

P.P.S. My website is finally up, and I mean it this time! Don't believe me? Check out www.jonlandbooks.com.

Justice consists not in being neutral between right and wrong, but in finding out the right and upholding it, wherever found, against the wrong.

—TEDDY ROOSEVELT

PROLOGUE

THE RANGER'S PRAYER

O God, whose end is justice
Whose strength is all our stay,
Be near and bless my mission
As I go forth today.
Let wisdom guide my actions,
Let courage fill my heart
And help me, Lord, in every hour
To do a Ranger's part.
Protect when danger threatens,
Sustain when trails are rough;
Help me to keep my standard high
And smile at each rebuff.
When night comes down upon me,
I pray thee, Lord, be nigh,
Whether on lonely scout, or camp,
Under the Texas sky,
Keep me, O God, in life
And when my days shall end,
Forgive my sins and take me in,
For Jesus' sake, Amen.

—Pierre Bernard Hill,
Texas Ranger chaplain

"Smell that?" Texas Ranger captain George W. Arrington asked from the top of the hill he'd pushed his horse up to better search for water.

William Ray Strong sniffed the air, catching an aroma that reminded him of a rank buffalo carcass left to spoil on the range. "Yes, sir, I do. Dead bodies for sure."

"It's coming from the settlement over by that creek bed," Arrington said, eyeing the horse-drawn wagons surrounding a small nesting of tents and tables.

"Pioneers?" William Ray raised.

"This far out? Not likely. You see anybody moving?"

"Not a soul."

"Me neither. You may have caught the Frontier Battalion at the close of its days, son," Arrington said, referring to the combination of Texas Rangers and local militiamen founded to track down the Apache and Comanche making war along Texas's expansive frontier known as the Panhandle. "But it looks like we got ourselves something that needs tending to."

William Ray turned his horse to follow Arrington's stallion back down the hill. The eight-man Texas Ranger detachment William Ray had just joined had been looking for water for most of the day now, an effort that seemed hopeless with nothing but the arid plains before them. But then the ground began to harden underfoot, the nature of the country changing dramatically as they climbed this short hill to find a dry salt lake off in the distance. Arrington told William Ray that in the West Texas desert such lakes often held freshwater in the form of streams or creeks on their western sides.

Arrington lapsed into silence and William Ray rode alongside him all the way to the edge of the camp where the smell thickened until it was all the air seemed to carry. The legendary Ranger captain dismounted and led his company forward with guns drawn.

The first bodies came into view with the buzzards swooping down from all angles to pick at the dead flesh. All but Arrington covered their mouths with bandannas as they approached, the most wizened ones holding their rifles extended.

"No need for that, boys," Arrington told them as he strode into the makeshift settlement, scattering the buzzards. "Whatever happened here's long done."

"Renegades, you figure, Captain?" one of the men asked.

William Ray watched Arrington kneel by one body, move on to another, and then a third before responding. "None I've ever seen. These wounds ain't from arrows or tomahawks and the bodies ain't been stripped. Nope, somebody cut these folks down as they stood."

"Put up a heck of a fight by the look of things," William Ray heard himself say before he could stop himself.

"You see a single defensive posture or rifle in evidence?"

"No."

Stepping over a blood patch, Arrington moved to a wagon and pulled a Winchester from its rear.

"There you have it," he said, tossing William Ray the rifle.

"It's full," William Ray told him, sniffing the barrel. "Ain't even been fired."

"Dozen men, eight women, six children," the company scout, a half-breed who called himself Bear Claw reported. "Whatever happened here happened quick, sometime yesterday by the look of things."

"How long you figure they been here?" Arrington asked him.

"Six, eight weeks at least. Wait out the heat with all the water they needed. Found a map indicates they came from the north."

"Must not've known this was still Injun country," another member of the company said, spitting tobacco.

"This wasn't Indians," Bear Claw said, staring up into the sinking sun as if it might hold the answer. "Wasn't anyone near as I can tell, being that I can't find a single track either coming or going."

"Any idea what that leaves us with exactly?" Arrington asked him.

"*Mishotunga*," Bear Claw muttered.

"In English, please."

"*Mishotunga* means evil spirit in Comanche. It's said that such a spirit haunts the land in these parts, seeking vengeance on those who violate it."

Captain Arrington's expression soured. "Evil spirit, eh?" He found a barrel full of water and dunked his head into it, coming out with his hair twisted into tight gnarls with the texture of twine. "We're gonna bury the bodies, water the horses, and set ourselves up our own defenses," Arrington told his men. "Make sure we're ready when whatever it was that did this comes back."

SAN ANTONIO; 1984

"Another, Grandpa, another story!"

Earl Strong shifted his granddaughter, Caitlin, from his left knee to his right, wincing from the effort. "So which one you want to hear next?"

"Sweetwater!"

"Again?"

"Again! How you cleaned up the town way back when."

Suddenly Earl didn't feel the pain that clung to him almost all the time these days. He might not have looked eighty-five, but mirrors could be terribly deceitful things.

"Way back when, little girl," he chuckled.

"Sweetwater, Grandpa, Sweetwater!"

Earl settled back in the easy chair, eight-year-old Caitlin's head nestled against his chest smelling like the first flowers of spring. He loved telling his old tales of the Texas Rangers, just as his father, William Ray Strong, had done with him.

"All right, little girl," Earl started, "it was like this. By the time I rode the train into that town . . ."

SWEETWATER, EAST TEXAS; 1931

. . . Sweetwater had been struck hard and fast by the oil boom. The poverty resulting from the drought that killed the cotton crops had barely receded when the Great Depression hit. Then black gold stitched a thick swatch of desperate hope across the state of Texas through Ranger, Cisco, Breckenridge, Burkburnett, Eldorado and Amarillo before finally spilling out of the ground in Sweetwater.

Overnight, Sweetwater had swelled from a farming klatch of five hundred to a boomtown of ten thousand wildcatters, speculators, and Depression-starved laborers desperate for work. Cities made of tents instead of lumber sprouted across mud-soaked fields in clear view of the wooden oil derricks climbing for the sky. Before long, these tent cities overflowed onto land both public and private. The most popular place to settle was the courthouse directly across the street from six town businesses, their rear walls sliced away to allow six wells to be sunk into the ground. Canvas flapped where two-by-fours and windows had been just days before.

Constable Hollis Tyree, as close to a lawman as there was in Sweetwater, had to step across sleeping bodies blanketing Courthouse Square's grass every morning on his way to work. The incessant spring rains had turned Sweetwater into a vast mud pit that added to the rancid stench of unwashed men in air already choked with the tarry smell of ground oil. It had been enough to make Tyree gag on more than one occasion, leaving him to wonder if there were somewhere else he'd be better off being.

Tyree was a banker by trade who'd only become constable after drought and the Depression had killed his bank, since the job allowed him to keep the home and stretch of land that had been in the family for generations. But the boom made him severely regret that decision. The crowds and clutter he could handle well enough, along with the constant clanking of the churning derricks that sucked the black gold from wells that littered Sweetwater like giant rabbit holes. With those crowds and clutter, though, came an ornery lot of thieves, prostitutes, gamblers, and gunmen swarming into the town. Hollis Tyree had never seen a more unsavory assortment of humanity, utterly indistinguishable from the oil field workers who became victim to all manner of robbery and scam.

He'd never been trained as a lawman or even carried a gun, leaving him out of sorts and ill-equipped to deal with the complaints from residents and ruffians alike. Watching Sweetwater literally dissolve before his eyes, Tyree finally sloshed across the mud-soaked road into the Western Union telegraph office, its windows boarded up after some gunplay got out of hand.

"Where you want this sent?" Fred Hatchings, the operator, asked him.

"Don't know for sure, since I never had a call to send one like it before," Tyree replied. "Governor's office, I suppose."

"Town's going to hell, Hollis," Hatchings said, beginning to tap his fingers across the telegraph keys.

"True enough, Fred, but it ain't there yet."

A return wire from the office of the governor said to expect help on the noon train on Wednesday, help in the form of none other than the Texas Rangers. Tyree was there to greet the train and stood anxiously on the depot's plank platform, eyeing the few men who disembarked. Not one wore the cinco pesos badge or Stetson of the Rangers. He lingered, hoping against hope that the saviors of Sweetwater would emerge last. But the last man off was as scruffy and unshaven as all the rest, though Tyree sensed something different about the stranger when he passed. Something about the way he carried himself, enough to make Tyree suspect he was some kind of regulator or professional gun hired by speculators to police their fields. Instead of things getting better with the coming of the noon train, they may have gotten appreciably worse.

Tyree was making his rounds Friday night when a chair tossed through a window drew his attention to the local saloon that had been bought out for a song by a greedy land baron. He entered to find a man being beaten with a splintered chair leg.

Tyree drew his nightstick. "That'll be enough there," he said, as bravely as he could manage.

"Says who?" demanded the big man holding the chair leg.

Tyree made sure his constable badge was in plain view. "The law."

A hefty portion of the saloon broke out into spontaneous laughter.

"The law got a name?" the big man asked, still grasping the chair leg.

Tyree saw how the squared-off top section had splintered and gulped down some air. "Constable Hollis Tyree."

The big man dropped the chair leg and brushed back his jacket to reveal the gun holstered on his hip. "Well, we caught this dung heap here cheating at cards and done deputized ourselves to dispense justice. Sound fair to you, Constable Tyree?"

"I'm afraid it don't."

The big man took a step closer to him. "Pardon my rudeness. The name's Rawlins, Jack Rawlins."

Tyree felt the breath bottleneck in his throat; a collective gasp coursed through the saloon.

"Guess you've heard of me," continued Rawlins.

"Heard of a gunman went by the name Fast Jack Rawlins some years back."

Rawlins tipped his cap. "That'd be me, Constable. Pleased to make your acquaintance." He grinned, before his face hardened into a sneer. "Now be on your way and let us handle this."

Tyree held his ground, trapped between thoughts and intentions. If he walked out of the bar now, he might as well keep walking until Sweetwater was behind him. If he stayed, they'd likely be carrying him out instead. He'd heard lots of stories about what the old west in these parts had been like. Just never figured he'd be living in it.

"Look here, sir," Tyree started, finding his voice and then losing it again when the clack of boot steps across the floor froze him.

He watched the tight crowd part to allow a man to sift through, Tyree recognizing him as the stranger who'd been last off the noon train on Wednesday. But he looked taller, his shoulders straight instead of hunched, his dark eyes filled with the kind of menace Tyree wondered if he'd misinterpreted on first glance.

The stranger stopped twenty feet from Tyree, leaving Jack Rawlins centered between them.

"You're under arrest, Jack," he said.

"Says who?" Rawlins sneered.

As the entire bar watched, the stranger pushed back both sides of his great coat to reveal a pair of pearl-handled revolvers holstered on either hip and a dull badge pinned to his vest.

"Texas Rangers in general. Ranger Earl Strong, Company D, in particular."

Another gasp rose through the crowd, as whispers were exchanged.

The sneer slipped from Jack Rawlins's expression, replaced by nothing at all.

"Guess you heard of me," Earl said. "Now listen to me, Fast Jack, you got a couple of choices here, some that'll get you dead and some that won't. You think you're good enough to take me on, let's have at it. Otherwise, slip your gun out and drop it to the floor. There ain't no third option, by the way."

The moment froze, nobody in the bar moving an inch. Tyree used the time to study Earl Strong's face—leathery, yet surprisingly young. The dispatches and magazine articles that followed his many famed exploits pegged his age in the early thirties, though his gravelly voice and harsh, dark eyes suggested a man of considerably more years or, perhaps, no measurable age at all. Earl "Strong-as-they-come," as some called him, was thinner and lankier than in his pictures, the muscles wrapped over his frame sinewy and lithe. His narrow waist exaggerated the breadth of his shoulders and at that moment those shoulders looked preternaturally broad.

Hollis Tyree watched Jack Rawlins smirk and shrug.

"Guess we got no call for violence between us," he said, lifting his pistol slowly from its holster.

"No, Jack, we don't." Then, once Rawlins's gun was deposited on the floor, "And that goes for the rest of you too. Pistols out and on the floor before you for Constable Tyree to confiscate and inventory."

Earl Strong turned back to the assembled mass that had frozen in place, letting his eyes hold briefly on Jack Rawlins.

"On behalf of the governor of the state of Texas, I

am hereby declaring martial law. That means no whoring, no fighting, and no gun carrying inside town limits." He ran his gaze about the faces before him, stopping on a boy wearing an apron and leaning against a broom. "What's your name, son?"

"It's Bobby Parsons, Ranger, sir."

"Earl'll do well enough, son. Now stow that broom somewhere and help Constable Tyree collect the firearms." Then, to the assembled crowd, " 'Less anybody wants to voice a complaint about that, of course."

No one did.

"Good enough." Earl nodded, walking amid them. "I got a prisoner in custody now and I'll get another two thousand if that's what it takes to keep Sweetwater safe for those who came here to pursue a living and respect the law. I am that law here and I don't fancy much whether you respect me or not." Earl continued to circle about the crowd, ending up by the front door. "Just toe the line I give you and we'll get along just fine regardless. But know there ain't no compromise to my words and anyone who crosses them best be prepared to explain his reasoning to the devil," he said backpedaling. "Now I got business elsewhere to attend to, so please hand your sidearms over to the constable and the boy, and don't make them call me back here on your account. Pleasure meeting y'all," Earl finished, sticking a big cigar into his mouth just before . . .

SAN ANTONIO; 1984

". . . the door closed behind me. Next thing I knew . . ."

"Why'd you stop, Grandpa?" Caitlin asked, nestled up to his chest.

"Time to go to sleep, little girl," Earl said pushing himself up out of the chair, holding his granddaughter against him.

"But we didn't get to my favorite part!"

"Doesn't change the hour. And your daddy be plenty riled if he found out I let you stay up this long."

"I won't tell."

"Good thing for both of us, little girl. Now let's get you off to sleep."

Caitlin fidgeted. "What about the rest of the story?"

"We'll pick things up tomorrow. Story's as done as it's gonna get tonight."

"Can we go shooting tomorrow too?"

"Which gun?"

"The Colt. And maybe the 1911 model .45."

Earl would stand behind Caitlin, cupping her hands in his to steady them when she fired. Showing her how to work the gun's kick, to squeeze the trigger instead of pull it.

"Sure thing," he said, carrying her to her room. His arms ached from the effort, his creaky knees threatening to give way. He'd been feeling old lately, damn old. Best thing he had was these babysittings while his Ranger son, Jim, was out doing pretty much the same thing he had for over forty years.

Earl laid Caitlin down in her bed and pulled the covers up to her chest. "We gonna finish the story tomorrow?"

"Absolutely, little girl," Earl lied, knowing he never would; not the parts Caitlin didn't need to hear anyway, the parts he'd never told a single soul. "But only if you close your eyes and get some sleep."

"Grandpa?"

"Yes, little girl?"

"Someday I'm gonna be a Texas Ranger, just like you and my daddy."

"And a damn fine one you'll make, better than either of us."

"You really mean that?"

"Cross my heart," said Earl Strong.

"And hope to die?"

"I could say that, little girl, but it'd be a lie for sure. Nobody hopes to die, least of all a Ranger."

"Nobody messes with the Rangers, do they, Grandpa?"

"Well, truth be told, some do, little girl," Earl told Caitlin. "But they always live to regret it, those that live anyway."

PART ONE

The character of the Texas Ranger is now well known to both friend and foe. As a mounted soldier he has had no counterpart in any age or country. Neither Cavalries nor Cossack, Mameluke nor Moss-trooper are like him; and yet, in some respects, he resembles them all. Chivalrous, bold and impetuous in action, he is wary and calculating, always impatient of restraint, and sometimes unscrupulous and unmerciful. He is ununiformed, and undrilled, and performs his active duties thoroughly, but with little regard to order or system.

—Luther Giddings, *Sketches of the Campaign in Northern Mexico, 1853*

I

Caitlin Strong approached the police command post set up behind the ring of squad cars bearing the markings of both the El Paso Sheriff's Department and Texas Highway Patrol. The cars formed a makeshift perimeter, essentially barricading the city's Thomason Hospital. Above, clouds raced across the sky, leaving the sun to come and go over the scene.

El Paso's sheriff Bo Reems and Captain Rafael Mercal of the highway patrol saw her coming at the same time, sharing a glance that dissolved into a sneer.

"Took your sweet time getting here," Mercal said between lips now pursed into a scowl.

"Rangers covering the area been sent to watch the border," Caitlin told him.

The blazing sun slid out from beneath the clouds again and she studied herself briefly in the reflection off Mercal's mirrored sunglasses. Free of her Stetson, her black, wavy hair tumbled past her shoulders, evidence of a broken promise to herself for weeks now to cut it. Her skin was naturally tan and unblemished, save for the scar left on her cheek a year before when a Mexican drug lord had bitten down in a fight that had left him dead. At first glance her dark-blue eyes seemed too big for her face. But Caitlin had learned from her grandfather how to hold them wide enough to see things people would never have thought she could, like the sheriff's deputies snickering and whispering just out of earshot.

"You boys wanna join us up here?" she asked them and, embarrassed, the deputies quickly turned away.

Caitlin felt a sudden breeze kick stray patches of her hair across her face. "Austin figured watching the border was more important under the circumstances," she said, brushing the hair aside, her back to the snickering deputies now.

"Austin," Sheriff Reems started, "didn't need to send nobody here at all."

"Procedure, Sheriff."

"More like bullshit, if you ask me."

"I didn't," Caitlin said and swept her gaze about the ring of officers watching the cordoned-off access road, wielding shotguns and M16s as if they expected an attack any moment. "Looks like you're fixed to fight a full-scale war."

"These drug cartels out of Juárez want to get somebody, no border's gonna stop them," said Mercal. "No Ranger either."

Mercal had been an all-conference defensive end for the University of Texas. His record for tackles had stood for some time and he would have gone pro if not for tearing up his knee in the Cotton Bowl. Caitlin noticed him grimacing now, but not from the pain, she thought.

"Sandoval?" she asked, referring to Fernando Lozano Sandoval, a commander with the Chihuahua State Investigations Agency who'd survived an assassination attempt and was being treated inside.

"Mexican gangsters cut through six of his guards

that were fronting the building and four more inside," Sheriff Reems answered. In stark contrast to Mercal, he looked as wide as he did tall. One of Reems's officers had once told Caitlin that the sheriff had never once left the state of Texas. He breathed noisily through his mouth and she could never recall a time when the underarms of his khaki uniform shirts weren't darkened by sweat, today being no exception.

"They killed a bunch of bad guys in the process," added Mercal, turning his gaze back on the building. "But the rest took Sandoval hostage in the intensive care wing."

"How many bad guys left?"

"We got no eyes inside the building to tell us. Best guess is three or four of the original dozen come to finish the job on Sandoval that started in an ambush on the other side of the border in Juárez. This being the only level-one trauma center for three hundred miles, he got brought here."

Caitlin joined Mercal's gaze on the hospital, holding her eyes on a third-floor bank of windows. "Snipers?"

"Four of them," Mercal added, "best I've got. But the Mexicans left inside know enough to stay clear of the glass. SWAT team on site and ready to go."

"But no communication with anyone inside."

"Not a peep," said Sheriff Reems. He pulled a wad of tobacco from his cheek and tossed it to the ground. "We been calling every phone on the wing and used the bullhorn to tell them to call us." He shook his head, his bulbous jowls flapping like twin bowls of Jell-O. "Nothing."

Caitlin dug a finger into her hair. "You mind if I try something?"

"Matter of fact, I do," Mercal said, spine straightening to give him back the height that was mostly a memory. "Austin says we gotta have a resident Ranger, that's fine. They don't say we need to let you involve yourself in our affairs."

Caitlin returned her gaze to the windows. "People in that intensive care wing might feel otherwise. And you been at this too long already for it to end any way but bad."

Mercal exchanged another glance with Reems, whose cheeks puckered as if he were readying to spit the tobacco he'd already discarded.

"I'm offering you cover here, Captain," Caitlin resumed, paying deference to the man in charge while ignoring the sheriff. "Things end bad, it'll fall on the Rangers."

"What exactly is it you're fixing to do, Ranger?"

Caitlin pulled the SIG Sauer from her holster and handed it to him.

"You'll know soon enough, Captain."

Holster empty and Stetson back in place, Caitlin stretched her hands into the air and walked straight for the hospital's main entrance, feeling the gazes of the deputies and highway patrolmen following her the whole way. But it was something else she felt even stronger coming from the third floor: the eyes of other men upon her, likely perched behind some wall cover where a glimpse was all they could grab unless they decided to expose themselves to a shot.

Caitlin passed members of the SWAT team camouflaged by the bushes set in a small strip garden just before the glass doors, but didn't acknowledge them for fear of alerting the men watching from the third-floor windows to their presence. She walked slowly through the glass doors and then straight to the elevator, doing everything possible not to conceal her presence.

Inside the cab, she tightened her Stetson over her hair so it rode lower on her forehead and pressed 3, then stood right in front of the doors with hands raised again as the door slid open.

A pair of wide-eyed gunmen sweating in the air-conditioned hall greeted her, holding Heckler & Koch submachine guns—expensive hardware for simple drug gang members.

"Acuéstese en el piso!" said one with a deep scar that looked like an exclamation point down the right side of his face. "Down on the floor!"

Caitlin lay facedown on the tile just beyond the elevator.

"El Rinche," Scar spit out.

He checked to make sure the elevator cab was empty while the other gunman patted her down roughly through her jeans and denim shirt, paying special attention to her boots to make sure no pistol was holstered to her ankle.

"¡Levántate! Get up!"

Caitlin rose, hands back in the air.

"¿Qué te quieres?"

"I want to make your lives easier, that's what I'm doing here," Caitlin said in Spanish. Then, when her remark produced only a confused stare from Scar, "I'm gonna take the place of those kids over there." She gestured toward a pair of boys and a girl trembling so hard beneath their bedcovers their IV lines were jiggling. "Means you can let them go."

Caitlin could see eight other beds occupied, all set against the windows with only terrified faces visible above the bedcovers, one of which belonged to Fernando Lozano Sandoval. A third gunman stood against the wall nearest the windows while a fourth man, the youngest of the bunch, sat in a growing pool of blood with his shoulders propped by an empty bed, bleeding from both leg and shoulder wounds.

Caitlin's gaze met Sandoval's briefly before moving on to a pair of children a few beds down. Arms still raised, she started slowly forward, sliding between Scar and the other gunman.

"¡Para te! Stop!"

"You're in better shape than you think," she told him, her gait purposely deliberate. "Once we get the kids out, I'm gonna talk you through walking out of this as protected witnesses in the service of Mexico instead of perps. Right, Mr. Sandoval?"

The man from the Chihuahua State Investigations Agency nodded fearfully, looking like a disembodied head resting atop the pillows.

"I'll shoot you, el Rinche!" Scar threatened.

"Do that and I won't be able to help you and your wounded young friend down there. Two of you look alike. You brothers or something?"

She reached a young boy's bed and laid her Stetson down atop the bedcovers. "Let's get you ready to move," she said as reassuringly as she could manage to him.

Caitlin began to unhook the monitoring machines. She heard Scar yelling at her, glimpsed the third gunman lurch away from his perch against the wall.

"No!" Scar screamed at him too late.

The first sniper bullet caught him in the face, the

second in his throat, resulting in twin plumes of blood splattering over Caitlin and the bedcovers. She felt the sting of splintered bone smack her cheeks, as she dug a hand into her Stetson and yanked out the .40 caliber pistol she'd taped under the dome.

She saw Scar twist his submachine gun on her, finger finding the trigger an instant after Caitlin jerked hers twice. She put two bullets into his chest, and he dropped like an oak tree, getting off a single wild spray that found nothing but wall.

Caitlin felt the hiss of a bullet surge past her ear and swung toward the final standing gunman, dropping into a crouch. She registered the pistol trembling in his hand as she shot him dead center in the forehead.

He fell at the feet of the wounded man, more of a boy really, who was fumbling a pistol into his off hand. Caitlin could still feel the surge of adrenaline rushing through her, electricity dancing along the surface of her skin, turning her nerve endings raw. Instinct took over before thought could intervene. She'd shot the wounded kid three times before she even felt the pistol reheating in her grasp, muzzle flashes flaring like shooting stars she used to wish on as a little girl.

The blare of the gunshots deafened her to the screams and sobs of the hostages, all safe and alive, as Caitlin turned toward the window, raised her arms, and waved them to signal Captain Mercal and Sheriff Reems that it was over.

"You Rangers sure know how to make a mess," Mercal told her, huge beads of sweat still dappling his face.

He and Caitlin watched the body of the last gunman being carted away.

"Gotta make a mess sometimes to get things cleaned up," Caitlin said.

Mercal swiped a forearm across his brow, leaving a patchy wet streak upon his sleeve. "Well, you got the biggest set of balls I ever seen, woman or not."

"Stop, please," Fernando Lozano Sandoval told the orderlies wheeling his bed from the room when they reached Caitlin. "I know who you are, *señorita*."

"You can thank me later, sir."

Sandoval's expression wrinkled in displeasure. "I would rather thank you now. Many in Mexico know of you. They believe it would be better if you stayed out of our country."

"It's out of my jurisdiction anyway, Mr. Sandoval."

"I'm talking about your most recent investigation into missing Mexican girls."

Caitlin felt heat building behind her cheeks. "You mean the ones being sold as sex slaves?"

"These are dangerous men, Ranger."

"I thought we were talking about the girls."

"You saved my life. I'm trying to return the favor. You do not want these men as your enemies."

"If they're bringing kidnapped children across the border, they're already my enemies. Why don't you just tell me where to find them?"

"You want to die that much?"

"Funny how you didn't ask me that when I was gunning down your captors. I'm starting to think I've been looking in the wrong place, Mr. Sandoval. Instead of warning me off, just point me in the right direction. Do that, sir, and we'll call it even."

Sandoval looked around him, picturing a different outcome. "Nuevo Laredo," he said finally.

"That where I'm going to find what I'm looking for?"

"Only if you're *loco* enough to try." Sandoval's gaze recovered its focus as quickly as it slipped away. "The men you are looking for have much of Mexico in their pockets."

Caitlin backed away from Sandoval's bed, so the orderlies could slide him on again. "Then I guess it's a good thing I'm from Texas."

2

ALBION, TEXAS; THE PRESENT

Like all fourth-grade teachers, Faye Magruder hated rainy days. A bunch of nine-year-olds being cooped up inside for recess was a recipe for disaster if ever there was one. In the late spring, when it grew especially hot, she'd conduct her class outside beneath the thick canopy of a cottonwood tree. It got so her students prayed for the heat it would take to move their studies outside and, for her part, Faye Magruder didn't blame them. She'd spent her whole life in the southwest Texas she loved in spite of the droughts, stifling heat, and crazy storms that turned the air thick with ozone. She'd done plenty of traveling in her time and it was always the smells she missed the most. Other places smelled fake and unnatural to her. The smells of Texas, especially this close to the desert, had likely been the same since the Ice Age had shifted the continents about.

But lately things had been smelling funny to her,

enough so that she'd seen the doctor, who quizzed her about allergies and colds and inquired whether she'd been using any different cosmetics that may have affected her olfactory senses.

Faye Magruder told him she hadn't changed her cosmetics in fifteen years, even stopped using them altogether after her husband was killed by an IED in Iraq and she'd buried her favorite perfume with him in the ground. Anyway, cosmetics couldn't explain the pounding headaches that had been racking her as of late. She'd never suffered from migraines, but imagined this must have been what they felt like. They were at their worst in school, especially bad by the end of the day.

And having her young charges stuck inside while hailstones pounded the classroom windows wasn't helping things either. The kids were wild and unruly and Faye Magruder was willing the day to end when Molly Beaumont approached her desk holding a pair of scissors and a cutout floral design she'd traced herself.

"Now, what have we here?" Magruder said, spreading the floral design out before her.

She never noticed the little girl raise the pair of scissors she was still holding, much less see them come down. Not until the blades had pierced the back of her hand and dug deep did she realize something had gone terribly wrong—and then only because her hand was literally stuck to the desk by the scissors that had dug into the wood beneath it.

She felt her ears bubble and it took a moment for her to realize it was her own scream doing it, as little Molly Beaumont looked on, giggling with glee.

3

"You understand why I asked you to meet me here, Meeks?" Hollis Tyree III said to the man keeping pace with him down Main Street of Sweetwater, Texas.

"No, sir, I don't."

"That's right, you haven't been with me long enough. I walk like I own the town, don't I?"

Meeks remained silent.

"That's because I do pretty much, the real estate anyway. This is home, Meeks, where it all began, where I come when things need sorting out and I need to be left alone." Tyree gazed about almost whimsically. "Only place people just let me be, besides a friendly hello. You see, my grandfather was constable of this town when the oil boom hit. To hear him tell it, it was the most lawless time imaginable. But he stuck it out and a good thing too, since the biggest strike of all was found smack dab on his two-hundred-acre spread. Birth of the Tyree family fortune. Now it's the only place in the world I can walk around like normal without a parade of bodyguards and business suits following me."

"You do have me, sir," the man walking at Hollis Tyree's side said. At six-foot-two they were the same height, but Meeks was by far the broader. He kept his hair somewhere between short and long, a man neither comfortable with his military background nor able to embrace the civilian lifestyle that had replaced it. His face had an unfinished quality about it, ridged and angular as if a sculptor had fashioned the broad strokes but never got around to adding the detail work. The result was pocks and gaps like a natural rock formation where flesh should have been. Some of it was scarring, some of it wasn't, and even Meeks himself couldn't tell which was which.

Hollis Tyree, on the other hand, had the rawboned, sunburned features of the derrick workers and riggers who'd flooded Sweetwater over eighty years before. He looked like a man who was comfortable in the field because he'd been there from land to sea and had the scars and pain to prove it. Like his grandfather and father, Tyree had learned the oil business from the bottom up, standing side by side with laborers whose yearly salary he now made in a nanosecond.

"You like working for me, Meeks?"

"I do, sir. You speak your mind, make it clear what it is you want accomplished on your behalf."

Tyree nodded and stopped suddenly, Meeks gliding to a halt by his side. "Over there, across the street," he said, gesturing toward a chain drug outlet, video franchise, and local bookstore. "There used to be a dozen derricks. They knocked out the backs of buildings to drill them. They're all gone now, not a single one left. I figure we should have left at least one rig standing to remind this town of its heritage."

Meeks gave Tyree his space, let him continue without interrupting.

"My favorite place in the world is still my grandfather's spread. Been in the family since his grandfather came to Texas after the revolution. He had to defend it from Indians more than once, Comanche streaming across the plains like a storm the way he told it. You've got history in these parts too, don't you, Meeks?"

"My ancestors were Pinkerton men come west for entirely different reasons, sir."

"They worked for Hearst I seem to recall."

"They did."

"Killed some men in his employ, I imagine."

"First for gold. The oil came later. Military men like me before they signed on as Pinkertons."

Hollis Tyree swung away from the spot where oil derricks had once spiraled upward while ravaging the earth. "Tell me about Albion, Meeks."

"A half dozen incidents now, the latest being this teacher who nearly lost a hand to a nine-year-old wielding scissors."

Tyree's face wrinkled in revulsion. "No connection found yet."

"None that my people have been able to detect. Just an elected sheriff and his deputies handling things. Easily contained." He paused, holding Tyree's stare. "For now."

Tyree's gaze swept over the main drag of Sweetwater, imagining it choked in mud and men in the time of his grandfather. "You have children, Meeks?"

"They live with their mother."

Tyree's hands clenched into fists. "I had two, a son and a daughter, both in college. They went to Mexico on spring break two years ago and disappeared. Just dropped off the face of the earth, along with a couple of their friends. I spent the first week waiting for the ransom call and the last two years still praying it'll come. So here I am with all the money in the world to buy their lives back and nobody gives me the chance." Tyree's eyes misted up, his sagging shoulders shrinking their breadth and making him look suddenly frail. "I never told you this before?"

"I read about it, Mr. Tyree."

"Here's something you didn't read. I sent an army of investigators down there and paid off enough government officials to start my own country." Tyree shook his head, slowly with no emotion in his gaze. "Nothing. Not a single shred of evidence linking the disappearance of my kids to anyone. I haven't stopped looking, I'll never stop looking."

"I've got some contacts down there myself, sir. Glad to use them if you'd like me to."

"Of all the things you could do on my behalf, that'd be the most important. I'm looking at the end of the line for my family name. I spent the first two months my kids were gone moping. What brought me back was knowing I had to find something to put myself into. Something worthwhile that could make me something other than money. That's what we're doing in Tunga County is all about. And now you're telling me it might be going to hell too." He paused. "Albion's about the same size as Sweetwater, isn't it?"

"Give or take a thousand, I guess so."

Hollis Tyree's eyes roamed the center of town again, seeming to cast his gaze well beyond it. "A lot of people."

"Everything's relative, Mr. Tyree."

"I suppose it is."

4

Caitlin entered San Antonio's Central Police Substation with her Stetson held by her side, the haircut she'd been promising herself put off yet again. The clerk behind the glass reception counter, a pudgy middle-aged Latino with black hair dye leaking onto his temples, regarded her and the Texas Ranger badge pinned to her denim shirt and rose almost reverently. The building's air-conditioning was fighting a losing battle with the ninety-degree temperatures outside, accounting for the sweat that had begun to bleed the combed-in color from the clerk's hair.

"Caitlin Strong for Captain Alonzo. I'm here about Dylan Torres."

The clerk's gaze remained fixed upon her, lingering on her breasts. Caitlin's stomach was flat, her arms and shoulders well muscled from all the riding she'd done as a little girl and gym time later. She'd taken up boxing more recently, found it to be the perfect workout for keeping her body toned and her mind off things she was trying to put aside.

"Sure thing, Ranger," the clerk said. "It's a pleasure to make your acquaintance."

"Likewise," Caitlin started, brushing some stray hair from her face as she read the clerk's nametag, "Officer Ortega."

"The captain's expecting you," Ortega said, lifting a phone to his ear. "I'll tell her you're here."

"Thank you."

"Sorry to bother you with this, Ranger."

"No need to apologize, and I appreciate the call."

Ortega still had the phone pressed against his ear. Caitlin hadn't seen him hit a number yet.

"Is it true what they say about that town down in Mexico back last year?"

"Don't know. They say lots of things."

"That a hundred men died in the gunfight."

"I didn't stop to count, Officer."

"Casa del Diablo—something like that."

"The House of the Devil," Caitlin acknowledged, her gaze lowering to remind Ortega about the phone.

Ortega pressed a key and spoke quickly before replacing the receiver. "Captain Alonzo is waiting for you. Fourth office down on the right. I'll buzz you in."

Caitlin heard the buzz followed by the click of the security door snapping electronically open. She grabbed the latch and started to pull, turning back toward the clerk.

"It wasn't a hundred men at all," she told Ortega, whose face drooped in disappointment. "It was ninety-five," Caitlin followed with a wink.

Captain Consuelo Alonzo greeted Caitlin with a cursory handshake, as cold and impersonal as it got. The substation commander's office was plain and neatly furnished with the modern amenities the building's relatively recent construction allowed. Alonzo didn't smile and closed her office door after ushering Caitlin inside. She was a stocky, muscular woman who wore her hair up in a bun that would fit neatly under her cap. A Hispanic whose features looked more Indian than European.

"I want you to know that this is all by the book,"

she said, settling back into her desk chair. "The boy had a phone call coming to him and he chose to call you."

Caitlin took one of the two chairs set before the desk. She noticed the wall behind it was lined with professionally mounted citations and awards. "I understand, Captain."

"I want no suggestion of favored treatment here because you're a Ranger."

"I appreciate that."

"We'll release the boy to you under his own recognizance, which is standard protocol."

Caitlin waited for Alonzo to continue, spoke only when she didn't. "You mind telling me what charge he was arrested on?"

"You mind telling me how you know him?"

"Through his father."

"That'd be Cort Wesley Masters?"

"With all due respect, Captain, I suspect you already know the answer to that question."

"I just find myself curious as to why a Texas Ranger would be bailing out the son of the most famous outlaw in modern Texas history."

"I'm not bailing him out at all, ma'am. The boy's being released on his own recognizance, like you said."

Caitlin watched the veins riding Alonzo's temples bulge a bit. "We got him in here on drug dealing charges."

"Was he holding when your officers picked him up?"

"Are they ever?"

Caitlin leaned forward, her holstered SIG Sauer seeming to keep pace with her right hand. "Excuse me, ma'am, but just who are 'they'?"

Alonzo's spine stiffened in her chair. "A patrol car

spotted him in East San Antonio during school hours. When the officer drove toward him, he ran."

"You ask him why?"

"That officer did and then one of my detectives once the boy was brought in. He wouldn't talk to either of them. Said he wanted his one phone call instead. Well-schooled, Ranger."

"By which you mean . . ."

"Do the math."

"Like you arresting a boy on drug charges who's not holding and then keeping him in custody on account of his father. That's how it adds up to me."

Alonzo stuck her chest out, forcing the flabby stomach straining the folds of her uniform over her belt. "He was with a girl," she said after a pause. "She ran too, managed to get away."

"You ask him who she was?"

"Only thing he told us was his name and address. I thought I told you that already."

"I'm sorry, ma'am."

Alonzo's stare grabbed hold of Caitlin and wouldn't let go. "Cort Wesley Masters is a killer."

"We were talking about his son, Captain."

"Son of a man everyone knows you've been cavorting with."

"My personal life an issue here?"

"Not at all."

"Then I'd appreciate you not raising it. Keep things professional."

"Keeping time with a man like Masters can't help but affect your profession, if you don't mind me saying, Ranger."

"Actually, Captain, I do mind."

Alonzo's expression wavered as she tried to form

her next thoughts into words. "I'm not gonna ask you what really happened in Mexico, or how many people you and Masters killed down there. I'm not gonna ask you about him shooting up a bar and leaving a pair of dead bodies behind a day or so after he was released from prison on a case the Rangers botched. I'm just gonna tell you that the only thing stopping me from hauling Masters's sorry ass in here to retrieve his devil spawn offspring was the mention of your name. That kind of courtesy to a fellow law enforcement officer trumps all else, regardless of my personal feelings."

"I appreciate the consideration, Captain," Caitlin said, rising from her chair. The heat she'd felt building behind her cheeks began to recede, the slight twitching in her fingers stilled with the level of common ground between her and Alonzo holding for now.

Alonzo rose too, straightening her gun belt. "Truth is, I truly admire you having the guts to go after whoever's behind the kidnapping of these young Mexican girls who end up enslaved as prostitutes."

"So far I haven't done all that much," Caitlin said, thinking back to Sandoval's lead about Nuevo Laredo, wondering again what he'd left out in their brief conversation, "except arrest a few of the drivers bringing the girls into Texas."

"You made sure the girls they were carrying got home safe too. I got nieces back over the border. Makes me sick thinking of them being victimized like that."

"Not if I can help it, ma'am."

Alonzo looked as if she were waiting for Caitlin to say more, seeming disappointed when she didn't. "Well, anything this department can do to help you out, just let us know."

Caitlin started for the door, stopping to look back

at Alonzo before she got there. "One thing, Captain. Releasing a minor on his own recognizance isn't standard protocol at all."

"Must've slipped my mind," Alonzo told her.

5

Caitlin stood waiting back in the reception area while one of Captain Alonzo's sergeants escorted Dylan through a door leading up from the holding cells. It had been six weeks since she'd last seen him and he already looked older, dressed in baggy jeans with white shirt hung outside the waistband over well-worn sneakers. Caitlin wondered if he ever wore the cowboy boots she'd gotten him for his fifteenth birthday at Allens Boots in Austin four months ago, but decided not to ask. Too busy feeling guilty over having not been around for so long. She knew there'd be hurt lurking in the boy's dark, deep-set eyes if the kind of dread fear that comes with an arrest hadn't swallowed up everything else.

His escort retrieved Dylan's belt, wallet, and shoelaces from the duty officer and handed them back before leading the boy the rest of the way to the entry door that opened with its distinctive click. Dylan passed through and let the door close behind him, tossing the black wavy hair from his face with a shake of his head.

"Let's get you out of here," Caitlin said.

The boy brushed the black hair back over his shoulders and followed her out the door. "You gonna tell my dad?" he asked her, threading the belt through the loops of his jeans.

"Once he finds out, I don't know which one of us he's gonna kill first," Caitlin said when they were inside her SUV.

Dylan's eyes remained fixed out the window as Caitlin pulled out of the parking lot.

"Anything you got to say on that subject?"

"Thank you."

"Just thank you?"

"Thank you, *ma'am*."

Caitlin studied the road just long enough to realize she couldn't just sit quiet. "Captain told me you were picked up on drug charges."

"You believe him?"

"It's a her, and not for one damn minute."

Dylan finally looked toward her. "Thanks for that too." He reached over to the console and turned the air-conditioning higher. "I'm still hot from that cell. Was like being stuck in a box with holes cut in the sides. Now I know how a trapped rabbit feels."

"Let that be a lesson to you." Caitlin glanced at him across the seat.

"Where you been anyway?"

"You trying to change the subject?"

"Just asking you a question."

"I think it's my time to do the asking," Caitlin said, as much to avoid answering Dylan's question as anything. "What was it you wouldn't tell the police about what brought you to the east side of town?"

"That's for me to deal with."

" 'Til I got dragged into this, you mean. Sorry, son, but it's not so easy to drag myself back out."

The boy stiffened, his dark eyes taking on the familiar harshness of his father's. "Don't call me son. You're not my mother."

"No, I'm not. And my guess is whatever it is you're holding inside, you wouldn't tell her either. Doesn't exactly help us figure what to tell your dad, though, does it?"

"Why we have to tell him anything?"

"Because I'd expect the same. Discussion might come easier if I could help you make sense of it for him."

Dylan huffed out his breath, started playing with the buttons on his shirt. "He's away, down in New Orleans. On business."

"He said that?"

"Far as I remember. I didn't have anyone else to call."

Caitlin made sure he could see her smile. "I'm kind of glad for that."

"You haven't been coming around as much. My brother misses you."

"Does he now?"

"He smiles more when you're around. Only time pretty much."

Caitlin felt something heavy settle in her throat. "You taking care of Luke while your dad's away?"

"That's right."

"Think about that before you skipped school and got yourself arrested?"

"Something else I was thinking about."

"That girl the police saw you with, I'm guessing."

Dylan kept his eyes from her, saying nothing.

"San Antonio PD's still looking for her."

Dylan turned back her way. "Why?"

"Captain Alonzo's not about to let go."

"On account of my dad?"

"Part of the reason, yeah. Other part is cops see a couple of kids running around the east side of the city in the middle of the day, first thing comes to their mind is drugs. Since they didn't find any on you, they'll set their sights on the girl."

Dylan's dark eyes widened, then narrowed again. "Drugs got nothing to do with this."

"What does?"

"Maria—"

"Maria?"

"That's the girl's name," Dylan said, squirming in his seat as if the upholstery was boiling his skin. "She was running away, from men a lot worse than my dad ever was. Men who stole her and put her in some kind of human stockyard so they could sell her to freaks to have sex with."

Caitlin felt her heart skip a beat and leaned forward in the driver's seat. "Maybe you better start at the beginning."

6

NEW ORLEANS; THE PRESENT

Cort Wesley Masters raised his hands in the air, submitting to a frisk by Frank Branca Jr.'s bodyguards as Frankie himself looked on grinning.

"Tell me something," Frankie said to him in the living

room section of the St. Louis Hotel's Fleur de Lis Suite. "In prison, did anybody try and touch you?"

"They knew better." Two of the three bodyguards backed off while the third looked on, their job complete, and Cort Wesley lowered his arms. Bright sunlight streamed in through the open balcony blinds, making him squint. "Just like you, Junior."

The glistening white smile slipped from Frank Branca Jr.'s face. "Nobody calls me that anymore. It's Mr. Branca now."

"Sorry, your father's the only Mr. Branca I know," Cort Wesley said, eyeing the figure frozen in a wheelchair placed by the open French doors that offered a sprawling view of the French Quarter overlooking Iberville Street. Katrina had mostly spared this area from the catastrophic damage still afflicting so much of the city. And those trees that had been uprooted had all been replaced now, though the new shadows were substantially smaller than the old, more sun left to bake the asphalt in unforgiving fashion. The suite, meanwhile, was furnished exquisitely with handmade traditional furniture upholstered in rich fabric with perfect stitching. It smelled of the lush foliage sprouting from Iberville Street beyond and was bathed in light spilling in through the windows and exposed balcony.

"Five years is a long time, Masters."

"Six now."

"Things have a way of changing, don't they?"

Cort Wesley glanced again toward Frank Branca Sr. The last time they met, Frank Sr. was still playing golf and tennis and worked out every day. A stroke had robbed him of that and plenty more, confining him to a wheelchair wired to portable monitors and breathing with the help of a ventilator. The elder Branca wheezed occasionally through a mouth that no longer functioned. His skin was pale and sallow, the work of some twisted artist, it looked like, redrawing his visage in milk on dried parchment a stiff wind might tear. His once thick flesh had melted away to leave him almost skeletal. But the old man's eyes were the worst. Utterly blank and unresponsive, lacking the very capacity for thought and flicker of amusement Cort Wesley had always seen in them, belying the murderous and brutal business he had chosen for himself.

Frank Jr. noticed the direction of his stare. "My old man survives every attempt by New York and Chicago to take him out and look how he ends up. Fucking shame. You know how many times I thought about taking a pillow to him myself?"

"Why didn't you?"

"I talk to him, something tells me he's still there. I dress him myself every day. Get his tie tied the way he likes, even stick his old .38 in a holster he bought off a collector claimed it belonged to Dutch Schultz. Just having him around gives me the kind of security I'll never have again once he's gone."

The Branca crime family had pulled out of Texas a few years into Cort Wesley's stay inside the brutal Huntsville prison known as The Walls. A combination of violent Mexican drug mobs moving into the state, along with the return of organized crime to New Orleans in Katrina's wake, had chased them back to their roots here and in southern Florida. They had rented this suite on a permanent basis because, according to Frank Jr., his father had always enjoyed the view.

"Come on, Masters, take a load off," the new head

of the Branca crime family told Cort Wesley, plopping himself down on a cream-colored couch with cushions thicker than clouds.

Cort Wesley took the chair opposite him, hating the moment. Last thing he wanted to do was come to the Branca family, especially under Frank Jr.'s auspices, for the money they owed him. After what went down yesterday, though, he needed it and needed it fast.

7

San Antonio; the day before

Marianna Silvaro, the social services worker assigned to his case, had been waiting for him in the health club lobby when he emerged still sweaty from his workout.

"Didn't know you were a member, Ms. Silvaro," he asked, throwing her a smile. He'd focused on back and chest today, leaving his muscles straining the bounds of his shirt. The muscle heads and juice monkeys loved the mirrors that rimmed the free-weight room upstairs. Cort Wesley hated them for the message of age they imparted. He never thought of such things until his boys fell to his responsibility. Suddenly the creases and worry lines he hadn't even noticed before reminded him of every bad grade and missed parent conference with this teacher or that. He looked around the room filled with clanking iron and grinding cable and wondered how many other men here had a couple kids they were still getting to know.

More recently, Cort Wesley had started wearing

sunscreen, and last week he'd used the gift certificate to a hair salon Caitlin Strong had given him for his birthday before it expired. The only difference he could see, besides the price, was a shampooing, and he hated the feeling of someone else wetting down his hair and running their hands through the lather. Then the stylist asked him if he wanted the gray at the temples touched up.

So this is what raising kids does to you . . .

He told the stylist to leave the gray and decided to go back to a barber.

Silvaro pushed her considerable bulk up from a chair that creaked under the strain, making Cort Wesley instantly regret his comment. Her skin, colored a deep shade of beige from too much makeup, seemed stretched to its limit by the simplest of gestures. But as his Department of Social Services representative she'd been mostly fair with him and deserved better than the admonishing stares those coming and going through the door cast her.

"You're a tough man to track down, Mr. Masters. And you missed our appointment yesterday."

"I plum forgot, ma'am."

"You also forgot to file your means of support forms, along with proof of income and employment with the department."

"I'll get to it right away. That's a promise." Cort Wesley noticed her eyes straying to the tattoos that dominated both his shoulders. "You like my tats, ma'am?"

"I recognize the skull and crossbones," Marianna Silvaro noted, studying him closer. "What's the other one?"

Cort Wesley angled his body so she could better see his left shoulder. "Bloody dagger being stuck back into its scabbard."

"Oh," Silvaro said, face wrinkling in displeasure. "Mr. Masters, I want you to understand how precarious your situation is becoming."

"Precarious?"

"You need me to define the word for you?"

"I was in the Gulf War, ma'am. I think I know what precarious means."

She took a step closer to him, Cort Wesley not at all used to someone narrowing the gap that way. "In this case it means you're in very real danger of losing custody of your sons."

The sweat cooling on Cort Wesley seemed to freeze in an instant, making his pores feel as if someone had jammed icicles in them.

"Mr. Masters," Silvaro continued, "since you were granted provisional custody, you haven't complied with a single request from the department. I've stood up for you as best I can, but a man with your past has to expect additional scrutiny."

"What kind of past would that be, ma'am, I mean, considering I've never been rightfully convicted of a crime in my life?"

"The lack of a female influence in your sons' lives is also a concern."

"Since their mother got murdered, you mean."

Silvaro still didn't back off, leaving Cort Wesley feeling tense and awkward. He'd never known a man tough enough to stand up to him this way, and here he was cowering before a social worker as wide as she was tall.

Another thing raising kids will do to you, Cort Wesley thought.

"I'm on your side, Mr. Masters. I've interviewed your boys and have no reason to believe you're anything but a good father to them. But that does nothing about the glaring omissions in your file we need to resolve before I'm forced to make a decision none of us wants. What are you doing to make a living, for example?"

"Been doing a bit of bodyguarding."

"Is that how you put five people in the hospital in the past six months?"

"Sometimes bodyguarding requires it. An occupational hazard, I guess."

"Is that what you call it?"

"The men who hired me to protect them are just fine," Cort Wesley said by way of explanation. "I'd call that a job well done."

"I'm not sure my department would agree. I tracked you down to tell you that you need to better demonstrate you're financially capable of taking care of your sons. Am I making myself clear?" Silvaro asked, eyes lingering on his tattooed shoulders once more.

"You like my tats that much, ma'am, you should get your own."

"Mr. Masters, I don't see—"

"They're Disney press-ons. My youngest boy picked them up when we were in the park a few months back and stuck 'em on me yesterday." He turned sideways again, giving Silvaro a better look at the dagger. "See how when I flex the muscle, it looks like the knife's moving?"

Marianna Silvaro looked down, then away.

"Those Disney folks are really something, aren't they?" Cort Wesley asked her.

8

NEW ORLEANS; THE PRESENT

"You said this was about business," Frank Branca Jr. was telling him.

"That's right."

"Because we're about to make a move back into Texas, you know. Cut a deal with the Mexican cartels to move product for them."

"That's not the business I came about."

"No?"

Cort Wesley pictured the lavish garden beyond the window to help steady his breathing. "We had a deal when I went in. You were supposed to take care of my kids and their mother."

"Me?"

"The family."

"Which in those days would mean my dad. You got a beef, Masters, you'll have to take it up with him. Hey, Dad, you taking visitors today?"

A thick, gurgly wheeze emanated from the old man's mouth, frothy drool emerging to dribble down his chin.

"Guess not." Frank Jr. turned back to Cort Wesley. "Guess you'll have to come back, try again tomorrow."

"I just want what's coming to me, Frankie."

"Heard the mother of your kids got herself killed."

"Through no fault of her own."

"No, I'm guessing that was yours and, look at this, now you got all the responsibilities of a dad. Got a couple of kids myself, a boy and a girl, with my wife, Rosie. You remember Rosie?"

Cort Wesley nodded, but recalled instead the various showgirls and prostitutes with whom Frank Jr. kept company. He was popular with them for his power more than his looks, which were never much to speak of. He had pearl-white teeth, wore his coarse black hair slicked back with hourly applications of gel, eyes he tried to make hard, and skin so smooth and unmarked that the Branca family soldiers used to call him "Francie" behind his back. Since he was insulated under the protective umbrella provided by his father, they'd never think of saying it to his face any more than the women he bedded would dare comment on his physical shortcomings.

"Rosie loves Texas," Frankie Jr. continued. "Claims she hasn't been happy since we left there. The kids too. But the schools are better here. Cost me some green to get them into the best parochials. Fifteen and my son's got to wear a tie and dress shirt every day, you believe that."

"I'd like to be able to afford the same for mine."

"Good luck."

Cort Wesley turned his gaze on Frank Branca Sr., the angle of the sun making the old man's eyes water. "Why do you leave him out there like that?"

"He loves the sun."

"Looks like he's in pain. Or maybe it's because he knows his son is a low-down dirty welcher."

Frank Jr. shifted in his seat quickly enough to draw the attention of his bodyguards. "Talk like that's a good way to make your kids orphans."

"You really think me not having a gun makes any difference?"

"Maybe you didn't notice my bodyguards are ex–Army Rangers, some shit like that, just like you."

Cort Wesley glanced at the three men again, having trouble picturing that. "I was Special Forces, and I just want what's coming to me, Frankie."

"Don't we all? Only solution I can see is you coming back to work for us, like I said before."

"Already told you I'm not interested. Sorry."

Frankie Branca leaned back, stretching his arms out so they cracked at the elbows before lacing his fingers behind his head. "You go Boy Scout on me or something? 'Cause I heard stuff about you hooking up with a Texas Ranger. First time I hear it said, I'm thinking can't be, since no way Cort Wesley Masters is a faggot. Least he wasn't before he went inside. Then I hear it's a woman Ranger. True or false?"

"That she's a woman or a Ranger?"

"I knew you before you became a wise ass, Masters. Trust me, it doesn't suit you."

Cort Wesley jammed a hand into the pocket of his jeans, causing Frankie Branca to flinch and his bodyguards to tense. But all he came out with was a piece of paper.

"I wrote you a bill. Back payment for services rendered, just like I said."

He rose from his chair and extended the paper toward Branca. When Frankie didn't take it, Cort Wesley dropped it in his lap.

Frankie acted as if it wasn't there, pretended he couldn't see it. Crossed his legs so it would slip to the floor.

"Oops," he said, making no move to retrieve it.

Cort Wesley remained standing, hands coiling by his sides, unable to get the thought of the punk's father, who'd always treated him square, roasting outside. Then, ignoring Frank Jr.'s bodyguards, he started toward the balcony.

"Where the fuck you think you're going?" Frankie asked him.

"Get your father out of the sun."

A knock fell on the suite door, one of the bodyguards moving to open it.

"You don't mind, I got another appointment."

"This won't take long," Cort Wesley said, kneeling in front of Frank Branca Sr., ignoring his son.

Pfffft . . . Pffffft . . . Pfffffft . . .

The sound alerted Cort Wesley to what was happening an instant before the first bodyguard's body was blown backward, midsection shredded by silenced submachine-gun fire. The three gunmen who stormed the suite focused on Frank Jr.'s other two bodyguards, giving Cort Wesley the opportunity to tear the old man's .38 from Dutch Schultz's holster.

The revolver felt strange in his hand, just six shots, he reminded himself, as the three gunmen started blasting away at the weaponless Frank Jr., who'd taken refuge on the floor behind the couch. Cort Wesley lurched back inside the suite, still unseen until he dropped the first man with a pair of headshots. A second spun his way to be greeted by two bullets that found his left cheek and right eye, while the third ducked back into the dining room portion of the suite, opening fire wildly.

The bullets stitched a jagged design through the balcony doors' glass, just missing Frank Sr. who reacted not at all. But the mere thought of the old man nearly perishing in the spray was enough to fuel Cort Wesley into motion. He hurdled the couch, ready to shoot as soon as the final gunmen twisted around from his wall cover to right his barrel.

The man appeared just as expected, thinking the advantage to be his, never anticipating Cort Wesley to be right upon him. Cort Wesley saw the shock and fear in his eyes as he shot him in the throat and chest, the man's final barrage stitching a jagged design across the ceiling that sliced a crystal chandelier from its mount and sent it smashing downward.

Cort Wesley discarded the pistol and retrieved the piece of paper Frankie Jr. had let fall to the rug. He stepped over the shards of shattered glass and watched Frankie rise from his position of hiding, twin patches of urine staining his linen trousers.

"I take checks, Junior," Cort Wesley said, tossing the bill back at him. "And you should take better care of your father."

9

SAN ANTONIO; THE PRESENT

"I don't wear the boots you gave me to school," Dylan told Caitlin, as they sat down at the lone canopied table on the patio of Starbucks's Riverwalk location on West Crockett Street. "I saw you looking before. They're cool, but not for school."

Caitlin found herself embarrassed by him noticing. "Tell me about Maria."

Dylan looked up from the pedestrian traffic crowding past the Hard Rock Café directly below. "She was brought up here against her will."

"You said she was kidnapped."

"Uh-huh." Dylan nodded. "On her way home from school one day maybe six months back by men in a van. They blindfolded her and took her to this place where she was held prisoner, forced to do things until they drove her across the border with some other girls in the back of a truck with no windows. Said she almost roasted to death; could feel her skin ready to melt from the heat."

Dylan sipped his iced cappuccino, his lips coming away speckled with froth. Caitlin had suggested they talk over ice cream, which had drawn a caustic stare from him. He'd ordered the medium size with an extra shot, still no more caffeine than the energy drinks boys his age seemed to live on these days. He fell silent briefly and turned his gaze on a tour boat cruising past the Montezuma Cypress trees that rimmed this part of the channel.

"How old was Maria when she was kidnapped?" Caitlin asked him as she watched a night heron swallow a crawfish whole on the other side of Riverwalk. The day's blistering heat had already melted most of the ice in her cup of iced coffee, in spite of the stiff breeze that had blown welcome cloud cover over the sun.

"Her English is about as good as my Spanish, but it was just after she turned fifteen."

"Your age."

"Yeah, I thought of that too. Yesterday, Maria says, these men she'd never seen before came to the place where she'd been kept prisoner and picked a dozen of the girls including her out of a row. Stuck them in the back of a panel truck and headed north. Way she described one of them made my hair stand on end, Caitlin."

Funny how she liked how Dylan said her name, confident enough to use it now like a man but still sounding pretty much like a boy. Mostly he was starting to sound like Cort Wesley, not just in pitch but also tone, the way he held his words and the confidence with which he spoke them. Dylan had his late mother's dark brooding looks and his father's intensity and magnetism; it was no wonder girls flocked to him like pack rats. Caitlin had been there when his mother, Maura Torres, was killed and had saved Dylan's life, along with his younger brother's. The bond forged between her and the two boys that day was the strangest and strongest she'd ever felt, different certainly from her feelings for Cort Wesley but just as deep.

"And when I saw him," Dylan was saying, "I can tell you her words didn't do him justice."

That was enough to snap Caitlin all the way alert again. "Wait a minute, you say you *saw* this man?"

"Just after I met Maria. She was hiding out around my school."

"Smart girl. Easy to hide among other kids."

"Well, it didn't work. She stuck out."

"Why?"

"Her clothes didn't fit. Looked like she'd plucked them off somebody's clothesline or something. Turned out she stole them off a rack at a sidewalk sale."

"Okay," Caitlin said, leaning forward as Dylan took a sip from his cup that left foam on his upper lip, "where does the man you said made your hair stand on end come in?"

"He was the one in charge when they picked out the girls and brought them across the border. I saw him outside my school while I was talking to Maria. She came up to me first, asked to borrow some money when I was walking up to bus my lunch tray. I'd just handed her a five when I could tell something spooked her. Then I noticed the guy."

"Describe him."

"Weirdest-looking man I've ever seen," Dylan said, voice wavering slightly at the mere memory. "Had a head that looked pumped full of air, hair that didn't fit his scalp, and shiny skin."

"You say shiny skin?"

"That's right." The boy nodded. "I don't know how else to say it. He was wearing a sleeveless vest with no shirt and he had muscles bulging everywhere, enough to make my dad look small. But that wasn't the real strange thing."

"What was?"

"He had something clipped to his belt that ran into his arm like— What do they call those things they stick in you when you need fluids?"

"An IV."

"That's it. He had one of those. Thin, clear plastic tube. I'm sure of it." Dylan hesitated. "Don't you wanna know what happened next?"

"I already do. You grabbed the girl and ran."

"Hopped a bus to East San Antone where I figured we could lay low 'til I got things sorted out."

Caitlin's gaze narrowed a bit. "How'd Maria get away in the first place?"

"Well, they crossed the border last night and headed north across the desert. Panel truck the girls were jammed into stopped so they could get some water and go to the bathroom since they'd been cooped up in there ever since they left Nuevo Laredo."

Nuevo Laredo . . .

Caitlin felt her neck hairs stand on end. "Can you reach her, Dylan?"

"I gave Maria my cell when the cops showed up. Knew they'd chase me instead of her. They always chase the boy, not the girl."

Smart kid, Caitlin thought, handing Dylan her BlackBerry cell phone. "Call her."

IO

SAN ANTONIO; THE PRESENT

"She's not answering," Dylan said, uneasy. The phone was still pressed to his ear, shaggy hair covering the casing.

"Try again."

Dylan dialed again to no avail but held fast to the BlackBerry.

"So Maria got away when they pulled over."

"It was early this morning. She waited until they left again, then started hitchhiking and got lucky after ten minutes or so. Driver left her off a few miles from my school and she just happened to walk near it around lunchtime. How the hell the weird guy find her, Caitlin?"

"This kind of thing's more common than you think."

"What kind of thing's that?"

"Young Mexican girls being forced into prostitution. It's a kind of slavery, and more of it goes on than any of us can imagine."

"That's goddamn sick!"

"All that and more, son. Thing is, the wranglers—"

"Wranglers? I thought they were called coyotes."

"Not the ones responsible for shepherding kidnapped girls like this across the border."

"Sounds like cattle."

"And it pretty much is. Anyway, the wranglers like this weird guy figure at least a few of the girls will try to run off at some point, so they outfit all of them with locators, GPS beacons no bigger than a quarter, to track them once that happens."

"That's how he found her at my school," Dylan concluded, his eyes starting to drift anxiously.

"Be my guess. What's wrong?"

"Means he can still find her, no matter how well she hid." Dylan raised Caitlin's phone back to his ear. "I'm gonna try her again."

"She's on Hacienda," Dylan said, relieved Maria had answered this time. "Says she's mostly just been walking up and down the street."

"Good. Tell her to take off her belt."

"She changed clothes."

"What about her shoes?"

"Kind of like sandals. They looked pretty beat up."

"Have her ditch them."

"Why?"

"Because wranglers usually plant the locators in belts or shoes, sometimes both."

Caitlin listened to Dylan relay her instructions, in a combination of Spanish and English. She could see the boy getting red in the face in frustration when the girl had trouble understanding him, looking so much like his father right at that point it almost scared her. Then his expression lengthened suddenly, his deep-set eyes growing uncertain as he cut off his words mid-stream. Suddenly boyish again and fearful.

"What's wrong?" Caitlin asked him.

Dylan lowered the phone to his shoulder. "Maria says that guy's back."

II

EAST SAN ANTONIO; THE PRESENT

Macerio kept his eyes on his transponder, honing in on the position of the small flashing light now almost dead center on the screen. He looked up at the street and tried to impose a mental grid over it to pinpoint the girl's position. She was close, very close.

Beep . . . Beep . . . Beep . . .

He'd turned the volume down so passersby would think he was simply text messaging someone. He could feel the dark metal hot in his hands, superheated by the sun that reddened his skin on contact and left his nerve endings raw and inflamed. The side effects of the drugs were to blame for that along with the hair loss that left him wearing an ill-fitting toupee he'd taken off a man he'd killed in Chochilla. This double-sided tape Macerio bought in a drugstore was supposed to make the toupee stay on, but sweating inevitably loosened it and he'd been doing a lot of that lately.

Macerio's father and grandfather had both died of

cancer before they were forty-five. He never expected to live that long, but crossing forty left him reasoning that he hadn't survived so much violence to let himself be stricken down as his relatives had. So he sought out an oncologist named Nobrega who practiced at General Hospital on Paseo Triunfo de la Republica in Juárez.

"I want you to give me chemotherapy."

"But you're not sick," the doctor told him, mystified.

"I will be, just like my father and grandfather. I can feel the cancer growing inside me now just as it did them. I want the chemotherapy to kill it before it kills me."

"I cannot do this," Dr. Nobrega insisted.

Macerio pulled a wad of cash from his pocket and started peeling off hundred-dollar bills.

"This isn't about money," the doctor said. "I must follow protocol or risk losing my license."

Macerio took a picture of Nobrega's family from his desktop and dropped it on the floor. Then he looked up and met the doctor's gaze, grinning. "Nice-looking kids."

Macerio started the treatments the following day. The side effects were much worse than he'd been expecting. To combat some of them, especially the weakness, lethargy, and loss of appetite, Dr. Nobrega prescribed cortosteroids. When they proved to be of little help, Macerio replaced them on his own with daily injections of anabolic steroids. The weakness vanished and Macerio actually felt stronger than he ever had. So much so that he made Nobrega teach him how to rig the steroids to an IV that would keep them dripping into his body on a constant basis.

That had enabled Macerio to continue working through the entire six weeks of his treatment. It had ended a month ago now, but most of the side effects, especially his lack of taste and sensitivity to the sun, had not abated. Even if they had, he doubted he would have stopped his IV treatments. The steroids had added fresh layers to his already heavily muscled frame, making him all the more effective at his work, especially with the women who fell into his charge. All told he had never felt better, taking great comfort in the fact that he had beaten the cancer before it had a chance to beat him. He didn't like his ill-fitting, recycled hair or baby-sensitive skin, but those were things he could live with.

Normally, neither Macerio nor his employers would've cared about the loss of a single *puta* destined to vanish into the streets or the immigration system. But he had special plans for this one. She had the look he liked: dark with almost Indian features and big, full eyes. Innocent and sensual at the same time. His employers would never miss her.

But Macerio would.

Beep . . . Beep . . . Beep . . .

Straight ahead to the right, just a hundred feet away, Macerio judged, starting across the street.

12

San Antonio; the present

Caitlin sped up to pass a rolling wreck of a car driving with its flashers on. She was just a few blocks from the corner of Rozan and Andujar, not far from a coin-operated laundry with big plate windows where Maria was hiding so she could have clear view of the street beyond. She felt Dylan tense next to her as she screeched into a left-hand turn and undid the strap on the holster holding her SIG Sauer.

"You got another gun in your truck?" the boy asked her.

"Couple of them."

"Maybe you should let me have one. I'm pretty good with a twelve-gauge."

"What do you think your dad would make of me doing that?"

"He's the one who taught me to shoot the twelve-gauge. My brother too."

"Luke? What in hell for?"

"So if anyone ever comes gunning for us again, we'll know what to do."

Caitlin nodded, feeling stupid and insensitive, a fifteen-year-old boy's answer holding far more wisdom than her question.

"We spot this weird-looking guy," she told Dylan, "I just might do that."

Macerio stood in the shade of the alley, holding the dull, quarter-sized steel plate. He'd found it in the Dumpster near the girl's sandals, which meant someone had told her to discard them. He'd searched the Dumpster while the afternoon sun baked his skin, ten minutes that left him feeling he'd been roasting in the fields for a whole day. His face came away red and raw from the effort, his weakened nerve endings so frazzled no amount of shade could relieve a sensation akin to someone scraping at his flesh with sandpaper.

Macerio thought of his young, missing *puta*, one clever enough to shed the beacon that normally allowed him to track down his runaways with little effort. It happened, not often, but it did happen, he thought, as an SUV tore around the corner and flew past him down the street.

Caitlin felt her front tire smack up against the curb directly in front of the coin-operated laundry, the SUV barely stopped when Dylan lunged out to meet a slim, dark-featured teenage girl wearing cuffed jeans that clung to her ankles. She watched the girl scan the street nervously as she lurched with Dylan back toward the SUV, had never seen more fear in any pair of eyes in her life.

"*¡Apure, por favor!*" she wailed, ducking low in the backseat.

"Hurry!" Dylan added and slammed the door behind them.

Macerio watched the SUV tear off with its tires bleeding smoke and rubber, a very pretty woman with shoulder-length black hair behind the wheel, the boy he'd glimpsed earlier with the *puta* next to her in the backseat. It was unmarked, not law enforcement then, and watching it shrink in the growing distance made him want to find this *puta* all the more. Add her to the long list he kept tucked in his memory.

Macerio knew that earlier in the day local police had arrested the boy he'd seen with the *puta*. Find him and he'd find her.

13

"He's not behind us," Caitlin told Dylan.

The boy finally turned away from the SUV's rear window. "Just making sure."

"You can sit up now," Caitlin said to Maria. "You're safe."

The girl remained hunched low until Dylan eased her upright and slung an arm around her shoulder to draw her in close. "She's on our side. She's going to help."

"My name's Caitlin, Maria."

"*Sí.*"

"I know you're scared, but Dylan's right, I'm going to help you. You need to believe that. You need to speak to me."

"Where's that twelve-gauge?" Dylan asked suddenly. "Just in case."

"It wouldn't work against Macerio anyway," Maria chimed in.

"Macerio?" Caitlin repeated.

Maria looked toward Dylan instead. "The man you saw." Then, to Caitlin, "Back in Nuevo Laredo, when he entered the house, the older women, they crossed themselves and whispered to each other. They called him Demonio behind his back."

They came to a stoplight and Caitlin studied Maria in the rearview mirror. The shadows cast by the tinted windows made her look older, Caitlin suddenly feeling she was looking at a woman instead of a girl, a twisted dichotomy exploited by those who'd stolen her youth. Then Maria drew her hair back behind her ears, revealing the features of her gaunt face that tightened every time they slid past a pedestrian. A young girl again, innocent and frightened, hunkered low to avoid being seen from the street.

"They told stories of how Macerio was fashioned from hard-packed clay and then a *bruja* witch said a spell and brought him to life," the girl continued. "He has no heart, the older women say, and the magic liquid in the pouch on his belt gets pumped into his veins to keep him alive."

The light turned green and Caitlin started on through the intersection. "Let's get you someplace safe."

14

SHAVANO PARK; THE PRESENT

Caitlin stood at the front window of the house where Dylan and Luke Torres lived with Cort Wesley in Shavano Park.

"Your father tell you how long he was gonna be gone?" she asked Dylan, while Maria used the upstairs bathroom.

"Until he got back I think was his exact terminology." Dylan regarded her closer. "So what's the problem?"

"He could have let me know he had business to attend to. I could've checked in."

"He said to call you if we needed anything."

"Like getting sprung from jail or helping rescue a runaway girl?"

She looked toward the front door, replaced, frame

and all, with a steel security one after the gunfight that had claimed the life of Maura Torres, Dylan and Luke's mother. Maura had been shot as she opened the door, Caitlin getting there a moment too late to save her but just in time to save her kids. She imagined she could smell the blood in the air, see it pooled on the floor and speckled across the walls. Caitlin was about to say something else to Dylan but the sight of Maria padding down the carpeted stairs silenced her. Her feet were bare and dirty. She'd uncuffed her jeans and tousled some kind of shiny gel in her hair that Dylan clearly noticed as well. Caitlin had seen more than her share of girls not much older than Maria who'd been beaten and broken down from their years as a virtual sex slave. But Maria's tenure had not yet sapped the innocence or hope from her eyes, in contrast to those whose gazes were neither sad nor fearful; just empty and dead.

She stopped at the bottom, holding the banister. "I want to go home. To my family."

"They live near Nuevo Laredo?" Caitlin asked her.

"No. A small village outside Mexico City. A few times I tried to steal men's phones so I could call them. It didn't work, and they beat me."

"Can you describe the place where they kept you for me?"

Maria clutched the banister tighter. "*Sí*, a building with many rooms and many girls in each of them. They would leave us in there for days at a time with little to eat and drink and nowhere to go to the bathroom. It smelled so bad, some of the girls got sick. If you were lucky you got a corner to yourself and you could push your face against the wall. If you were lucky."

Caitlin hesitated before posing her next question. "Do you remember where this building was?"

"*Sí,*" Maria nodded.

"And you can tell me where to find it in Nuevo Laredo, where I can find the rest of these girls?"

Maria nodded again.

"Had you seen this man Macerio before last night?" Caitlin asked Maria.

"A few times when he came to drop off other girls. Or choose one to take with him." Maria's eyes lowered and held on the bottom step. "None of those ever came back."

Caitlin stiffened. "How many?"

"I'm not sure."

Caitlin shivered, felt a cold draft slip up her shirt and chill her spine.

"Caitlin?" Dylan said.

"Las Mujeres de Juárez," she muttered.

"What's that mean?" Dylan asked her, "the Women of Juárez."

Caitlin tried to ignore him. "You have any notion of where they were taking you?" she asked Maria instead.

"You didn't answer my question," Dylan persisted.

But Caitlin held her gaze on Maria until the girl finally responded.

"Not when we left and we couldn't see anything in the back of the truck. It was so dark and the ride was so bumpy. One of the girls got sick, and then another. The smell got so bad, we all got sick, and finally they pulled over. Let us out and gave us water."

"Any landmarks?"

"I remember road signs for someplace called Uvalde and, after I ran off, San Antonio."

"Sounds like U.S. 90. Runs along the southern part of the state, hugging the border for a ways."

"Maybe. And I remember something else. After they let us out the back of the truck, the stink was so bad one of the men said to the other it was a good thing we only had twenty miles left to go."

"Twenty miles."

"*Sí.*"

"You look hungry," Caitlin said, feeling guilty over not realizing it before.

Maria nodded. "Very."

"I'll see what's in the fridge, make you a sandwich."

Dylan headed into the kitchen. "I'll do it." Then, to Caitlin, "I've tried your sandwiches. You put too much stuff on them."

"That's the way my dad made 'em for me."

Almost to the kitchen, Dylan stopped and turned back and around. "Yo, Caitlin."

"What?"

"I really do like those boots."

Caitlin felt her insides slacken at the simple comment, something feathery floating through her gut when the front door to the house opened and Dylan's younger brother, Luke, entered. His eyes passed over Caitlin, falling on Maria.

"Who's she?" the boy asked.

15

Cort Wesley saw the two San Antonio cops standing at the end of the Jetway and knew they were waiting for him.

"Well, lookee what we got here." One of them grinned, as he drew closer. "A genuine celebrity. Wish I'd brought my autograph book along. Jerry," he said to the other one, "you got your memo pad handy?"

Jerry handed one over. "Here you go, Bib."

Bib flipped it open as he and Jerry followed Cort Wesley into the terminal. "Lookee here, says a man meeting the description of one Cort Wesley Masters was involved in a hotel shooting earlier today in New Orleans. You think we should question him on that, Jerry?"

"I do."

Cort Wesley stopped, centering himself between the two cops to keep both of them in his field of vision at any time, as more passengers continued to file past them.

"You shoot anyone today, Mr. Masters?" the one named Bib asked him. It could have been a nickname, based on the fact that this cop had a uniform shirt stained with enough food types to have made wearing a bib advisable.

"Not that I recall, Officer."

"But you don't deny being in New Orleans."

"Well, that is where the flight I just got off came in from."

"You don't scare us at all, Masters," Bib insisted,

straightening his spine as he redonned his mirror shades.

Cort Wesley looked at his reflection cast wider to the point of making his lean, angular face look fat and his gray eyes look black. Neither of the cops was enough of six feet two to look him in the eye, though Jerry seemed to be balancing himself on his toes at times to make it close. He appeared to be Hispanic, meaning the name was probably short for Gerardo or something. The flow of disembarking passengers had stopped, leaving them with the gate all to themselves.

"We just thought this might be a day for the record books," Jerry said, back on his toes, "what with an opportunity to see two members of the Masters family behind bars at the same goddamn time."

"Guess he hasn't heard about his son yet," added Bib. "How he got himself nabbed on drug charges and spent some time in lockup."

Cort Wesley stood there calmly, while inside his stomach churned with stale airline peanuts and soda mixed with melted ice.

"Good thing the boy got sprung 'fore the jailbirds had their way with him," Jerry taunted.

"Yup, pretty kid like that be a good candidate to have his ass plowed wide as Interstate 75. I heard social services was ready to put your kids someplace where there ain't no killers in the house, Masters. This oughtta speed the process up considerably."

Bib was still grinning when a lurching step by Cort Wesley brought them face-to-face.

"I can see your partner's hand on his gun in your sunglasses, Officer Bib." Cort Wesley could smell the dried sweat rising off him, along with the odor of fast-food onions that had clung to his uniform since lunch. "And I'm here to tell you I could leave you dead and have your weapon in hand ahead of Officer Jerry being able to draw and fire. Either of you ever shot a man made out of more than white cardboard? I have, back in the Gulf War, and it's a lot harder than it seems, 'specially the first time. So if you got call to arrest me, slap on the cuffs and lead me out. If you don't, I'm gonna do you boys the favor, just this once, of forgetting you spoke of my son in that manner. So we got ourselves an understanding, or not?"

Cort Wesley checked the reflection in Bib's sunglasses, Jerry's hand frozen over his holstered pistol as if it were painted on the air there. Then he backed off, close enough to both cops to move on either if it came to that. But Bib looked down and Jerry finally eased his hand away from his pistol, flexing his fingers to push the blood back into them. The stale sweat stench had gotten much worse while Cort Wesley had been face-to-face with him, turning his stomach sour anew.

"I'll take that as a yes," he said and walked off.

PART TWO

As strange as it may seem in some quarters, the Texas Ranger has been throughout the century a human being, and never a mere automaton animating a pair of swaggering boots, a big hat, and a six-shooter all moving across the prairies under a cloud of pistol smoke. Surely enough has been written about men who swagger, fan hammers, and make hip shots. No Texas Ranger ever fanned a hammer when he was serious, or made a hip shot if he had time to catch a sight. The real Ranger has been a very quiet, deliberate, gentle person who could gaze calmly into the eye of a murderer, divine his thoughts, and anticipate his action, a man who could ride straight up to death.

—Walter Prescott Webb, *The Texas Rangers:*
A Century of Frontier Defense

16

Guillermo Paz crossed himself before entering the Templo Bautista Jesus de Nazareth church, placing him in the right mind-set for the purpose that had drawn him here today.

Construction on Templo Bautista Jesus de Nazareth had been completed in recent months as part of continuing efforts undertaken by Casas Por Cristo, a charitable group dedicated to building homes and churches for poor families to help ease the blight threatening to consume the entire city. Paz liked standing on the banks of the Rio Grande and gazing across it toward El Paso, thinking of Texas Ranger Caitlin Strong, who'd haunted his thoughts for a year now.

Paz threw both of the church's double doors open to accommodate his vast bulk. The doorframe itself stood seven feet in height, Paz barely clearing it in his boots. Inside, the church still smelled of raw lumber and recently poured concrete. The plywood pews had yet to be varnished or stained, the concrete flooring the very same shade as the building's dull exterior construction. But it was the windows Paz noticed the most; clear instead of stained glass and fronted by inlaid bars that created streaming checkerboard grids across the floor and walls when the sun passed through them.

The confessionals were located to the right, in an alcove off the building's apse. Just one, it turned out, that had been richly stained in stark contrast to the unfinished rows of wood beyond. Paz swiped a finger across the surface, half expecting it to come away sticky. But the touch revealed wood weathered and worn, leading him to believe the confessional itself had come from another church, perhaps one of several shut down by the escalating violence that had claimed the lives of some priests too devoted and stubborn to flee.

Paz opened the confessional door and squeezed himself inside atop the built-in seat. Immediately a panel slid open, revealing the shadowy form of the resident priest's face.

"Bless me, Father, for I have sinned. It has been over a year now since my last confession."

"Why so long, my son?"

"I thought I was past it, that I had outgrown the need to take comfort in the words of strangers."

"Do you see God as a stranger?"

"Well, that's a good question, and I go back and forth on it. A year ago He and I were pretty tight. Not so much lately, though."

"Have you strayed from His path in that time?"

"This is Juárez, Padre, the capital of strays. That's why I came here: for the familiar scent."

"I'm not sure I—"

"Gun smoke, Padre. I figured this was the perfect place to lose myself for a while. Can't argue with me there, considering a couple thousand people got killed here last year alone, just the ones we know about. There's always work for a man like me in a place like this."

"So you've come here to confess those acts?" the priest said, voice cracking. He tried to clear his throat, failed, and tried again.

"No, I'm fine there. I think you got me wrong, what it is I've been up to. Sure, I thought there might be a place for me in the violence. Given my history and all, what better place than one where you can smell blood in the air? Literally. But I wasn't in Juárez for more than a couple hours when a guy at the next table over in a cantina got machine-gunned through the window. His blood sprayed up all over me and I realized, nope, this isn't for me anymore."

"And yet here you are, my son, all these months later."

Paz took a deep breath, began peeling away the finish on the wood forming the ledge before him with a fingernail. It had become a habit since his childhood; to carve his name into the confessional, leave his mark behind along with his words. But there'd been a very long gap between carvings.

"You know the many *barrio bajos* that litter the city?"

"Juárez has become a world of slums, my son."

"The homes there are built of pallets and cardboard. The lucky ones are wrapped in tarpaper for insulation and topped with tin roofs. So I passed one of these *barrio bajos* on my way out of the city and I see a drug gang standing around one of the shanties after lighting it on fire. You ever see tarpaper burn, Padre?"

"No, I haven't."

"It goes fast and takes everything else with it," Paz said, finishing the straight line in the "P" and going to work on the loop at the top with his nail. "You ever hear the screams of people as they're burned alive, smell their flesh roasting?"

The priest shivered. "No again, my son."

"You know why the gang burned those people, Padre? Because they could. No other reason. They just could. I followed the drug gang to their headquarters and you know what I did?"

"Is that what you've come here to confess?"

"No, but I'll tell you anyway: I did the same thing to them they did to that family living with tarpaper walls. I grew up in a place just like it in Venezuela, a village named La Vega. There was a church at the foot of the hill where a priest like you taught me to read and write before he was shot down in the street. So the last few months I've been living in these *barrio bajos*, trying to make sure no one else gets roasted alive."

"Ángel de la Guarda," the priest muttered in disbelief. "The Guardian Angel . . ."

"I see you've heard of me, Padre."

The priest's voice became lower, hesitant. "I . . . I did not think you were real."

"Well, here I am."

"The people do not believe you are human. They believe you are an avenging spirit sent to protect them." The priest's tone changed, becoming almost reverent. "If you'll excuse me for saying, it sounds like you were on the other side of such things once."

Paz was working on the "A" now, switching to a different nail. Amazing how important leaving his mark in other ways on places had become for him. "And for a long time too. That all changed just before I came to Juárez."

"Is that what has brought you to me today?"

"Sort of," Paz told him. "Because I can't let it go."

"Can't let what go, my son?"

"This woman, a Texas Ranger. I thought I'd gotten her out of my head, Padre. Then I read about how she saved a big Mexican government official in an intensive care ward at an El Paso hospital from Juárez gangbangers like the ones who roasted those people alive. I've been too angry to sleep, angry over these drug gangs nearly costing the Ranger her life. So yesterday I found one of the biggest drug stashes in Juárez and burned it."

Paz could hear the priest's breathing pick up. "You're a wanted man now. Burning their drugs is much different from killing a few of their dealers. The cartel will hunt you to the end of the earth."

"Let them, Padre. Truth is, I'm headed out of here anyway. Got business elsewhere."

"Regarding this Texas Ranger?"

Paz went to work on carving the "Z," trying to do it in a continuous motion without raising his nail off the wood. "I think I became Ángel de la Guarda because I wanted to be like Caitlin Strong. I need to know why I feel what I feel for her. There was something in her eyes . . . I thought it was just the passion lacking in my own. Now I think it was something else, the thing that brought us together in the first place." Paz stopped and took a deep breath. "I think she's in danger . . ."

"So are you."

". . . and I think it's my job to save her."

"From what?"

"I don't know, not yet anyway. It's something from a long time ago—that's what I've figured out."

The priest thought briefly. "You being here in Juárez, being Ángel de la Guarda, was your penance for the man you left behind. The new one forged in his image seeks kindred spirits in the way the old one could not. Perhaps in saving this Ranger's life, you'll also save your own."

"I was hoping you'd say that," Paz said, finishing up the "Z" and brushing the wood flakes free from his handiwork.

"You are doing God's work, my son."

"When you spend your whole life with the devil, Padre, it's nice to join the other side for a change."

17

Shavano Park; the present

Caitlin was sitting on the porch when Cort Wesley pulled into the driveway, lunging out of the truck the moment it came to a halt. He mounted the steps and stormed toward the door, barely aware of her presence until she took up a stance before him.

"Get out of my way, Ranger."

"Some things you need to hear before you go inside, Cort Wesley."

"You mean besides what a couple San Antonio cops told me at the airport?"

"Stand still and catch your breath."

Cort Wesley hadn't realized he was breathing hard. "I don't see you in, what, two months, and now you're telling me what to do?"

"On account of Dylan needing me to get him out of jail, yeah."

"Back up."

"Not until you slow down."

"If you were a man—"

"You still wouldn't be able to outshoot me. Not the first time we met and not tonight either." Caitlin met his dark, charcoal-colored eyes. "You can blink now."

"I'm sorry," said Cort Wesley, his breathing settling.

"I don't know what makes me madder, Cort Wesley; you taking off and leaving your boys on their own, or not telling me so I could look in on them."

"After two months, I didn't want to impose."

"I've been busy."

"Chasing missing Mexican girls—you told me all about it."

"Yeah, the prevailing opinion is not to give a shit about them, just like you."

"Got my own kids to worry about, in case you forgot."

"Actually, I thought *you* did."

Cort Wesley's face started reddening again, putting Caitlin strangely at ease. He had a strange quirk of going pale in the moments before violence became inevitable. Only man Caitlin had ever known, or faced down, whose rage didn't deepen and darken his features. She recognized this as his frustrated look, the way he got when things piled up too high to see over.

Caitlin watched his gaze keep shifting from the door to her, then back again.

"You mind if I go inside now?"

"Tell me what those cops told you first."

"Now you're giving me orders?"

"Just tell me."

Cort Wesley's features started to relax and lighten a bit. "That Dylan got arrested on a drug charge today."

"True enough on the surface. But it hardly tells the whole story."

Cort Wesley's eyes blinked and flashed, as if he were recording the scene for the first time. "Whole story having something to do with why you're sitting out here on the porch with the strap undone over your SIG."

"That's right."

He smacked his lips together, watched Caitlin twirl a finger through her hair, tightening the strands into a ringlet. "Yeah, I should've known."

"Known what?"

"You got your trouble look."

"What's that supposed to mean?"

"You ever face off against a bull when he's ready to charge?"

"Can't say I have."

"Well, Ranger, he gets this look in his eyes, all focused and intent, but calm, like he's in his element and nothing and nobody can take him down."

"Should I take that as a compliment?" Caitlin asked him.

"Take it whatever way you want. The boys missed you, Ranger," Cort Wesley added, softer. "They've seen you, what?, all of twice since we took them to Disney. Wouldn't surprise me if Dylan got himself arrested just to have an excuse to call."

"He wouldn't have had to, if you hadn't taken off and left him and Luke to fend for themselves."

"I told them if there was a problem to call you."

"You might've alerted me to that fact."

"Guess it didn't cross my mind after so long."

"Good thing it crossed Dylan's."

Cort Wesley took a deep, labored breath. "So if it wasn't drugs, what was it?"

"Sit down."

Cort Wesley's eyes darted up to Dylan's window, the boy's shape shrinking away too late to avoid being seen. Then he sat down. "I'm listening."

After Caitlin had finished, Cort Wesley leaned back, suddenly reflective. "I'm not sure whether to smack him or hug him."

"Yeah, boy's a regular chip off the old block."

"You didn't say that with a smile, Ranger."

"He put himself in real danger today, Cort Wesley."

"And saved that girl's life for sure."

Caitlin frowned, forced her hand from her hair again. "So you approve."

"Part of me does, yeah."

"Which, the part that went to New Orleans?"

"Needed to collect on an old debt if I'm gonna keep the boys fed and all. I hated doing it, I'll tell you that much. But the Brancas owed me the money and I needed it to take care of my boys the way they deserve before social services yanks them out from under me."

"Social services?"

"They got a caseworker all over my ass about whether I'm a fit parent or not. Who knows, maybe she's right. Me moving in here and impersonating a father. What the hell was I thinking?"

"I ever criticize you for that?"

"Wasn't that what you were doing a minute ago?"

"For not calling me so I could look in on the boys

while you were gone. Make the social services lady happy."

Cort Wesley swept a hand over the sweat cooling on his brow. "Ranger, she had a look at your history, she'd probably think you were more likely to shoot them than mix up some pancakes."

Caitlin rocked her chair back even with his. "Tell me why you didn't call."

" 'Cause you would've asked me where I was going and then told me not to go there. Maybe I get tired of the lectures."

"That's why I'm making up for lost time tonight."

"How long you gonna stay away this time?"

"I didn't see you rushing to the phone to find out what I was up to."

"Maybe I figured it was none of my business."

"Then I guess it's a good thing for us Dylan thought it was still his business."

Cort Wesley pushed himself out of his chair. "Think it's time I went inside."

18

SHAVANO PARK; THE PRESENT

Cort Wesley opened Dylan's door without knocking, his eyes falling on the girl sobbing softly atop the bed-covers while Dylan sat on the side of the bed stroking her hair. He cleared his throat, waited for his oldest son to look his way.

"You got a minute to talk?"

The boy nodded and lifted himself off the bed after

whispering something in the girl's ear. He closed the door again himself, after joining his father in the hallway.

"I'm trying not to be too critical of what you done here," said Cort Wesley. "I like a man who stands up for things, not afraid to take a risk if it means helping somebody else."

Dylan smiled slightly. "I was afraid you'd put me over your knee."

"Nah, I'd never spank you. I might shoot you, but I'd never spank you."

Dylan watched Cort Wesley wink and widened his smile.

"You being a good student with no history of such things matters for something too. Trouble is word's out in the city, among the cops anyway, that you're my son. The upshot of that bit you this afternoon for the first time, but it might not be the last. That's something I want you to take out of this, how extra careful you got to be in choosing your situations."

"Nothing in this case I could've done different anyway."

"You could've called me."

"You were in New Orleans."

"Would you have if I wasn't?"

"What do you think?" Dylan asked him, not missing a beat.

Cort Wesley's eyes flashed concern. He started to take a deep breath, then stopped. "She's a pretty girl, Dylan."

"She was in trouble."

"Dangerous combination, trust me on that."

"What is it you wanna tell me?" Dylan asked him.

"Not tell you, son, warn you."

"So go ahead."

"I just did, didn't I?"

Dylan whipped the hair from his face with a snap of his head. Then he ran a hand through it. "Am I supposed to answer that?"

"No, this: how you plan on explaining your actions to the folks who run your school?"

"Lots of kids take off early sometimes."

"They don't belong to me. You do."

Dylan rolled his eyes.

"Don't do that."

"Do what?"

"Look, I'm just trying to talk to you here."

"You finished?"

Cort Wesley looked at his oldest son, thinking of what he'd done over the years to others who'd taken that tone with him. He felt his fingers twitching, eager to be curled into fists out of instinct.

Dylan blew some stray strands of hair from his face, his expression growing tentative. "What's Las Mujeres de Juárez?"

"Huh?"

"Something Caitlin said when Maria was telling her story. The Women of Juárez."

"You heard her say that?"

"Pretty sure I did, yeah."

Cort Wesley's spine seemed to arch. Dylan always had to look up to meet his eyes, but suddenly it seemed he had to cast his gaze higher.

"Make sure the window in your room is locked," Cort Wesley said, and headed back for the stairs.

19

"Las Mujeres de Juárez," Cort Wesley said, standing over Caitlin on the porch. "You forget to mention that to me?"

"I didn't forget. I'm just not sure."

Cort Wesley's eyes seemed to stop blinking again, the color draining from his face. "Sure enough to be sitting out here with your SIG unstrapped."

Caitlin looked at the shotgun he had brought outside with him. "You ever wonder why times like this bring us the closest?"

"You mean that spending time with Mickey and Goofy just doesn't seem to hold? Nope. I was too busy wondering why every time I've got us figured out, you pull a disappearing act." Cort Wesley stopped, then started again just as quickly. "Two months this time."

"I explained that."

"And now, maybe thanks to Dylan, you got a line on what you're really after."

"That's not fair."

"Yes, it is. That girl upstairs is what you been chasing for months. Tell me there's not a part of you wouldn't like this Macerio or whatever to show up here and now."

"Got me figured out for sure, don't you, Cort Wesley?"

"I think so."

"Which explains why you didn't bother to say thank you."

Cort Wesley shook his head, looking disappointed.

"You don't thank family for doing what family does, unless you were doing it as a Ranger, in which case I am in your debt. So?"

"So . . . what?"

"Which is it?"

"If you need to ask, I've got no intention of telling you."

Cort Wesley smirked and finally took the wooden chair next to her on the front porch, laying the twelve-gauge over his legs.

"How'd the talk go with Dylan?" Caitlin asked him.

"Like most of them these days. Got no idea if I accomplished anything at all. Boy always leaves me scratching my head."

"Wonder who he takes after. You set him straight about his actions today?"

"Depends on your meaning."

Caitlin flexed her eyebrows. "That answers my question."

"I'm kind of new at this," Cort Wesley told her. "Don't know if I'll get the chance to get old at it, if social services has their way."

Caitlin looked at him closer. "That's twice you've mentioned that."

"Department's thinking seriously of taking my boys away from me. No visible means of support, no woman in their lives . . . you want me to go on?"

"I'm sorry."

"Not your responsibility, so you got nothing to be sorry for." Cort Wesley tried to take a deep breath but stopped halfway, his frustration showing in the furrows suddenly dug into his forehead. "I never been scared of anything in my life like I'm scared right now.

Why you think I hauled ass to New Orleans to make my case to the Brancas?"

"How about you give me the social worker's number, lemme see what I can do?"

Cort Wesley fished the card from his wallet and handed it to Caitlin. "Texas Rangers got authority over Department of Social Services now?"

Caitlin stuck the card in her pocket. "You'd be surprised."

"Maybe you won't make the best character reference under the circumstances."

"Meaning?"

"When she asks you how often you're around and you say once every two months to bail the oldest out of jail."

"Thought you might've been pissed over what happened the last time we were together."

"You mean, you breaking my nose?"

Caitlin was sparring with a Golden Gloves lightweight at Castillo's Boxing Gym on Pleasanton Road a couple weeks after they got back from DisneyWorld, when Cort Wesley approached the ring between rounds.

"Hopefully you're not picturing me when you throw that right cross."

"What are you doing here, Cort Wesley?" Caitlin asked as some of the other cops and Rangers who used the gym for recreation looked on.

"Got some of your souvenirs in the car. Figured I'd give them to you when you stopped by, but since you haven't I was curious where you been keeping yourself."

"Now you know," Caitlin said and spit some water into a bucket. "You don't mind, the next round's about to start."

Cort Wesley started to climb into the ring. "Anybody got some gloves I can borrow?"

"It still hurts," he told her from the chair next to hers on the front porch.

"I warned you I was good."

"Figured you'd take it easy on me."

"That was before your right hook nearly broke my jaw."

He'd come at her with his cocky smirk, figuring he'd just have his way when . . .

Thump . . . thump . . . thump.

. . . Caitlin's jabs snapped his head back and sent him reeling. Cort Wesley charged back in, going at her with brute force that backed her up into the ropes. She covered up, cross-stepping away from the corner, and then landed an uppercut that opened him up for the hook in question. She felt the heavy glove mash bone and cartilage on contact, both of Cort Wesley's nostrils spewing blood that left a speckled trail across the mat. He doubled over, then bounced back up ready to go at her again to be greeted by the towel Caitlin had extended toward him.

"You should've been wearing protection," she told him now.

"Not my style."

"So I've seen."

"Off and on."

"Off and on," Caitlin agreed.

Cort Wesley's eyes continued to sweep the night

before them, the streetlights bathing the minivans and SUVs stacked in the nearby driveways. "How about a rematch?"

"You want your nose busted again that bad?"

"I'll be ready this time."

Caitlin waited for him to look at her before responding. "You want me to talk to social services for you or not?"

"Rather you go a few rounds with this Silvaro woman. Knock some sense into her head."

"How about knocking some into Dylan's? Or is putting himself in a killer's sights by taking off from school with a runaway girl acceptable from your standpoint?"

"She's upstairs crying on his bed. What about her parents?"

"Number she gave us isn't in service anymore. I got one of our office guys trying to track the new one down." Caitlin heard her BlackBerry beep the signal for an incoming text message and checked the screen. "You mind holding down the fort for a bit?" she asked Cort Wesley, rising.

"Something happen?"

"Our office guy tracked down that number."

20

SHAVANO PARK; THE PRESENT

"You mind giving me a few minutes?" Caitlin asked Dylan after he opened the door.

The boy shrugged his shoulders and nodded, retreating into the hallway. Caitlin closed the door behind him and moved to the bed, Maria turning to look up at her.

"I wanna go home."

"And we'll get you there soon enough."

"Why not now? I could take a bus or something."

"Well, there's reasons why you can't do that, but I got the next best thing in mind," Caitlin said and raised her phone. "We found your parents' new phone number. Turns out they moved since you've been gone."

The girl threw herself into Caitlin's arms, hugging her so tight it hurt Caitlin to breathe. She hugged Maria back, the girl's ribs and shoulder bones protruding from malnutrition. She felt Maria's tears against her cheek, her hair rich with the smell of Dylan's shampoo she'd used during a second shower in which she'd nearly scrubbed her skin raw as if to wash away the filth of the past six months.

Caitlin waited for Maria to break the embrace, then handed her the BlackBerry. "Number's already displayed. All you gotta do is hit the send button here."

"When can I tell them I'm coming home?"

"Soon," Caitlin said, starting for the door. "Soon."

She rejoined Cort Wesley on the front porch, aware of him studying her as she sat back in her chair.

"Looks like you been doing a little crying yourself, Ranger. Hope it wasn't on account of me being so tough on you."

"That girl's been through hell, Cort Wesley. I just can't imagine."

"Yes, you can; we both can, kind of things both of

us have seen." He thought for a moment. "Maybe that's the problem."

"What?"

"You and me. We faced down death enough times, Pirates of the Caribbean and Space Mountain just didn't measure up."

"You think that's why I haven't been around for two months?"

"Haven't called either."

"I've been—"

"I know, busy chasing down missing Mexican girls. You figure out why, maybe the rest will fall into place."

"How many times you want me to say I'm sorry?"

"It's like you're on some kind of quest or something and now Dylan's become a part of it."

"So all of a sudden you're the concerned parent. . . ."

Cort Wesley shifted his chair to better face her. "I don't like thinking about my son being face-to-face with the man behind the Women of Juárez."

"He did that all on his own."

"Am I missing something here?"

"Just the point," Caitlin told him. "Maria didn't come to Dylan looking for help, she came looking for money. He took the rest from there, didn't hesitate when this Macerio showed up."

"Guess I am missing the point."

"He's fifteen, Cort Wesley."

"I was sixteen when I killed my first man."

"More of a boy too, I seem to recall."

"The knife made him older, Ranger. 'Sides, I couldn't tell, given I was more interested in protecting my girl at the time." He hesitated, dropping his eyes almost shyly. "Same way I feel about you. You remember the last time we were together before you busted my nose?"

Caitlin nodded. "That motel just off the interstate. The bed shaking every time a semi went by."

"Oh, is that what it was?" Cort Wesley said with a wink, his face quickly sobering. "You woke up screaming."

"Must've had a nightmare."

"Wasn't the first time." Cort Wesley leaned forward, holding the twelve-gauge barrel up on the porch floor. "And you never told me what they were about."

Caitlin's gaze narrowed, as if she were trying to see something out of her range of vision. "I'm a little girl running from something in the rain. It's night, I'm alone, and there's someone after me."

"That's it?"

"I ever remember anything else, you'll be the first to hear."

21

YUCATÁN PENINSULA, MEXICO; THE PRESENT

Colonel Renaldo Montoya gazed down at the four Americans tied to the pillar before him. That pillar supported the lone surviving watchtower of the Mayan temple beyond that the colonel had discovered himself upon taking refuge in the jungle. The jagged remnants of its stepped pyramid structure were camouflaged by overgrowth and the protective canopy of trees that had outlasted the centuries. The ruins featured ornate graystone steps climbing toward the now open front wall that had once held the entrance. Like the Mayan culture itself, the temple was no longer alive, but neither was it dead, clinging stubbornly to life.

"*Buenos días,*" Montoya said to the two boys and two girls who were shaking in eerily synchronized motion. Montoya watched the sacks pulled down over their faces expanding with each labored breath until he signaled his men to strip them off.

The American college students looked up at him fearfully, lips trembling, eyes struggling to adapt to light again. Montoya noticed lines of tears staining their faces with streaks of grime, one of the boys trying to tighten his features into something defiant and strong.

"My name is Colonel Renaldo Montoya. It is important to me that you know that, important that you know where you are. Look around you."

None of them did.

"Look around," Montoya ordered again.

The four college students turned about, still reluctant to take their eyes off Montoya.

"You came down on vacation to my world, eh?, the world of my ancestors. We call that trespassing, and now you must be punished," Montoya continued calmly, standing stiff and sure as always.

Montoya ran his gaze from one of the Americans to the next, only the defiant boy meeting his eyes hatefully enough to pass as brave. He had close-cropped, straw-colored hair and weight-lifting muscles that formed his bravado. The other boy was tall and lanky with a nest of matted sun-bleached hair and a surfer's tan. The girls looked the same to him, uniform in their sniffling and sobbing. Montoya crouched down to face one of them, freezing her in midsob.

"I do not mean the Mexican culture," Montoya told them. "I mean my own, the Mayan culture. My ancestors, my *olom,* settled this country right here in the Yucatán, and for centuries our warriors of pure blood thrived until the Europeans came. For twenty years we fought back the advances of the Spaniards." He slid over to the second girl, waited for her to look up at him before resuming. "Twenty years, and when we finally succumbed it was not to their spears and arrows, but the wretched diseases they brought with them. For centuries we endured in smaller and smaller patches of land, until the new Mexico decreed those were to be taken from us too, that Mayan independence was no longer to be tolerated."

With that, the colonel withdrew the nine-millimeter pistol from his holster and racked the slide back. "But I'm going to give you the opportunity my people were never given."

The colonel's stubble-laced square head rode his shoulders with barely any neck in between. And what little neck there was stood stiff and immobile, thanks to vertebrae surgically fused together after a bullet nearly severed his spinal cord. His face was pitted with acne scars and a larger one that ran through his eyebrow all the way to his cheek, barely missing one of his two eyes so light a shade of blue to seem almost indistinguishable from the pupils. As a boy, the oddity had branded Montoya a freak. As an adult, he had come to see it as a gift that gave him the vision others lacked.

"Please," one of the girls managed, "don't kill us."

"That is not my intention at all," Montoya told all of them. "In times past, Mayan kings were expected to participate in our ritualistic sacrifices themselves. I have come up with my own version of that with you as my *sib,* my offering. Blood has been spilled in this very place before and so it will again."

Four of his soldiers looked on from the shadows with weapons steadied, as Montoya extended his pistol downward. "There are three bullets in this gun, one of them already in the chamber. Three of you must die. Do that and the survivor gets his, or her, freedom. *Comprende?*"

Montoya moved from one American to the next, offering each of them the pistol. None offered to take it.

"I don't think you understand," Montoya said sharply. "I'm giving you control of your destiny, a much better chance than the one given my people by the invaders who polluted our blood and victimized our people. The rest is up to you. How you decide who lives and who doesn't." He stopped in front of the weight lifter. "What, you're not strong enough to go first; show your friends how it's done?"

The boy shriveled, slumping backward.

"Now you know what it feels like to have your world stripped from you," Montoya said and cast his gaze on the temple ruins. "What little land we had left, in Chan Santa Cruz, was invaded one hundred fifty years ago by a Mexican colonel named Pedro Acereto. He took three thousand men into the jungle and came back with only fifteen hundred. More soldiers came, then more and more, attacking from both land and sea, driving us into the swamps where pestilence and famine further decimated our people. And when we surrendered they slaughtered us and left our bodies to rot in the sun."

The colonel slid past the two girls and stopped in front of the surfer. "But enough of us survived to keep the old ways close in our hearts, even as we were reduced to little more than slaves, peasants, and now itinerant labor for you Americans and rich Mexicans who are no better. We pick your crops, clean up after you, keep our eyes from meeting yours in a display of subservience not befitting our warrior heritage. You represent those who've victimized us for generations now, turned those who founded this very earth into slaves fit for no more than tending it."

"We didn't do shit to you, man!" the surfer managed, his voice cracking.

Montoya continued to hold the gun out to him. "I should be a general, I should be commander of the Mexican army. But as a full-blooded Indian, I'm looked down upon, shunned, considered inferior. Me, commander of the Zeta Special Forces, the best soldiers Mexico has to offer. Me, descended from kings who tore the beating hearts from the chests of their enemies, not even able to use my true family name of Chibirias that my grandfather had no choice but to disown. And now I'm going to tear the beating heart from your country."

The surfer took the gun from the colonel's hand and for an instant, just an instant, Montoya thought he was going to turn it on him.

Go ahead, he thought, *try.*

Instead, though, the surfer's eyes turned blank and he started the pistol upward, angled for the sky until he jammed it against his temple.

"Fuck you, man. *Fuck you!*"

The surfer's hand was still trembling when he squeezed his eyes shut and pulled the trigger.

Click.

The gun slipped from the surfer's grasp, plunked to the ground.

Montoya grinned as he stooped to retrieve the empty pistol. He patted the surfer's head almost tenderly and then moved down the line, meeting each of the other American's eyes until they looked away.

"My men will take you back to where they found you," Montoya told them all. "Tell everyone that I'm here. Tell them I'm coming."

22

SAN ANTONIO; THE PRESENT

"You wanna give me that again?" Captain D. W. Tepper of the Texas Rangers told Caitlin, leaning so far over his desk, she thought he might fall.

His office was brightly lit now in comparison to the dimness he usually worked in to keep the heat down so he wouldn't have to run the air-conditioning all day. But D. W.'s eyes had begun to go and he found himself unable to use the computer anymore without both the overhead light and desk lamp fired up. Today he was wearing a freshly starched white shirt, string tie, and pressed slacks over a pair of boots unmarked by scuffs. Last time Caitlin saw him dressed like that was her husband's funeral a year before.

"Nuevo Laredo, Captain," she repeated. "I think I know where a whole bunch of these kidnapped girls are being held."

Tepper's expression took on that of a man swallowing bile back down. "Thought I told you to give up on that. We got enough trouble handling what comes into our own jurisdiction."

"Once they're sold as sex slaves, these kidnapped girls end up in a whole lot of jurisdictions."

"I got that much," said Tepper. "It's the rest I wanna make sure I heard right, you mentioning Las Mujeres de Juárez."

"I think I know who's been killing them," Caitlin told him.

In the past thirteen years, since 1997, the bodies of over four hundred Mexican women, many of them unidentified to this day, had been found along the border with Texas in various stages of dismemberment, beginning in the area between Juárez and El Paso.

The Rangers had been involved in the case off and on since then, but the lack of cooperation from Mexican authorities had stymied any efforts that might have otherwise proved fruitful. In addition to their own incompetence and apathy, the Mexican *federalés* and local officials had never been able to totally put aside their hostility toward the Texas Rangers, thanks to a past that had seen them on opposite sides of too many battles. Some still referred to the Rangers derogatorily as *el Rinche,* and Caitlin supposed the animosity had too much history behind it to ever go away entirely.

Her own involvement with Las Mujeres de Juárez investigation dated back to 2003. She and fellow Ranger Charlie Weeks were looking for drug-running tunnels dug out of the desert floor east of El Paso when they came upon the body of a young woman that had been rolled down an embankment of a two-lane highway amid stray tires, broken bottles, and fast-food wrappers. She was naked save for a pair of lace-up sandals that must've been knotted too tight to remove. A pool of dried blood had painted the ground beneath the body, spreading outward from the woman's rectum, where a sharp object later identified as a railroad spike had been wedged to shred her intestines while she was bleeding to death from a knife wound.

It had surely been, the coroner reported, an agonizing death in keeping with the pattern already developed for Las Mujeres de Juárez. Evidence of torture and rape were present in virtually all the murders, Caitlin learned, in spite of which virtually no progress at all had been made on either side of the border.

Until yesterday.

"I'll bring the girl in later to write up her statement," Caitlin finished.

"Seems to me you should've done so already."

"Figured it be best to get her status clarified first, Captain."

"Meaning?"

"She may have evidence against the worst serial killer in history, along with a sex slavery ring south of the border that's ruined thousands of lives."

Tepper's face crinkled with concern. "I know that look, Ranger, and I know what you got in that mind of yours. But, like I said, south of the border's not exactly our jurisdiction."

"Didn't stop my granddad."

"Sure, back when he used to hunt dinosaurs in his spare time." Tepper cleared his throat and shook his head. "You wanna tell me why you're all over this sex slave thing like a pit bull on a poodle?"

"That Mexican girl I picked up yesterday, Maria

Lopez, said the kidnappers packed their victims into rooms tighter than a sardine can. She told me one of the girls choked to death on her own vomit and it was more than a day before they removed the body. That answer your question?"

"It would if all this hadn't started long before yesterday."

"Feels like something I gotta do, Captain, but I can't tell you why exactly. Sometimes I have dreams about a girl just like these victims. She's handcuffed to the slats on an old freight car somewhere. I don't know who she is, but she always looks so sad. All I wanna do in the dream is help her, but I never can. I wake up in the morning glad I might be able to do better in real life."

"A dream?"

"Feels like more than that, but, yeah, pretty much."

Tepper frowned. The light made the furrows in his leathery face seem even deeper, some more like crevices in which he was accustomed to losing the tip of a finger. He'd finally given up smoking six months back, leaving him with a dry cough instead of a wet, mucus-laden one. But his teeth were still stained brown and skin yellowed by the residue of a habit that had nearly killed him.

"What if I told you to let it go?" he asked suddenly.

"I'd tell you I couldn't."

"Even if it was for your own good?"

"Why would that be exactly?"

Tepper looked away, as if afraid to let Caitlin see his eyes. "Wish you could just trust me on this."

"On what?"

"You're not your granddad, Ranger. And trust me when I say you don't wanna be."

Caitlin felt one of her fingers start to dig around in her hair and yanked on it. "You're talking in circles, Captain."

"Maybe you're just not hearing what I'm telling you."

"Maria Lopez can help me break this case wide open," Caitlin insisted.

Tepper drummed his fingers amid the clutter of papers strewn over his desk blotter. "You really believe *one* man could be responsible for four hundred murders, Ranger?"

"That's what the evidence I looked at suggested. But too much of it had been compromised to be sure."

Tepper shook his head and stripped the string tie from his collar. "Just got back from a meeting of all Ranger captains in Austin where these Washington types talked their tongues off. We're supposed to be on the lookout for Mexican guerrillas crossing the border, the hell you make of that. Listening to them go on and on was like giving myself a hot pepper enema." He frowned. "Didn't expect I'd be coming home to something like this neither."

"The girl says she overheard the wranglers saying they had just another twenty miles to go, heading north not far out of Uvalde on U.S. 90."

D. W. Tepper's eyebrows rose, digging ditches out of the furrows along his brow. "North of Uvalde you say . . ."

"Mean something to you, Captain?"

Tepper nodded as if he'd prefer not having to. "You ever heard of a man named Hollis Tyree III?"

23

"Prairie dogs?" Hollis Tyree III asked, holding the gnawed-through husk of flexible rubber tubing.

"Yes," his foreman Weaver told him, as Tyree rolled the tubing about in his hands.

"Prairie dogs," Tyree repeated from the middle of what had been a desert just a few months before, now bustling with the activity of men, machines, and a city of bright white prefab structures that shined in the sun. "Costing me time and money. I don't give a damn about the money, but the time's something else again. You got a solution?"

"Well, we can't use poison and they seem to have figured out our traps."

"Of course, being the geniuses that they are."

"Sir—"

"Issue guns to the off-shift men. A bonus for whoever shoots the most of the little bastards. How about ten thousand? You think that might coax their aim a mite?"

Before Tyree, the orange drilling rigs stretched as far as the eye could see, the modern-day equivalent of the oil derricks that had made his family rich in Sweetwater. Unlike those immobile, unwieldy structures, these were sleek and versatile. When erect, their truck-mounted housings stretched a hundred feet into the air, looking like shiny steel sentinels guarding the horizon. If a rig's efforts yielded nothing, the workers simply lowered it mechanically back to the truck bed and drove on to the next ping on the geothermal map.

Tyree's scientists had spent six months plotting the locations, while his technicians supervised the design and construction of the rigs themselves. Interesting how eighty years after oil was struck in Sweetwater, many of the challenges remained the same.

Except these fields had nothing to do with oil.

Weaver was still standing before him, trapped between thoughts and words.

"You got a problem with that, Weave?"

"No, sir."

"See Meeks to arrange for the guns, then." Tyree could sense the man's reluctance. "How long you work for my father, Weave?"

"Long enough to teach you the fields."

"Worked my ass off too, didn't you?"

"You wouldn't have it any other way, sir, and you know it."

"Back then I called *you* sir. Liked it better that way. Remember what you called me?"

"Number of things, as I recall."

"Punk, turd, lazy-ass, rich boy, and pond scum being among them."

"A few, anyway," Weaver smiled.

"You remember we had the locust problem down in Brownsville?"

"I do. Your daddy strapped a flamethrower on his back and went at them himself." Weaver hesitated, letting his mind drift. "I seem to remember you walking 'longside him."

"Until I sneezed and lit one of the rigs on fire. He took the damage out of my salary. Six whole goddamn months." Tyree took in a deep breath and let it out slowly. "What'd you think he'd make of what we're doing here?"

"I think he'd say you were fucking crazy."

Weaver grinned and Hollis Tyree grinned back at him. "Oh, you're right there for sure. Where's the money in it, he'd ask? Tell people we're running out of oil and they'll rush out to fill their tank. Tell them we're running out of water and they'll just look at you funny. But it's true. The Southwest has already lost sixty percent of its irrigation supplies and Lake Mead is going down twenty feet a year. In twenty years, if we don't do something, the whole Southwest is destined to become a wasteland. But folks won't see the problem until they turn on their faucets and nothing comes out. That's what this job's all about, Weave, making sure something *does* come out."

The two men stood side by side in the dry wind, the generations bridged between them.

"You trying to save the country, Hollis, or something else?" Weaver asked suddenly.

Tyree looked toward him but didn't answer.

"It wasn't your fault, sir."

"What, burning the rig?"

"What happened to your kids down in Mexico."

Tyree spoke with his gaze on the rigs so Weaver couldn't see his eyes. "You mean 'cause I spoiled the shit out of them instead of working them to hell like my dad worked me? You think they would have been better off if I'd made them spend spring break working on an off-shore?"

"Hard to say now, under the circumstances."

"But they're gone. That's not hard to say, is it?"

Weaver shrugged. "I best be getting back at it."

"I'll tell Meeks about the guns, Weave," Tyree said, waiting for the work foreman to take his leave before pulling the report he'd commissioned on the situation in Albion into the light of the sun, reading it as the morning breeze flapped the pages about.

He read the first page of the report, the summary, again. The schoolteacher who'd been stabbed with the scissors, Faye Magruder, was resting comfortably at home and expected back in the classroom in a matter of weeks. But similarly inexplicable incidents continued to plague the town.

A man beat a paperboy senseless for tossing the morning paper on his wet lawn.

Two women got into a major tussle in the aftermath of a PTA meeting. One remained in the hospital after the other tossed a mug of scalding black coffee into her face.

A local cop shot a man in the leg during a routine traffic stop.

On the surface these could have been regarded as isolated incidents, the product of bad luck and tough times and nothing more. But Tyree knew better. These incidents told him so.

Tyree walked along the freshly paved road he'd laid atop the desert floor to allow smooth passage for his construction and rigging vehicles. It glistened in the warming sunlight, the smell of tar still plain and thick in the air. The road had the look of a vast black ribbon stretching from one end of the world to the other, almost eerie in its desolation with only Tyree-sanctioned vehicles traversing it since it didn't go anywhere else.

The drilling rigs swallowed up the land on the west side of the road, the community required to man those rigs dominated the east. That community consisted of a nest of trailers housing the offices and communications facilities, arranged in rectangular fashion like an

old-fashioned army fort. Beyond them, trailers unused and left over from any number of natural disas-
ters, purchased for pennies on the dollar from FEMA,
dotted the barren landscape. These trailers housed
the field's workers, mostly three or four in each.

His grandfather had left Sweetwater long before
Hollis III was born, so he had no actual memory of
what that town had looked like back when the oil
boom hit. What he knew, he knew only from pictures
and, again, the comparisons were striking. Right down
to the prefab buildings that had been hastily erected to
take care of the men's needs, including a store that sold
food and sundries on credit, a bar, and a restaurant. It
was his security man Meeks who suggested bringing in
the women, warning in a none too cryptic fashion the
upshot if Tyree failed to provide this basic need as
well. They occupied a building identical in all respects
to the prefab church, except for the wooden crucifix
missing over the door.

Meeks had arranged for the camp's private security
force too. Regulators, he called them, every bit as mean
and as tough as the Pinkertons from which Meeks was
descended who enforced the law on the gold claims
of George Hearst, cementing his fortune and legacy.

Nothing had changed, Hollis Tyree mused. From
Hearst in the nineteenth century, to his grandfather in
the twentieth, to himself in the twenty-first, things had
remained remarkably the same. Only the object of the
strikes was different, since both Hearst's and his grandfather's strikes had been about making money, while
his was about spending it. Tyree had once figured he
could spend a million dollars a day for a thousand
years and still not go through his entire riches.

He stopped over a bespectacled man assiduously

taking soil samples a few feet away. "Morning, Dr. Lamb," Tyree greeted.

"Sir?" Lamb asked, startled.

Lamb's voice was nasally and on closer inspection Tyree realized one of his eyes was blackened, his nose swelled up on the same side.

"What happened to your face?"

"Pardon me?"

Tyree pointed toward his own eye. "Your face. Looks like somebody busted you up. Your nose is the size of a grapefruit."

Lamb forced a laugh. "That? Well, sir, it's rather personal. If you don't mind . . ."

"Not at all."

Lamb, looking out of place in his shirt and tie, stood up and tried to brush the stubborn desert dust, damp with mesquite, from his knees, as his thinning hair blew about in the stiff breeze.

Tyree flapped the pages so Lamb could see what he was holding. "Explain to me exactly what's happening in Albion without the fancy jargon."

"Well, those aquifers we found here are down so deep nobody knew they were there until this latest generation of seismic equipment told us so," said Lamb. "By all indications the contents of one of the aquifers we struck leached into the ground wells serving that town."

"We poisoned their water. That's what you're telling me."

"Not according to the results of the field report."

Tyree flapped the pages he'd been reading before him. "You mean this? Seems a little vague to be considered conclusive."

"It's a complicated situation," Lamb told him. "We're

testing for an unknown mineral or toxin. Could be anything or nothing."

"No, it couldn't be nothing."

"Let me rephrase: nothing we're aware of."

"Huh?"

"Mr. Tyree, the aquifers we've struck in your fields here date back tens, even hundreds of thousands of years. It could be there's something in them that for all intents and purposes can't be identified because we've never seen it before. But chances are the toxin, mineral, or whatever is isolated to one specific area. I'm expecting this latest batch of samples I've been taking will produce something more definitive."

"You're saying we can keep a lid on this. Button up the contamination by just capping the site in question."

Lamb nodded.

"EPA gets wind of this before we get it handled, a whole lot of people are gonna go thirsty down the road. So you call that lab of yours, Doctor, and you tell them they better light a fire under their ass. That clear?"

"Yes, sir," Lamb told him, breathing noisily through his mouth.

"Where exactly is Albion as the crow flies, Lamb?"

"Twenty miles due west. Eight thousand residents, give or take."

Tyree found his gaze listing in that direction. "Like prairie dogs . . ."

"Excuse me, sir?"

"Nothing, Doctor," Tyree told him.

24

"Water," Caitlin said, when Captain Tepper had finished.

"The new oil, some folks in the know say."

"So we got a town sprouting up in the middle of the desert of Tunga County where they made the find."

"Old-fashioned tent city, I hear tell, or trailers in this case. Not much different from eighty or so years ago when your granddad cleaned up Sweetwater after they struck oil."

"He used to tell me the story all the time when I was a little girl, along with another about his father William Ray Strong coming upon a bunch of murdered pioneers when he was riding with George W. Arrington and the Frontier Battalion."

"I don't recall that one."

"By a creek bed somewhere in what we call Tunga County today."

Something in D. W. Tepper's expression changed, growing pained and sad.

"Something wrong, D. W.?"

He seemed to snap out of whatever had struck him. "Got another PET scan scheduled for later today. Docs can't find a single thing wrong with me and I never felt worse in my life. Hell, I'm thinking about taking up smoking again."

"You've looked the same for as long as I've known you."

"Guess I was old when I was young and even older now that I'm old." Talking that way turned his gaze nostalgic and reflective. "You had lots of favorite stories, as I recall."

"That one my granddad used to tell me about Sweetwater was something special."

"Hollis Tyree's grandfather was constable at the time. He was the one sent the wire that brought Earl Strong to town." The pained look resurfaced, gone before Caitlin could question Tepper about it again. "An oil strike on his spread gave birth to the family fortune. His grandson's a billionaire now. But it was his dad who bought up that land in Tunga County years ago with no purpose other than to make sure no one else did. Geological survey revealed the aquifers maybe nine months back and Tyree's crew set up shop pretty much the very next day."

"Lots of men."

"As I've heard told anyway."

"Explains the prostitutes called up from Nuevo Laredo. A whorehouse on wheels, inside a rank panel truck driven by this Macerio, or whatever his goddamn name is. Maria Lopez was on her way there when she fled."

Tepper caught the look in Caitlin's eyes, his own flashing concern. "You stay away from that place until we make better sense of this. That clear?"

"I notice you didn't warn me to stay clear of Nuevo Laredo, Captain."

"'Cause I know it wouldn't do any darn good." Tepper glanced down at his gnarled fingers in search of a cigarette that wasn't there. "You just keep your gun in your holster, Ranger."

Caitlin flashed Tepper a smile. "'Less somebody draws theirs first, Captain."

25

Guillermo Paz was climbing the steps of the Sweetwater Public Library when he saw the squad car slide to a halt in a no-parking zone at the curb. Paz watched a deputy climb out, having trouble closing the door and putting his hat on at the same time. His uniform was caked with brown dust kicked up from the mud that seemed ready to swallow the town, so much so that Paz noticed the town's residents had uniformly painted their front steps the same dirt-brown color.

"Good afternoon," the deputy said, approaching him.

"*Buenos dias, ayudante.*"

"You mind speaking English?"

"Not at all, Deputy. Is there a problem?"

The deputy stopped ten feet from Paz as if he'd struck an invisible wall. "Someone from the diner called. Said a customer had just been in they never saw before."

"So this is your way of welcoming visitors to your town."

"The customer spooked them pretty bad."

"I have that effect on people sometimes," Paz told him, his feet placed on separate steps.

The deputy chanced a few more steps forward. "So what brings you to Sweetwater?"

"Research. I'm writing a book on the oil boom of the 1930s."

The deputy relaxed a bit. "Folks in the diner said you were asking a lot of questions. That's what spooked them. You don't mind me saying, sir, you don't look much like an academic."

"You don't have to be to write a book these days. I had relatives who worked the fields here in Sweetwater. The tales have stuck with me ever since I was a boy."

"So you're Mexican?"

"I am."

"Excuse me for saying you don't sound Mexican."

"My father was from Venezuela, descended from a long line of Indian warriors. I apologize if I bothered anyone, *ayudante*."

"You got some ID?"

Paz pulled the well-worn billfold from his pocket and extended it forward. Watched the deputy approach him tentatively to take it, extending a hand the way a man might raise a stick toward a hornet's nest.

The deputy opened the wallet, compared Paz's face to the picture, and handed it back to him.

Paz stuffed the wallet back in his pocket. "I'm especially interested in the Texas Ranger who cleaned up your town after it was invaded by a collection of bad men, the likes of which hadn't been seen in these parts before and haven't been since."

"You'd be talking about Earl Strong."

"I would."

"Library's got lots of photos and news clippings from the era."

Paz let his shoulders slump, feigning disappointment. "I was hoping to speak to someone who actually lived through it. That would speed up the process considerably. Allow me to move on that much faster."

The deputy weighed his words. "Well, sir," he said,

still having trouble meeting Paz's eyes, big and dark as eight balls wedged into his face, "there's one man still here now who was alive then, named Robert Roy Parsons. He was just a boy at the time, had a job at the local saloon where Earl Strong first showed his guns."

Paz thought of his own boyhood, much of it spent in just such a place working for the local crime boss known as Carnicero, Spanish for "butcher," thanks to his proficiency with all manner of blades. But Paz was good with a knife too, and stabbed Carnicero as he sat grinning on a bar stool after refusing to give Paz the money due him to take care of his pregnant mother. To make his point Carnicero had bent Paz's finger back until it snapped, so Paz used his other hand to ram the blade deep into his chest. The crime boss was bleeding to death on the floor when Paz reached into his pocket and extracted only the money he was owed. He fled his slum community of La Vega after giving the bills to his mother.

"Where can I find Mr. Parsons?" Paz asked the deputy.

"Same place as all those years back, 'cept he owns it now."

Paz noticed a squad car already parked across the street from the Sweetwater Saloon when he got there, the same deputy behind the wheel pretending to busy himself with other things.

"Call me R.R.," Parsons greeted, surprising Paz with a firm handshake for a man near ninety years old. He was tall, straight spined, and surprisingly robust for a man of that age, moving about nimbly without the tentative nature Paz was accustomed to seeing in old people. He had a full head of white hair, a pleasing manner, and welcoming spirit more fit for the age he'd grown up in than the one in which he was living now. "Deputy told me you might be coming. Seemed a bit spooked."

"I lied to him," Paz admitted.

"Come again?" Parsons asked, eyes narrowing.

"I told him I was here researching a book. Truth is I'm here on a matter of life and death."

"Sounds serious."

"It is," Paz said, picturing Caitlin Strong in his mind. "A person I care about is going to die, unless I find what I'm looking for."

"And what's that?"

"I don't know yet. I was hoping you could help me."

Parsons pulled back a bit, putting as much distance between him and Paz as the wall would allow. "Deputy said it had something to do with Texas Ranger Earl Strong."

"Everything," said Paz. "I don't think the deputy has much appreciation for history."

"Well, sir, then it's a good thing I do, considering I lived it."

"You remember Earl Strong, then."

"Like he was standing in front of me instead of you. I followed him around like a puppy from the first night he showed up in this very same joint. Of course, it was a much different place in those days."

"So I imagine."

Parsons thought for a moment and took a long look at Paz, having to crane his neck to look him in the eyes. "What do you say we get ourselves a table."

. . .

The Sweetwater Saloon was more of a restaurant now, with a nest of tables rimmed by wood-frame booths along the walls. And centered amid it all, set back near the kitchen, was a horseshoe-shaped bar outfitted with a quartet of televisions. It would be another hour before the place opened for dinner, meaning Paz had Parsons all to himself for at least that long. The old man had chosen a table against the far wall, a nearby window overlooking the street beyond where Paz could see the deputy's car was gone.

"That bar," R.R. Parson told Paz, "was built from the same wood as the original. Couldn't bring myself to discard anything with that many memories soaked in, if you know what I mean."

"I do," Paz replied, wondering if Carnicero's blood still stained the floor of the bar where he'd killed him.

"Floor's the original too. Every pair of boots that clacked against it came with a story, and I like to think people still get a sense of that, even if they don't realize it." Parsons reached up and lifted from the wall a framed picture of a man wearing the badge of the Texas Rangers over his starched white shirt, holding a Winchester rifle in hand. "This here's Ranger Earl. What was your name again?"

"Paz," he said, running a thick finger along the glass guarding the image of the man captured within. Earl Strong was tall and lean, not carrying a lot of muscle on his frame but no fat Paz could see either. Everything about him, from his boots to his trousers to the tawny skin of his face fit him perfectly. It was his eyes, though, that Paz focused on the most, because they were Caitlin Strong's eyes, brimming with the same fury, resolve, and intensity. He was certain that somewhere in this picture, in this man, he'd find the source of his fascination with Caitlin Strong, as well as the means to save her.

"Well, Mr. Paz," R.R. Parsons continued, "what is it I can tell you about old Earl to help save somebody's life?"

"Everything," Paz told him.

26

SWEETWATER, TEXAS; 1931

Earl Strong had wasted no time in letting the miscreants, roustabouts, and derelicts gathered in Sweetwater know who was in charge. The next morning he was seen riding up and down the town's lone ruddy, muck-ridden commercial thoroughfare atop a black horse, his twin pearl-handled revolvers laced to his hip and an old lever-action Winchester slung through a slat in the saddle.

Hollis Tyree couldn't believe how much the attitude of the motley assortment of humanity drawn to Sweetwater had changed at one man's hand and reputation. Those who'd never heard of Texas Ranger Earl Strong before need only lay an ear open to hear more than they wanted about the exploits that had spread his name across the entire state. If he wasn't the toughest, most respected man in Texas, he came very close.

Tyree heard the heavy pounding of hoofbeats while he patrolled the street atop the wood-plank sidewalk,

turning to see Earl Strong looming over him, silhouetted by sunlight. The horse had sprayed mud onto
Tyree's trousers, a few flecks splattering his face as
well.

"Morning, Constable."

"Morning, Ranger Strong."

"Call me Earl, Constable."

"Thank you, Ranger Earl."

"Never did ask you about the location of the town
jail."

"Town don't have one, sir."

"Don't have one?"

"Never saw the need before."

"Well, that puts us in a bit of a pickle now, don't it?"

But not for long. Earl commandeered the abandoned
town church and instructed Hollis Tyree to chop holes
in the rotting wood floor.

"Be back presently," Earl told him, after scratching
the places where he wanted the holes with a knife.
"Gonna fetch us some chain."

He returned not only with a hundred-foot heavy
steel chain salvaged from the work yard, but also a
hundred or so trace chains to connect up with it and
padlocks to go with them. Jack Rawlins was the first
prisoner to be rigged to the chain by affixing the trace
around his neck with a padlock and then fastening it
to a section of the hundred feet of steel he'd already
looped through the chopped holes. In and out, in and
out, in and out . . .

A week into Earl's stay in Sweetwater, there were
forty men attached to one end of the chain and six
women to the other. Earl showed the ladies kindness
by looping the trace chains around their ankles instead

of throats. The odor was a mix of rank bodies, putre-
fied sweat, and the residue of unwashed pails the pris-
oners used for a commode.

"Watch this, Constable," Earl told Hollis Tyree when
a fresh trio of bearded undesirables appeared in town,
making no secret of their guns.

And Tyree did just that as Earl worked his horse to
a halt sideways before the new arrivals, blocking
their path. "Welcome to Sweetwater, gentlemen. Now
show me your hands."

The men saw no reason not to hold their hands up
where Earl Strong could see them.

"Just like I figured," he said. "You got smooth skin,
no calluses, and there's no dirt under your fingernails.
Means you're not field workers; only other reason
you'd come to a godforsaken place like this is if you're
a pimp, gambler, petty thug, or just an old-fashioned
outlaw looking to hole up for a while. So to spare us
all the trouble, I'm placing you under arrest and putting you on the chain."

"Who the hell you think you are?" demanded one,
spitting a thick wad of tobacco near the front hoof of
Earl's steed.

"Texas Ranger Earl Strong. Any other questions?"

The men looked at one another, perhaps in search
of their bravado.

"We ain't done nothing, Ranger," another of them
protested.

"But you will, that's for sure. Could be you're
stickup men or contract killers and you've come
here to make some kind of mischief and mayhem
and behave in a form of unlawful manner that won't
be tolerated. So you boys should thank me for doing
you all a favor."

The men looked at one another again before Earl continued.

"See, by putting you on the chain, I won't have to shoot you."

Hollis Tyree watched as Sweetwater continued to fill up. With the rooming houses renting out hall space, cities of tents and sleeping bags continued to appear, stretching the town's bursting borders. Two more Rangers joined Earl to keep things even from the law's perspective and they stayed under control, until Tyree summoned him to the office of an overwhelmed local doctor pushed back off the wagon by the influx of business.

"Doc sent for me soon as he did the examination," Tyree told Earl, holding the door of a room open for him. "Wanted you to see what they done to the poor girl for yourself."

Earl entered the room ahead of him and saw a young Mexican woman with fair skin and black hair seated on the exam table trembling from fear and pain. She wore a flimsy white dress with a torn strap and a line of dirt the size of a man's hand from her breasts down through her torso. One of her arms was in a sling and her right knee was wrapped tightly. Her right jaw was swollen red and hung lower than her left. Her eyes were wide and terrified. Black eyes, Earl noted, the same shade as her hair. Her teeth were chattering, face squeezing into a taut grimace every time a bolt of pain surged through her. Earl figured her for eighteen, nineteen at the most.

"I know how you feel about violence against women, Ranger Earl," Tyree said from behind him.

Earl removed his Stetson and walked up close to the girl. "Who did this to you?"

When she didn't respond, Earl repeated the question in Spanish. The woman's eyes flickered, but she made no response.

"It hurts to talk, don't it?"

The young woman nodded.

"Don't try talking then. Just nod or shake your head. Okay?"

The young woman nodded.

"That's fine," Earl said. "You're being forced into serving the needs of men, is that right?"

A nod.

"And the sumbitches who did the forcing are the same ones who messed up your face and arm, aren't they?"

Another nod before the young woman looked past Earl now, as if there might be something better waiting for her beyond a wall papered with a human anatomy poster and generic eye-test chart.

"And this happened down at the railroad freight yard where they turned those rusted cars into bedrooms with red lights flashing over their doorways, right?"

The young woman nodded, just a single time before her face filled with fear again.

"You did just fine," Earl told her, smoothing a hand down the unswollen side of her soiled face, her cheek clammy to his touch. "I'd like to know your name if you don't mind telling me."

"Juanita," the girl managed. "Juanita Rojas."

"Well, Juanita, nobody's gonna lay a hand on you in this town again, and that's a promise."

Bobby Parsons followed Earl Strong to the freight yard that night. He walked there across town with a fellow Ranger on either side of him. They carried 1911 model .45 caliber pistols and twelve-gauge shotguns, Earl content with his pearl-handled revolvers. The lawlessness that had been on the verge of consuming all of Sweetwater was now isolated to the freight yard. Earl tolerated it because the yard was outside proper town limits, and he figured letting the men think they were getting away with something kept them from trying to get away with more. He looked on the freight yard as a cesspit where all the shit went when you flushed and, one way or another, it had to collect somewhere.

Earl arrived just as a hulking man who was so fat it took two strung-together belts to hold up his pants was taking a leather belt to a woman who kept giving him lip in Spanish no matter how much he struck her. Her face was an unrecognizable patchwork of welts. The fat man wheezed with each strike, breathless from an effort that left sweat streaming down his face and turning his blue shirt black with moisture.

"That'll be enough!" Earl bellowed.

"You mind your business!" the fat man shot back, raising his belt anew as the woman finally crumpled to the tracks.

Earl shot the belt out of his hand, the sting from the vibration so bad it flopped uselessly to the fat man's side.

"Who the fuck are you?"

"The man who's gonna shoot you dead if you give me the slightest provocation."

"You know who I am?"

"Fattest piece of dung I ever laid eyes on in my life."

The Rangers on either side of Earl couldn't help

but laugh. Neither could Bobby Parsons from his position peeking out from behind a rusted freight car.

"I come from Chicago," the fat man said. "Ever heard of it?"

"City somewheres north of Dallas. I don't get out much."

"How about Al Capone? You heard of him?"

The other Rangers stiffened. Earl took a few steps closer to the fat man, pistol angled low now.

"'Cause I work for him," the fat man continued, sensing a weakness. "Everyone in this here yard works for him. Chicago runs this yard. You need to know that, yokel."

"Yokel?"

"G-men are no match for us up in Chicago and you're no match for us down here."

"That remains to be seen, don't it?" Earl said.

"You got a family, yokel? Mr. Capone takes special pleasure in hurting families."

Earl snapped his gun into firing position and shot the fat man in the leg. He went down with a force that seemed to shake the earth, the woman struggling to her feet and limping away.

"You son of a bitch!"

Earl came forward and stood over him. "Answer is no, I don't have a family. I shot you just for the implication. And if you imply anything of the sort again, it'll earn you another bullet."

The stench rising off the fat man was worse than that of the church-turned-jail. "This ain't over, yokel!" the fat man rasped. "Tomorrow I'm sending for an army!"

Earl started to walk off.

"The wrath of Chicago is gonna be brought upon you until you wish you were never born!"

Earl looked back at him one last time, longing for one of the cigars wedged in his shirt's lapel pocket. "You tell 'em to bring their own coffins or I'll charge Mr. Capone for the wood."

Back in town, Earl made straight for the telegraph office. Puffing at last on his cigar, he wrote out his message to Austin slowly, making sure Fred Hatchings would be able to read all the lettering.

"What's this?" Hatchings asked anyway.

"B-A-R. All capitalized. You gotta send it exactly that way."

"Says two of them here."

"That's what I need."

Hatchings began tapping out Earl's message. "Anything else?"

"Yeah. Tell 'em to get the damn things here double quick."

27

SWEETWATER, TEXAS; THE PRESENT

"B-A-R," Paz repeated, whimsical smile stretched across his face.

"That's what I heard the next day. Mean something to you?"

"It does indeed. Tell me more about this woman."

"Juanita Rojas—that was her name," R.R. Parsons told him, his eyes all misty and dreamlike from the memories the tale had stoked. "Earl sat up with her all night, holding her hand so she knew she'd be safe. Juanita was pretty busted up, all right, but once the swelling went down, I don't think I ever saw a more beautiful woman. Earl Strong," Parsons said reflectively. "Yup, he sure was something."

"What else can you tell me about Juanita Rojas?"

"Nothing, other than the fact she was from Mexico, because that was where all the whores the Chicago Outfit brought in were from."

"Did she go back home?"

Parsons shrugged. "Don't rightly know, mister. See—"

"What about Al Capone?" Paz asked, eager to hear more. "Did more men show up as promised?"

"You didn't let me finish, mister. Couple days after Earl saved Juanita Rojas's life, my parents fled town and dragged me along. We didn't come back until Earl was long gone and Sweetwater was back to being a real town again, 'cept it had paved streets by then paid for with oil money."

"You must've heard something."

"Sure, lots of things. But never could figure out what was true and what wasn't. A war did come, I can tell you that much, and Earl didn't run from it neither. What more there is, you'll have to find it somewhere else, I'm afraid." He gave Paz a long look, letting his eyes wash over him. "You look like you could have been fit for those times, a match for Earl Strong even. Say, how 'bout I have the kitchen fix you a steak? There's lots more to tell about those days none've heard in quite a while now."

Paz saw the longing in the old man's eyes. "I think I'd like that," he said. *"Muchas gracias."*

"I'm the one should be doing the thanking," said Parsons. "You wanna know the rest of what happened when Al Capone's boys hit town, I'd recommend stopping at the Texas Ranger Hall of Fame in Waco. But if you don't mind me asking, mister, what's a Mexican whore got to do with this life-and-death matter of yours?"

Before Paz could respond, he saw the sheriff's deputy enter the restaurant and head straight to the table he was sharing with R.R. Parsons. The deputy's expression had gone dour and he carried himself stiffly, as if weighed down by some invisible burden strapped to his shoulders.

"Something wrong, *ayudante*?" Paz asked him.

"There are some men in town asking about you."

"Me?"

"Not by name, just description. Whole carload of them. Mexicans, I think." The deputy took off his hat and tried to look stronger than he was. "Look, I don't know who you are or what really brought you here, but whatever it is we don't want it in Sweetwater. So I'd be obliged if you could leave town before those Mexicans find you."

So the priest had been right; the Juárez cartel, whose drugs Paz had destroyed, had tracked him here. His nature told him to make a stand, confront the Mexicans now to send a message to their employers. But a bloodbath in a sleepy little town like Sweetwater would undoubtedly claim innocent lives and attract the kind of attention Paz could ill afford. Not if he wanted to stay on the trail of the information he needed to save Caitlin Strong as well.

Paz rose slowly, eyes on the windows to see if the Mexicans were waiting outside. "I guess I'll have to take a rain check on that steak," he told R.R. Parsons. "Thank you for your concern, *ayudante*. You won't be seeing me again."

28

El Paso; the present

Dr. Alvin Lamb was sipping his beer, alone in a honky-tonk bar called the Highpoint, when the door opened and Frank Branca Jr. entered accompanied by a new pair of bodyguards. Branca dispatched the men toward a table by the old-fashioned jukebox and joined Lamb at his table, flipping the chair around so he could straddle it. Country music, Hank Williams he thought, rose through unseen speakers, just soft enough to provide background he didn't have to raise his voice over.

"Nice to see you, Professor. Hey, the swelling went down."

Lamb pushed his mug aside.

"Something wrong with the brew? You want me to get you another?"

Branca had started to look for a waitress when Lamb's voice called back his attention. "I don't drink. Just figured I was supposed to order something as long as I was here."

"Lots of things people are supposed to do they don't always." Branca eased himself further over the chair back. He was wearing too much aftershave, enough to unsettle Lamb's already queasy stomach. "Like making good on their gambling debts."

"That's why I called, Mr. Branca."

"You said what you had for me was bigger than money. Fucking pot of gold at the end of the rainbow."

"Bigger than that too," Lamb said, placing a manila envelope he'd been sitting on atop the table.

"What's this?"

"A lab report from the site in Tunga County I've been working for Hollis Tyree. He's got no idea of its contents."

Branca's face crinkled in displeasure, marring his otherwise smooth features. "What the fuck that's supposed to mean?"

"Read it and you'll see, Mr. Branca."

"I look like a scientist to you?"

"You don't have to be. Trust me on that."

"Trust a man who's into me for twenty large plus the vig, interest building up every day? Now why would I want to do that?"

With a trembling hand, Lamb slid the envelope still damp with the moisture shed from the seat of his pants toward Frank Branca Jr. "Because this is gonna make us even."

29

Caitlin found Marianna Silvaro in Ruby's Diner down the block from the State of Texas Department of Health and Human Services, on Brady Boulevard where her office was located. She wasn't hard to spot, given Cort Wesley's description, seated at the counter alternating between her coffee and a homemade Danish pastry the size of a shoe box, the stool barely large enough to accommodate her bulk.

"Ms. Silvaro?"

The woman spun slightly, her stool creaking as she regarded Caitlin's badge and face at the same time. "What can I do for you, Ranger?"

"You mind if I sit down, ma'am?"

"Please."

"I guess you could call this a character reference," Caitlin said, accepting a freshly poured coffee from a waitress.

"For Cort Wesley Masters, no doubt."

Caitlin didn't bother hiding her surprise. "Well now, how'd you come to know a thing like that?"

"We do our homework too, Ranger. We're well aware of your relationship with Mr. Masters."

"Along with his children, ma'am. Might even go so far as to call me the female influence in their lives."

Silvaro's gaze dipped to the SIG Sauer holstered on her waist, whether approving or disapproving Caitlin couldn't tell. "I'll note that in my report."

"I was hoping we could talk a bit about Mr. Masters."

Silvaro sipped her coffee, leaving her plate-sized Danish in place. "We could certainly schedule an appointment."

Caitlin forced a smile. "Thing is, ma'am, I'm never quite sure where I'm gonna be from day to day, so if you don't mind how about we schedule it for right now?"

Silvaro broke off a piece of her Danish and didn't say no.

"I want you to know I'm looking out after Mr. Masters's boys," Caitlin continued.

"I thought you wanted to talk about Mr. Masters."

"I am. We are, ma'am."

"And what would you say about his parenting skills?"

"Well, his kids are doing just fine, both top of their class at school."

"I'm aware of that. You a parent yourself, Ranger?"

"No, ma'am, I'm not."

"Then what exactly qualifies you to comment on Mr. Masters's capacity as one?"

"I was there when his boys' mother got killed."

Silvaro turned her stool to better face Caitlin, ignoring her Danish for now. "That have something to do with Mr. Masters's inadequacies as a parent?"

"Sounds like you're making a judgment there."

"Just like you are, in spite of the fact you've got no standing on the subject."

"Maybe not, Ms. Silvaro," Caitlin said, feeling sweat start to push its way through her shirt in spite of the diner's air-conditioning. "But I do have standing on what violence does to people, especially children. The way these boys lost their mother is going to stay with them forever, and the only reason they're doing as well as they are is that their father makes them feel safe."

"I understand," said Marianna Silvaro, dabbing the corners of her mouth with a napkin.

"I don't think you do, ma'am."

Silvaro started to reach for her Danish again, then stopped. "We deal with many children who've witnessed or been victims of violent crime, Ranger. More than you could possibly realize. Had a girl last year whose father took a steam iron to her mother's face. Poor thing just stopped herself from sleeping because of the nightmares. So don't tell me what I know and don't know."

Caitlin felt her fingers throbbing, clenched the left ones into a fist, held low so Marianna Silvaro wouldn't notice. "You know the names of Mr. Masters's boys?"

Silvaro's lips puckered. She let out some breath. "I have a lot of cases."

"It's Dylan and Luke, and they sleep just fine, ma'am. That's because they got a father who's there for them in ways neither of us can possibly imagine. Now I understand all about the need for income verification, proof of employment and the like, but there's no box to check for what Cort Wesley Masters has done for his sons. He kept them living their lives because they know he can stop the monsters from coming back. If I thought some foster home or juvenile facility could do that, I wouldn't be here now." Caitlin removed an envelope embossed with the Texas Ranger logo from her pocket and tucked it under the plate holding Silvaro's Danish. "This here's an official personal reference for Mr. Masters. I know you want to do right for him, ma'am, and I'm hoping this puts another bullet in your chamber."

"We're on the same side here, Ranger," Silvaro said, easing the envelope into her pocketbook.

Caitlin left a pair of singles to pay for her coffee and slid off the stool. "Let's hope so, ma'am. That letter's for anyone who's not." She held Silvaro's stare. "You tell them my phone number's on the bottom, they want more details."

Caitlin had barely stepped outside the diner when her cell phone rang, D. W. Tepper's name lighting up on her Caller ID.

"Don't worry, Captain, I'm still north of the border," Caitlin greeted.

"That's a good thing, Ranger, 'cause I just got a call from a local sheriff requesting immediate help with a hostage situation."

"You say hostage situation, Captain?"

"I did and you're the closest Ranger I got to the scene. Town called Albion on the outskirts of Tunga County. Ever heard of it?"

PART THREE

The stars have gleamed with a pitying light
On the scene of man a hopeless fight,
On a prairie patch or a haunted wood
Where a little bunch of Rangers stood.

They fought grim odds and knew no fear,
They kept their honor high and clear,
And, facing arrows, guns, and knives,
Gave Texas all they had—their lives.

—W. A. Phelson

30

"Why can't I go?" Cort Wesley's younger son Luke protested.

" 'Cause you got school."

"Dylan's got school and he gets to go."

"Dylan's older."

"What about that girl?"

"What about her?"

"You taking her shooting too?"

"I'll take you tomorrow."

"You always say that."

"And don't I deliver?"

Luke shrugged. "Mostly, I guess."

"There you have it."

"I wanna shoot the Glock, not just the twenty-two."

"Deal."

"And the twelve-gauge."

"Not allowed on the range. You know that."

"How am I supposed to learn to shoot a gun better if I can't shoot it?"

"With a twelve-gauge, if you can aim and find the trigger, you've learned all you need."

That was how Cort Wesley's day had started, the conversation with his younger son held over eggs, toast, and oatmeal, but just cold cereal for Maria. He'd gone back upstairs when Caitlin Strong left just before dawn to find the girl sleeping in Dylan's bed with the boy curled up with a blanket and pillow on the floor. Cort Wesley noted Dylan had positioned himself so opening the door would clip his feet, thereby rousing him.

"What?" he muttered groggily.

"Go back to sleep."

His first inclination had been to sell the house where his boys' mother had been killed and start fresh without the awful memories conjured up each time Luke or Dylan walked through the very door where she'd fallen. But they'd objected to his suggestion and, truth be told, he was glad for it. Not only would facing the awful violence that had transpired here better help them accept the reality, but it might also help make them steer clear of the lifestyle that had caused their mother's death. His lifestyle.

Cort Wesley dropped Luke off at school on the way to the shooting range, the boy slamming the back door of the extended cab truck behind him to further voice his displeasure.

"I never shot a gun before," Maria said, as they pulled away from the drop-off zone.

"You want to?"

"No, they scare me."

"They shouldn't," Dylan told her from the front seat. "Hell, if you'd had a gun you could've plugged this Macerio good."

"I don't think bullets can kill him," said Maria.

31

SAN ANTONIO; THE PRESENT

"I don't like this city," Macerio told the plainclothes cop who'd sat down next to him on a bench seat near the rear of the Riverwalk tour boat. "Too many people smiling."

Detective Joe Youngblood tried not to look at the man. But the wide breadth of his shoulders and the head that looked swollen with pus made sight of him hard to avoid. The smell wafting off the man was just as bad anyway, something bitter and somehow antiseptic. Youngblood had paid many a visit to the coroner's office and, best as he could fix it, the human chunk of muscle seated next to him smelled like a corpse. Formaldehyde pumping through his veins instead of blood. Youngblood had caught a glimpse of what looked like an IV bag poking out of a pouch affixed to the man's belt, connected to plastic tubing that ran below his shirt, so who knew, maybe he was a corpse, after all.

"That's right, take a good look, *amigo*," Macerio said after the tour boat had set off from the dock, adjusting the hat currently holding the dead man's toupee in one place. The new double-sided tape he'd tried hadn't worked any better than the old, and the hat helped keep the sun off his chemo-ravaged skin anyway. "You're an Indian, aren't you?"

"Comanche," Youngblood nodded. With two wives, four kids, and two mortgages, no one could really blame him for taking some side work occasionally, even if that side work usually meant providing information to the elements of society he was paid to incarcerate. They were beyond the reach of the law anyway, so Youngblood found it easy to rationalize his actions. It was amazing what a man could convince himself of, life being relative and all.

"That gives us something in common," the big man was saying, ignoring the voice of the boat pilot narrating the tour, "the fact that this state was stolen out from each of our peoples."

"The boy you're looking for is named Dylan Torres. Arrested yesterday afternoon in East San Antonio and released three hours later. Arrest report didn't stick."

"Why?"

"He was signed out by a Texas Ranger. But you got bigger problems than that."

"Why?"

"Because the kid's father is Cort Wesley Masters."

"Who's that?"

"Masters used to work for the Branca crime family when they had the exclusive franchise for Texas," Youngblood told the man who smelled like a corpse. He could see tiny rivulets of sweat beading up on the man's brow and cheeks, seeming to carry more of the odor with them. "Did a five-year stretch in Huntsville on a bad beef. People say he's killed over a hundred men."

"A lot of killing."

"He was a Green Beret or something in the Gulf War."

Macerio looked the cop square in the eye, the guide droning on about how New Deal money had paid for the Riverwalk's original construction. "How many you think I've killed? Come on, take a guess."

Youngblood looked to see how far up the river they were, saw the Bexar County Courthouse looming before them, which meant not far enough. "A lot."

"That's not a guess."

"I came here to do a job," Youngblood said, as a family of ducks swam past them. "It's done."

"Not quite. I need the address where I can find this Dylan Torres."

32

SAN ANTONIO; THE PRESENT

The outdoor range was empty when they arrived, and Cort Wesley hung two targets from side-by-side brackets set before the hay bales that served as bullet stops. He made sure Dylan and Maria had their earplugs in before he emptied the first magazine, all but one of the fifteen bullets finding the kill zone.

Cort Wesley ejected the spent mag and handed the Glock and a fresh one to Dylan. The boy methodically went through the well-practiced routine of making sure the gun was cleared, popping the magazine home, pressing the slide release lever, and readying his stance after making sure the range was clear. Maria held her hands over her ears in spite of the plugs, as Dylan fired off shot after shot with his left hand curled naturally under his right for support.

Having been taught to shoot by Cort Wesley left his form pretty much mirroring his father's. But the boy was starting to develop his own quirks and style based on his sighting ability and size. He'd gotten his exceptionally good looks from his mother, but these had come with her smaller stature, at least when compared to Cort Wesley's. He doubted Dylan would ever see six feet, figured five-ten might even be a stretch. He was wearing the boots Caitlin had given him for his birthday, which added more than an inch to his height, brought him closer to eye-to-eye with his father. Cort Wesley liked that.

The Glock's slide locked open and Dylan effortlessly ejected the magazine as he checked his target.

"Not bad," Cort Wesley complimented. "Nice, neat spread. Just three shots outside the black."

"Missed the target whole with another."

"It happens."

"Could cost in a real shooting fight."

"Not something you ever want to find out, son," Cort Wesley said.

"Can we go now?"

"We just started."

Cort Wesley could see the impatience in the boy's eyes, his mind on Maria instead of the Glock, explaining how he'd missed the target. There he was, changing right before his father's eyes. Cort Wesley figured Dylan had worn the boots for the girl, wanted to be taller for her.

"What you wanna do instead?"

"I don't know," the boy shrugged. "The arcade maybe."

"To shoot make-believe monsters and bad guys."

"Just today, Dad, okay?"

Cort Wesley wanted to stay and shoot some more, catch the smell of sulfur drowning out the scent of some body spray Dylan had doused himself in.

"Okay," he said anyway, catching Maria stiffen out

of the corner of his eye. He swung in the direction she was staring to see Frank Branca Jr. standing at the edge of the tall grass of the range, a fresh pair of body-guards just behind him.

"Who's that?" Dylan asked.

"Nobody," said Cort Wesley, racking a fresh magazine into the Glock as he started toward Branca.

33

ALBION, TEXAS; THE PRESENT

Caitlin found the sheriff of Albion behind the make-shift barricade formed to cordon off the town's lone supermarket, an H.E.B. The holes and spiderweb patterns in the glass above one sign advertising a special on flank steak and alongside another for snapper told her there'd been some shooting done already, from the inside out by the looks of things.

"Thanks for coming, Ranger," Sheriff Tate Huffard greeted, not seeming to care she was a woman. He looked too young for the job, his straw-colored hair trimmed thin at the temples and eyes looking over-whelmed by what they'd been seeing lately. Huffard must have set the barricade up before the angle of the sun changed enough to roast him and his deputies with its rays. Huffard's uniform shirt was soaked dark with sweat in more places than it wasn't.

"Hostage situation is the report I got," Caitlin said, taking up a position alongside the sheriff behind the cab of his department-issue SUV. She shielded her eyes, feeling the sun singe her skin.

"My deputy who responded to a shots-fired call took a bullet," Huffard told her grimly through a dry mouth that made his words crackle. "He's still inside and we can't raise him on his radio."

"Any idea how many hostages?"

"Between eight and ten, as best we can figure. Another pair of my deputies got chased back by gunfire when they tried to enter."

"What kind? Automatic, pistol, shotgun?"

"Pistol. Big magnum by the sound of things and holes in the windows," Huffard continued, gesturing toward the glass lining the front of the building. "Been a few more shots fired since then, but nothing else we can make sense of. We got eyes on the place from all angles, including those rooftops behind us. Trying to do this thing by the numbers."

"Single shooter?"

"Near as we can tell." Huffard took off his hat and swiped a forearm across his damp brow. "Damn town's flat gone crazy lately. We got things happening now never happened before and they're all happening at once. Guess we gotta blame the economy for that." Huffard's expression, which had gone distant for a moment, quickly found its focus again. "There's kids inside there, Ranger."

"No contact whatsoever from the suspect?"

"Not a peep, and we been calling the store phone number every few minutes just to see if we can get somebody to pick up."

"Don't suppose you got a SWAT team anywhere in the vicinity, Sheriff?"

Huffard shook his head. "Nope. That's why we called the Rangers."

"There's six more of us en route now. My advice is we wait for them before—"

A fresh series of loud *pops!* followed by a single scream cut off Caitlin's words.

"You were saying?" Sheriff Huffard asked her, after they finally receded.

34

SAN ANTONIO; THE PRESENT

"You put that money I gave you to good use yet?" Frank Branca Jr. said smiling, when Cort Wesley reached him.

"You mean the money you owed me?"

"Whatever you say, Cort Wesley."

"My sons' educations, house payments, that sort of thing."

Branca squeezed his lips together and shook his head. "Somehow that doesn't sound like you at all."

"How's your father?"

"Still alive, thanks to you."

"My point exactly."

Branca swung his gaze about the range, holding it on Dylan as he took a target rifle in his grasp. "That your son?"

"And he's a damn good shot too."

Branca looked at the Glock wedged into Cort Wesley's pants. "Takes after his father then. But you've got nothing to worry about from me. I came here with a business proposal."

"Already told you I wasn't interested in what you were selling."

"How long do you think that money I gave you is going to last?" Branca asked, unperturbed.

"I'd rather work behind the counter at McDonald's than work the streets again on your behalf."

"Who said anything about the streets? What I'm here about today is different. Bigger, maybe the biggest thing we've ever done. Calls for a man of your skills and expertise."

"Those skills and expertise are usually good for nothing but landing men in jail, Junior."

Branca bristled at the use of the nickname he loathed, but this time he didn't correct Cort Wesley on it. "You hear about that billionaire digging for water in the Tunga County desert? Man named Hollis Tyree invested millions in developing new technology to find and bring it up. Enough, he claims, to irrigate all the land in the Southwest that's drying up and a good portion of southern California and the plains too."

"What's that got to do with the Branca family, Junior?"

This time Branca didn't bristle at all. "Because, Masters, water wasn't the only thing Tyree found."

35

"You sure about this?" Sheriff Huffard asked her.

"We got a wounded cop in there and who knows how many civilians."

"You go in, we could end up with a bloodbath on our hands, Ranger."

"I'd say you got one of those already."

Sheriff Huffard and his deputy took up positions on either side of Caitlin in front of the rear loading dock's bay door. The plan was for them to hoist it up enough for her to slide through once she gave the signal. Caitlin palmed her SIG and dropped down in a crouch. Then she nodded to Huffard and his deputy who tucked their hands into the slight groove between the bottom of the bay door and loading dock surface.

The deputy, though, hoisted too hard, drawing a grimace from Huffard and a grinding squeak certain to give Caitlin's presence away to anyone near the storage area. She tucked herself through anyway, ready to shoot at the first motion she saw. Once inside, Caitlin was immediately relieved by the clanking hum of refrigeration units that would have dulled the sound of the door being jerked upward, at least to anyone inside the H.E.B. itself.

Caitlin heard nothing as she reclaimed her feet and started forward, and only a few hushed whimpers when she closed on a swinging door that led into the store proper. She pressed herself to the side of that door, easing up to its window plate to peer outward. The perspective, limited to one whole aisle and part of another, revealed four hostages huddled at various points against a frozen food container, dry goods display, and refrigerated milk and juices.

"This is Sheriff Tate Huffard," boomed the sheriff's voice over a megaphone from the parking lot beyond, fulfilling another part of the plan to draw the captor's attention away from the rear of the store. *"Whoever you are in there, we just want to talk. Nobody else needs to get hurt now."*

Charging into the store without better knowledge of the gunman's position was a fool's errand, especially until she was certain it was just one gunman and not more. The closest hostage to Caitlin's line of sight was a woman pressed up against a shelf crammed with an assortment of crackers, chips, and jars of salsa. Twenty feet away on a straight diagonal line.

Caitlin lifted her SIG and rapped it ever so lightly on the glass, the pinging much louder to her than it would have sounded beyond the door. She tried a second series of raps, slightly harder, before the woman finally turned her way. The shock of acknowledgment spread over the woman's features, her eyes quickly squinting to make out the Texas Ranger badge Caitlin had pressed against the glass. Whether or not the woman could distinguish that or not, Caitlin couldn't be sure, but the look on her face had turned from terrified to desperately hopeful.

Caitlin pinned her badge back into place and held one finger up against the glass, then two, and finally three. She had to repeat the process several more times before the woman in the snack aisle grasped her unspoken question and raised a single finger in the air, holding it there for Caitlin to see.

One gunman, then. Sheriff Huffard's deputies had been right about that much anyway.

Caitlin waited for the sheriff's next call over the megaphone before emerging.

"Whoever's in there, this is Sheriff Huffard again. If you got a cell phone on you, dial nine-one-one and they'll patch you straight through to me."

The woman's eyes clung to her, as Caitlin eased the swinging door open and slid her boots across the tile floor into the air-conditioned cool of the H.E.B. She slithered to the head of the snack aisle and pressed a finger on her free hand against her mouth to keep the woman silent. Then she crept out to the head of the aisle, trying to tune out the hushed whimpers and sobs to better place the lone gunman's position in a store that suddenly seemed cavernous, its aisles like vast gulleys between hills laden with all manner of food products.

She caught the coppery scent of blood in the air; someone was dead here—Caitlin sensed more than smelled that, though she couldn't say exactly how.

"I want my mommy," a young, cracking voice uttered two aisles up.

"Shhhhhhhhhhhh," came the response, enough of the sound audible to picture an adult male behind it.

Caitlin readied her SIG in both hands, dragging her boots across the tile now to avoid detection. She stopped and pressed her back up against a display of kitchen cleaners at the head of the next aisle. The overhead lighting was radiant and bright, not about to give up any shadows that might have further helped her pin down the gunman's precise position.

"This is Sheriff Tate Huffard again. . . ."

Caitlin used the distraction to peel out from the head of the aisle, edging toward the next one.

"Everyone out here, all of us, want to resolve this peacefully without any further harm to anyone. . . ."

Caitlin stepped over a slick of blood spreading from beneath a man's body, the sound of a young girl's soft sobbing growing louder. She passed a shot-out meat display case, shards of glass looking like tiny pieces of ice atop the sirloin, chuck, and tenderloin.

"That includes you and you got my word on it. . . ."

She reached the head of the deli, prepared foods, and produce aisle, the last one down, SIG ready as Sheriff Huffard's voice echoed through the supermarket.

"So now get out your phone, dial nine-one-one, and let's sort our way through this."

Caitlin spun out, pistol raised and ready.

36

ALBION, TEXAS; THE PRESENT

Caitlin's mind raced to process the scene before her:

A bearded, hairy shape of a man holding a young girl who looked seven or eight years old tight against him with a cannon of a revolver pressed against her head. The girl's position blocking any kill shot she could try. The man uttering high-pitched, pained whimpers that made Caitlin wonder whose sounds she'd actually been hearing from aisles over.

The bearded man started to twist toward her, exposing a bit more of himself for a shot, but not enough. Such decisions, her grandfather had once told her, might feel slow in coming but were actually made within a half second or less. The brain recording all evidence and rendering a verdict in the gap between breaths.

Caitlin lowered her gun to control the situation with calm. Not much of a sacrifice, considering she could jerk the pistol up and fire from her hip with only a millisecond's difference in lag.

"I'm just here to talk, sir," she heard herself say.

"Spiders," the man muttered between trembling lips and Caitlin discerned the neat outline of the pistol's bore drawn into the little girl's temple, as he jammed the gun against her cheek, bending the skin inward. "Gotta get the spiders outta this one like I did the others."

Caitlin thought of the blood slick that had nearly tripped her up. She kept her SIG angled down, far from comfortable with a shot that could cause the gunman to blow the little girl's head off on reflex.

"What spiders?" Caitlin asked, able to think of nothing else.

Drool leaked down both sides of the man's mouth. "Can't you see them? They're *everywhere*! Crawling out of the cereal boxes and the meat case."

She thought of the shot-up glass in front of the meat case.

"Coming down from the ceiling on their goddamn webs!" the man continued, his gaze turning upward.

For a moment, just a moment, Caitlin thought she might have a shot. Then it was gone again.

"I can help the girl," Caitlin told him.

"You can?"

"Can help you too. I'm here to kill the spiders. Need your help first, though."

"Been helping already. Shooting them where they stand. Bang, bang, bang!"

"Send the girl over to me," Caitlin tried.

The man's features reddened with rage, fury replacing consternation on his expression. "Can't! They breed inside us while we sleep and pour out when the time's right. This little one's a breeding ground, I tell you, a breeding ground! I take this gun off her for a second, just a second, and out they'll come and neither one of us can get them all. This is the way it's gotta be!"

Caitlin saw the little girl's cheek depress farther and thought the man was going to shoot her for sure right then. "When'd you first notice them?"

"What?"

"The spiders. When you first notice them?"

"At my house, crawling all over the walls. First noticed them last week; just a few, though, like an advance team scouting the enemy. 'Cause what we got here, we got ourselves a war. Us versus them. Last species standing."

"That's why they sent me."

"You?"

"Texas Rangers been put on alert all across the state. War's on and you're a genuine hero for saving your town."

The man seemed to take some solace in that. "Started pouring out of my kids just this morning. I knew then the war was on, what I had to do and I done it. Bang, bang, bang!"

Caitlin shuddered, chanced a side step to better her shooting angle.

"Whatcha doing?" the man barked.

Caitlin froze. "Thought I saw one climbing up on your arm. Just wanted to be sure."

The rage returned to his face, aimed at his young hostage this time. "Spiders be pouring out of her any time now, I don't finish this before they do!"

Caitlin could see his finger start to curl across the trigger. "Let me."

"No!"

"I got a full mag here," Caitlin said, flashing her SIG at him casually. "How many you got left in that hand cannon of yours?"

"I don't . . ."

"Only takes six. How many you fire so far? When you have the chance to reload?"

The man glanced down at his gun, fear overrunning his features.

"You fire your last bullet, they'll take you for sure. Can't afford to lose any more soldiers in this war. That's why you've got to let me do this one. So move aside real slow, before the spiders start spouting from her mouth."

The man swung his glance upon her. "They don't come through the mouth. It's through the skin they come."

His grasp on the girl was so tight, Caitlin could see he'd squeezed the blood from his hand. No way she could risk a shot with so little clearance.

"Know what?" Caitlin said, easing closer to the man as she crouched to lay her pistol on the floor. "You should take mine."

She slid the SIG across the shiny linoleum, bright from the fluorescent lights burning overhead. The man dropped the magnum to his lap and started to reach for it.

Caitlin was on him before his finger even got close to the trigger, moving as the man's attention remained riveted on the SIG. She felt his face mash inward at impact with the heel of her boot, the kick coming up and from the side. The man's head rocked backward and slammed into neatly stacked jars of spaghetti sauce, scattering them downward as Caitlin jerked the girl from his grasp. She saw his eyes roll upward dazedly as she snatched her SIG back up and steadied it on the man's now unconscious frame.

"Easy there," Caitlin said, trying to soothe the little girl in her arms. "Everything's gonna be all right now."

Even as something told her that was as far from the truth as it got.

37

TUNGA COUNTY; THE PRESENT

Hollis Tyree III lifted the pickax again and slammed it down into the patch of half-dug earth, his teeth rattling as the edge chipped into more of the ledge before slipping free. His shirt was hung from the remnants of an old, stubborn fence post that had managed to weather the years. His upper body muscles ached and he felt the beginning of sunburn across his shoulders.

Tyree caught a family of prairie dogs scuttling about the brush off in the distance, stuck the pickax in the ground, and yanked the old Springfield 1911 model .45 from his belt. He deliberately kept both eyes open, sighted down its stainless-steel barrel, and fired off all eight shots in rapid succession. Blood bursts sprang from three of the varmints, one thrown six feet through the air on impact. Tyree watched the rest of them scamper desperately away, wondering if he had time to snap in a fresh magazine and start firing anew. Instead he simply stuck the gun back in his belt and rubbed his ears as if that might relieve the fluttering the percussion had left behind.

Tyree glimpsed Meeks standing behind him, jacket on in spite of the heat to conceal the pistol holstered to his belt. Only man Tyree had ever known who didn't seem to sweat under the sandblasting Texas sun.

"Care to join me, Meeks?" Tyree asked him, leaning on the shaft of the pickax and mopping his brow with his sleeve. "Pound some ledge." Only then did he notice that Meeks was holding a sack, weighted down at the bottom. "What have you got there?"

"Dead prairie dogs, a half dozen."

"Good."

"Maybe not, Mr. Tyree, because we don't know what killed them. One of my men found them in the southeast quadrant when he started his rounds this morning."

"Southeast quadrant," Tyree repeated, turning his gaze in the direction where Professor Lamb had taken the bulk of his soil and ground water samples. "Any idea why I'm out here pounding ledge, Meeks?"

"No, sir."

"Truth is I wanted to see if I could still do it. This is pretty much how I started in the business as a boy. My dad paid me five dollars a week. He didn't believe in an allowance. Made me work for every penny from the time I was seven years old. He didn't want anything coming easy for me. He bought this land forty years ago and swore his head off when he couldn't find oil on it anywhere."

Tyree started to hoist the pickax once more, then

thought better of it. "He was truly a visionary, Meeks, but even he couldn't see that twenty-five years from now, maybe less, it's not oil people will be desperate for, it's water. That's why we're here, that's what that billion dollars is for. To make sure nobody has to fill a glass in the morning and make it last all day and make sure everybody always finds produce when they go shopping. You got any idea how many gallons it takes to irrigate a southern California orange grove or Arizona orchard? The day they go dry is the day this country stops being the country we know. That's why we can't stop, no matter what."

"Still no word from Dr. Lamb, sir. I've got a man waiting at his house."

Tyree dropped his gaze to the sack clutched tight in Meeks's grasp. Dark sodden patches had begun to soak through the bottom and, just for an instant, he thought he glimpsed something moving within, as if scratching to get out.

"Lamb lied to me about those test results, Meeks. That's why I came out here. Pound some ledge and try to figure out why. Lab says they never even received the samples he claimed he sent."

Meeks's cell phone beeped, signaling an incoming text. "Excuse me." He cupped a hand over the screen to read the message, looking up somberly at Tyree when he was finished.

"What is it, Meeks?"

"Albion again, Mr. Tyree."

38

Cort Wesley eased past an ice cream truck and pulled into the driveway, Luke next to him in the front seat with Dylan and Maria in the back. He'd adjusted the rearview mirror to keep his eye on them and, once, caught Dylan's hand curling over the girl's until their fingers locked.

He wasn't at all sure what he was supposed to do or say at this point. The older Dylan got, the more he reminded Cort Wesley of himself in too many of the ways that mattered. Same bullheaded fearlessness and willingness to take on all comers. Cort Wesley didn't know how most fifteen-year-old boys would have responded to a Mexican runaway fleeing a human monster of a man, but he had a pretty good idea no other one would have spirited her off to safety.

While Dylan may have matched him in temperament, resolve, and intensely brooding stare, the boy was saddled with his mother's lithe frame that couldn't even hold his jeans to his hips. Dylan had balance and agility that made him a magician with the skateboard, but lacked the capacity to back up his words and intentions with the kind of physical attributes that made intimidation and the very preemption of violence possible. When violence came, Cort Wesley was sure the boy wouldn't back down, but was substantially less confident in how that would play out.

He hated the worry that came with being a real father. Cort Wesley couldn't figure how parents coped with normal issues, never mind protecting their kids from a serial killer. What was it Caitlin Strong had said after he'd first moved into the house he'd purchased years before with Branca family money for Maura Torres?

"You've got to trust him, Cort Wesley."

"I don't even know him."

"One leads to the other."

"Maura's got a sister in Scottsdale. Maybe the boys be better off with her."

"You really believed that, they'd already be there."

"So what's it mean to trust him?"

"Giving him the freedom to make his own mistakes and backing him up when he does."

"That the way it was for you, Caitlin Strong?"

"Nope. It was quite different. My mom died when I was four and my dad was out being a Texas Ranger. My granddad was around, Earl Strong, maybe the most famous Ranger of them all. But I grew up quick mostly."

"My boys witnessed their mother being gunned down. They did a lot of growing that day."

"They'll never get past that living in Scottsdale."

"Says who?"

"You ever run from anything in your life, Cort Wesley?"

"Not a single time."

"Then what makes you think your boys should?"

Yup, Caitlin had things figured right. And Cort Wesley figured if he had to question the wisdom of saying something, he was better off saying nothing at all. So he had let Dylan keep hold of Maria's hand, glad that finally pulling into the driveway would make the boy break his grasp, if nothing else.

Luke was out of the truck almost before it came to a halt, off sprinting down the street.

"Luke!" Cort Wesley called after him to no avail. So here he was, one of the most feared men in modern-day Texas, having one son with hormones bursting out of his jeans and another trying to run down an ice cream truck before its annoying speaker-fed jingle hit its next loop.

"Two of you get in the house," he told Dylan and Maria.

"Can't we go get a—"

"Get in the house," Cort Wesley repeated, already chasing after Luke. "I'll bring you back something."

...

Dylan took Maria's hand again, as they headed up the walk. It felt tiny and warm in his grasp, and the way she squeezed his back made him ache in places he was just beginning to know he had.

As he unlocked the door and held it open for Maria, Dylan was struck by the fact that it was the first time he had mounted the front steps since his mom died without thinking of her being shot here a year ago. It made him feel peculiar and a bit guilty. He stiffened and something made him pull his hand from Maria's when they stepped over the spot where she'd fallen, as if he was being disrespectful of her memory.

Once inside, Dylan locked the door behind him and peered through the nearest window to look for his father until he heard Maria gasp.

The boy swung toward her and saw the human monster he'd glimpsed yesterday from afar now up close and personal, sitting casually on the living room couch with hands cupped behind his head.

"*Buenos dias, señorita*," the monster said to Maria.

39

"I'm not scared of you," Dylan said, planting himself in front of Maria who shrank back against the drapes.

"Then why are you shaking?" the man monster asked him, revealing a knife with an eight-inch blade in his grasp.

Dylan tried to find more words, but couldn't form any with his thoughts.

"Where's your father?"

Dylan's hands balled into fists. "I'm not talking."

The man monster stood up, revealing a glimpse of the IV bag tucked into a pouch on his belt, the afternoon sun glistening off his blade through the windows. Its rays framed him like a spotlight, making his skin look milky and corpselike, tissue-paper thin.

"Where's your father?" he repeated, his tone not changing at all.

"You'd best be gone when he gets here."

"I saw him pull the truck in the driveway. What did he do, send you in here first in case there was fire to draw?"

Dylan dry swallowed some air, felt something heavy

in his throat at the same time his eyes started to mist over with tears.

"Do you know how many people I've killed?" the man monster asked him.

"What should we get for Dylan and his girl?" Luke asked at the ice cream truck.

Cort Wesley's gaze was fixed back on the house, something tugging at his senses. "She's not his girl."

"What should we get for Dylan and *the* girl?"

"Think you're funny, don't you?"

The boy swiped at the cone with his tongue. "Yup."

"Make sure you get yourself a napkin."

"Why you keep staring at the house?"

"Something's not right."

"What?"

"Don't know."

Luke went back to his ice cream cone. "You got that look on your face."

"What look?"

"*That* look."

Cort Wesley glanced at his younger son, amazed the boy could read him better than he could read himself. "What's Dylan always do soon as he gets home?"

"Open a window, even when the air-conditioning's on."

Cort Wesley realized that was what was bothering him, all of the windows on the first floor he could see from here still closed. "Yeah."

. . .

"You didn't answer my question," Macerio said, gaze locked with Dylan's as if Maria wasn't there.

"It's not gonna work."

"What?"

"You staring me down so Maria will try to run and you can get her in the back with your knife." Dylan felt his cell phone vibrating in the front pocket of his jeans, ignored the hip-hop ring tone, felt the tips of his boots rubbing against each other.

Macerio grinned, showcasing twin rows of teeth turned yellow-brown by the chemo. "I don't kill them that fast. Would you like to hear how I do it?"

"No," Dylan managed.

"Different ways. Depends on my mood." The man monster stopped, something seeming to occur to him. "You know, nobody ever asked me why, what I do it for. Ask me."

Dylan opened his mouth but nothing but air came out and then that stopped too. He'd never wanted to see anyone as much as he wanted to see his father come crashing through the door right now with guns blazing to drain the man monster's blood, though he wondered if it'd be red. And against that scene pictured in his head, the ice cream truck's jingle started sounding again.

Di-dah-li, dah-li, dah-li . . .

"Ask me why." The man monster's tone a bit firmer.

"You wanna tell me, just do it."

"I'd rather show you," the man monster said and rose from the couch. He started forward, the fluid sloshing about his IV bag as he angled toward Maria.

Di-dah-li, dah-li, dah-li . . .

Louder, as Dylan sidestepped to remain between them.

The man monster looked at him curiously, knife flashing in his grasp. "You don't want to do that."

Dylan found a place in his mind where it didn't matter anymore; his hatred for this pasty assemblage of a man who smelled like a lab project gone bad in fifth period chemistry was there and nothing else.

The man monster's expression remained utterly flat. "She has to go first, so you can watch me."

Di-dah-li, dah-li, dah-li . . .

Really loud now, which just wasn't right, all wrong.

What happened next unfolded before Dylan like a splotchy video recorded on his cell phone, jumping from one scene to the next with part of the middle left out.

First, the man monster surging forward with an arm that looked like a knobby tree branch sweeping toward him.

Then *di-dah-li, dah-li, dah-li* sounding like the ice cream truck was right against the house.

Because it was. Because in the last moment before the man monster's arm brushed Dylan aside with a force that rattled his teeth and sent his brain ping-ponging against his skull, the boy saw the living room wall cave inward under the ice cream truck's charge.

He was sure he saw his father leaning out the truck's side, covered in plaster and glass, firing his Glock in what felt like a dream, because it had to be a dream. And in the dream the man monster had somehow avoided the bullets, and the truck, flying through the air as if he'd sprouted wings.

Dylan's eyes were closed by that point but somehow, somehow, he heard glass shattering ahead of the rapid clack of more bullets pouring from the Glock,

accompanied by the rattle of the expended shells pinging against the hardwood floor.

Cort Wesley couldn't know, couldn't be sure. Closed
windows weren't much to go on.

But it was more than the windows. It was like sensing the blistering heat outside while the air-conditioning
purred quietly, spreading its chill. You couldn't really
feel it, but you knew it was there all the same. Your
senses told you. Instinct told you.

Instinct.

And right now instinct told Cort Wesley something
was very wrong in that house. He'd honed that sense
while inside The Walls, when any moment you let your
guard down could find a shank drilled through your
kidney. You even learned to sleep awake, rousing at
the slightest sound or stirring and learning to fall back
into what passed for sleep just as quick.

Yup, something was all wrong.

Instinct.

But a fine line separated it from imagination. Cort
Wesley reached into his pocket for his cell phone,
coming up empty since he'd left it in the truck.

"Damn," he mumbled.

"Here," Luke said, "use mine."

Cort Wesley took it and pressed in Dylan's number.
It rang unanswered until voice mail picked up.

"He didn't answer?" Luke wondered.

"Nope."

"He always answers."

"Yup," said Cort Wesley, eyeing the closed windows and wishing he could see through walls.

Instinct.

"Sir," he said to the man scooping out a fresh cone for another customer, "I'm gonna need to borrow your truck."

Dylan was sure he was unconscious and yet he smelled gun smoke wafting over the room.

Do you know how many people I've killed?

"Dylan, Dylan . . ."

Ask me why?

"Wake up, son, wake up now!"

I'd rather show you.

"Open your eyes, boy. Come on, open your eyes."

Dylan finally did, meeting his father's, expecting the man monster to be there too, and finding his breath when he wasn't.

Cort Wesley started to lift Dylan back to his feet and felt the boy crumple up against him. He clutched his son tightly, holding his gaze on the window Macerio had plunged through, as if expecting him to leap back inside.

PART FOUR

You may withdraw every soldier . . . from the border of Texas . . . if you will give her but a single regiment . . . of Texas Rangers.

—Sam Houston

40

"Sir?" the woman's voice called, disturbing Paz from his reverie. She was small and slightly hunched with a bee's nest of gray hair and a nametag reading CLARA BEEKS. "You said you were looking for information about Earl Strong."

Paz turned from viewing the contents of the display case toward her. Since entering the museum, he'd been captivated by the displays of old Samuel Colt pistols, saddles, Winchester rifles. Each of the exhibits held behind polished glass made him understand Caitlin Strong better, his fascination with her legacy taken to a whole other extreme. Paz was more convinced than ever that whatever he was looking for could be found here, where the past was beautifully preserved forever.

"I am," he said politely to the woman.

"Well, normally an appointment to research on site is required."

"This is an emergency."

The woman's face flushed with concern. "How's that, sir?"

"His granddaughter's life is hanging in the balance. That's why I'm here, to find out why. Something in the past, Earl Strong's past."

The woman nodded, even though it was clear she

didn't totally grasp what Paz was saying. "Well, it's not hard to find answers to questions about Earl Strong. Know quite a bit about the great man myself. Everybody here does."

"Really?"

"Uh-huh. Had the privilege of setting up a special tribute in his honor some years back. His son was still alive, as I recall, and donated a box of letters, correspondence, commendations, even Earl's original holster and pearl-handled Colts. As a matter of fact . . ." Clara Beeks slid sideways to another display case. "Yup, here they are, and that picture there's of Earl himself."

Paz joined Clara Beeks in front of the case, dwarfing her in his shadow. The holster was draped over a wooden pallet much like an old-fashioned horse tie. The pearl-handled revolvers Earl had brandished in Sweetwater lay angled against each other atop a dark-wood stand just below a retouched picture enlarged to poster size featuring Earl wearing both guns with rifle slung casually over his shoulder. Different from the one hanging on the wall of the Sweetwater Saloon.

Twenty minutes before, Paz had driven the stolen truck up the paved dirt entryway of the Texas Ranger Hall of Fame and Museum set between twin waist-high stretches of rock slab walls. Those walls extended higher at the entry, creating the effect of a nonexistent gate. The one-story building stretched well back into a thick grove of elm trees, what looked like a wing added after the original construction angling to the left into the grove itself. Pillars braced a shaded overhang extending out from the sloped roof. The building could have been a fancy home, a school, or, from a distance, an assemblage of corrals and stalls.

"It's Earl Strong's time in Sweetwater that interests me the most," Paz told the woman.

"Lots of legend there mixed in with the truth, I'm afraid."

"Did Al Capone really send gunmen out of Chicago after Earl raided his freight yard whorehouse?" Paz asked.

Clara Beeks grinned. "I see you've done your research.

"Some."

"Well, that's one of the parts of the story where legend and fact get mixed together. But I'll tell you what I know, if you want to hear it."

"I'd love to," said Paz.

41

SWEETWATER, TEXAS; 1931

Earl Strong's challenge to The Outfit out of Chicago put the Rangers in a difficult spot. With their diminished ranks already stretched thin by the spread of boomtowns throughout Gregg and other counties, the Rangers just didn't have the spare men to give Earl the support he required. The hope in Austin was that the threats lodged by the fat pimp Earl had shot were all bluster and no army would be coming from Chicago to reinforce his efforts and make an example of the man who had crossed Al Capone.

That hope didn't last long.

The Outfit saw the string of East Texas towns swollen with oil and bursting at the seams with all manner of men as prime fodder for the wares they dispensed from women, to booze, to gambling. Sweetwater was just the first place where Al Capone had staked his claim and, as such, it had to work as the prototype for The Outfit's plans to expand the model. With no law enforcement to speak of, at least not staffed to the point of offering viable resistance, the gangsters saw a dream come true, especially with the efforts of federal authorities substantially curtailing their efforts up north.

For his part, Earl Strong just went about his business, his efforts supplemented by his two Ranger deputies who, like Earl, came from stock bred off a frontier ethic. Tim Bob Roy and Frank "Sandman" Sanchez were both rawboned, strapping men who'd worn out their welcome in every rough-and-tumble town to which they'd been posted. They were not at all adverse to violence and were as much prone to causing it as cleaning it up.

One day, maybe a week after Earl's one-man raid on the freight yard, a young boy came running up to the shack the Rangers used as an office next to the church-turned-jail, huffing for breath.

"Easy there, son," Earl said, laying a hand on the boy's back.

"They're here," the boy gasped.

"Who's here?"

"Bunch of men in suits. I was tossing stones in the freight yard when they come in."

Earl took his hand off the boy's back and stiffened. "How many you figure?"

"I think eight, but it could've been more."

"Carrying bags?"

"Uh-huh," the boy nodded. "More like satchels or duffels, though. Plenty heavy, too."

Earl turned his gaze down the street as if expecting the men to be there.

"Who are they, Mister Earl?"

"Nobody good, that's for sure," Earl said, patting the boy's head. "But don't you worry none. Rangers got things buttoned up tight in your town. One thing, though, son."

"What's that?"

"Be best not to play in the freight yard for a time."

It was late that afternoon, the sun burning lower in the sky, before the eight men walked straight down the main thoroughfare into the center of town, abreast of one another with every other man holding a tommy gun at the ready. Their suits were sprayed with dust and dirt, their Florsheim shoes already ruined by muck and mud. Their feet actually swished as they walked, adding to the clear displeasure on faces streaked with the grimy residue that had coated the Sweetwater air since the oil drilling began.

The Chicago men found Earl Strong sitting in a rocking chair on the porch of the doctor's office, double-barreled shotgun laid over his thighs and pearl-handled revolvers splayed to either side. The men took up a wide berth directly before him, big and broad enough to block out a portion of the lowering sun that had been shining in Earl's eyes. One of them stepped forward while the others remained in the line, their tommy guns held casually in the crooks of their arms with tips pointed downward.

"Mr. Capone sends his regards, Sheriff."

"That's good, 'cause I hear he might be going away for a while. And, by the way, it's Ranger, not sheriff."

"Think you're a big-time badass, don't you?"

"That's what some will tell you."

"That might be true down here in Shitsville, but you're dealing with Chicago now. You may have made your bones killing Indians and Mexicans, my friend, but we are not Indians or Mexicans."

"I'm not your friend," Earl told him.

"I'm trying to do this the easy way, not the hard. Those are my orders, Ranger, whether I approve of them or not. That makes this your lucky day."

"Really now?"

"You don't know how lucky you are," the man said. Earl noticed his eyebrows were so thick and bushy they seemed to grow together into a single long piece stitched across the bridge of his nose. "Because all we want is the girl back you're keeping in the doctor's office."

"That all?"

"The bitch belongs to The Outfit and Mr. Capone takes his property seriously." The man took two more steps forward, stopping just short of the steps to the porch where Earl was seated. "So you just stand aside, let us go inside and retrieve the bitch, and we can all go about our business."

"Juanita Rojas."

"Huh?"

"The girl's name is Juanita Rojas. And she's a young woman, not somebody's property."

"Not to me."

"Then I guess we can't just go about our business, can we?"

Earl heard the distinctive clack-clack of tommy gun bolts being jerked backward into firing position. These were drum-fired, not magazine fed, notoriously inaccurate, but at this distance the rounds could splatter him against the building.

"You stand aside, Ranger, let us take back what's ours, and we can be on the morning train outta here."

"But not back to Chicago, I imagine, not with all the great pickings for the gambling, whores, and liquor you boys want to control in camps like this."

"That's none of your affair."

"This is my town now and anyone in its limits falls under my protection."

The Chicago man sneered. "Even a Mexican whore?"

"Lincoln freed all the slaves, sir."

"And me thinking it was just the niggers."

That drove Earl to his feet. "I'm glad we had this opportunity to get acquainted. You can be going now."

A twitch from the Chicago man had the tommy guns snapped upward, all four of them angled on Earl. "Not without what we came for. You really want to die today that bad?"

"Was just about to ask you the same question, Chicago. See that old general store 'cross the street?"

The Chicago man didn't look or nod.

"You ever hear of the BAR?"

Again, no response.

"Stands for Browning Automatic Rifle. When Samuel Colt's company couldn't handle production, the Winchester Company took over manufacture of the M1918 version. Hell of a weapon, I gotta tell ya. Lightest machine gun to fire the .30.06 Springfield cartridges that can put a hole in a man the size of a soup saucer."

Earl moved to the edge of the covered porch's top

step, so the toecap of his boots eased over the lip. "I'm telling you this because I got two Rangers up in the storage loft of the general store armed with BAR M1918s." Earl watched the Chicago man's neck stiffen as he resisted the temptation to confirm the sight for himself. "Now, Chicago, you may be able to gun me down, that's for sure. But you and your men will all be dead before I hit the ground, that's for sure too. You ever seen what a BAR can do to a man? Lemme tell ya, it ain't pretty. Cut him near in half. Makes those tommy guns of yours look like pea shooters, no offense to General Thompson neither."

The men from Chicago exchanged looks with one another, a few risking a glance upward across the street. Through the streaming sunlight they could make out something dark and deadly poking out of each of the open windows.

"So, Chicago," Earl asked, "how you wanna play this? It's your call entirely. But that young woman recuperating inside this building, who you'd turn out to the awful smelling rabble who inhabit this town, ain't going nowhere with you or anybody else. Truth be told, right now I'm of a mind to shut down the whole operation your Outhouse, or whatever it's called, got going in the freight yard. You boys turn tail and leave town now and I just might let things be there and not put the lot of you on the chain."

The Chicago man swallowed hard, his expression one of a bad meal coming back up.

"You can still be on the morning train for other parts," Earl continued, "with no harm done at all. Got a piece of advice for you on that account: whatever town you climb off in, make sure there's no resident Texas Ranger on patrol."

42

Clara Beeks stopped, settling herself with a deep breath. "Yup, Earl Strong sure was something, he was."

Paz reacted with a start, snapped back to the present time. He carried very few memories of his boyhood, most prominent of which was his mother rocking one of his infant brothers or sisters in her arms while she told him a story. That was the feeling he had right now, like he was a little boy back in the slum of La Vega, Venezuela, listening to his mother's soft, sweet voice while wind rattled their shanty's clapboard walls and rain drummed down on its tin roof.

"What about the Chicago men?" he asked, again much the way a little boy would. "Did they ever come back to town?"

"Well, sir, here's where the legend and the facts become somewhat of a muddle. But you seem like quite a well-read man."

"I am."

"Then tell me, have you ever read or heard anything about the Chicago mob down here in Texas during the boom years?"

"Nothing at all."

"There you have it then. But if you want to hear how things turned out direct from the horse's mouth, then come with me."

Clara Beeks led Guillermo Paz into the section of the Museum and Hall of Fame reserved for archival exhibits and document storage. She introduced him to another woman on duty there who retreated behind the locked door of a storage room, while Paz busied himself with a check of the documents, letters, and correspondence sealed within an L-shaped, wall-length glass display case. Each was accompanied by a detailed explanation of its historical context.

Paz felt Caitlin Strong behind that glass as well, not the woman exactly but the long tradition from which she had come. In those moments he came to realize she was no different from her grandfather in manner and sensibility. While the Texas Rangers had changed the way they operated with the times, they had not changed one bit at the core, upholding the tradition of men like Earl Strong every step of the way.

"Here we go," he heard Clara Beeks say, turning to see her standing with a slim pile of old, weathered pages held fast in her hand. "This is a report written by Earl Strong to Ranger headquarters in Austin five days after he met the Chicago men for the first time. It details everything that happened from that point on, separating fact from legend."

Paz looked down, feeling Earl Strong himself in the pages that smelled like old straw.

"Our copying machine's down right now, but if you can come back around the close of business this evening, I'll have a photocopy waiting for you. Say six o'clock. Just keep knocking on the main door until I hear you."

"I'd appreciate that very much."

Guillermo Paz approached the main entrance to the Texas Ranger Hall of Fame and Museum promptly at six o'clock, the parking lot now deserted save for a single compact car. He was about to knock when he saw the door was cracked open, shattered at the latch.

Paz drew his pistol and entered, easing the door closed behind him without making a sound. The scents of stale perspiration and oily, unwashed hair clung to the air, evidence that the Mexicans who'd found him in Sweetwater had trailed him here as well.

By the time he entered the records center where he'd last seen Clara Beeks, he smelled gun smoke as well. The old woman's body lay on the floor near a still humming photocopying machine. Paz approached warily and eased her gently over. Clara Beeks's sightless eyes gazed up at him, a jagged splotch of blood staining her white blouse, looking doubly bright when contrasted against the crumpled folds of her pink sweater.

Paz rose, heart hammering in his chest. He wished the Mexicans had laid in wait for him, wished he had the opportunity to make them all pay painfully for this. The fact that they hadn't could only mean the old woman had made no mention of his expected return. He looked toward the photocopying machine's print tray and saw a nest of pages gathered there— Earl Strong's report to Austin, no doubt, that Clara Beeks had promised him.

Paz turned back toward her body and felt the heat of anger raise sweat to the surface of his skin. His breathing picked up. The men who had killed Clara Beeks worked for the same Juárez cartel that had nearly cost Caitlin Strong her life in El Paso. Having missed him in Sweetwater, they had managed to track him here, and Paz felt a twinge of anxiety over the fate

of old Robert Roy Parsons, owner of the Sweetwater
Saloon.

Lots of accounts to be settled not too far down the
line then, Paz thought as he gathered up the photo-
copied pages from the tray.

43

SHAVANO PARK; THE PRESENT

Caitlin Strong and Captain D. W. Tepper screeched to
a halt outside Cort Wesley's house within seconds of
each other. They'd gotten the word about Cort Wesley's violent run-in with the killer suspected of being
behind the serial murders of Las Mujeres de Juárez
while still in Albion where Tepper had met her to help
sort out the aftermath of the supermarket shootings.
Three dead in all, the little girl she'd rescued thankfully
not among them.

Caitlin noticed Captain Consuelo Alonzo standing
in the shade cast by the ice cream truck Cort Wesley
had driven through his own house. He'd been cryptic
in describing to Caitlin exactly what had happened.
And based on the somber look on Alonzo's expression,
Caitlin figured Cort Wesley had been equally cryptic
with her. She appeared to be coordinating the investigation between San Antonio local police and Bexar
County's sheriff's deputies when she saw them coming.

"This is local jurisdiction, Captain," she said to Tepper, ignoring Caitlin. "But I do appreciate the show of
support."

Tepper took off his Stetson, slapped it on his side,

and took a long look at the ice cream truck parked halfway into Cort Wesley Masters's living room. "I believe what we got here is a joint effort."

"Did I miss something?" Alonzo asked, jamming her hands against her hips.

"The suspect involved is part of an ongoing investigation."

"You talking about Masters, Captain?"

"I'm talking about the psychopath he chased out of his house with the help of twenty-one all-natural flavors."

"Psychopath?" Alonzo repeated, unable to disguise the change in her tenor.

"Make you a deal: you tell me what your crime scene people got in their back pockets, and I'll get more specific."

"We're working on a sketch of this psychopath of yours. Already ran his prints and came up with a blank. Lifted them off as big a knife as I've ever seen a man carry."

Caitlin and Tepper looked at each other.

"We also got some residue of the contents of a plastic pouch your psychopath must've had rigged into himself with an IV. Mr. Masters claims he put two bullets from a Glock into the man and we're going on the assumption that a third separated your psychopath from his bag."

"We're gonna need that big knife once you're done with it," Tepper told her.

"Time for you to get specific first."

"It may have been used in a number of murders," Caitlin said, even though Alonzo continued to ignore her.

"And how many would that be?"

"Four hundred. Maybe more."

That brought Alonzo's hackles down and took the stiffness from her spine. "We talking about Las Mujeres de Juárez here?"

Caitlin waited for D. W. Tepper to respond.

"That's what we need the knife to tell us, Captain," he said.

44

SHAVANO PARK; THE PRESENT

"I didn't go looking for the trouble this time," Cort Wesley said in the kitchen after the sun had set, only a skeleton police crew and Captain Tepper left behind.

A tow truck had winched the ice cream truck from the living room, more chunks of plaster and split beams crumbling when it finally came free. Cort Wesley had given his account of what had happened three times to three different cops and sat in while the same cops took detailed statements from both Dylan and Maria. The boy had grown furious when those cops impugned his father's character and somehow tried to imply things had not happened exactly as reported, suggesting that the man named Macerio was actually an associate of Cort Wesley's and had shown up here after they'd had a falling out.

"I don't want you folks to try and pin this one on me," Cort Wesley had warned. "This interview is over," he continued, laying a hand on Dylan's shoulder to tell him it was time to go.

"We're almost finished here," the detective taking Dylan's statement told him.

"No, we're finished now."

He'd sent Dylan upstairs with Luke and Maria, then joined Caitlin in the kitchen once the detectives had moved back outside the house.

"You might not have been looking for trouble," she said, "but it found you all the same."

"Just like it keeps finding you. Ain't we a pair?"

"Don't know," Caitlin said, letting her eyes hold on Cort Wesley's. "Are we?"

"Thought I asked you the same question yesterday."

"In so many words."

"How many are there? Tell me something: why you keep pulling away?"

"You see me sitting here?"

"I'm talking about when things slow down and there's time to think. We get back from DisneyWorld and you're off to Neverland like Peter Pan."

"In which case, I must've used up all my fairy dust."

"Way I figure, it's gonna take more than magic to make my boys and me enough for you. You gotta feel like you're protecting us, saving us." Cort Wesley hesitated. "Tell me if I'm wrong."

"I don't know."

"That's not an answer."

"It's the best I can do, Cort Wesley. For now anyway."

"How about this, then? Times that bring us closest are always over guns."

"Maybe they just bring out the best in us," Caitlin offered.

"Considered that, but I think it's something else. I think they bring out the real person in each of us. Expose our ilk," he added, paraphrasing a jailhouse philosopher named Leroy Epps he met inside The Walls. "You know, our cores."

"That bother you, Cort Wesley?"

"I'll tell you what bothers me, Ranger. It took a killer to bring you back into my life. Only good thing about the asshole getting away is maybe it'll keep you around for a while."

"Is that supposed to be a joke?"

"You see me laughing?"

Caitlin gazed out the window. "Macerio's been getting away with killing for years. This is the first time we've been close to him."

"He's just the start of your problems now."

"How's that?"

"Frank Branca Jr. came to see me at the firing range today."

"Firing range?"

"I was with Dylan."

"You pick up his homework at school while you're at it?"

"Guess I was too busy remodeling my first floor and he got his homework on the Internet. Classes do that now. You were a real, honest-to-God parent you'd know that."

"Like you, you mean."

Cort Wesley bristled, his dark, deep-set eyes chastising her. "Frankie Junior offered me a job."

"Doing what?"

"Not quite sure of the specifics yet, just the general notion, which somehow involves Hollis Tyree III's water dig in Tunga County."

"How?" Caitlin asked, leaning forward.

"There's something else on that land, Ranger, besides water. Frankie wouldn't tell me what, but he wouldn't be interested if it didn't hold some kind of profit for him."

Caitlin's gaze suddenly went distant, her mind drifting to another place entirely.

"What?" Cort Wesley asked. "What is it?"

"Just remembering a story my granddad used to tell me about his father riding with Ranger captain George Arrington. They found a bunch of pioneers all murdered and mutilated right around the spot where Hollis Tyree is digging."

"Murdered and mutilated by what?"

"Never did find out. Whole thing became something of a legend, a kind of spook story of some angry Indian spirit taking its revenge after the pioneers violated the earth somehow."

"You believe that?"

"I believe you're telling me Hollis Tyree's dug up something besides water. Connection bothers me."

Something in Cort Wesley's expression changed. Caitlin couldn't put her finger on what exactly. It was like flipping the lights on in a familiar room, the scene looking entirely different for a reason no more complicated than a blown bulb.

"Tell you what bothers me," he said finally. "What social services is gonna say about all this."

"Well, driving an ice cream truck into your house doesn't exactly qualify as a stable home environment. But maybe Marianna Silvaro doesn't watch television."

Cort Wesley flashed his cell phone at her. "She's already called four times. Message says she's going to submit her final report in forty-eight hours if there's anything I want to add."

"Doesn't sound good."

"No, it doesn't. Guess I could pack up the boys and take off for a time."

"You ever run from anything in your life?"

"Never."

"Enough said, Cort Wesley."

"First time for everything." He looked at her closer. "Is that blood on your shirt?"

"Spaghetti sauce." Caitlin felt the late-day sun burning her cheeks through the window. "Crazy man was about to shoot a kid in an H.E.B. in Albion because he thought spiders were breeding inside her."

Cort Wesley blew some breath into a whistle. "That's crazy, all right."

"There's more. The town sheriff mentioned an elementary school student stabbing her teacher in the hand with a scissors when the kids couldn't go outside for recess. Another man got in a fight with the manager of the local coffee shop because the coffeepots were filled with blood. A woman played demolition derby in a used car lot when they didn't get her air-conditioning fixed right." Caitlin held Cort Wesley's stare, reading the look in his eyes. "And I'll tell you what's craziest of all: how you knew I'd been in a scrape to begin with."

He shrugged. "Can't explain how I knew it. Guess I'm starting to know you as well as myself."

"Starting?"

"You know where my middle name comes from?"

"John Wesley Hardin would be my guess."

"Last of the great Texas gunfighters and outlaws."

"Until Texas Ranger John B. Armstrong shot him and his men down in a train."

"True enough, Caitlin Strong. My dad had five sons with three different women, but he only named one of them after an outlaw, like he already knew how I was gonna turn out. How you suppose that can be?"

"I really couldn't say, Cort Wesley."

"Just like I can't say how I knew you got yourself into a scrape today. Maybe it's something different in your eyes or the way you're carrying yourself. Maybe I smell something on you—gun smoke, blood, whatever—my conscious mind can't quite register. All I know is what I know. Just like I know I put two slugs into Macerio."

"We won't find him north of the border, Cort Wesley," Caitlin said and pulled a folded-up piece of paper from her pocket. "Maria drew me a map of where to find where they had her stashed in Nuevo Laredo."

Cort Wesley regarded the childlike drawing scrawled in Magic Marker still fresh enough to bring its scent off the page. "Then what are we waiting for?"

Gazing at Maria's crude map made Caitlin think of something else, a picture forming in her mind that chilled her blood.

"Where you going?" Cort Wesley asked, when she bounced up from the table.

Outside, Caitlin found Captain Tepper talking on his cell phone. He snapped it closed as soon as he saw her coming.

"What's on your mind, Ranger?"

"Those bodies of Las Mujeres de Juárez, four hundred or however many."

"What about them?"

"I need the locations where they were recovered along the border with accompanying dates."

"We'll get right on it. You wanna tell me your reason?"

Caitlin shook her head. "You wouldn't believe me if I did, Captain."

45

YUCATÁN PENINSULA, MEXICO; THE PRESENT

"I wasn't expecting to see you again so soon," Colonel Montoya said to the two men walking alongside him through the dense foliage of the southern Yucatán peninsula.

The jungle was thick to the point of being almost impassable. Montoya walked confidently, as if his feet had memorized the narrow route through the dark green flora, multiple varieties of overhanging trees, and garden plants turned feral by the rich soil and nutrients found nowhere else in the world. A bittersweet smell that reminded Montoya of fresh mulch and ivy clung to the air, growing stronger with the heat.

"Something has changed," Vincente Carillo Guzman explained, fighting to keep the low-hanging branches off him as if they were snakes ready to snap. Guzman was head of the Sinaloa drug cartel based in northwest Mexico; in the estimation of many, the richest man in the entire country. He was wearing khaki-colored cargo pants that looked stiff and clean enough to be freshly purchased from one of the American catalog companies in which he owned substantial stock.

"An opportunity that is in our best interests to seize now, Colonel," added Fernando Leyva, chief of the Juárez cartel. He was short and squat, a man forever at war with his weight. He wore light trousers but a black shirt that had gone shiny in the places where the sweat had soaked through. His combed-back hair looked matted to his skull.

Leyva had been at war with his Sinaloan counterpart for years, leading to the unprecedented surge in violence throughout the country, especially his base in Juárez. The resulting mobilization by the army had cramped their previously unfettered criminal enterprises, while curtailing the sales and distribution efforts of both cartels. Montoya's Zeta Special Forces commandos had initially led that effort and now supervised the uneasy peace brokered by the colonel himself. Consolidating the two previously warring cartels under a single unstoppable unit had set the stage for his greater plans, although even Montoya found himself wondering what it was that had brought the two of them together to see him in the jungle.

Montoya felt mosquitoes fat with blood buzzing around him. He swatted one that landed on his forearm, leaving a thick stain behind. "Only the females bite. I've always wondered why. I want to show you something," he said and pushed through a final patch of thick brush immediately before him.

Montoya led the way through the patch toward the ruins of the Mayan temple, passing the pillar where the American college students had been tied the day before. He led the two men up the stairs inside what remained of the stepped pyramid, instantly welcoming the dark and cooler confines, the still-whole roof forming a shield from both light and heat. "I discovered these ruins myself. My Mayan ancestors offered sacrifices in this very spot. In return they were granted glimpses of the future they managed to record."

Guzman and Leyva accompanied Montoya to the far wall where the light streaming in through the open front proved sufficient to reveal the first in a sequence of ancient drawings etched intricately into the stone structure. Surrounding each individual drawing were the imbedded letters, known as glyphs, of the ancient Mayan language. Montoya ran his eyes over them, his lips moving silently as if he were reading the words almost reverently to himself.

"This place is where the past and future intersect," the colonel said finally. "I had archaeologists brought down here to clear these. They've still got a ways to go, but I wanted you to see what's been revealed so far."

The sequential panels of drawings all pictured bloody battle scenes featuring a big bullheaded figure leading one army against another. The drawings were detailed to the point of including blood splattered over the warriors on both sides, though far more was displayed on the larger army being vanquished by the smaller.

"The blood you see depicted is real," Montoya explained. "My ancestors baked it over an open flame, so it would harden to an enamel-like texture once brushed into place."

Guzman and Leyva took turns swatting at more mosquitoes that had followed them into the temple and turned their gazes from the smaller army's square-headed leader to Montoya and then back again at the first panel.

"The resemblance is uncanny, Colonel," Guzman noted.

"An incredible likeness," agreed Leyva, as if not to be outdone.

"An army to the south triumphing over a much larger force to the north," said Montoya. "I'd call it fate. It's all here on this wall; the future of man, the future it is my responsibility to make. Twenty-twelve, the year the future ends according to the Mayan calendar, marking the onset of the End Times, at the close of the final Katún, the Time of No-Time. I am the bringer of that time, as foretold on these very walls."

Montoya swung all the way around to face the two men. "The profits our arrangement has produced have allowed me to buy the rest of the soldiers I need, all loyal to me now instead of Mexico. They've become my guerrillas and soon they will infiltrate U.S. cities and unleash a war like none the Americans have ever known. They will not see us. They will not know where we are coming from. And we will fight them on our terms until their entire country is held hostage by fear."

Guzman and Leyva exchanged a look, the first time Montoya had ever seen them so close without at least a dozen armed men backing both of them up.

"The opportunity that has brought us here," began Guzman, speaking for both of them, "can aid that cause substantially."

"Immeasurably," added Leyva, turning his attention on the final uncleared sections of wall. "Flames, the world to the north consumed by them—that's what I believe you'll see revealed in the final drawings. That is what this opportunity offers, Colonel. The true End Times."

Montoya caught a mosquito out of the air and squeezed it between his thumb and forefinger, wiping the blood off on his pants. "Keep talking," he said.

46

NUEVO LAREDO; THE PRESENT

"Tell me again what exactly we're looking for?" Cort Wesley asked from behind the wheel of the Dodge Dakota pickup truck cruising along the darkened, ruddy street lined on both sides with decrepit buildings. Occasionally, lights flickered through jagged holes that had once held windows.

Caitlin glanced down at the crude, but surprisingly accurate map Maria Lopez had drawn of the slum-dominated outskirts of the city of Nuevo Laredo. Rangers had moved the girl, Dylan, and Luke to a nearby motel under twenty-four-hour guard until they got back.

"Birds," she said.

"Birds?"

"A building with birds on it big enough to house a lot of people. If you wanna call that a house." Caitlin looked up from the map at Cort Wesley. "Tell me again why we're driving a stolen truck?"

"Borrowed."

"Okay, borrowed."

"This is Nuevo Laredo, Ranger. We don't want anybody we piss off to have a license plate or vehicle description to track."

True to Cort Wesley's word, most of their route thus far had been concentrated in the area of La Zona, or Boy's Town, a walled compound of five intersecting streets dominated by any number of brothels and cantinas that catered to both natives and Americans crossing International Bridge #1. Strangely enough, this was a relatively violence-free area of the crime-ravaged city.

"I still had any contacts," Cort Wesley continued, "they'd be the ones to tell us where we can find this storehouse for stolen girls you're looking for. Right now they're just as likely to take a shot at us for being out at night."

"I think we got our bearings crossed," said Caitlin, eyes on Maria Lopez's map again. "I think south is north and vice versa."

"Meaning the other side of the slums."

"Yeah. Gang territory."

Cort Wesley smirked. "This is Nuevo Laredo, Ranger. Whole city's gang territory."

Caitlin had the same feeling moving from Laredo into Nuevo Laredo that she had when passing from El Paso into Juárez: mere yards apart in distance but encompassing an entirely different world in every other respect. More than a century before, Mexican cattle rustlers and thieves had crossed the Rio Grande here to do battle with Rangers and their deputies over the Texas border. The city then had formed the center of what was essentially a full-scale border war that had resulted in any number of violent gun battles leading to atrocities that haunted the Texas Rangers to this day. Vastly outmanned and outgunned, the Rangers had adopted a vigilante mentality that had nearly cost the legendary lawmen their very existence. Some went as far as to say that men like her grandfather and the equally great Lone Wolf Gonzaullas had almost single-handedly saved the Rangers' future and preserved their legacy.

"Would've thought the place we're looking for be closer to Boy's Town," Cort Wesley noted, cruising a fresh set of streets paved in flattened gravel that seemed to conform better to the markings on Maria Lopez's map.

"I think the girls they bring here are used mostly for export."

"Seems like a lot of export, Ranger."

"Not just north of the border, Cort Wesley; south of it too. And east and west. These men look at young girls as slabs of meat with breasts and vaginas they can attach cash registers to."

"That bad?"

"We're so focused on drugs down here, sometimes it's hard to see anything else."

Cort Wesley slowed the truck, angling it suddenly to the right. "Well, I think I just saw the birds we're looking for."

47

"That adobe-looking building over there behind the fence," Cort Wesley said, pointing.

"Looks like an old school, bus and all."

"See those things on either side of the front door?"

"Parrots," Caitlin said, comparing what she saw to the scale of Maria's drawing.

"Yeah," agreed Cort Wesley, "birds. Notice the guard posted behind the bus?"

"The one who just lit a cigarette?"

Cort Wesley parked the truck on the side of the road. "You don't miss much, do you?"

"Let's go get what we came for," Caitlin said, opening her door.

"What exactly is that, Ranger?"

Caitlin froze, the door half open. "Macerio if he's inside. Where to find him if he's not."

Cort Wesley lurched drunkenly up to the fence gate, Caitlin making a show of trying to stop him from rustling it.

"Hey! Hey! You over there, let me in; I went to this school!" he called out in Spanish.

The guard awkwardly unslung the assault rifle from his shoulder and stormed forward, barrel twisted sideways and slightly upward—a trademark of poor training. "Get out! Go away!" the guard ordered.

"Just wanna show my girl here the inside. Come on, it'll only take a minute."

The guard forced his rifle barrel through a link of the fence and started to poke Cort Wesley with it. Cort Wesley responded by jerking the barrel all the way through until the guard was pressed against the links, while Caitlin jammed a gun flush against his cheek.

"How many other guards inside?"

"Three," the man muttered.

"If you're lying, I'll shoot you in the face."

"Four," the man corrected. "Five including the one at the desk."

"Now, hand me the key to this lock here."

Cort Wesley clipped the guard's crude walkie-talkie to his belt and donned his bulky jacket and cap, while Caitlin used plastic cuffs to fasten him to a fence post. A kerchief found in the glove compartment of the stolen truck made for a perfect gag.

"We got two cameras to contend with," Cort Wesley told her. "You ready to do this?"

Caitlin mussed her hair. "Damn right."

Cort Wesley took her by the shoulder and led her forward, making a show of getting rougher as soon as they came within range of the camera while keeping his face tilted low.

"*¡Abra!*" he said, hitting the door buzzer. "Open up!"

A click followed a buzz and the door snapped open. Cort Wesley shoved Caitlin inside ahead of him and righted the assault rifle on a fat Mexican man rising from behind a desk in the corner.

"Move a muscle and I'll kill you. Just sit yourself back down."

Arms raised in the air, the man did as he was told. He was wearing carpenter's overalls and his desk was strewn with tools, screws, and nails. Caitlin noticed the smell of sawdust was heavy in the air as she approached him alongside Cort Wesley.

"We're looking for a man named Macerio," she told the Mexican. "Know him?"

The man just sat there, glance shifting between her and Cort Wesley.

"I'm gonna ask you again. Do you know a man named Macerio?"

The man swallowed hard, still didn't speak.

"Let me try," Cort Wesley said, as he came around the desk and grabbed a hammer. He hoisted it into the air and brought it down hard on the back of one of the man's hands while covering his mouth to drown out his scream. "You don't answer the lady again, I'm gonna start in with the nails. You scream when I take my hand off your mouth, I'll start anyway."

The man breathed heavily and noisily when Cort Wesley pulled his hand away. His eyes swam with fear and pain, his face now dripping sweat onto the desktop.

"I know him," he grimaced. "But he is not here."

"But he's expected back, right?" Caitlin demanded.

"No, he will not be back. Please, that's the truth."

"I believe you. Problem I got is how it is you're so certain."

The man looked down, too late to stop Caitlin from seeing the truth in his eyes.

"You know he's not coming back because you're shutting this place down, right? That's what the bus is for. Yes or no?"

The man nodded, still afraid to meet her gaze.

"Where are you taking the girls?"

The man didn't respond, didn't move, didn't look up.

"Goddamn," Caitlin started, realizing. She stopped when she felt a heat building inside her as if her very bones had caught fire, pushing flames out her pores. Electricity danced at the edges of her fingertips, forcing them to quiver before she grabbed hold of the fat man's head and yanked it up so she was eye-to-eye with him. "They're gonna disappear, aren't they? Dumped in some mass grave out in the desert because all of a sudden this little fun palace has become a liability." Caitlin jerked the man's head backward hard enough to nearly spill him from his chair. "You son of a bitch. . . ." Then, thinking fast, "Four other men inside besides you, is that right?"

The man nodded rapidly.

"How many girls?" Caitlin followed.

Silence.

"How many girls!"

"Sixty."

She pushed another walkie-talkie resting atop the desk toward him. "Tell the others you need them down here. Quick."

When the man resisted, Cort Wesley grabbed a tenpenny nail and started to line it up over the back of his swollen hand.

"I will do it! I will do it!" the Mexican gasped, finally snatching up the walkie-talkie.

"Good choice," said Cort Wesley.

The others came down the stairs together in single file, Caitlin and Cort Wesley easily boxing them in before they could try for their weapons. Then they herded all five men into a supply closet that still held empty composition books and boxes of chalk.

"Make yourselves comfortable," Caitlin told them. "Anybody asks, tell 'em the Texas Rangers stopped by for a visit."

And with that she slammed the door.

"You find the keys?" she asked Cort Wesley.

He flashed an assortment pulled from the fat Mexican's desk. "So what happens once we get them out of here, Ranger?"

Caitlin started for the stairs, holding his gaze. "You know how to drive a bus?"

48

SAN ANTONIO; THE PRESENT

Captain Tepper called in additional support and custodial personnel to company headquarters to get the girls processed and take all their statements the next morning.

"You're an hour late," he noted after Cort Wesley parked the school bus in front of the main entrance.

"Decided to stop at a Denny's on the way," Caitlin told him.

"Hope you're not expecting me to pick up the bill."

"Restaurant was glad to perform a public service on behalf of the state of Texas. And the manager's got some Rangers as regular customers."

"How'd you get them across the border exactly?"

"Told the Border Patrol it was a field trip."

"And they believed you?"

"They believed the Texas Ranger telling them that's the way it was."

Tepper cast his gaze back at the girls disembarking from the stifling bus in favor of a shady spot beneath a pair of cottonwoods where a clerk was handing out bottles of water. "I called social services. We're gonna need their help in figuring out what to do with these girls from this point."

"What'd you tell them?"

"That they'd been rescued south of the border in a joint operation with Mexican authorities."

"Oughtta hold for a while. Long enough anyway."

"Long enough for what, Ranger?"

"To find Macerio."

Cort Wesley was gone by the time two carloads of social services workers arrived, led by Marianna Silvaro, who was driving the lead car. She spotted Caitlin straightaway and lumbered over through the heat, her skin shiny in the sun. Thunder boomed in the distance and Caitlin smelled ozone in the air, a storm building for sure.

"Mr. Masters hasn't returned any of my calls, Ranger Strong."

"He's had other matters to attend to, Ms. Silvaro."

"I appreciate you standing up for his character, Ranger, but my final report is due in less than forty-eight hours now. And after what happened yesterday it's hard for me to believe his two boys are safe in his custody."

"What if I told you none of that was his doing at all?" Caitlin said, thinking of how Dylan's rescue of a runaway girl had started the whole thing.

Thunder rumbled again and Silvaro looked to the west as if to search for its source in the dark clouds forming well away from the sun. "I'd need more details."

"Afraid I can't provide any more than my word, ma'am."

"And in any other case, Ranger, that would be more than enough to suffice. But not when the lives and safety of children are deemed to be at stake."

"Meaning they'd be safer with strangers or someplace where the sheets gotta be washed every day just to stop a kid from dying of dysentery or staph."

"That's not fair," Silvaro said, showing no signs of backing down, "especially coming from somebody who just ferried a busload of endangered children across the border."

"Take a good look at those girls, ma'am," Caitlin said, and waited for Silvaro to do just that before resuming. "Because the man I saved them from is the same one who came after Cort Wesley Masters's kids yesterday. Somebody should've performed an abortion on him outside the womb to spare a lot of people the kind of pain you don't want to hear about."

Silvaro's face wrinkled in distress. "Was that necessary?"

"Ms. Silvaro, I've got great respect for what you and your department do. But right now your nose is stuck in something that would make any normal person gag from the stench. It's a place people are normally happy pretending doesn't exist. I've seen it and smelled it long enough to know you can't possibly understand the kind of person it takes to survive the long-term exposure."

"I know there's a point here somewhere."

"You want to ruin a man's life, you should understand the circumstances first. And since you're not ready to do that, I'm asking you to take my word."

"Your word?"

"That's right."

The wind picked up, blowing in the leading edge of the front that would shake trees and rattle buildings. Caitlin half expected emergency sirens to wail any second to warn people inside away from the windows and into their basements.

"Just doing your job," Marianna Silvaro was saying, "like I've got to do mine. You may not have meant to, but you just proved my case for me. Please have Mr. Masters call me so I don't have to get a court order to remove the children from his custody."

"I'm not sure I wanna be the one passing him that news."

"Something happens to one of those kids, it's on me now, Ranger Strong, and I take what I do seriously."

"So does Cort Wesley Masters, ma'am."

"Think we finally got this under control," Captain Tepper said to Caitlin, mopping his brow with the Stetson held by his side, as the first raindrops began to fall. "Oh, almost forgot," he resumed, pulling a manila envelope from his inside jacket pocket. "Locations where all the bodies of Las Mujeres de Juárez were recovered along the border and corresponding dates. Ready to tell me what you're looking for?"

"Nope," Caitlin said, holding the envelope even with her hip.

Before them, a combination of Rangers and social services personnel under Marianna Silvaro's direction were interviewing the rescued girls at small tables and chairs set up in the shade. Caitlin guessed their statements would be fairly uniform, pretty much mirroring that of Maria Lopez, although she suspected from the wan, lost expressions that a number had been held captive much longer than she.

"Hopefully they can beat the storm," Tepper continued. "All told, I'd call it a successful rescue."

"Rescue's not finished yet, Captain," Caitlin said, looking at him. "Still a dozen or so girls unaccounted for."

Tepper's expression turned stern. "You're not fixing to pay a visit to Hollis Tyree's worksite in Tunga County, I hope."

"Did I say that?" Caitlin asked. "But it's about time a resident Ranger stopped by, don't you think? Can I borrow your truck?"

Tepper handed her his keys and fastened his Stetson back in place, as he watched Caitlin slide off. He turned his attention briefly to the shady area beneath the cottonwoods, then back to Caitlin as she climbed into the driver's side of his truck.

"Man, I love that girl," he said, jamming a cigarette into his mouth but stopping just short of lighting it.

49

WACO, TEXAS; THE PRESENT

Guillermo Paz sat in the truck cab as rain pounded the windshield hard enough to threaten the glass. He held the photocopy of the report Texas Ranger Earl Strong had filed with headquarters a few days after he had faced down Al Capone's men from Chicago tight in his hands. The cab was stuffy and the air stale, forcing Paz to crack a window even though it allowed a neat sliver of the storm inside. He was accustomed to taking several showers throughout the day, but the lack of one in more than a day now left him smelling his own rank sweat and skin oil that brought a light sheen to his face and arms. Made him feel like he should step out into the storm long enough for it to wash him clean.

Earl Strong's report was written out in longhand in the form of a letter, the penmanship surprisingly neat, as if Earl Strong's words were as precise as his aim. By the time Paz took to reading the report yet again, he had practically memorized the words. Such a clear picture painted in his head of the gunfight that had made Earl Strong a true legend that Paz felt he was there standing alongside him. . . .

Sweetwater, Texas; 1931
Captain Franklin Kershaw
The Texas Rangers
Austin, Texas

Report filed by Ranger Earl Strong

Dear Captain Kershaw:

This ain't a pretty tale I have to tell you. I want to get that straight at the outset, and if anyone in Austin is looking to dispense blame for the events I am about to describe, all that blame should come down on me and me alone.

First, I want to thank your office mightily for re-

sponding to my request for the BARs in a fashion
timely enough, I fully believe, to save plenty of lives,
mine included. That kind of firepower in the hands of
those as practiced and skilled as us Rangers makes me
feel the fifty or so of us left could fight the next big
war all by ourselves and come out just fine. Don't
know who it is we might be fighting right now but
whoever it is, I don't reckon the battle could be any
bloodier than the one just fought here in Sweetwater
and that's the God's honest truth.

Now, as I left off in my last correspondence, it was
my fervent hope that those boys from Al Capone's
Chicago Outfit would hop the next train out of Sweetwater and head back where they belonged. But I guess
I knew in my heart they had no aim of doing any such
thing on account of them being gunmen of a sort, and
a gunman never runs away from a challenge; he can't,
if he ever wants to face his bosses again, never mind
himself.

Point is if I had it to do all over again, I'd have put
those sumbitches on the chain with the rest of the
scum gathered in Sweetwater. See how they felt after
a week of living in a space no bigger than their own
person, crapping and pissing in a pail they had to
share with another two men. Yup, that probably
woulda fixed things for sure and, to speak the God's
honest truth, I believe I may have done what I did
because I wanted the fight they was offering. I'd come
upon so many lowlifes and bottom scum that I had
found a place in my head that made me no better than
them and that's the God's honest truth too.

I say this to you here 'cause I believe it to be a concern for future Ranger deployments in these modern
times. There's too many of us reared on a frontier

tradition where the enemies were more clear-cut and the fights didn't call for so much pondering in their wakes. Back when my daddy and granddaddy were riding the range, their biggest problems were thieves, rustlers, Mexican bandits, and renegade Indians. They were guardians of a land still making its borders and just about all the battles they fought were about territory and ownership one way or another. Guess it's still about that now pretty much, only the enemies and the weapons have changed mightily, Captain, and if us Rangers and the great state of Texas is going to survive, we've got to change too.

But let me get now to the events that followed the Chicago men laying down their tommy guns and walking back to the freight yard with their tails between their legs. Coulda walked all the way back to Chicago for all I cared, but I knew they'd be back.

What tricked me was my own pride on account of my figuring they'd come back for me. Was the night after the initial confrontation that Tim Bob Roy was on night patrol down the main thoroughfare when six of those Chicago boys ambushed him. They shot him in both legs and then took to him with clubs and mallets, and by the time Constable Tyree came and fetched me, his face was so mashed to pulp you couldn't even tell he'd been a man.

Now I'm not saying Tim Bob was the best man I'd ever known. He'd had occasions when he took a belt to his boys and a hand to his wife. Going home always left him hitting the booze hard because, truth be told, he was born for the range and was never happy away from it. But he was a damn fine Ranger who'd saved my life least as often as I'd saved his and I was proud to call him a friend. He was in Sweetwater, because, as you know, I requested his presence, so the responsibility for his murder fell on me.

I wrote his family to that effect, glad in those long moments I didn't have no wife or kids of my own. Always thought that's why I never got scared of nothing, having nothing to lose and all. So I told Sandman Sanchez, who had a wife and two girls, to get on home and let me handle the finish with the Chicago boys. Of course, he wasn't hearing a nickel of that. Said if he left Sweetwater then, you might as well sew a dress around him and give him a wooden pistol in place of his Colt.

Now, and this is important, there was still the law to consider here, so Sandman and I collected statements from the witnesses we had, men who smelled so bad I paid a boy to swab down the floor and walls of our office to rid it of the stench. But they gave us the descriptions we needed and it wasn't hard to figure the next step, since what other men in town were wearing wool suits and ties?

So Sandman and me headed over to the freight yard on horseback the next morning. We stood outside the old train car the Chicago boys had claimed as their quarters.

"Chicago," I yelled, meaning their leader you will recall I referenced in an earlier letter. "Come out here, Chicago. This is Texas Ranger Earl Strong talking."

The door to the car opens to reveal the man with the eyebrows looked stitched together in his skivvies reeking of booze and cigarettes. "You fixing on putting me on your famous chain, Ranger?" he asks me, grinning up a storm.

"Nope," I said back. "That's just for all manner of lowlifes and scum, the worst of which still rank far above the backstabbing, murdering likes of you."

So he grins at me. "You must have me confused with someone else, Ranger. I was here all of last night and have the witnesses to prove it."

"Who said that me paying you this visit concerns last night, Chicago?"

He stiffened up and narrowed his eyes to slits, and right then I saw where this was going and, truth be told again, couldn't wait for it to get there.

"If it was up to me," I went on, "I'd hang the lot of you here and now. But these are civilized times and the law has got to be upheld even for devil spawn pieces of dung like you. You Chicago boys come down here to my state with all your whores so you can get drunk and butt love each other all night long."

Now I know what you're thinking, Captain, and you're dead on right. I was indeed provoking the sumbitch because, like I said, I already knew what was coming. And there was no reason to put it off. By this time Sandman had backed up to our horses, indicating we might be talking a good game but in the end were prepared to turn tail and run against such lousy odds, especially with them Chicago boys tight inside a steel freight car. I saw a bunch of them in the window, including the glint of their weapons. Guess I didn't get all the tommy guns after all, 'cause I was certain I caught a few of them being lifted into position behind the car's cracked window glass.

The one I called Chicago pushed his hairy arms up into the doorframe. "So you come to arrest me?"

"I come to arrest all of you."

"And to think we were preparing to leave on the noon train just like you suggested, Ranger."

"I'm afraid that option's off the table now. It falls on me to arrest the lot of you on the charge of murdering Ranger Tim Bob Roy. And, in case you didn't know, we still hang murderers in Texas."

If Chicago was perturbed by that at all, he sure didn't show it. "There's more of us now than a couple days ago, Ranger. More guns too."

"I figured as much."

"But you don't figure yourself for the damn fool you are, do you? You talk about Chicago like it's a million miles away and we got no right to be here. This country's a different place these days, all connected and interdependent. Chicago and Texas might as well be side by side on the maps they put in geography books. Los Angeles and New York too. Only thing separating such places is distance and that's not really very much at all anymore."

"It might not be," I told him back. "But right now you're in Texas and I'm the law in Texas and I'm placing you and your men under arrest."

He must've figured I was playing right into his hands and, truth be told, he coulda been right. Once word got out that this Outfit of his had whipped the Texas Rangers, they'd pretty much own the boomtowns stretched up through the east. But he was playing into mine too. Because once word got back to Chicago that the Rangers had whipped the best Mr. Al Capone had to offer, I don't figure any more of them would be following.

I see that now but, truth be told, I didn't really see it then. All I saw in my head was Tim Bob Roy lying broken in the street with a face like bloody mashed potatoes. It was a fairly cool morning and the windows on that old rail car were all closed. I knew when the first glass broke what was coming and drew both my Colts, firing before the Chicago guns could to give

Sandman the time he needed to rip his BAR from its saddle strap.

I coulda shot Chicago himself first but kept my fire on the windows to chase his men back instead, which was when Sandman opened up with the BAR. And, let me tell you, it might be classified as a light machine gun but there's nothing light about it when you start firing the damn thing.

But here's where the Chicago men went wrong. They figured they had the upper hand inside that railcar they must've thought to be like a bank vault. Figured they could cut Sandman and me down in a hail of bullets that would tear us apart. What they didn't figure on was the BAR's .30.06 shells pulverizing that steel and banging all around the car's innards en route to somebody's flesh.

The screams started sounding ahead of their return fire, which was hapless as any I've ever seen. These boys might have thought they were tough, and probably were the way bullies are with those that are smaller and afraid to fight back in any meaningful way. They was used to gunning down men who didn't have guns of their own or weren't well skilled in using them, especially when somebody was firing back. But Sandman and I had seen the other side of enough gunfights to neither fear nor delay, and I can't even now imagine what was going through those Chicago boys' minds with a pair of Rangers standing clear in the open taking the upper hand on them.

Sandman kept firing, turning that car into Swiss cheese, while I made my way around to the other side to deal with those who tried to run out the second door. My confession to you today, Captain, is that I shot all of them, each and every one fixing to do the same to me. As I best recollect, I took out five that way, which means Sandman covered the rest numbering six in all with the BAR.

First time I ever been in a gunfight where every man hit ended up dying, three of them taking their sweet time to do it and not in a pretty way. Chicago himself, we found him alive inside the car, squeezed underneath a couple seats. It took both me and Sandman to yank him free amid all the blood and guts spilled in that car.

"I ain't gonna kill you," I says to him, " 'cause then there'd be no one to take the word back to Chicago that the Texas Rangers are not to be messed with. Any more of you come following, they gonna go back the same way as these. You tell that to Mr. Al Capone and anybody else in The Outfit needs to hear it."

Right then I heard a whistle blow.

"Believe that's your train, Chicago," I told him, lighting up my cigar. "Things here are as done as they're gonna get. I'd get a move on if I was you."

He boarded that train in his skivvies, Captain, never looking back at Sandman and me even once, and I don't expect he'll be filing any police report or complaint once he gets back home.

That's the way it happened, Captain. It wasn't pretty or fun or anything worth a dime novel someday. And, truth be told, the whole fight was over in not much more than thirty seconds, so if there is a dime novel they might have to make it a penny. I got no more to say on the subject and you can consider this—

Oh yeah, I need to add one more thing. By the time this reaches you I will have set off on a journey south into Mexico, little town called Majahual inside Costa Maya, to bring Juanita Rojas home. I'm leaving

Sweetwater in the able hands of Sandman Sanchez and Constable Hollis Tyree. I'm gonna leave the rest of the paid women here with them that brought them, since it's easier to control a town full of men when they can have their fun, once the local doc checks the girls out. Better making use of their private parts than taking out their aggressions elsewhere, least ways that's always been my experience.

I will report in as soon as I'm back from my journey to resume my post here or any other where you feel I'm needed.

Until then, I remain

Earl Strong, Texas Ranger
Sweetwater, Texas, 1931

Guillermo Paz studied the signature at the letter's bottom in the dim light of the damp cab, trying to know the man better from it. He sensed deep down in a place he didn't quite understand himself that he was getting very close to a terrible truth that would cost Caitlin Strong her life unless he uncovered it in time.

He checked both the truck's mirrors, hoping to see the approaching headlights of the Mexicans' car. Paz would have liked nothing better than to wait here as long as it took for them to find him. The Mexicans needed to pay for killing an innocent woman who'd died because she tried to help him. But not now, not today.

Tomorrow, when he reached the village of Majahual inside Costa Maya.

50

Tunga County; the present

"It's worse than we thought originally," Hollis Tyree said to Meeks, sounding sad and drained. He held the newspaper open to the article in question for both he and Meeks to see in the office's light. The article featured a photo of a Texas Ranger conferring with the local sheriff in the aftermath of a hostage situation inside an H.E.B. supermarket. Outside the trailer office the sounds of machinery had dulled, while the smell of lubrication oil and baked earth remained strong even through the air-conditioning. "Texas Ranger saved the day this time."

Meeks's face wrinkled in displeasure.

Tyree's brow furrowed at that. "Texas Ranger named Earl Strong saved Sweetwater, Meeks. Take him out of the equation and my grandfather would've likely been gunned down and left in the gutter to die." His gaze drifted, all at once somewhere else entirely. "The Texas Ranger who saved those lives yesterday in Albion was Earl Strong's granddaughter, if that doesn't beat all."

Meeks's gaze drifted out the window before he could respond. "You say the Ranger in Albion was a woman?"

"Yes. Why?"

"Because I think she's here."

The first sight of the sea of drilling rigs that claimed the landscape and stretched to the horizon had made

Caitlin figure for the first time in her life she knew what her grandfather felt when he stepped off that train in Sweetwater. But these fields had been erected over finds of water instead of oil, and the apparatus were high-tech steel instead of wood-frame structures that rocked in the wind.

The orange Day-Glo rigs were mounted on the rear of massive double-axle trucks. When fully extended, they rose a hundred feet into the air, affixed with black tubing laced to armlike appendages that made it look like Texas was under siege by mechanical monsters from outer space. The rigs stretched as far as Caitlin's sightline could follow, a long movable line of them thunking deep into the ground in search of the aquifers Hollis Tyree's geologists had discovered here amid arid desert land.

Caitlin wondered if her grandfather's first view of the wooden derricks cluttered through Sweetwater had left him similarly overwhelmed. Unlike Earl Strong, though, she made no effort to disguise her presence and hide her badge and gun as she stepped down from the air-conditioned cool of Captain Tepper's truck into the sun-baked heat of the desert day.

The sky held threat of the same storm that had descended upon San Antonio, but so far anyway it was keeping its distance besides a few dark clouds looking like scouts in the sky. Strangely, no one approached her as she walked toward the collection of trailers that must have served as the site's offices. The trailers had their external engines firing to push cool air through their hotbox interiors. Outside the air was so dry, Caitlin's skin felt like it was about to crack, giving her fresh respect for the generations before her grandfather whose labor in impossible conditions had built the state of Texas from the ground up.

She passed a fenced, makeshift depot lot containing an assortment of massive yellow loaders, excavators, and conveyors. There were also other pieces of equipment she didn't recognize that looked like huge cylindrical vacuum cleaners with steel instead of rubber tubing, powerful enough to suck up the world.

She continued on to the nearest trailer and was about to climb the steps when the door to the next one down opened and none other than Hollis Tyree III himself emerged, accompanied by a broad-shouldered man who had military written all over him. They both approached Caitlin, the bigger man positioned so he could stay between her and Tyree at all times.

"Mr. Tyree," Caitlin said, extending her hand, "I'm—"

"I know who you are, Ranger Strong," Tyree said, taking it enthusiastically. "This is the head of my security team, Meeks. Meeks, meet Caitlin Strong, who I understand is becoming quite a legend in her own right. You ever hear of a Mexican drug lord named Emiliato Valdez Garza?"

"Can't say that I have, sir," Meeks told him.

"And you never will, since word is this Ranger here shot it out with his men down in Mexico and ended up killing Garza herself. She's a genuine hero. Isn't that right, Ranger?"

"Well, sir, what you said about Garza is right enough. The hero stuff I don't pay much attention to."

"It's a true pleasure to meet you in any event. I noticed you admiring our setup."

"I'm not sure if admiring is the right word, but it's certainly impressive."

Tyree cast his gaze out toward the fields where workers continued to align the drill heads of the massive apparatus with the ground in search of the elusive water deep below the surface. "We had the rigs custom manufactured by the Dando Corporation. What you're looking at is the Watertec 100, capable of drilling nearly a mile below the surface, twice as deep as any previous water drilling rig."

"I'm sure that made Dando's shareholders pretty happy."

Tyree grinned at her, the folds of his sun-darkened face crinkling. "That would be primarily me at this point. What you're looking at is the means to preserve the future of this country as we know it. And believe me when I tell you, I am not exaggerating."

"Neither am I when I tell you your good intentions carry considerable weight, but not enough to balance some concerns I've got."

"I'm listening, Ranger."

Caitlin's eyes sought out Meeks and held his stare. "Might be best if we spoke in private, Mr. Tyree."

"Whatever you have to say to me, you can say in front of Meeks."

Caitlin took off her Stetson and flopped it in the air to toss the dry dust that soaked the air from it. "Then I'll speak as plainly as I can. Rangers have reason to believe three days ago a panel truck dropped off a dozen or so girls here. These girls had been kidnapped in Mexico to be sold into prostitution, which, I suspect, was their intended purpose at this site."

Tyree looked honestly horrified, turning his attention to Meeks. "You know anything about that?"

"Nothing at all, sir," Meeks replied with his gaze still boring into Caitlin's. "It's an outrageous accusation."

"What led you to such a conclusion, Ranger?" Tyree asked.

"One of the girls managed to get away when the truck pulled over maybe twenty miles from here."

"That's all?"

"I'm afraid so."

"Then I'd assume," said Tyree, "that you're checking all possible destinations in the area."

"That's just it, sir," Caitlin said, fitting her Stetson back on her head. "As far as possible destinations go, this site is about it. Perhaps you wouldn't mind if I had a look around."

"Actually," said Meeks, "we would."

"He speaking for you, Mr. Tyree?"

"He is, Ranger," Tyree said, with no hesitation at all.

"Do you have a warrant?" Meeks asked her.

"Guess you're not from Texas, are you?"

"No, I'm not."

"'Cause the thing is, Mr. Meeks, only warrant Rangers normally need we carry in our gut. And right now mine's telling me those girls are here for sure. Underage illegals brought in for the pleasure of your workers can buy you, and your noble intentions, the kind of trouble you don't need."

"Which is why we'd never break the law, Ranger."

"That's a good thing, being that the rest of the girls in the same bunch were targeted for killing down in Nuevo Laredo. I got to them just in time and now I'm here telling you the same thing is likely planned for the girls who came in that panel truck. So if they're here, my advice would be to fess up now and let me do my job, no other questions asked."

Meeks lapsed into silence, Caitlin joining him without ever breaking his stare until Hollis Tyree laughed.

"Man oh man," he grinned. "I never got to meet Earl Strong but I feel like I'm looking at him right now. We got family history between us, you know, Ranger."

"I do indeed, sir."

"My grandfather lent yours his 1930 Plymouth Model U to take a Mexican girl the great Earl Strong had rescued from some Mob-supported pimps back home. Now here you are looking to help out Mexican girls too."

"Just doing my job."

Tyree's eyes seemed to catch fire at that, his lips quivering in repressed rage. "Rangers couldn't help me find my children a couple years ago."

"I read about that, Mr. Tyree, and I'm sorry."

"Isn't that supposed to be your job too?"

"Happened in Mexico, as I recall. A bit out of our jurisdiction."

"Not your grandfather's, Ranger. Man like him would've done something about it," Tyree said, his eyes boring into hers now in place of Meeks's, "no matter where that took him."

"That doesn't give you an excuse to pack Mexican girls even younger than your son and daughter into a panel truck and smuggle them into the country."

Tyree's features flared anew, the look on his face that of a man unused to the simmering rage he could barely contain. "As Mr. Meeks has told you, those girls aren't here. I'm not questioning the righteousness of your pursuit, Ranger. I just think you need to take it elsewhere."

Caitlin sidestepped closer to Tyree, angling herself to leave Meeks no longer between them. "I'll do that, Mr. Tyree, but truth be told you got other problems here it's my duty to make you aware of. You're doing a great thing here drilling for water to keep the Southwest from going thirsty and the whole damn country from going hungry. But there's something else under this ground that's bringing some old nightmares back to life. You ever hear how Tunga County got its name?"

"Can't say that I have."

"Has to do with a place called Deadman's Creek where a bunch of folks got killed a long time ago. My great-grandfather William Ray Strong came upon the bodies when he was riding with Ranger captain George W. Arrington's company of the Frontier Battalion back in 1881."

"A group of pioneers got themselves massacred by Indians on the bank of a creek bed, as I recall the story," Tyree said.

"Wasn't Indians," Caitlin told him. "Not according to Arrington anyway. And he had a scout with him who couldn't find any tracks in or out."

"Where you going with this, Ranger?"

"Deadman's Creek would've been located in today's Tunga County, pretty much smack dab where you're drilling for water. Way my grandfather told it, the massacre stuck in Indian folklore. As a matter of fact, it's where this county got its name; Tunga was shortened from *Misho*tunga, Comanche for evil spirit."

"You saying this land's cursed, Ranger?"

"No, sir. I'm saying something in the water of Deadman's Creek made those settlers crazy and they killed each other, the same thing that's making the people of a town called Albion crazy."

"Our tests have confirmed you're wrong."

"With all due respect, sir, I believe it's your tests that are wrong. So if you want I'll come back here with a warrant, the EPA, National Guard, and Sam Houston's army if that's what it takes to satisfy Mr. Meeks here. Be advisable, then, to stay on my good side by cooperating in every way possible, because if I find you got kidnapped girls serving men on the premises, I'll shut you down and stop all the good you're doing here and now."

Tyree still hadn't taken his eyes off her, although the tilt of his gaze made Caitlin wonder exactly what it was he was seeing. "Ever hear how your grandfather put men on the chain?"

"I have, sir."

"You're just like him, aren't you?"

"Well, he taught me how to shoot, ride, and ranger, so I guess you could say yes."

"Think you could have found my children?"

Caitlin shrugged. "I would've given it my best, just like my granddad." She backed up slightly, keeping Meeks in her sights. "Difference, Mr. Tyree, is that the only backup Earl Strong had when he came to Sweetwater was his pearl-handled Colts and Winchester rifle, while I've got the whole state of Texas."

Tyree tilted his head to the side, half grinning. "Your grandfather only needed the backup he carried on his hip, Ranger. The backup you need doesn't exist. Not in Texas, not anywhere. You'd be well advised to keep that in mind."

A tense silence settled between them, broken by the echoing clatter of gunshots coming from the fields beyond. Caitlin turned that way, catching wisps of gun smoke rising from the barrels of rifles wielded by men who were mere specks from this distance.

"We got a pest problem here, Ranger, prairie dogs," Hollis Tyree told her. "That's how we deal with them."

Caitlin held his stare. "Lucky for you they can't shoot back."

Hollis Tyree watched Caitlin Strong's SUV head back down the road, disappearing into the distance.

"How you want this handled, Mr. Tyree?" Meeks asked.

Tyree finally turned away from the road toward him. "Albion's the key. Button the town up, Meeks, whatever it takes."

PART FIVE

If the Civil War emancipated the slaves, so did Reconstruction emancipate the Texans from dependence on the federal arm, it made them ready at last to protect their own borders. The people, resenting the presence of federal troops and hating the "buffalo soldiers" in the army posts, were ready to call their Rangers and willing to pay them.

—Walter Prescott Webb, *The Texas Rangers:*
A Century of Frontier Defense

51

"You stuck it right in Tyree's face?" Captain D. W. Tepper asked Caitlin from across the table in the Blue Bonnet Café in Marble Falls, near his old farmhouse, where he'd met her the next morning for breakfast.

"Figured the truth might provoke a rise in him."

"Except we don't know it to be true yet."

"I figure we will soon enough. Frank Branca Jr. knows whatever's under that land besides water, and Cort Wesley Masters intends to find out what we need to know from him."

"Why don't we just deputize the son of a bitch?"

"I was thinking about asking you to make a call to the Department of Public Safety on his behalf."

"What the hell for?"

"Social services is threatening to take away his kids. Papers are halfway drawn up."

"What's public safety supposed to do about that?"

"I was thinking you might get creative on account of Cort Wesley practically being deputized an' all."

Tepper shook his head, frowning. "Jesus H. Christ, Ranger. What is it with the two of you?"

"Not what you think."

"And what *do* I think?" Before Caitlin could answer him, Tepper shook his head. "This place has a pie happy hour every afternoon. Best slices you ever ate, priced two for one. Too bad life can't be that simple."

Caitlin nodded her agreement. The previous night, Cort Wesley and she had checked into adjoining rooms in a roadside motel. He and his boys took one, while Caitlin and Maria took the other in accordance with his instructions. Dylan saw the look on his face and didn't bother to protest. The plan was for him and Caitlin to take shifts sitting out on the covered portico that ran the length of all the rooms. But Cort Wesley couldn't sleep and ended up staying outside through her hours as well as his, leaving Caitlin free to match the contents of the envelope Captain Tepper had given her earlier in the day to a foldout map of Texas and Mexico pulled from a dust-riddled display in the motel office.

Her head had just hit the pillow when a thunderstorm sprouted from the sky, first smacking the roof with the clatter of hailstones and then saturating the air with rain. It fell in buckets too deep for the gutters to handle and split the last of Caitlin's night in rough halves divided between listening to the torrents pouring to the ground and the familiar nightmares of her as a little girl, this time being trapped alone under her favorite cottonwood tree with lightning flashing all around her. In the first of the dreams, she wasn't scared because she knew her father would come get her. In the last of them, she was terrified because he hadn't, waking up with a start drenched in her own sweat and feeling for the empty space in the bed next to her in the hope Cort Wesley would be there.

"Putting all that aside for a time, I put a rush on the forensics report on that knife," Tepper resumed, after the waitress had set a heaping portion of bacon and eggs with a side of hash browns that spilled off the plate down before him. "If the blade matches the cut marks on the previous victims, this Macerio's our man for sure." He leaned forward, leaving his food untouched. "You ready to tell me what it is you been fixing to say about Las Mujeres de Juárez?"

Caitlin took that as her cue to lift the foldout map from her pocket and straighten it out on the tabletop, coming right up to the rim of Tepper's plate. With each exposed fold, more of the thick red dots she'd drawn along the Texas-Mexico border appeared.

"What the hell am I looking at, Ranger?"

Caitlin used the butter knife from her place setting to further enunciate the jagged line made by the killings' locations. "Roughly four hundred bodies found, going east to west." She placed the tip of the knife atop the first dot she'd drawn. "Starting here, farthest to the west about even with Juárez, and ending here, farthest to the east, one after the other."

Tepper looked as if he'd forgotten his food altogether. He leaned back in his chair, continuing to study the map as he picked at his eyebrows. "You saying what I think you're saying?"

"Each body recovered farther east than the one before."

"Man's drawing a line in blood across the whole goddamn border."

"And look at what's next," Caitlin said, using her knife again to draw an imaginary line from an unblemished spot on the map north.

"San Antonio," Tepper realized, whistling under his breath.

"Maria Lopez, Captain."

"Well, I'll be damned."

52

"Hey, Doc," Macerio greeted the man who opened the door. "It's good to see you again."

Hector Nobrega's mouth dropped. He gazed at the massive, muscle-laden figure before him through the house's steel grate, as the rattle of his sons' playing with their toy trucks sounded behind him. Nobrega thought about slamming the door now, wondered if the grate was strong enough to keep Macerio out. He doubted it.

Nobrega smelled a stench rising out of the man, a fetid odor of decay mixed uneasily with an astringent scent powerless to disguise it.

"I think they're infected," Macerio said suddenly.

"What?"

"The bullet wounds, two of them. Got both of the slugs still stuck inside. Couldn't get to them myself. *¿Me puede ayudar usted, el médico?*"

"Help you?" Nobrega parroted, buying time to think. "We'd need to do it at a hospital, in sterile conditions where I can—"

"No need for all that, Doctor. Not if you got a pair of pliers, some antiseptic, and antibiotics handy."

Macerio sensed the doctor's resistance, just as he had after demanding the chemotherapy. "Those your kids I hear inside?"

"*Usted tiene suerte,*" Nobrega said, dropping the second slug he'd pulled from Macerio's flesh into the bathroom sink.

"Lucky? I suppose that's true enough."

Macerio couldn't help wondering what the doctor might have found inside him. Certainly normal flesh and blood couldn't account for the man he was, especially after the constant drip of steroids flowing into his system. Nor could they account for a pair of powerful shells getting waylaid by simple muscle en route to pulverizing bone and vital organs. Truth was Macerio had indeed poked around with one of his knives, intending to dig out the slugs had they not proven to be so deep and difficult to budge. The best he could do was bite his lip through the pouring of alcohol into the wounds to forestall the rapid infection Macerio had seen eat through men like acid. Even then, he was certain a rank odor of putrefaction had begun to leak from the wounds by the time he reached Nobrega's home.

"You're lucky," Nobrega resumed, "because another day or so without treatment and the infection would've killed you."

Macerio repositioned himself on the toilet seat to give the doctor a better angle with which to clean, stitch, and dress his wounds.

"I don't have any more local anesthesia. This is going to hurt."

Nobrega soaked a thick gauze pad with alcohol and went to work.

"My hair hasn't started to grow back yet," Macerio told him.

"It will."

"Eyebrows too?"

"I'm sure."

That seemed to perk Macerio up, even as Nobrega began stitching his wounds. "Hey, Doc, I ever tell you where I got this toupee?"

"No," Nobrega said, not bothering to disguise his disinterest as he continued stitching, drawing not so much as a flinch from his patient.

"*Nada mas.*"

Something chirped and Nobrega watched Macerio pull a sleek black cell phone, like none he'd ever seen before, from his pocket.

"Keep stitching," Macerio said, adjusting his massive shoulders to block Nobrega's view of the screen.

But Nobrega could feel those shoulders tighten at Macerio's reading of the message, stretching the thick skin through which he was trying to stitch. It was like trying to push a needle through steel.

Macerio pocketed the cell phone and twisted enough to meet Nobrega's gaze. "I've got business across the border."

Nobrega thought he saw something like fire dancing in the big man's eyes, as close as Macerio could get to happiness.

"Hurry up, Doctor. *Apresúrese.*"

53

SAN ANTONIO; THE PRESENT

Cort Wesley strolled into the lobby of the Hyatt Regency Hotel with Maria, Dylan, and Luke in tow.

"I got some business upstairs," he said, finding a reasonably secluded spot in the lobby to leave them. "I wanna see all three of you right here when I come back down." He fished a ten-dollar bill from his pocket and handed it to Dylan. "Get some snacks if you want." Then, to his younger son Luke, "But don't let me catch you with any chocolate on your breath, you hear?"

The boy nodded, puffing out some breath.

Cort Wesley was halfway to the elevator bank when a broad man in a black suit approached him. His name-tag identified him as Eugene.

"Excuse me?"

"What can I do for you?" Cort Wesley asked with a smile.

"That boy you came in with, the one with the long dark hair."

Cort Wesley tensed slightly. "What about him?"

"Well, this may sound crazy, but he looks an awful lot like that rock star kid on the cover of all them magazines my daughter reads."

Cort Wesley leaned in closer to the man and lowered his voice. "It's not crazy at all. Can you keep a secret?"

"Uh-huh." Eugene nodded.

"Kid's in town on the down low. The young lady's his girlfriend. Younger boy's his little brother. Are you reading me on this?"

"I believe I am."

"You work security?"

"We call it Loss Prevention."

"Sure thing." Cort Wesley clamped his arm across the man's broad shoulders in friendly fashion. "I'd be most appreciative if you could keep an eye on him while I'm upstairs getting the lay of the land," he continued, sliding a fifty-dollar bill into Eugene's lapel pocket. "Anything happens I should know about, I'll give you my cell number."

"I'm on it, sir," Eugene continued, handing the bill

back to him. "Be my pleasure. Wouldn't mind the kid's autograph, though. For my daughter."

Frank Branca Jr. had reserved the Riverbend Suite overlooking the Riverwalk itself. The suite featured no balcony, so Frank Sr. sat in his wheelchair set by a spacious window instead, straw hat draped over his head to keep the sun from his eyes and a light blanket covering his legs.

"Glad you're on board, Cort Wesley," Branca said, drinking from a liter-sized bottle of water misty with condensation. Seated on the couch, he looked taut and fit, his skin smooth enough to appear as if someone had sprayed it on. He wore a silk shirt so perfectly rolled up at the elbows Cort Wesley figured it might have come that way.

"Didn't say I was on board yet. Just said I wanted to talk."

"Not much to talk about until you're on board, is there? You want a water?"

Cort Wesley shook his head. "All right, what's my role in this?"

"Your specialty: intimidation."

"How's that?"

Branca gulped down some more water, a few stray drops dappling his silk shirt. "What we're selling here is information. That's the product. Nice clean score."

"This goes back to Hollis Tyree's water fields again."

"Did I say that?"

"You did yesterday. Said water wasn't the only thing they found."

"And the beauty is they don't know about it and we do."

"About what exactly?"

Branca stole a quick glance at his father and lifted a thin leather briefcase from the cushion next to his. "Contents of this are gonna make me more money than my dad ever made on any single deal. We collect the money and turn the case over. Simple as that."

"It's never as simple as that."

Branca grinned. "That's what I thought. Figured it'd take a kind of auction to get the right price. Then, lo and behold, the first buyer I spoke with made me an offer I couldn't refuse."

"So to speak."

"Yeah," Branca winked.

"Who's the buyer?" Cort Wesley asked him.

"Meet's set for noon tomorrow," Branca answered, ignoring his question. "I want you here at ten." He looked toward his three bodyguards, two of whom Cort Wesley recognized from the firing range the day before. "The boys here already been told you'll be running that part of the show."

The bodyguards all nodded to affirm Branca's statement.

"And I'm supposed to, what, stand around and look menacing?"

Branca grinned again, showcasing twin rows of overly white teeth. He toasted Cort Wesley with his water bottle. "Fucking Green Beret, what do you think?" Then he swallowed the rest down. "There's big bucks in this for you, Cort Wesley. We're not talking about moving junk or smack here, like the old days."

"What are the chances more than just my presence will be required?"

"I figure the buyers will be bringing their own heavy artillery. That makes you my equalizer. Only man I know up to the job in the current circumstances. This goes down like the French Quarter the other day," Frank Jr. continued, "I want you there. You want to bring in extra muscle, feel free."

"Extra muscle tends to get in the way, Frankie."

Branca flashed his grin again. "I was hoping you'd say that."

Cort Wesley's cell phone rang.

"I'm sorry I couldn't do more, sir," Eugene, the hotel security guard, told him.

"What happened?" Cort Wesley asked, Luke shielded behind him now with neither Dylan nor Maria anywhere to be seen.

"Two cops came into the lobby like storm troopers, and tried to take the rock star kid's girlfriend into custody."

"You get their names?"

Eugene shook his head. "Caught one calling the other 'Bib' is all."

Cort Wesley felt his spine stiffening. He thought he heard thunder rumble outside, then realized it was in his own head. "Bib . . . You're sure?"

"I am, yes. He and the other cop started dragging the girl away, so the rock star kid throws himself at the one called Bib and cold-cocks him right in the face."

"Cold-cocked a cop?"

"Busted his nose from what I could see, based on the blood. Then the other cop maces the rock star kid . . ."

"They maced him?" Cort Wesley said, fire burning in his belly.

"And slapped cuffs on him, while the girl takes off

and the cop with the busted nose chases her through the lobby. Second set of uniforms caught her at the door."

Cort Wesley's vision tightened, the narrow world before him shrinking in size while tightening in focus. He felt each breath like a rumble in his chest.

"I'm sorry, sir," Eugene was saying. "It all happened so fast, there wasn't nothing I could do except call you. I'm sorry."

Cort Wesley fought to steady his thinking. "So the cops took the kids away."

"Threw each one in the back of separate cruisers. One who got his nose busted left with a handkerchief against his face. Sir, I feel just terrible that I let you down so."

"Wasn't your fault, Eugene."

"I got one good thing to report anyway," Eugene said, producing a high-end cell phone from his pocket.

"What's that?"

"While all this was happening, a guest snapped a picture of the rock star kid. I figured the least I could do was confiscate it to keep this from getting any more worse than it already is."

"You done good there."

"Keep the kid's face out of the snot rags anyway."

"You got that right, my friend," Cort Wesley said, cell phone back in one hand keyed up to Caitlin Strong's number, while the other clung to Luke, keeping him in close.

"Don't forget that autograph," Eugene called after him. "Whenever you get the chance."

54

"Her name's Molly Beaumont," Sheriff Tate Huffard told Caitlin, as they pulled to a halt in front of a modular one-story home with an old Mercury Marquis parked under a carport.

"Why isn't she in school?" she asked.

"Mother decided to home school her, at least until her teacher's hand heals all the way."

Huffard led the way up a walk flanked on either side by yellowing crab grass.

"Mother's expecting us," he said, ringing the doorbell. "She's kind of at a loss these days."

The door opened to reveal Blanche Beaumont dressed in cheap jeans that were too tight and wearing an extra layer of makeup. "This must be the Ranger," she said dryly, eyeing Caitlin. "Thought it be a man."

"Can we come in, Mrs. Beaumont?"

"Sure thing. Excuse the mess, if you don't mind. My cleaning lady's got the week off."

The remark was meant to be funny, but it came out sounding sad. Blanche Beaumont stepped aside, so Caitlin and Sheriff Huffard could enter.

"I don't get back to work at Walmart next week, I'm gonna lose my gig as assistant manager there. Means I'll have to send Molly back to school whether she's ready or not."

"You afraid she'll do something like this again, ma'am?" Caitlin asked her.

"Ranger, I never would've expected it the first time, so who's to say?"

They found Molly Beaumont seated behind a tiny, prefab plastic desk set in the corner of the room, filling in the features of Dorothy and the Wicked Witch in a *Wizard of Oz* coloring book. The little girl turned when she heard her door open, staring emotionlessly at the two strangers standing behind her mother. Her hair looked stringy and unwashed, her stare as colorless as the black-and-white outlines on the page before her.

"Molly," Blanche Beaumont started, "these folks wanna have a word with you. You tell the truth and be polite, okay?"

Molly nodded and watched her mother backpedal from the doorway, disappearing. "My mommy doesn't want me going back to school," she said softly.

"Do you know why?" Caitlin asked her, as Sheriff Huffard eased the door closed.

"Because of what I did to my teacher."

"You remember why you did it?"

The little girl was working on the Wicked Witch's face now. "Did what?"

"Hurt your teacher."

"I didn't mean to," Molly said, keeping her focus on the coloring book.

"You mean it was an accident?"

Molly shrugged her tiny shoulders that were little more than flesh-tinted bone.

"You don't remember doing it at all, do you?"

Molly shook her head. "I know I did it because my mommy told me I did."

"What do you remember?"

"The rain and walking up to the teacher's desk. Then she started screaming and I saw there was a scissors stuck in her hand. It looked funny."

"Funny?"

"I laughed because it looked so funny."

Caitlin crouched down so she was even with the little girl. "Was something bothering you that day?"

"My cat."

"What about your cat?"

Molly began coloring more feverishly, her crayon drifting outside the black lines to destroy the neat order of that drawing and the one on the facing page. Caitlin touched her arm and felt it stiffen.

"Did something happen to your cat?"

The little girl continued to ignore her.

"Molly?"

"My mommy killed him."

Caitlin looked up at Tate Huffard.

"His litter box smelled really bad, so my mommy took a broom to him. Kept whacking and whacking, whacking and whacking . . ."

The little girl's voice drifted off, her hand gyrating madly now, further spreading the color outside the outlines of Dorothy and the Wicked Witch.

"Then she stuffed him in a Hefty bag," Molly resumed again suddenly, "and buried him in the backyard under the elm tree. Later on she told me he ran away."

"You tell anybody else this?"

Molly's hand had slowed again, but she seemed to have forgotten about the lines entirely. "Nobody asked me."

"So your mother doesn't know you saw her do it."

"You're not gonna tell her, are you?"

Caitlin slid her hand up the little girl's back and stroked it gently. "Not if you don't want me to."

"I just wanna go back to school. Can you tell my mommy to let me go back?"

"You miss your friends?"

A nod.

"And your teacher?"

Another nod. "But I think she's mad at me."

"You love your mother, Molly?"

"Sure do."

"She'd never hurt you, would she?"

The little girl shook her head vehemently. "I want her to let me play with my friends again."

Caitlin stood back, glancing down at the coloring book on the way. Dorothy's little dog Toto was in the lower right corner, colored totally black.

"Molly say anything particularly helpful to you?" Blanche Beaumont asked Sheriff Huffard and Caitlin back in the small living room where she'd set up an ironing board in front of the television.

"She seemed upset about her cat," Caitlin told her.

"Mr. Whiskers. Damn thing ran away and flat disappeared." Blanche Beaumont's expression grew furtive and tight. "Molly tell you anything different?"

"Just that he disappeared right before she took a scissors to her teacher's hand."

"You think there's a connection?"

Caitlin forced a shrug. "Anything's possible."

55

"Well?" Huffard asked her on the way back to his cruiser.

"You see a litter box anywhere in that house?"

"Nope."

"Because there isn't one anymore. Blanche Beaumont knows that cat isn't coming home."

They reached the car, Caitlin climbing in just ahead of him.

"You wanna tell me what this has to do with a man thinking spiders were invading the world?" Huffard asked, as he closed his door.

"This all started two weeks ago."

"Near as I can figure things. Seven, eight incidents of violence that don't make no sense." Huffard frowned and eased the car away from the curb. "It's getting worse, Ranger. After the spiders, I'm losing sleep wondering what's coming next."

"Where's your town get its water, Sheriff?" Caitlin asked him.

He seemed not to be listening. "Huh?"

"Where does Albion get its water?"

"Wells, like just about everywhere else in these parts. In dry years, some folks gotta drill down and start a whole new one."

"That include the Beaumonts?"

"Couldn't say, Ranger."

"What about the man from the H.E.B.?"

Huffard's hands started to jitter on the steering wheel. "You want me to check?"

"Yes, I would."

"Care to tell me why?"

"Not ready to yet."

Caitlin measured things off in her mind. Albion was twenty miles due west of where Deadman's Creek had resided until the land had gone bone dry. Now Hollis Tyree had discovered the underground source for the creek that had led to the deaths of twenty-plus settlers in 1881 and unleashed it again, this time in Albion.

"Something else," Caitlin resumed, after a pause. "All those people who've behaved strangely and violently, I want you to draw blood samples from them."

"*All* of them?"

She nodded. "As many who oblige, starting with that little girl we just talked to. I'll be back to pick them up tomorrow. And don't forget to have a couple of your deputies stop by here and dig around that elm tree in the back."

"Why?"

"To see if you should add the girl's mother to the list."

Caitlin switched her cell phone back on, finding a voice message from Cort Wesley Masters waiting.

56

SAN ANTONIO; THE PRESENT

"*. . . just tell this cop calls himself Bib and his lame ass of a partner to try making me.*"

Caitlin came through the door of the Central Police Substation to find Cort Wesley arguing up a storm with the dispatcher on the other side of the glass. Two officers stood to either side of the dispatcher's stool, hands cheating close to their sidearms.

"Sir, your son was assaulting a police officer at the time."

"I got a witness says otherwise."

"Then you should file a formal complaint."

"I prefer to do it with the officers in question." Cort Wesley gazed over the dispatcher's shoulder. "Bet the two of them are back there right now, pissing themselves like genuine hard-asses."

The dispatcher spotted Caitlin approaching, no idea what to make of her presence.

She joined Cort Wesley at the counter. "Tell Captain Alonzo I'd like to see her."

"Captain's busy."

"You tell her to get her ass out here, or I can place a call to the Department of Public Safety to have it hoisted up the flagpole. You straight on this?"

The dispatcher sneered at her as he lifted his phone.

"I'd like the full name of the officer who maced Dylan Torres in the face," Caitlin told Alonzo from the other side of the glass, as Cort Wesley looked on like a tightly wound spring.

"That the way you want to play this, Ranger?" Alonzo's police-issue trousers looked tighter than the pair she'd been wearing the other day, her muscular thighs and butt ready to tear them at the seams. "Because if you do I can put in a call to the administrator in charge of Mr. Masters's case at social services."

"You don't wanna do that, Captain."

"And why's that?"

"Because I don't think you want to go on the record about your officers storming into a hotel lobby to arrest two innocent kids and macing one of them in the face."

"We only came for the girl, Ranger, who I understand is here illegally. It's called doing our jobs."

"That what you call it, bitch?" Cort Wesley demanded, stopping only when Caitlin squeezed his steel band of a bicep as best she could.

"Well now," Alonzo said, half-smiling, "you just bought yourself a ticket out of my station house. How that happens, Mr. Masters, is your call. But I look forward to discussing our conversation with Marianna Silvaro at social services." She swung toward Caitlin. "I'm having that girl driven back to Mexico to be left with the authorities in Nuevo Laredo. That freak show of a man comes gunning for her again, it'll be on their dime."

Caitlin heard the door behind her rock open and Captain D. W. Tepper enter, accompanied by Rangers Steve Berry and Jim Rollins.

"Not anymore," he said, having heard the last of Alonzo's words. Stetson on the verge of swallowing his increasingly gaunt head, Tepper strolled straight to the counter and slid a crinkled set of pages through the opening. "This here's a writ signed by the public safety commissioner transferring Maria Lopez in our custody."

"Bullshit," said Alonzo, not bothering to read it.

"This is our case now, Captain. But we intend to continue working cooperatively with you," Tepper followed politely in stark contrast to Alonzo's tone, flashing a wink that further enraged her.

"Something change I don't know about, Captain Tepper?"

"Forensics report came in on that killing knife recovered from Mr. Masters's home. Turns out to be a match to the wounds in the body of a Mexican woman Ranger Strong here found near the border in 2003. One of Las Mujeres de Juárez."

57

Tepper paused to let his point sink in. "We'll take Mr. Masters's son with us at the same time, if you don't mind."

"And what if I do?"

"I'd remind you he's a material witness and you'd be giving no choice but to relieve you of your command, put a Ranger in your place."

"The hell you think you are?"

"Got a peek at your jacket, Captain Alonzo," Tepper said, instead of answering. "Real sorry to hear about those pending complaints. You ask me, they're singling you out just for being a woman. And while I put no stock whatsoever in these rumors about your sexual preferences, others might. I was you, I wouldn't haul off giving them more against you than they already got."

The officers brought Maria out first, her eyes wide with fear and resignation marking the flatness of her expression. Dylan came through another door a few moments later. His face was red and irritated from the mace, his eyes bloodshot and still tearing. He kept sniffling as the officers led him forward, his hair damp with patches of it stuck to his forehead. His frayed jean bottoms curled under the bottoms of the boots Caitlin had bought him, dragging across the floor. His skin seemed to glow.

Caitlin could feel the suppressed tension uncoiling in Cort Wesley as he watched the boy approach. Dylan emerged and froze before his father, their stares locking wordlessly, neither knowing what they were supposed to say.

"Let's go," Cort Wesley said, leaving it at that.

"Can I have a word with you?" Captain Alonzo said, emerging through the security door when Caitlin was halfway out the exit.

Caitlin stopped and turned back around to face her.

"I cut you slack I shouldn't have the other day. Now I regret it."

"Ma'am, there's never sufficient call for a man to take a can of mace to a boy. Doesn't say much for him and even less for whoever might be holding his ticket."

"Guess we're just lousy paid bureaucrats here. The Ranger code doesn't apply."

"Then maybe it should."

"Kid with a wild streak throws himself on you, you gonna take him out for ice cream?"

"Guess not," Caitlin conceded. "But my mace can would stay clipped to my belt, I can tell you that much."

Something changed in Alonzo's expression, the anger

and prideful distress over being one-upped by higher powers bleeding away. "Word is you bussed a bunch of kidnapped Mexican girls across the border."

"That what you heard?"

"Is it true?"

Caitlin held her gaze, not responding.

"Maybe I got you all wrong, Ranger, but more likely I haven't got you at all and I'm beginning to think nobody does."

"That's the first thing you've said I agree with, Captain."

58

Outside, Dylan's gaze stayed locked with Maria's until D. W. Tepper's truck pulled away with her sandwiched between Rangers Berry and Rollins in the backseat. Caitlin and Cort Wesley had both parked their vehicles in an area labeled AUTHORIZED PARKING ONLY, and she could see Cort Wesley's younger son Luke peering up from a video game in the front passenger seat of his truck.

"You want to explain yourself?" Cort Wesley snapped at Dylan suddenly.

"What was I supposed to do?"

"Anything that didn't land you in jail for the second time in less than a week for starters."

"You would've done the same thing and you know it."

"You really believe that?"

"No, guess you're right," the boy said thoughtfully. "You would've done more, and the cop who did the macing be in considerably worse condition right now."

"I don't even know what you're talking about."

In that moment, Cort Wesley saw himself as Marianna Silvaro must have: totally out of place as a parent and role model. He wanted to break something over his knee, anything to give the stress building up in him a vent.

He watched Dylan climb into the backseat, not bothering to rouse his younger brother from the front. The clock in Cort Wesley's head started ticking down from twenty-four hours, the time he had left before Marianna Silvaro came to take the two of them away. He wondered what Silvaro would make of the scene inside the substation. She'd probably have Dylan and Luke placed as far from him as possible, in another state if not planet.

Caitlin was ready to drive off when she saw Cort Wesley and Dylan arguing up a storm. Distance kept her from making out any of their words, but she could see Dylan leaning up over the truck's bench seat and his father pouring out so much heated breath with his words that the windshield was beginning to fog up.

Caitlin tried to focus on Macerio and the neat line of blood he'd left spilled along the border with Mexico. Somewhere in that line lay the point behind all the killings, the bizarre pattern taking the randomness out of Las Mujeres de Juárez and accounting for how one man could be responsible for so much death. More than four hundred murders committed over nearly fourteen years now. Macerio making his point, whatever that was, for a long time.

Caitlin turned her engine on, then off again, and climbed out of her SUV. She walked toward Cort Wesley's truck through the cooling air and wind rattling the posted parking signs, foretelling the approach of yet another spring storm, and rapped on his closed window. He slid it downward, as Dylan slumped in the backseat to avoid her gaze.

"Something I'm missing here," she said to Cort Wesley.

"Say what?"

"About Macerio and Las Mujeres de Juárez. How's a man get away with killing that many people over so long a period of time?"

"What, you figure I'm an expert on the subject?"

"Just want to hear what you think."

Cort Wesley resisted the temptation to swing back toward Dylan and continue their argument. "A man kills that long in the same area, it's because he's got no fear of getting caught. Understandable under the circumstances, I suppose."

"Is it?"

"What are you getting at here, Ranger?"

"Goes back to what you said, 'cause *everybody's* got fear of being caught. Macerio—doesn't for another reason entirely."

"You suggesting he's *protected* somehow?"

Caitlin tried to hold fast to her thinking against the seeming implausibility of it. "Plenty say Jack the Ripper being British royalty explains how he got away with his murders."

"That's quite a leap, even for you, Caitlin."

"I'm just thinking out loud here."

Cort Wesley opened the truck's door and climbed out.

"Dad," Dylan protested from the back.

"Shut your mouth son. I'm not done with you yet either."

"We need to talk about Frankie Branca," Cort Wesley told Caitlin after they slid away from his truck. "The buy's set for tomorrow. Whatever Junior found out about Hollis Tyree's land in Tunga County is stuffed inside a briefcase he's selling. Maybe we just raid his hotel suite now."

"Raid's a good idea, but not until the buyer's present."

"I was thinking about handling it myself."

"Past tense, since you just came clean to me."

"Remember I told you I wanted to be a Texas Ranger when I was a kid?"

"Sure do."

"This'll probably be as close as I get."

59

SAN ANTONIO; THE PRESENT

Back in her SUV, Caitlin called Thomason Hospital in El Paso. It took several minutes for authorities to get Fernando Lozano Sandoval, commander with the Chihuahua State Investigations Agency, on the line.

"It's nice to speak to you again, Ranger," Sandoval greeted.

"I'm glad to hear you're doing better, sir."

"They've closed off half a floor here to keep me safe. I think I'd rather have you."

"I appreciate the thought."

"You saved my life."

"Just doing my job, sir."

"Is that why you're calling me now?"

"Truth is, when we last spoke you said something I just can't get clear of."

"You recall what?"

"Not the words, just the look in your eyes when you spoke them. You probably don't even remember what I'm talking about."

A long pause followed, Caitlin listening to Sandoval's deep breathing the whole time before he finally spoke. "Have you ever heard of Colonel Renaldo Montoya?"

"Can't say that I have."

"Montoya used to be commander of the Zetas, the Mexican army's Special Forces."

"Used to be," Caitlin repeated.

"A year ago he was stripped of his command and his rank for suspected complicity in the murder of several American tourists at the hands of his men. We were moving to arrest him when he disappeared."

"Montoya's the man who set up the assassination attempt on you," Caitlin realized.

"*Sí*. And we believe he's used the Zetas still loyal to him to take over our nation's drug cartels and the smuggling rings."

"Smuggling, sir?"

"Of young women, like the ones you rescued in Nuevo Laredo, Ranger."

"Guess you heard about that."

"We believe Montoya's hiding somewhere in the jungle. Hundreds of his former commandos have disappeared. For a time, we feared a coup, financed by the money he's making running drugs and girls. Now I'm not so sure."

"I'm still listening, Mr. Sandoval."

"It goes back to his murder of American tourists. Montoya's a full-blooded Mayan. Feels his career was derailed because Indians are looked down upon in Mexico, considered second-class citizens. He blames your people and the Europeans for that, for corrupting the native culture and all but destroying it. He wants Mexico returned to its original roots."

"Doesn't seem to be much anyone can do about that, ultra-nationalist or not."

"Montoya's no nationalist, Ranger, he's a psychopath. Trust me when I tell you he poses a far greater risk to your country than men flying airplanes into buildings. You believe your worst enemies are far away when they're actually parked right on your doorstep."

Caitlin felt the sweat heating up the phone in her grasp. "He came after you because you stood up to him. That's right, sir, isn't it? You were willing to take Montoya on, while the rest of the government, from the president on down, was too afraid to try."

"I was lucky he sent drug soldiers instead of Zetas. I may not be as lucky next time."

"You leave that to me," Caitlin told him.

PART SIX

When at the age of sixteen,
I joined a jolly band.
We marched from San Antonio
down to the Rio Grande.
Our captain he informed us,
perhaps he thought it right,
"Before we reach the station,
we'll surely have to fight."

—www.legendsofamerica.com

60

"You must see this for yourself, *jefe,*" his chief lieutenant said to Ismael Jose Alvarez in the back room of the restaurant his family had owned long before he became one of the chief narcotics producers in the country. Alvarez was a businessman first and foremost who did not play favorites and always delivered the best product available for the best price.

A late-model American sedan was parked in the small square outside. Dust covered the finish and flies buzzed in and out of its open windows. As he drew closer, Alvarez saw four dead bodies slumped inside the car, the stench reaching him yards before he got there.

"They are from the Juárez cartel, *jefe,*" his chief lieutenant explained. "I recognized two of the men myself."

Alvarez moved as close as his nose would allow. "Who would have done this, Miguel?"

As if on cue, Alvarez's cell phone rang and he jerked it to his ear.

"Me," a deep voice said, before Alvarez could say a word.

. . .

"I'm watching you now," Paz continued.

"What do you want?"

"Information."

"You leave four bodies outside my restaurant for information?"

"And to make sure you understand you'll be held responsible for the murders by the Juárez cartel if you don't furnish it."

"Who are you?"

"In Juárez they call me Ángel de la Guarda."

"*Ma Dios . . .*"

"I see you've heard of me."

Alvarez's eye swept the street, trying to buy time for his men to search it. "Why have you done this?"

"Because they were planning to do the same to me. And if you don't call off your men moving to search the street, I'll kill them too. And then I'll come after you. Feel free to ask your friends in Juárez about me before making your decision."

Located in the Mexican state of Quintana Roo, Costa Maya had become a popular tourist spot for the cruise ships that had made it a regular stop thanks to its convenient proximity to the Mayan ruins in the Yucatán. To accommodate the massive vessels, a modern deep-water port had been built between a pair of ancient fishing villages, Majahual and Xcalak, that now relied on tourism for the bulk of their commerce. Whenever ships were in port small shops and jewelry stores battled pushcarts and hastily erected souvenir stands for business.

Paz's first day in Costa Maya had yielded nothing. No one in or around the village of Majahual knew anything about any family named Rojas matching the facts Paz gave them. Suddenly, he feared his search for the truth behind Caitlin Strong's past would end here and now. The best information he could glean was that the former home of Juanita Rojas in Majahual was now an upscale shopping plaza. The trail had stopped there.

The Cadillac Escalade Paz had stolen from the Cancún International Airport rental lot was still parked in the shade in view of that plaza, when a late-model sedan turned the corner and slid toward it. Paz stepped out after spotting it, waited until he saw the gleam of weapons being raised through the open windows before he yanked his pistol out and opened fire.

He emptied his magazine as the gunmen's wild automatic fire dug divots from the road and sidewalk and sprayed him with the chips of concrete. Killing his pursuers, the men who had gunned down an innocent old woman back in Texas, excised the demons of his frustration, revealing to him a potential next step in the gunfight's wake.

He'd shoved the driver aside and deposited the car outside the headquarters of Ismael Jose Alvarez, the only man with the contacts to help him in his quest and who now would have a reason to.

"I believe I've tracked down this family for you," Alvarez told Paz over the phone two hours later. "I'm not sure, but it's the best I can do. It was so long ago, señor."

"If you're right," Paz told him, "our business is done." He could hear Alvarez's labored breathing on the other end of the line. "Si no, volveré."

61

"*Buenos dias,*" Guillermo Paz said to the young woman who had opened the front door of the mud brick and adobe home to which he'd been directed by Ismael Jose Alvarez. He'd waited several hours before approaching to be sure Alvarez hadn't sent anyone to greet him, finally satisfying himself that the narcotics supplier's reputation for discretion in such matters was well deserved.

"My father is at his shop," the young woman said, gazing up at him in wonder. "If you have a problem with your car, you can find him there. . . . Señor?"

Paz hadn't realized how long he'd been staring at her until that moment. But he couldn't help it, because the young woman standing in the doorway was the spiting image of Juanita Rojas as described by Earl Strong. Her features were fair and strong, her hair straight and black. Her skin was the color of fresh grain with nary a blemish. Paz looked at her and immediately thought of the Mayan tribes that had so long dominated Mexico, just as an offshoot had settled the mountains of Venezuela where he was born. The Mayans were born warriors, a hemisphere away from the famed Spartans in distance but much closer in tradition and attitude.

He doubted the girl in the doorway had any idea of her likely heritage or of the resemblance she bore to a young woman who'd dominated Paz's thoughts ever since Clara Beeks had spun the tale of Juanita Rojas's rescue at the hands of Earl Strong. Then again, maybe he was looking at a ghost.

"This is the Nieves home, *sí*?"

"*Sí*," the young woman replied, still clearly anxious.

"But it was once Rojas and it's a Rojas I'm looking for, specifically Juanita."

The young woman's eyes widened. "Juanita Rojas was my great-grandmother."

"What do you want?" Rosario Nieves asked him, clearly unsettled by his unbroken stare.

"I'm sorry," Paz said, his trance broken. "I'd just like to ask you about your great-grandmother."

"It's not like I ever met her."

"Of course not."

"And you're not a cop or anything."

"Nothing like that. I just want to know what happened after a Texas Ranger named Earl Strong brought her home from Texas."

Suddenly Rosario Nieves's expression grew warmer and more inviting. "You're talking about the man who saved my great-grandmother's life."

"*Sí*, in Sweetwater, Texas."

Rosario Nieves pushed the flimsy door open enough for Paz to enter.

62

Hollis Tyree's Plymouth had proven a loyal friend through the first leg of the journey southwest toward the Mexican border and the province of Costa Maya beyond. The car wasn't even a year old when Constable Tyree handed Earl Strong the key and sent him on his way.

"You understand this is a favor, not an order," Earl reminded him.

"Ranger Earl, I wouldn't even be alive to drive this car if it weren't for you, so I figure letting you borrow it leaves me well ahead of the game."

"Well, I do appreciate that and I promise to bring it back in the same condition as I took it."

Earl had already parked the Plymouth in front of the doctor's office and eased Juanita Rojas gently across the backseat. The doctor had suggested providing a bottle of ether to make the long journey more tolerable for her, but Earl didn't trust himself with chemicals and the girl insisted she wanted to stay awake for the duration. Just feeling the fragility of her bones and pain at his touch from the beating she'd taken at the hands of The Outfit's pimp made his blood boil. Once he got her safely home, Earl was even giving strong consideration to using some of his vacation time to take the train to Chicago and pay Al Capone himself a visit.

"I don't figure those Chicago boys be bothering you none, Constable," he told Hollis Tyree. "But if they show their pug noses anywhere within a hundred miles of here, the Rangers will know it and, rest assured, action will be taken."

"Thank you, Ranger Earl. It's been a pleasure working with you."

Tyree extended his hand and Earl Strong took it in a tight, callused grasp.

"You're as brave a man as I've ever stood with, Mr. Tyree. I'm proud to know you."

Earl was on the road minutes later. He kept looking back to check on Juanita Rojas, speaking with her in both English and Spanish despite the fact she was too tired to respond or maybe even listen.

The drive was long and, once south of the border, Earl could never remember a time when he'd felt hotter. The air outside seemed to sizzle, and driving through it was like pushing the car up a mountain. He'd topped off the gas tank at the last filling station and, just for good measure, filled three additional cans to store in the trunk in the likely event no more stations turned up along the way.

He'd intended to drive straight through the cool of the night, but opted to stay over at a roadside motel well south of the border halfway to the village of Majahual for Juanita's benefit. Earl laid her on one of the room's two beds, stretching out on the other with no intention of sleeping himself. In the back of his mind was the possibility, however unlikely, that the Chicago boys had tailed him here and were preparing to storm the room with tommy guns.

He came awake hours later in the pitch dark of the room, the one candle long extinguished, and the sensation of Juanita Rojas's soft body curling up next to him. It took all of Earl's resolve to leave himself just where he was, pretending to still be asleep, when she rolled over atop him and he felt her mouth upon his.

The remaining hours before dawn were the best Earl could ever remember, made even more so by the fact that he knew it would never happen again and shouldn't have this time. He was a lawman, after all, a goddamn Texas Ranger charged with the woman's protection. And no matter how exactly things had gotten away from him, the fact remained he hadn't resisted the young woman's overtures nor could he had he tried.

In those hours the dirt-stained, baked air of Sweetwater and the fiery bullets of the Chicago boys melted away behind a cloud of pleasure like none Earl had ever known before. He'd been in love with the Rangers for so long he'd forgotten it was possible to love something else too, much less a human being. Those hours changed him in ways too profound for him to fully understand, at least not then. He lay awake to the sound of birds chirping and Juanita still lying across his chest, hoping the sun would never rise and the day never came. But it did, the light on his face reminding Earl Strong of who he was and what he was doing in a godforsaken country in which his dad and granddad had each spilled more than their share of blood.

It took all the gas he'd stockpiled to get Juanita Rojas home, not a word spoken through the remains of a journey that ended just after night fell once more.

63

"He returned my great-grandmother to her parents," Rosario Nieves finished, "tipped his hat, and rode off with barely a word spoken other than to apologize."

"Apologize?"

"For what he'd done. He said it made him feel as dirty as the men who paid for sex back in Sweetwater's freight yard."

"Not true," Paz defended.

Rosario looked puzzled. "You sound as if you knew the man."

"But not what happened after he left here, after Juanita Rojas married a man named Nieves," Paz told her.

"She had three children, all boys, before she died of typhus," Rosario said. "One of them, Rafael, was my grandfather. His twin brother Luis moved to America, became a citizen, and was killed in the Korean War."

"What about the third?"

"Diego, my great-grandmother's first."

"Diego," Paz repeated, something occurring to him at the corner of his mind he couldn't quite get a fix on.

"Diego was just past one, the twins infants when Juanita passed. They say she went quietly and swore dead relatives had been surrounding her bed for days, ready to guide her journey to the next world."

"Do you believe that?" Paz asked Rosario Nieves.

"Believe what?"

"In angels, spirits."

"I believe there are things we're not supposed to understand until it's time."

"I believe there are things in this world we'll never understand," he told her.

Paz thought from the way Rosario looked at him that his words had unnerved her. Then she started speaking again in a voice that had gone suddenly hoarse and dry.

"Diego died just after Juanita; the poor boy had caught the fever from her. A little boy buried in the ground next to his mother. Is that what you meant by things we'll never understand?"

Paz cleared his throat, shifted on the chair that was compressing under the weight of his massive bulk. "Then your great-grandmother never saw Earl Strong again," he said, returning to the subject at hand.

"I'm getting to that," said Rosario Nieves. "She wrote him often, gave her mother all the letters to mail for her to him care of Texas Ranger headquarters in Austin."

"But her mother never sent them."

Rosario Nieves's eyes widened. "How did you know?"

"Because having a woman in the family taking up with an *el Rinche* would have disgraced them."

"Earl Strong wrote plenty of letters to my great-grandmother, but her mother hid them with the others she never sent. I think not hearing from Earl broke her heart. She gave up right around the time the twins were born."

"But that's not the end of the story, is it?"

Rosario shook her head. "Earl Strong came back to Majahual one more time after she died."

"Not for the funeral."

"No," the young woman said cryptically. "I never thought about it before. It didn't seem important."

"Does it now?"

Rosario Nieves rose from the chair and moved to an old maple desk, weathered by years of exposure to the harsh sea air nearby. She opened the bottom drawer on the left-hand side and removed an old cigar box; Cubans, Paz noted.

"Juanita's unsent letters are all in here. Plenty of Earl's unread ones too."

She extended the cigar box toward Paz.

"You never read them yourself?"

Rosario shrugged, revealing pointy shoulder bones beneath her shirt. "Even in death, a person has the right to privacy."

"Then why are you giving them to me, *señorita*?"

"Because something tells me you have the right to see them. For my great-grandmother's sake."

64

YUCATÁN PENINSULA, MEXICO; THE PRESENT

The jungle stank of men, Colonel Montoya thought as he climbed the steps of the ancient Mayan temple. Or, more accurately, men whose bodies had not adjusted to the tropical confines and the scorching humidity they brought. It was as if the jungle was marking them, rejecting them, wanting them gone from the world that had embraced Montoya. And why not? His own ancestors had been birthed in ruins much like these before they had crumbled. Back when Mexico was populated by those of pure Mayan lineage, before the Europeans led by the Spaniards descended to spoil the blood, and then the Americans to take everything else.

But all that, Montoya thought as he entered the temple, was about to change.

Inside, the officers he had culled from the ranks of the Mexican army stood studying the crude map of the United States he'd hung from the wall amid the drawings and glyphs Montoya had come to see as prophecies. The officers were roasting in their own sweat, so much so that Montoya could swear the sunlight revealed steam misting off their flesh. They saw him approaching and snapped to attention.

"At ease," Montoya told them.

A major's eyes remained riveted on the makeshift map. "These American cities that are highlighted . . ."

"Our targets," Montoya told him.

The officers looked at each other, befuddled.

"Please, do not worry," Montoya continued. "We will be fighting the Americans on our terms, not theirs. The drug cartels we now control have pipelines into every city in America for men and equipment. Already plans are being laid for our soldiers to move in right under the Americans' noses and strike them where they are weakest."

A colonel spoke for all the officers. "We do not understand."

"We will murder their police. We will attack their schools. We will kidnap their children. We will strike fear into their hearts and change their country forever, as they have changed ours. We will make their streets even bloodier than the streets of Juárez."

"We thought this meeting was about the coup," another of his officers said, "and the attacks you ordered on the American tourists."

"And now I'm ordering those attacks be halted. Once the government is ours, the Americans must feel safe here again so they do not suspect the truth."

"What truth is that?"

"That we are the ones who've gone to war with them."

"War?" raised the colonel. "War with the United States?"

"Two hundred men, even twenty, can do far more than two or even twenty thousand. Look at Mumbai. It took all of ten men to claim an entire city."

"Mumbai," said a captain who'd been educated in the United States, "is not New York or Los Angeles."

"Not at all."

"Then what is it you're not telling us?"

Montoya had been waiting for that question. His catlike eyes peered through the temple's half-light, meeting each of the officers' stares before responding.

"Our foe will be on its knees when our guerrilla war begins, already mortally wounded. The Americans have financed our plans with their appetite for our drugs, and now they will pay the ultimate price for that. Don't you see?"

It was clear from the men's expressions that they didn't.

"I chose you because, like mine, your blood runs pure and unpolluted. Like me you understand that the Mayan calendar predicts the world will end in 2012. It's here in the drawings made centuries ago, how we will lay waste to a vast army to the north. But the point of the prophecy is figurative, not literal. The world will end as we know it, and we are the instruments to bring that to pass. We are soldiers of God, fulfillers of the prophecy."

"What did you mean about our foe already being on its knees?" the major wondered.

"I'm glad you asked," Montoya said, grinning.

65

ALBION; THE PRESENT

Caitlin was on the road early in the morning, wanting to beat the traffic west to Albion. The quicker she got there to pick up the blood samples from Sheriff Tate Huffard, the quicker she could get the lab results back and determine what exactly Hollis Tyree's water project had inadvertently unleashed on the town. This as Captain Tepper led a raid on the hotel where Frank Branca Jr. was headquartered.

She parked amid the cream-colored squad cars emblazoned with the logo for the sheriff's department. Caitlin entered the sheriff's station to find a deputy she didn't recognize sitting at the desk behind the waist-high swinging door.

"May I help you, Ranger?" he greeted, rising.

"I'm looking for Sheriff Huffard."

The man sized her up, eyes holding on the SIG holstered on her hip. "May I ask what your business is with him?"

"That's between him and me, Deputy."

"Well, I'm afraid the sheriff isn't available. Left strict orders not to be bothered unless it was an absolute emergency."

Caitlin gazed about the room at the other deputies present, realizing she didn't recognize any of them either. "I believe this pretty much qualifies there."

"Can you be more specific?"

"Not to you, sir, no."

"Does this have anything to do with the incident at the H.E.B.? Because that's none of your concern anymore, Ranger."

She hitched her hands up to her hips. "I'm afraid it is, on account of the fact that the Rangers were called in on that in an official capacity."

"It's over."

"It's an ongoing investigation, Deputy. As resident Ranger, that's my call, not yours. Or didn't you know that?"

"Tell you what," the deputy said, advancing just enough to appear menacing, "leave me your number and I'll have Sheriff Huffard give you a call."

"Why don't you do that now and I'll just wait here?"

The other unfamiliar deputies rose from their chairs.

"You're not from Texas, are you, Deputy?" she asked suddenly.

"Excuse me?"

"Your accent's all wrong, the way you pronounce your words. You from back East or something?"

Caitlin could see the man stiffen. "I'm gonna have to ask you to leave, Ranger."

"We're just talking here."

"And now we're not."

The deputy stared at Caitlin. Caitlin stared right back.

"Why don't you just tell me where I can find Sheriff Huffard?"

"We're done."

"Whatever you say," Caitlin said, backpedaling for the door, letting the deputies see how close her hand was to her SIG. "You boys have yourselves a nice day now."

Caitlin waited until she was on the freeway, with the outskirts of Albion shrinking behind her, before calling D. W. Tepper on her cell phone.

"We're just pulling up outside the hotel entrance now," he told her. "You on your way back with those samples?"

"Not exactly, sir."

"Don't make the indigestion I already got worse, Ranger."

"Sheriff Huffard's gone."

"Say what?"

"Ran into a bunch of deputies I never saw before who said he's unavailable."

"Sounds bad."

"Exactly why I—" Caitlin stopped, a sound toying with the edges of her consciousness.

"Ranger?" she heard D. W. Tepper ask, as her eyes lifted to the rearview mirror to find one of Albion's squad cars tearing toward her with lights and siren both going. "Think I'm being pulled over, Captain." Caitlin studied the police cruiser's growing shape in her rearview mirror. "Just stay on the line."

She considered and reconsidered her options as the

cruiser continued to close. No way her V6-equipped SUV could possibly outrun it. And if, for whatever crazy reason there was going to be a gunfight, better to have it on still ground rather than from moving vehicles. She didn't know what kind of shots these men were, but she knew how good she was.

"How you wanna play this, Ranger?" Tepper asked.

"Let you know when I'm done. You smoke a cigarette this morning, sir?"

A brief silence followed her question, then, "How the hell you know that?"

Caitlin felt the shoulder gravel crunching under her boots and stood stark still outside her SUV, angled slightly to the side in a shooter's stance with right hand poised over her SIG. The squad car ground to a halt twenty feet from her, lights left on but siren extinguished. Another pair of deputies she didn't recognize climbed out but left their doors open, remaining poised behind them.

"You boys aren't cops," Caitlin told them. "You know it and now I know it. Cops would've already shown their guns, not draw them only to hold them low enough to figure they couldn't be seen. Show those pistols now and the next thing you boys see'll be the ground coming up hard. That clear enough?"

The men looked at each other, remained silent.

"Tell you something else. My nine-millimeter shells'll cut through those car doors like a knife through butter. You got a move you wanna make," Caitlin continued, "now's the time. Or maybe you should make a call to whoever you're really working for, ask him what you should do about the Texas Ranger ready to shoot you down as you stand."

The men looked at her.

"I'm gonna assume I wasn't speeding. I'm gonna assume you pulling me over was just a friendly gesture to remind me about that busted taillight I haven't gotten around to getting fixed yet. That's the way we can leave this. Just get back into our cars and go our separate ways, no harm done. Sound good?"

The men hesitated, right shoulders held a bit higher as if still thinking about raising their guns. Then the shoulders relaxed, and Caitlin stood there watching the two of them climb back into their cruiser. She waited for them to pull away before sliding back behind the wheel of her SUV.

"Captain," she said into her cell phone.

"Tell me I didn't hear what I just thought I did."

"Didn't hear any gunshots, though, did you?"

"I figured they were coming."

"Not yet anyway," Caitlin told him, watching the police cruiser disappear back down the freeway.

66

SAN ANTONIO; THE PRESENT

Cort Wesley watched Tepper's face darken as he pocketed his phone and moved gingerly to climb out of his truck parked outside of the Hyatt Regency.

"What Caitlin have to say?" he asked, when Tepper drew even with him en route to the dozen Rangers already holding inside the lobby.

"Stick to what we got before us here and now, Mr. Masters, if you don't mind."

"Glad to, sir," Cort Wesley said and followed Tepper into the lobby.

The night before he and Caitlin had checked themselves and the boys into two different motels, leaving his truck parked outside a room at the second before walking down the street to a third. Good thing about San Antonio was there was no shortage of inexpensive motels where both amenities and questions were kept to a minimum. Because a killer and God knew what else was running loose out there and the lives of his boys were in danger. And, if nothing else, holing up in motels for a time would keep Marianna Silvaro's social services Gestapo from coming to collect his sons.

He never thought anything would bring him back to the Branca family, but this was different—riding up in an elevator with Captain Tepper and five other Rangers, the rest dispersed strategically about the lobby and exits. They stepped out on the eighth floor and rounded a corner toward Frank Branca Jr.'s suite overlooking the Riverwalk with Cort Wesley taking the lead.

A strange feeling struck him even before he reached the door, almost like a residue hanging in the air he couldn't identify by smell but knew was there all the same. At the suite door, Cort Wesley saw instantly the latch had been blown. Scorched metal and wood marred the area where the key card slot and knob had been. He'd seen miniature shaped charges produce such an effect during raids in the Gulf War, but knew they were strictly military ordnance by definition.

He could tell from the way their drawn weapons

were now raised and ready that the Rangers had come to pretty much the same conclusion. He looked toward Captain Tepper who nodded, a signal for Cort Wesley to ease open the door, the stench of blood and death assaulting him immediately.

"Nobody touch a goddamn thing," Tepper ordered, advancing into the suite ahead of Cort Wesley when it was clear the shooters were gone.

Cort Wesley followed Tepper inside, running his eyes over the bodies of Frankie Jr. and his three bodyguards with the captain.

"You got an opinion on what you see here, Mr. Masters?"

"Wasn't a mob hit, that's for sure."

"How?"

"All four were dropped by controlled three-shot bursts, military-style with M16s or a more recent version maybe. They picked up the spent shells, so there's not much more to say on the subject."

"That's a lot to assume, sir."

"Not when you've been on the other side of this kind of work."

Tepper held his gaze on him for a long moment, giving Cort Wesley's eyes the time to wander toward the body of Frank Branca Sr. slumped in his wheelchair, the victim of a three-shot burst as well. Judging from the blood trail, he'd been wheeled back away from the window after he'd been killed.

Sons of bitches, Cort Wesley thought, feeling his hands tighten into fists.

"So how you figure this went down?" Tepper asked, snapping him alert again.

Cort Wesley saw it all in his mind, how quickly and expertly it had happened, based on the positioning of the bodies and how none of them had had time to draw their own weapons. The guards had been taken first while they watched television, followed by Frank Jr. since he'd been standing when hit instead of sitting. The shooters had shot Frank Sr. last.

"Guess that about sums it up," Tepper said, making Cort Wesley realize he had spoken all his thoughts out loud.

The suite hadn't been tossed. But things had been disturbed just enough to tell Cort Wesley, the shooters had come here with something else besides killing on their minds. The couch cushions were too even and all the chairs were tucked neatly under the suite's dining table instead of them being angled toward the fifty-inch, wall-mounted plasma television.

"The briefcase Frankie Jr. had with him yesterday is gone," Cort Wesley heard himself say this time. "Contents were what he was selling."

Tepper took off his hat and mopped his brow. "Well, guess it's safe to say he never got to complete the transaction."

67

TUNGA COUNTY; THE PRESENT

Hollis Tyree III listened to the light squeak the Watertec 100 made as it chewed through dirt, sludge, and rock in search of water deep below the surface. Its thick black tubing shook from the pressure, and Tyree thought he felt the very earth vibrating in protest beneath his feet.

He imagined that the wildcatters and speculators who flooded Texas in the time of his grandfather felt the very same way as the drill bits attached to their derricks churned through the sludge. They'd creak and groan, their wooden supports not always strong enough to withstand spring storm winds. Here, eighty years later, wood had been swapped for steel, oil for water. But little else had changed and Tyree found himself taking peculiar comfort in that.

He'd once seen his father take a bullwhip to a journalist who'd infiltrated his work force to uncover safety violations. Snapped the whip out a half-dozen times until the man's shirt was a tattered, bloody mess and he was lying in the mud. Hollis Tyree Jr.'s boots kicked up dirt as he strode over and jerked the journalist's head out of the muck.

"You write a single word about what you saw and I'll drop your family down a well. You hear?"

The journalist nodded, sending flecks of grime and blood flying. He remained true to his word because he knew Hollis Tyree Jr. meant everything he said, how far he'd go to preserve his dream. Well, now his son had no choice but to go just as far, no matter where exactly that took him. Albion for him had become what that journalist was for his father. Tyree didn't relish the prospects of going up against Caitlin Strong and the Texas Rangers, but she hadn't left him much of a choice. Too much was at stake here to lose it all thanks to the craziness infecting one goddamn town. He needed to buy the time required to get things buttoned up once and for all, even if that meant shutting this particular site down for a time.

Tyree pictured himself taking that same whip to Caitlin Strong. Losing his children had hardened him into the man he should have been in the first place. He understood now why his father had sought to toughen him up, to teach him nothing came without paying a price for it. He'd dispatched a veritable army to Mexico to find his children, when he should have taken his dad's bullwhip and headed down there himself.

Well, he wasn't about to make the same mistake again, not with Albion.

The rumbling around him got louder and it took Tyree a few moments to realize it was actually coming from an SUV tearing to a halt just a few yards from him. Meeks jumped out, followed by four of his guards wielding assault rifles, each taking up a ready position as if expecting an attack.

"What's happening, Meeks?" Hollis Tyree asked, approaching them.

"Professor Lamb was found murdered this morning, sir."

"*What?*"

"Single bullet to the head. Execution style. And there's something else." Meeks started to reach into his pocket. "The lab report you commissioned just came back."

Tyree saw worry flash in Meeks's eyes for the first time as he took the pages and unfolded them, scanning quickly until he came to the final conclusive paragraph.

"This can't be."

"Let's go, sir," Meeks prodded. "Now, please. You may not be safe here."

But Tyree read the report again; nothing changing, the results the same.

"What have I done, Meeks? What in God's name have I done?"

Part Seven

One day on the firing range, an FBI agent spotted a Texas Ranger with a 1911 model .45 caliber pistol shoved inside his belt; no holster, cocked and unlocked. The agent came up to the Ranger and tactfully asked if carrying a pistol that way wasn't dangerous.

"Son," the Ranger said, "if that damned old thing wasn't dangerous, I wouldn't be carrying it."

—Texas Ranger parable

68

Captain D. W. Tepper entered Cooper's Bar and Grill after Caitlin and Cort Wesley had already sat down at a corner table. Cort Wesley arranged his chair to keep an eye on Dylan and Luke who were playing video games on leftover machines supplied years before by the Branca crime family. The sight made him think of his last views of both junior and senior earlier in the day.

Tepper stopped to greet a singer named Mike Blakely who was tuning up his guitar and ramping up the sound system for that night's acoustic show; a CD release party with a band called The Rats opening, according to the marquee outside.

Tepper continued on to the table and removed his Stetson as he took a chair centered between Caitlin and Cort Wesley.

"I like this place," Cort Wesley said to him.

"Ex-Ranger's a partner, so it tends to attract a lot of law enforcement types."

"Makes me feel right at home these days."

"Well, now that we've dispensed with the pleasantries," said Tepper, "maybe we can discuss what the hell's going on in Albion. For starters, I can tell you the Department of Public Safety had no idea what the hell I was talking about."

"It's Hollis Tyree's doing," Caitlin told him. "For sure."

"Well, this stunt might buy him a little time, but that's it."

"Maybe that's all he figures he needs."

Tepper smoothed an eyebrow with his index finger and slid his chair closer to them until a candle jar set in the middle of the table cast a flickering glow across his face that got lost somewhere in the furrows. "One of you wanna explain to me how these murders on the Riverwalk are connected to fake cops taking over Albion?"

"Frankie Branca told me a scientist with a gambling problem slipped him a field report to pay off a debt," Masters told him.

"Contents of that missing briefcase?"

"That'd be my guess."

"It's all tied up tighter than a drum," Caitlin chimed in. "Tunga County, Albion, the Brancas. Bottom line being we stepped in some pretty mean shit here. Something's poisoning the water in Albion, turning folks there crazy just like it turned those pioneers who drank from Deadman's Creek crazy in my great-granddad's time. And whatever it is, it's clearly worth plenty to somebody."

"I think we're agreed on that much," Tepper told them both. "Question being what the hell we're supposed to do about it?"

"I say we keep up our own investigation into Tunga County, Captain," said Caitlin.

"Need grounds for that."

"Already got it: Las Mujeres de Juárez. Our suspect

was spotted on Hollis Tyree's worksite and expected to return."

"Well, that comes as close to working as we're likely to get."

Tepper fished a pack of Marlboro Reds from his jacket pocket and popped a cigarette up with a smack of its bottom. Caitlin recognized the pack as the same one stowed not so permanently in his desk drawer from the matchsticks wedged into the plastic. He plucked the cigarette from the others around it, stuck it in his mouth, and fired a wooden stick match to light it.

"How's it feel to be on the right side of things for a change, Mr. Masters?"

"I always felt I was on the right side of things, Captain. Everything being relative and all."

"True enough, I suppose," Tepper nodded, turning his gaze on Dylan and Luke. "You got a couple fine boys there. You have my sympathies things have been so difficult for them. And I appreciate you having my back this morning."

"My pleasure, sir."

Tepper gave him a longer look. "What you said about being on the other side of those kind of hits . . ."

"Service to country, Captain, and that's the God's honest truth."

"I figured as much."

"Didn't need a three-shot burst against those I came up against back stateside. I believe you busted my father up in a bar fight once, by the way."

"Son, I've busted up a lot of people's fathers in bar fights and, you ask me, that's what we're in the middle of right now."

"Ever lose one?"

"Don't know a man who ever won one, all things considered."

"My father said you and Jim Strong were the toughest men he ever came up against."

"That's only because he never met Caitlin's granddaddy Earl. But I'll still thank you for the compliment."

The table slipped into silence, the only sound in the otherwise empty space that of Dylan and Luke blasting away at space aliens. Tepper's cell phone rang and he pushed his chair back a bit before answering it. Caitlin watched his features tighten, the flickering light from the candle barely reaching him now, leaving the flat parts of his face as dark as the furrows. He just listened, not speaking again until a final, "Thank you very much. I do appreciate the courtesy."

He flipped the phone closed and looked back at Caitlin and Cort Wesley across the table.

"That was our friend Captain Alonzo at SAPD. Seems one of her patrols responded to a call at the Walmart Supercenter over on De Zavala about a suspicious customer. Suspicious on account of he was near seven feet tall and left without taking his change from a hundred-dollar bill when a cruiser drove by."

"Guillermo Paz . . ."

"Back in town for sure, Ranger."

"This just keeps getting better."

69

"Whether or not Paz saved your life in Casa del Diablo," Captain Tepper said to Caitlin, "he's still wanted for two murders in the city."

"SAPD wants Paz, they better call in the National Guard, Captain," she told him.

Tepper frowned, looking as if he'd just swallowed something rotten. "This just makes a big mess even bigger, Ranger."

"Only way I can see to clean it up," said Caitlin, "is to find out what got loose in Albion's water supply." She looked toward Cort Wesley. "And that means we pay a visit to Hollis Tyree's fields in Tunga County."

"They'll likely be tied up tighter than a drum," said Captain Tepper. "Don't see what we gain from the effort truthfully, 'sides risking a run-in with more of the kind pulled you over outside of Albion."

"We go in after dark and just see what we can see without starting a shooting war."

Cort Wesley's eyes had drifted to his sons again. "Not until I know my boys are safe."

"Been thinking on that," said Tepper, clearing his throat raspily. "About the Mexican girl too. I was planning on moving her to the care of the men I trust most in the world, those smart enough to get away from this before the writing dried on the wall."

"Ex-Rangers," Caitlin concluded.

"Not just any either. Men as ornery and tough as your dad who preferred the old school methods fit enough for what we're facing here. Hell, one of their daddies was taught to shoot by Wyatt Earp and another by Bat Masterson themselves."

"Whatever their price," Cort Wesley told him, "I'm paying."

Tepper stifled a laugh. "Hell, outlaw, they'll pay us for the privilege. Since giving in to retirement, none of them's done much else besides hunt, though one was a bouncer in a roadhouse until he hit seventy."

"Finally retire, did he?" asked Cort Wesley.

"Busted up a couple bikers and quit to avoid a lawsuit."

Caitlin's cell phone rang and she interrupted her smile to raise it to her ear. "Hello."

"Remember me, Ranger?" greeted Guillermo Paz.

70

San Antonio; the present

"You got the same phone number," Paz continued.

"I heard you were in town, Colonel Paz."

"It's nice to leave an impression. How's your outlaw friend?"

Caitlin's eyes darted between Captain Tepper and Cort Wesley, neither of whom was moving. "He's right here, if you'd like to say hello."

"No, I called to speak with you. It's been a long time, hasn't it?"

"I never got the chance to thank you, Colonel. For Casa del Diablo."

"There's no need. It's I who should be thanking you."

Caitlin remained silent, waiting for Paz to continue to make some sense of his words and reason for his return to San Antonio. "Who you working for this time?"

"No one. I'm here on my own to settle our debt."

"Last time I checked you saved my life, not the other away around."

"Along with the outlaw and his sons."

"He's thankful too."

"Enough to forgive what I did to his woman and garage friend?"

Both Cort Wesley and Captain Tepper were trying to get Caitlin's attention, but she waved them off. Even Dylan and Luke had stopped playing their video game. "You'll have to ask him."

"It's important to me that he understand I was a different man then. He saw my new self in Casa del Diablo and that man bears him no ill will. You'll tell him that?"

"I will," Caitlin said, eyes fixed on Cort Wesley now. "So what do you want, Colonel?"

"I already told you."

"Police know you're in town. I don't recommend staying any longer than need be."

"I'll stay as long as it takes to save your life."

"Save my life?"

"You're in danger."

"From who?"

Paz looked down at the cigar box resting between his legs on the church pew Rosario Nieves had given him in the village of Majahual. "A question better answered in person, Ranger."

71

"I'm glad you came," Guillermo Paz said, without turning toward Caitlin's approach down the center aisle of the San Fernando Cathedral on west Main Plaza.

"It's good to see you again, Colonel," she said, sitting down next to him in the pew and noticing the cigar box resting on his lap. "Never thought I'd be saying that."

Paz turned to look at her. "*La vida está llena de sorpresas.*"

"Life really is full of surprises," Caitlin agreed. "Now what'd you mean about mine being in danger."

"I'm not sure. But it has something to do with Earl Strong."

Caitlin felt herself stiffen. "What do you know about my grandfather?"

"This is for you," Paz said, handing the cigar box to her.

"What is it?"

"Letters your grandfather never got and letters he wrote that were never read."

"To and from who?"

"A young Mexican woman named Juanita Rojas."

"From Sweetwater," Caitlin said, recalling that part of her favorite bedtime story. "My grandfather saved her life."

Paz continued to hold her gaze. His eyes were the biggest she'd ever seen, dark and sure. Full of emotion that seemed at once reflective and melancholy.

"There's more," he said.

72

The letters had dried to the texture of parchment, the paper yellowed and the writing faded, some of it lost to the dampness that had penetrated the cigar box's flimsy structure. Caitlin handled them gingerly, unfolding each like a skilled surgeon while imagining she could smell her grandfather's aftershave baked into the letters he'd sent. The ones he'd never received were written in a scratchy scrawl that reminded her strangely of her own writing, evoking memories of the criticism she'd received at the hands of teachers grown weary of penmanship that seemed written on a whim.

As Caitlin read the letters, trying to recover the Spanish needed to make sense of Juanita Rojas's writing, the world around her dimmed, time converging as the present and the past became one.

According to his first series of letters, Earl Strong returned to Sweetwater only long enough to give Hollis Tyree back his Plymouth and learn he'd been reassigned. With the criminal element under control and Sandman Sanchez firmly in charge, Earl was dispatched thirty miles up the road to Gladstone. At that point the town was in similar straits to Sweetwater when Earl had climbed off the train and Austin was hoping history could repeat itself.

His first night in Gladstone, he was making his

rounds, getting the lay of the land when he saw a trio of men surrounding a barmaid who was dumping the trash in a back alley adjoining one of the saloons.

"Come on, bitch, this don't have to be so tough."

Earl watched that man strip off her blouse and then go to work on her skirt, while the others watched, chuckling. He stopped at the head of the alley, took out one of his pistols, and fired a shot into the air.

The three men swung, the one just about to force himself inside the barmaid still with his pants down.

"You boys wanna be getting back inside now."

"Mind your own fucking business."

Earl stepped forward into a thin shaft of light that just caught his cinco pesos badge. "It is my business. And if you're not gone before I blink next, I'm gonna shoot off your dicks." He drew his second Colt to further enunciate his point.

The three men crowded through the door back inside, their spokesman's belt left behind.

Earl headed down the alley to where the barmaid stood trembling with arms covering her exposed breasts. He made a point not to look directly at her and fished her bra and torn blouse from the alley floor, brushing the grime off them.

"Name's Earl Strong, ma'am," he said, tipping his hat to her as she dressed herself as best she could.

"I know who you are, everybody in town does. You coming here's all anybody's been talking about. I'm Molly Finlaw."

"Well, ma'am, I'm not nearly as mean as people say, but I'm even tougher than they think."

"Thanks for what you just did," she said, trying to fluff her hair back into shape. "And the name's Molly, by the way. Ma'am makes me feel old."

"Wish we could've met under better circumstances, Molly."

She brushed her hair back with her hands, revealing a softly contoured face and flawless complexion. Her skin tone was light for these parts, making Earl figure she was one of those who pulled up stakes to come to Texas and join the boom.

"Think I'll hop a train back home tomorrow," Molly said, as if reading his mind. "I've had enough of this place."

"No need to do that now, Molly. Once I put the bad element disrupting things on the chain, Gladstone'll be the safest town you ever saw in your life, and that's a promise."

"On the chain? What's that mean?"

"You'll see," Earl grinned.

In the ensuing days, she and the entire town did indeed see. Earl's job was made substantially simpler by word of his exploits in Sweetwater, especially chasing Al Capone's boys back to Chicago. Much of the bad element fled Gladstone upon getting word he'd hit town, and those that stayed moderated their behavior substantially to avoid the chain that had made Earl famous even before the shootout in the freight yard. Folks were calling it the most well known gunfight since the Earps and Doc Holliday battled the Clantons at the O.K. Corral. For his part, Earl listened to the substantially embellished versions of the tale, patiently and humbly responding to each.

He walked the streets of Gladstone with the same resolve and presence he had in Sweetwater, albeit with a new appreciation of the world that was changing around him. Earl had always held the true heroes of his time in the highest esteem and frankly didn't think he measured up against the Rangers who'd protected the whole of the Texas frontier from all manner of Mexican bandits and Indian renegades. Compared to their exploits, cleaning up a town or two was nothing. He slept each night with a roof over his head, communicating daily with Austin via telegraph and enjoying the security that came with a Browning automatic rifle as opposed to the Colt five-shooters the original Rangers carried into battle.

Earl also found himself quite happy to see Molly still at work in the saloon when he stopped in there for breakfast a few mornings later.

"You convinced me to stay, Earl Strong," she said, pouring him a cup of coffee.

"That makes it a good first week, it does," he smiled, toasting her with his mug.

Earl wasn't sure if that was the moment he'd fallen in love with Molly Finlaw, but it was pretty close. She was the first thing that took his mind off Juanita Rojas to whom he'd sent three letters now, while receiving not a single one back. He had an early dinner in the saloon that night and was there when the place opened for breakfast the following morning yet again.

"You keep looking at me like that, Earl Strong, and I'm gonna have to charge you extra."

Normally shy around women, Earl found himself smiling. "You charging me extra, Molly, means I might have to propose marriage to avoid going broke."

"I'm listening," she grinned back.

The first letter Juanita Rojas wrote to Earl Strong from Majahual was to confess she was pregnant from their night in the motel room. She started the letter by apologizing profusely for being such a burden after all he'd done for her, and finished it with a plea to come and get her so their child could be raised north of the border.

Caitlin pictured Juanita's mother dutifully promising to mail the letter, while keeping the truth from Juanita's father and working feverishly to rectify the situation by finding her a Mexican husband fast. If she bore a child out of wedlock, to an *Americano* no less and *el Rinche* to boot, she would be shunned, she and her child both left to live out their lives as outcasts.

The solution was to find a man who'd never know the child wasn't his and swear Juanita to secrecy about the whole sordid affair. She was a beautiful young girl and her mother felt terrible believing the men who'd taken her away with a promise she'd come back with riches gleamed from prosperous work across the booming border. Rectifying this situation would be her way of making that up to her daughter, while not compounding the problem she had created.

Juanita's letters indicated she'd grudgingly agreed, hosting an assembly of men even as she kept penning letters to Earl Strong in virtual diary form, not once questioning whether he could read Spanish or not. She never for a minute suspected the letters were going no farther than her mother's desk and continued writing them, even as she found a husband and Earl's baby inside her began to grow.

As marriage was being forced on Juanita Rojas with a man she barely knew and didn't love, Earl Strong's letters to her indicated he was finding quite the opposite with Molly Finlaw. She became the first real woman in his life and, just like his Ranger father and grandfather, Earl figured he needed look no further for a wife.

He was smart enough to know she'd stayed in Gladstone because of him, but not too smart to take her for granted amid the notoriety and platitudes thrust his way. The new West had been without a hero since men like Wyatt Earp had faded from memory of the old. To many, the booming resurgence of Texas in the early 1930s was more a step backward to the frontier times that had spawned gunfighters and outlaws than a step toward the future. Earl found himself with a foot firmly planted in either world, an old-fashioned hero in a newfangled time as Texas struggled to hold its own against the vast forces converging upon it.

Earl slept with Molly Finlaw for the first time a month after he'd saved her in the alley. He'd fashioned a small bedroom out of a loft storage area in the local sheriff's office. No room for a bed but plenty for a pair of twin mattresses Earl taped together.

Having the touch and feel of a woman refreshed him no end but it was nothing, he wrote, like the night he'd spent with Juanita in the motel. He claimed he missed her more and more with each passing day. Even promised to return to the village of Majahual someday to knock on her door once again, but this time to take her away with him.

But Caitlin sensed a boyish longing to her grandfather's words. As some of the dried paper came away as grit in her grasp, she had the sense that even as he was writing out his promises, Earl Strong knew they'd never come to be.

· · ·

Juanita Rojas had written Earl about how depressed she was over her pending marriage to a handsome and shy young man named Jesus Nieves whose family had been coaxed by a mutual friend into allowing a marriage to a native Indian of lesser standing. Juanita prayed every night there'd be a letter the next day from Earl Strong, as her belly began to bulge and her husband reveled in the fact that he'd soon be a father, having no reason to suspect the baby wasn't his. Sitting there in the church all these years later, Caitlin found herself feeling profoundly sad for this young woman who longed to see the letters from Earl her mother denied her. At least twice a month, she dutifully committed the daily goings-on in her life in correspondence her mother similarly never sent. Caitlin thought it was the saddest story she'd ever heard, although for his part her grandfather made out okay.

Earl married Molly Finlaw six months to the day after they'd first met. A simple ceremony held in a small San Antonio church attended only by his fellow Rangers. The peak of the oil boom had passed, law and order returned to East Texas through more traditional means than the ad hoc methods necessity and stature had allowed him to employ.

"I'm sorry, Earl," Molly said, after repeated attempts to have their first child failed.

"Maybe the fault lies with me and Rangering that have me everywhere but home most of the time."

She shook her head stoically. "I can feel the emptiness inside me. I know I'm barren and if you want to look elsewhere for the woman to keep your line going, I'll understand."

Earl had never loved her more than in that moment. "Molly, you ever known me to quit anything in my life?"

"Not once, not even close."

"Then why in the name of Sam Houston do you figure I'm fixing to start now?" He waited for her to smile, continuing once she did. "We'll try as many times as it takes and if that don't work, we'll just keep trying."

And they did, resulting ultimately in three miscarriages. Earl put up as brave a front as he could around her, but on the road their failure to produce a child was tearing him up inside. He could outshoot, outfight, and outwit anyone he came up against, only to have this black mark come up against his manhood. No matter which of them was to blame, Earl would never forgive himself if the Strong line ended with him. In the face of all he had accomplished that had rightfully earned him a fame and reputation thought gone forever, Earl felt it would all be for naught if there were no one to whom to pass the legacy on.

He tried to resign himself to the reality. Couldn't. Tried to stop sizing up every man lesser than he, except for the fact that they had borne children. Couldn't. Tried to reassure Molly that he was fine whatever God dispensed upon them. Couldn't.

And then one day, eighteen months into their marriage, a letter arrived from Juanita Rojas in Majahual.

Caitlin dabbed at her moist eyes, reading on. Juanita had penned the letter on her deathbed after the typhus had taken hold. They kept her infant twins and one-year-old son she'd named Diego in another room to keep the germs from them, and when the fever allowed Juanita would listen to her babies' cries, wishing she could be there to soothe them away. She was dying and she knew it.

In penning her final letter to Earl Strong, she begged him to come and take their son. She had confessed the truth of his being to her husband whose family wanted no part of a half-American child, the offspring of a dreaded *el Rinche* no less. Juanita knew the infant would be given up to the church as soon as she passed and made her mother promise, *promise,* to instead let Earl Strong take the child to be raised in Texas, America.

She died signing her name to the one letter her mother actually sent.

"You understand why we must do this, *señor,*" Juanita's father told Earl when he arrived.

"I'm just grateful you're giving him up to me," Earl said, holding Diego the way Juanita's mother had showed him. "And I'm very sorry for your loss."

"You saved my daughter's life, *señor.* For that you deserve this much. I assume you are *un hombre de su palabra,* a man of your word."

"*Sí,*" Earl said humbly.

"Then I want you to promise me you will never tell the boy the truth of his birth and that, no matter what, you will never return to Costa Maya with or without him. The world will be told he died of the same fever that took his mother."

Earl realized he was rocking the baby gently, instinct having already taken over. "I promise to do your courtesy justice by giving him the best life I can in Texas, sir. I promise to hold his mother's memory close to my heart, even if I can never share it with him."

Juanita's father reached out and grasped Earl's arm. "Promise me you'll never let down my daughter's child the way I let her down. Promise me you'll protect him as I failed to protect her."

"*Usted tiene mi palabra, señor,*" Earl told him. "You have my word."

73

SAN ANTONIO; THE PRESENT

"Diego is Spanish for James," Caitlin said as she closed the cigar box, thinking of her father, the great Jim Strong.

"I should have known it the first time I saw you," Paz told her. "It was there in your eyes, but I didn't know what I was seeing."

"I feel sick."

"I'm sorry I made you sad."

"You didn't. I'm not."

"The tears say otherwise. They come from a person who just found out a good part of her heritage lies in Mexico, lifelong enemy of the Texas Rangers."

Caitlin swiped the tears from her face. "A long time ago maybe."

"But what would it do to that heritage if people found out your legendary grandfather bedded a Mexican woman in his charge who gave birth to your legendary father?"

"That your intention, Colonel?"

"Not at all. I wanted you to understand we come from the same Mayan blood, among the greatest warriors who ever walked the planet. I wanted you to understand what I saw in your eyes the first time they met mine that changed me forever. And that makes me sad too."

"Why?"

"Because it's all I've thought about for nearly a year and now it's done. And I'm afraid that I'll end up going back to the man I was before."

"That man's dead and buried, Colonel. You're not the only one who can see things in people's eyes."

Paz thought for a moment, his eyes still big when narrowed. "Do you think your father knew?"

"Nope, not if Earl Strong gave his word to Juanita Rojas's father. Nothing would ever make him break a promise."

"His own wife never gave him any children?"

Caitlin shook her head and felt the tears brimming anew. "Six straight generations of Strongs, each having only the one child. Strange, isn't it?"

Paz shrugged. "My mother had six and couldn't provide for any. As a boy I swore to do whatever it took to never be poor again. I wonder if I made the right decision."

"I don't feel any different, Colonel."

"¿Perdón?"

"I might be a quarter Mexican, but I don't feel any different. And, thanks to you, I know the rest of a story my grandfather never could finish all the way."

"There's more," Paz told her. "I just haven't gotten to it yet."

"How can you know that?"

"Like you just said: I can see it in your eyes."

"I have these nightmares," Caitlin said, not looking directly at him. "I'm a little girl outside in the rain at night. Alone mostly. Sometimes my father finds me under a tree."

"Not your mother."

"No. Maybe since she died when I was real young."

Paz smiled, the action so foreign to him that he seemed unsure of it himself. "Your grandfather would be very proud of you today."

"Sometimes, when I'm at the range where he taught me to shoot, I feel him adjusting my grip. Laughing when I miss and whistling when I put a whole magazine in the center black. Sometimes I can smell his aftershave."

"My mother spoke with spirits all the time. The last time I talked to her, she told me she was going to join them in three days."

"And did she?"

"I came back for the funeral on the fifth."

Caitlin took a deep breath, blew it out slowly. "Guess you can be on your way now, Colonel."

"You still need me, Ranger. Your life is still in danger."

"This isn't your fight, Colonel."

Paz looked away from her as if he were considering that option. She watched his huge chest expand and contract in rhythm with his breathing. Then he spoke suddenly, after Caitlin had begun to figure he wasn't going to respond at all.

"Your grandfather chased Al Capone's boys out of Texas. Shot a bunch of them up in an old freight yard and sent the lone survivor back north on the next train."

"He did at that," Caitlin nodded fondly.

"Your Sweetwater is coming, Ranger," Paz continued. "I believe that's what brought me here now; to make sure you survive it. When you call, I'll be ready."

74

San Antonio; the present

Macerio sat in the East San Antonio bar sipping watered-down tequila. The chemo had destroyed his tolerance, his stomach set churning by the mere smell of alcohol. Tonight was the first time he'd been able to keep it down, and earlier in the day he felt the first pricks of stubble atop his bald dome. The chemotherapy's side effects, apparently, were finally tapering off and Macerio had come to this bar to celebrate.

The place was crowded everywhere except in his general vicinity, the only two stools open being the ones on either side of him. People might have been stupid and insensitive to the world around them, especially with a truckload of booze dumped down their throats. But they still knew enough to keep their distance from Macerio, some inbred defense system activated by his presence.

He figured the prostitutes who favored this bar would be arriving soon. He could smell the residue of their cheap perfume on the air from previous nights as if someone had burned the scent into his nostrils. Soon they would stroll in reeking of the stuff with a mask of makeup worn over their faces. Macerio would know they were here as soon as the stale air carried the stronger whiffs to him. And when one of them left with a stranger never to return again, people would say she'd moved on or say nothing at all.

He would dump the body south of San Antonio near the border, continuing the bloody line he was stitching across this part of the world. Even if anyone realized what he was doing, discerned the ritual within it, no one would ever figure out why, the reason rooted thousands of years in the past back to a more noble time Macerio was committed to restoring.

Las Mujeres de Juárez meant nothing to him. They were mere objects he took no particular joy in killing, their blood supplying the color he was adding to his world. Creating a literal and figurative bloodline the Americans would someday be loath to cross. Tonight he would add another to the list, extend the line.

He went back to sipping his tequila, enjoying it soaking his throat without forcing vomit up in its wake. A brief breeze told him the door had been opened and the scent it carried told him by whom.

Macerio grinned, then heard his cell phone ring, interrupting his reverie and his plans.

PART EIGHT

The operations of the companies will be directed, more than heretofore been the case, to the suppression of lawlessness and crime. . . . [Officers and privates] are expected to use unremitting diligence in hunting up and arresting all violators of the law and fugitives from justice wherever they may be or from whatever quarter they may come.

—Texas Ranger General Order 15

75

Caitlin and Cort Wesley sat behind some brush on the knobby hillside overlooking Hollis Tyree's worksite, trying to make sense of what they were seeing. The work before them, ongoing under the harsh glow of day-bright light arrays, was utterly different from just two days before and all wrong. Caitlin glimpsed Meeks and his private army patrolling the perimeter with assault rifles dangling from their shoulders. And Hollis Tyree himself seemed to be supervising the entire process.

"Those machines were in storage the other day," she said, handing Cort Wesley the binoculars.

He pressed them against his eyes to better watch the process of huge swatches of land being dug out and cleared for the vacuum cleaner–like machines to be lowered in. From there, tons of earth and gravel were sucked up onto conveyors that funneled the contents into massive dump trucks with tires the size of small buildings. The dump trucks were lined up in a wide arc within the work lights' spill, the process confined to the southeast portion of fields still dotted with the huge, truck-mounted water drilling rigs.

"I worked enough construction in my time to tell you I've never seen anything like this," said Cort Wesley. "But it seems akin to cutting tunnels out of shale from mountains rich in coal normally."

"Except Tyree's taking it out of the ground."

"Drilling straight down instead of sideways. Principle's the same, with one crucial difference. Tell you one thing, whatever he's doing now has got nothing to do with water. Makes me think . . ."

"What?" Caitlin prodded.

"They're filtering the stones and refuse out before the dirt hits the conveyor. Makes me think of mining for gold."

"Gold? You think that's what all this is about?"

"Not in these parts, Ranger, no."

She watched Cort Wesley go back to his binoculars as a white panel truck drove up to the gate built into the newly erected chain-link fence enclosing the lower portion of the property.

He looked over at Caitlin, tensing. "I think our serial killer just got here."

76

TUNGA COUNTY; THE PRESENT

Macerio's orders were to get the women. Plans, and priorities, had changed. The precise nature of his instructions were cryptic but clear enough: the women were not to return to Mexico alive.

He'd like to take a knife to the lot of them, a dozen for the price of one left on the border to lengthen his bloodline even more than planned. But that wasn't what tonight was about. Tonight he had a job to do and doing it right meant doing it quick and sure. Get them outside the truck to stretch their legs and drink some water and machine gun the lot of them. Choose the right place and all anybody would find once the sun, heat, and coyotes got to them would be bones, not more of Las Mujeres de Juárez.

As he approached the worksite, though, he saw everything was different since he'd last been here. Different machines, different job description. Priorities had changed. Clearly.

He watched the guards drag open the gate and drove the truck through, already planning where he would pull over once his charges were inside.

77

TUNGA COUNTY; THE PRESENT

Caitlin parked her SUV a quarter mile down the freshly paved access road well north of U.S. 90. She chose the spot for the thick nest of balled-up sagebrush pressed up against a rock formation just off the road. Perfect camouflage for the SUV, leaving Cort Wesley and her to figure out what to do from here.

"If the son of a bitch ends up staying there," Cort Wesley said, "we can make a fire and roast marshmallows."

"He'll be coming. Of course, what exactly we do about that remains an open question," Caitlin told him.

"Leave that part to me."

. . .

Macerio felt the hollow thump beneath him, the truck suddenly listing hard to the right, and knew one of his tires had blown. He cursed his bad luck, then figured maybe there was a way to make it work for him.

The shoulder along this part of the road fell off steeply into an irrigation ditch. The blown tire would give him an excuse to have the young women pile out to be killed en masse, a bullet or two for each. He'd order them to the rim of the shoulder, do the deed so their own momentum would take them over the side into the shallow pool of collected muck and water. The bodies would remain out of sight for some time and a hard rain in the next few days would conceal them for even longer.

Macerio steered the van off onto the soft patch adjoining the fresh pavement. Then he climbed out and jerked the truck's cargo door up, liking the way the girls' eyes glistened in the dark.

"*¡Todos fuera!*" he ordered. "Everybody out! *¡Apúrate!*"

Moonlight revealed the truck to Caitlin and Cort Wesley from several hundred yards away.

"Here we go," she said, unclipping her badge and dropping it into a cupholder.

"Don't like the idea of me sitting here, pretending I'm asleep," Cort Wesley said again.

"He recognizes you, we lose the advantage."

"You walking right up to a hardwired killer with your SIG out of sight. You call *that* an advantage?"

He'd found an ample supply of screws and nails in a toolbox stored in the back of Caitlin's SUV. Cort

Wesley hammered enough of those nails and screws into the thickest branches he could find and then laid them across the road in a pattern certain to snare at least one of the truck's tires and maybe two.

"You know there's only one way this ends," Cort Wesley continued.

"My intention is to arrest his sorry ass. But make no mistake about it, gunning him down runs a close second if things come to that."

"It'll come to that, all right. Men like Macerio don't stick out their wrists for you to slap the handcuffs on."

"You did," Caitlin reminded.

Once the trap was laid, they drove back down the road a half-mile or so and parked the SUV far enough into the brushy flatlands to let the night conceal it. Neither said much while they waited for the panel truck to pass; they didn't have to wait very long, just ten minutes by Caitlin's count.

By the time they came upon it angled on the shoulder, Macerio had already emptied the girls from the truck and was shepherding them around its front through the hazy spray of headlights barely making a dent in the ribbon of night ahead.

Macerio figured he'd kill the girls first, then change the tire, though he flirted with the idea of having them change it for him. For all his attributes, Macerio detested physical labor, especially loathing the peasant lifestyle that often came with it. Both his parents had been migrant farmworkers, making the trip north across the border every spring to join the harvests that would finance their meager existences for months to follow. He started hating the work as soon as he and his brother were old enough to do it, and killed for the first time during the second blistering summer of toil.

Macerio didn't remember the girl's name, just that she was flirtatious and big-breasted. They met in the middle of the fields, the girl reaching into his pants even before they started kissing. His pocketknife dug into her just as she found what she was feeling for. He had just turned thirteen at the time. He'd forgotten what he did with her body, but it had been years before he began drawing his line across the border.

Macerio was just reaching inside the truck's cab for the submachine gun tucked under the driver's seat, when the bright bluish tint of an SUV's xenon headlights caught him in their spray.

78

TUNGA COUNTY; THE PRESENT

Caitlin snaked her SUV to a halt behind the truck on the shoulder, angled to keep it in the hold of her headlights. Cort Wesley's head was already slumped downward in feigned sleep, Glock clutched firmly in his lap.

"I'll be watching as best I can," he told her.

Caitlin climbed out without acknowledging him, certain Macerio's eyes would be upon her now. She'd already made sure her SIG was tucked in her belt well back of her hip under her jacket. No reason Macerio would expect it to be there or have any reason to look for it.

"Hey, you need some help?" she called out to him, gravel spit from the path of her boots as she approached. "*¿Necesita usted alguna ayuda?*"

"*Todo está bajo control.*"

"*Sí. Beuno.*" Caitlin continued her approach, her gait that of the concerned, naïve Samaritan, no caution observed whatsoever to put Macerio on the defensive. "*Permita que mí lo ayude a cambiar el neumático.*"

"I told you, I don't need any help."

Caitlin stopped even with the back of the panel truck, no more than a dozen feet from the serial killer responsible for Las Mujeres de Juárez. She glimpsed the dozen or so teenage girls stealing anxious glimpses toward her from the road's shoulder. She knew Cort Wesley would've shot Macerio down as he stood. If coaxed to talk, though, he could provide potentially crucial information about the truth of what was happening on Hollis Tyree's land.

"*¿Señorita?*"

His voice brimming with suspicion now, Caitlin cursed herself for letting her gaze linger too long on his newly intended victims. She met Macerio's eyes, saw in them the reality that she had lost the sense of innocence she'd been depending upon. Her SIG was well out of easy drawing range. She'd need to twist a hand well back under her jacket and jerk the pistol free before she even thought about aiming it. Fortunately, Macerio didn't have a weapon in casual view either, creating a stalemate of sorts.

"How about some water?" Caitlin asked him. "For the girls. I've got a full cooler back in my truck."

That drew Macerio's gaze to her SUV, and she

watched him tense at the sight of another form inside it.

"They aren't thirsty. But do you have a phone I can use? The batteries in mine are dead."

"Sure do," Caitlin said, hand dipping into her pocket as she resumed her approach.

Asking for the phone bought Macerio time. Time to continue reconciling the odd feeling he had about this woman with her utterly defenseless attitude. The presence of the girls might have accounted for that, but the way she walked and moved alerted him to something else. And she seemed to be listing slightly to the right, the way gunmen of old did to facilitate a quick draw of their weapons from that side. He also found it strange she hadn't roused the man sleeping in her SUV's passenger seat, or that he hadn't roused himself.

The woman's boots graced the gravel of the shoulder, barely disturbing it. Macerio saw her extending the cell phone toward him, the moonlight catching her face.

Her face . . .

His mind flashed back to searching for his missing *puta* in East San Antonio, an SUV tearing away down the street.

This woman had been behind the wheel!

Macerio lurched toward her in the same instant that saw the woman twist her hips rightward even as a hand disappeared under her jacket. Macerio shoved the woman backward against the truck with one hand clamped on the gun and other digging into her throat.

.   .   .

Caitlin felt her cartilage contract, the breath squeezed out of her faster than air from a balloon. The hair riding atop Macerio's head had shaken forward, suddenly hugging his forehead over dark eyes blazing into her.

She tried to fire but felt his iron grasp holding her gun hand at bay, blocking the trigger as she heard the thunk of the SUV door being thrust open and lashed out with a boot toward the big man's knee.

Cort Wesley was a damn good shot, but not a great one. And the bodies twisting before him in the night left him fearing where his bullet might end up once fired. He drove himself forward, gun raised and ready, the night pierced by wails from the Mexican girls disappearing into it.

Caitlin felt the crunch of the big man's knee splitting from muscle and tendon. He listed slightly to that side, the pain bursting from him with an *ugggghhhh* a moment before he slammed her skull backward against the panel truck.

She felt the steel dimple at impact with her skull. The night brightened in a flash, then faded to a preternatural grayness, a misty shroud cast over her vision. She felt for her pistol only to realize it was gone along with the breath she'd forgotten where to find. Her lungs, starving for air, pressed against her chest, seeming to push against her thudding heart.

Then . . .

BOOM! BOOM! BOOM!

. . . something like thunder clapped, what felt like rain and hail hammering her at the same time.

Cort Wesley's first three shots were misses—on purpose to get Macerio off Caitlin. The move had its desired effect, the big man leaving her to slump down the side of the truck, while he disappeared behind it.

Cort Wesley threw himself into an all-out sprint, trying to sight in on Macerio through the darkness. His figure made for a dark speck against the moonlit night, then seemed to disappear altogether as it zigzagged beyond the figures of the girls fleeing as well.

What the hell . . .

Just like that, Macerio was gone, as if he had dropped into the prairie floor, leaving Cort Wesley nothing to shoot at.

He stopped and crouched warily over Caitlin.

"You get him?" she rasped.

"Nope," Cort Wesley replied, noticing the dark, shiny shape of a cell phone amid the gravel and dust. "But I got something."

79

SAN ANTONIO; THE PRESENT

Guillermo Paz unhitched the line fastening his safety harness to the San Fernando Cathedral's steeple. The crumbling roof was on the punch list the priest had given him to help pass the time, but he couldn't reach enough of the storm-damaged tiles encumbered by the safety line.

He'd never roofed before and, having grown up in a world where shanty homes were topped with corrugated tin tacked into cheap wood, he had no right to know what he was doing. Still, he'd fallen into an easy rhythm replacing the missing and broken slate tiles with fresh ones pulled from a stack uncovered in the church basement. The priest had explained that slate was a thing of the past, the only alternative to this patchwork being a total roof replacement even a historic landmark lacked the funds to manage.

Paz had started up here when the afternoon sun began to cool and continued his work under the moonlight. He carried a hammer, chisel, and wedge in his tool belt to remove the broken pieces and a glue gun with which to fasten the new tiles into place.

Paz worked as the night continued to cool, much more comfortable without the harness to contain him. Suddenly, though, the wind picked up, threatening to push Paz from his perch and topple him to the concrete below. The wind chilled him, carrying the promise of yet another spring storm. He looked off into the distance where it was brewing and sniffed the air, sensing something in the offing beyond wind, rain, and hail but equally calamitous.

Paz smiled, setting back to wait for that storm to come.

80

TUNGA COUNTY; THE PRESENT

The flashing lights seemed to stretch for miles, beacons in the Texas night. Highway patrol responders were first on the scene, reaching it in full understanding they were operating under Ranger auspices. Captain D. W.

Tepper had coordinated everything from his home in Marble Falls after Caitlin's call roused him from a dream in which he was peeling the paper off Marlboro Reds and eating the tobacco.

"I'm giving up on those damn patches," he explained. "I get off the phone with Austin, next thing I'm gonna do is flush the rest down the toilet. Nice work, Ranger."

Caitlin dry swallowed some air, the motion forcing a harsh ache through the cartilage Macerio had nearly crushed. She called Tepper back an hour later, the crime scene secure, the Mexican girls chased down, but no sign of Macerio whatsoever.

"Got a cell phone he left behind, Captain," she reported, "like nothing I've ever seen before."

"Touch screen, something like that?"

"More like what an astronaut might carry in his suit. We figure out how to dump the numbers we might know a hell of a lot more than we do right now."

"This man goes up against you and Masters and gets away, I'm not sure I wanna know any more," Tepper said, clearing the mucus from his throat.

"Highway patrol chopper sweeping the area hasn't found any sign of him and they won't either. But we got all the girls collected, safe and sound. I swear, Captain, this man must be able to make himself invisible. Who knows, maybe he really is some kind of demon."

"Any thoughts on what you saw on Hollis Tyree's land?"

"They're pulling something out of the ground, all right, and it's not water. Something's not right about the whole scene. How quick can the Rangers move on this, Captain?"

"Tomorrow morning soon enough?"

Caitlin found Cort Wesley seated in her SUV, regarding the crime scene with detachment, cell phone squeezed in his grasp.

"Was about to call my boys 'til I remembered the hour. Something like this happens, I wanna be sure they're safe, especially with Macerio still out there." Cort Wesley cast his gaze back toward the cordoned-off crime scene area where technicians were still measuring off distances and dusting for fingerprints around the panel truck. "What you think his role in this is exactly?"

"He comes back for the girls in his original capacity is all I can figure."

"They were outside the truck 'cause he was planning on killing them. That part of his original plan too?"

Caitlin turned her gaze out into the night. "You wanna drive to Pearsall, check on your boys?"

Cort Wesley kept his eyes on her, trying to figure out what she was looking at. "It'll keep. Don't want to take the chance of leading somebody there who might be watching."

Caitlin turned back toward him, started to speak, then stopped.

"Not like you to be at a loss for words, Ranger."

"My throat hurts."

Cort Wesley moved close enough to smell her lilac-scented shampoo mixing with the dank, sour smell of sweat frozen in her pores. "You wanna tell me what's really wrong?"

Caitlin's eyes emptied, her voice cracking painfully. "I don't want to be alone tonight."

"Me neither," Cort Wesley told her.

81

They lay in bed awake for a long time after it was over.

"Goddamn," Cort Wesley said, holding Caitlin's head against his chest and stroking her hair, "I feel like I'm back in high school."

"You mean 'cause we're sneaking around like this."

"Beats not seeing you for two months. Question being what happens when we put our guns away again."

"You got your boys to worry about too."

Caitlin felt Cort Wesley stiffen beneath her. He stopped stroking her hair. "You never told me how your magic worked with Marianna Silvaro."

"Haven't finished waving my wand yet."

She felt Cort Wesley's powerful chest lifting and lowering with each breath, heartbeat starting to settle.

"I read this essay Luke wrote for school about his dad's best friend," he said suddenly.

"Me?"

"You."

"Tell him I said thanks."

Cort Wesley tried to wet his lips with his tongue. "Is he right?"

"I don't know, Cort Wesley. I'd tell you if I did."

"Know what?"

"No."

"Feels like we're married right now. Something I never knew before. Ever."

"Me either."

"You were married for a time, Ranger."

"But we never shared much, not the way you and I do."

"Besides a bed being your meaning."

"Especially."

Cort Wesley started stroking her hair again. "So how is it we lost two months?"

"You already know the answer to that."

"I know what you told me. Doesn't make it true."

Caitlin eased herself off Cort Wesley so she could look him in the eye. "That's what you want, Cort Wesley, the truth?"

"It's what I just asked for."

"I was scared."

"Never seen anything that could scare you, Ranger."

"How about starting to figure I couldn't live without you and the boys?"

"Your answer being to just disappear?"

Caitlin shrugged. Outside, the motel's marquee pushed its flickering light through the room's thin blinds, casting alternating red and blue streaks across Cort Wesley's face.

"Find a reason to anyway," she conceded.

"These missing Mexican girls."

"Yeah."

"Figuring I'd still be here when you got good and ready to come back."

"I was right, wasn't I?"

Cort Wesley smiled and wet his lips with his tongue. "I think Luke was the one who actually got it right. Said we loved each other and it was good because it made him miss his mom less."

"Oh, man . . ."

"Also said you sucked at video games, especially one called Texas Ranger. Wrote he found that ironic.

Eleven years old and he's using the word 'ironic.' Hell, I don't even know what it means."

"I don't think anyone does really. One of those things you know when you see it, though."

Cort Wesley laid his hand behind Caitlin, easing her closer to him. "Like other things, I suppose." He glanced at the red numerals of the clock radio on the night table. Beyond the drawn blinds, the motel's marquee seemed to brighten, spraying backward letters through the flimsy material against the room's walls. "What I gotta say is I don't want you going missing again down the road. You start feeling wrong about things, take a walk or something. Or go to the gym."

"Maybe break another man's nose."

"So long as it's not mine," he said, cupping a hand over the right side of Caitlin's face. "So what do you say, Ranger?"

"About that rematch you asked for?"

"About not pulling another disappearing act."

"Nights like this oughtta make that pretty difficult, less something gets in the way."

"Like that old memory you can't fix in your mind."

"Every time I'm close enough to touch it, it runs away again." Caitlin glanced toward the window at the marquee flashing its way past the blinds. "Still got three hours until dawn. I fall asleep, there'll be nightmares for sure. You mind staying up with me?"

"Twist my arm," said Cort Wesley.

82

"You look tired," Captain Tepper said when Caitlin met him the following morning for breakfast at Denny's just up from the River Center Mall near the Riverwalk.

"I didn't get much sleep."

Tepper eyed her quizzically, then let it pass. His plate of steak, eggs, and home fries had just arrived when she got there and he was in the process of adding ketchup to the mix.

"Most important meal of the day, Ranger," he noted, swabbing butter onto his two pieces of Texas toast.

"It hurts to swallow right now."

Tepper looked up from his eggs. "You have the docs check out your throat?"

"No need. It'll heal."

"Hurt to talk?"

"And breathe. You don't mind, it's just coffee for me today."

Tepper pushed a forkful of eggs into the ketchup pile and swallowed it down. "Just heard from the highway patrol. Their sweep yielded nothing, as if Macerio just vanished into thin air, like you said. But a man was beaten ten miles down the road in a service station restroom and had his car stolen. You ask me, the man behind Las Mujeres de Juárez is back over the border already. That's the bad news."

"What's the good?"

"Already dumped the contents of the cell phone you recovered from the scene last night. Should have a report on the killer's calls in and out by this afternoon."

"We need to find out what Tyree was pulling out of the ground last night."

"Lieutenant Rollins is assembling the team now. Those fields will be in our hands before lunch."

"You mind going in without me?"

"Now I've heard everything. . . ."

"Need to do some digging of my own, Captain."

"Where?

"Better if you don't know, if that's not a problem."

"The problem is you're the only one we got knows the lay of the land."

"Cort Wesley Masters could draw that stretch for you blindfolded, you don't mind taking him along."

"Would it matter if I did?" Tepper dropped his fork down on the table and laid his elbows on either side of his still-heaping plate. "What else is eating at you, Ranger?"

Caitlin leaned back in her chair, suddenly needing some distance. "Did you know the truth about my father?"

"Depends on which truth you're speaking of."

"The one that starts with his given name really being Diego."

Tepper's milky eyes narrowed enough to straighten the furrows on his brow. "Where the hell you hear something like that?"

"Where do you think?"

"Paz?"

Caitlin let the question hover in the air between them briefly. "He told me the two of us are descended from the same Mayan warrior tribes. He knows more about my lineage than I ever heard told before."

"And you *believed* him?"

Caitlin nodded. " 'Cause he finished telling the story my granddad never could, and now I understand why."

Something changed in Tepper's expression. His upper lip quivered, his eyes going blank. "You're talking about Sweetwater."

"How much of it is real, Captain?"

"I wasn't even born at the time, Ranger."

"But you knew Earl and Jim Strong better than anyone. You telling me neither one of them ever told you about Juanita Rojas and Costa Maya and how my father was conceived?"

Tepper frowned. "Earl told me some, not all."

"Am I missing something here?"

"Leave it be, Caitlin."

"I can't, Captain. Maybe I want to, but I can't anymore."

D. W. Tepper looked the saddest she'd ever seen him, and that included at both her dad's and granddad's funerals. He glanced down at his eggs, steak, and home fries and shoved the plate aside.

"All right," he started, "but just remember I warned you. . . ."

83

JUÁREZ AND EL PASO; 1934

Earl Strong didn't see nearly enough of his son, Jim, in the boy's toddler years. The demands on the Rangers grew, and no matter how many times he resolved to make things different, there was duty to uphold and a badge to honor. As his own father had told him, there was no compromise in being a Texas Ranger. You either were or you weren't, and if you were it *was* your life. Plain and simple.

Earl had barely known his own father, William Ray, and found he couldn't live with the reality of that cycle repeating. His boy needed him. Problem was, the Rangers needed him more.

"This drug trafficking is a shit storm of a mess," Captain Tom Hickman told him at Ranger headquarters in Austin in 1934.

"I've heard that said more than once."

"Well, I'm here saying it's gotten worse. In the twenties we knew it was coming into Baja, California, through Tijuana. Marijuana mostly back then, which all changed when poor Mexican farmers turned to poppy growing."

"Where's that leave us?" Earl asked, feeling his arm hairs starting to get prickly.

"We got Mexican border agents telling us the farmers are beholden to opium traffickers known as *gomeros* for their very lives. Further complicating things is that these *gomeros* are in league with high-ranking Mexican government officials. We got some reports claiming that the mysterious head of the traffickers, a Chinese named Antonio Wong Yin, is a close *compadre* of both Governor Nazario Ortiz Garza of Coahuila and General Jesús García Gutiérrez, head of the state's military."

"Sounds like a mess all right, Captain. What is it you need done?"

"We need you to do what you did in Sweetwater, Ranger. Everybody knows you ran some pretty tough boys out of town there."

"The ones that lived anyway."

"Well, Al Capone's Chicago Outfit is where the opium's ending up. And most of it's coming in through Ciudad Juárez into El Paso." Hickman stopped there and regarded Earl tightly from across his desk. "You chased those boys out of Texas once, Ranger. We need for you to help do it again."

A few days later Earl and twelve Rangers of his choosing, including Sandman Sanchez, headed to El Paso to meet up with state detectives who became Texas's first antinarcotic agents. These detectives had developed a decent enough network of informants to pinpoint the timing and route of shipments across the border where agents of The Outfit would be waiting at prearranged rendezvous points. Captain Hickman's plan was to shut off the spigot at the source, but Earl figured the only way that strategy stood a chance of working was if The Outfit was similarly dissuaded from their current course of action.

Hickman had arranged a base in El Paso he had stocked with more firepower than Earl had ever seen in his life. For a man used to taking only what arsenal he could carry on horseback, the sight of heavy machine guns, carbines, and 1911 model .45 automatics, tommy guns, Brownings, and even hand grenades was quite a sight to behold. But he was smart enough to know if this came down to a shooting war, they were bound to lose based on sheer numbers and the enemy boasting an entire country as safe haven. The thing to do now was the same thing he had done in Sweetwater: make a strong enough example on both sides of the border to influence these Chicago boys and their mules to rethink their intentions. Earl knew enough about opium to know the number of lives it had already destroyed, cementing his resolve to get this job done while Molly stayed home with Jim. Doctors had pretty much assured them she wouldn't be able to bear children of her own, making her love Jim even more and leading Earl to be even more thankful God had brought Juanita Rojas into his life, however briefly.

The first raids, conducted in conjunction with the state detectives, concentrated north of the border and were spectacular successes. Communication being what it was in those days made it impossible for the various drug-running teams dispatched by the Chicago Outfit to get word out of what was happening. Earl's Ranger team arrested nearly a hundred runners without shooting a single man, waiting on each occasion until the shipment had been delivered so the Rangers could burn the opium for all to see.

What Earl could not fathom, given the limitation of his frontier mentality, was the power of money to buy betrayal. The state detectives to whom Earl was beholden for intelligence were similarly beholden to Mexican informants for information. This time, unlike Sweetwater, the Chicago boys used their brains instead of weapons by paying a few of the same informants more.

Two months into an assignment that left him sullen over missing his wife and son, Earl and his Ranger team were lighting out on foot through the southwest Texas desert saw grass to cut off yet another opium shipment when muzzle flashes lit up the night. Earl recorded them in the millisecond before two Rangers went down and a third doubled over, quickly sinking to his knees. He and the others pulled the wounded men into the meager cover provided by a dry rocky creek bed.

They returned fire to the east, only to have fresh rounds bursting at them from their exposed western flank. Earl swore under his breath, cursing himself out for delivering his team straight into an ambush. The enemy had chosen this very spot for the placement of the creek bed as an obvious point of cover. And once the Rangers had sought refuge there they had opened up fire from a secondary front.

Two more Rangers crumpled around him, one from a fatal headshot and another with a sucking chest wound that would see him follow before too very long. He had four wounded to deal with on top of that, but two of those could still fire a gun for the time being.

"This ain't working," Earl told Sandman Sanchez fifteen minutes into the fight.

"Say the word and I'm ready to take as many of these fuckers with me as I can."

"We're not there yet and never will be, I have my say about it."

"What you thinking, boss?"

"You know what I'm thinking."

Sandman shifted positions, grimacing. "Hope you don't mind me coming along."

"Matter of fact I do, 'specially with that bullet in your leg you didn't think I noticed. You just stay here and hold the fort. Get prepared to open up on the guns to the west soon as I deal with the ones to the east."

The gangsters firing at them from the high ground on both flanks were more killers than gunmen. First thing, Earl crawled on his belly along the rim of the creek bed, face pressed low to keep the lightness of his flesh from sight. A few hundred yards later, he rose to a crouch and scampered along the darkest patch of earth he could find.

Earl had dragged a tommy gun along with him to aid his cause. Hard to handle, difficult to aim, and not much good from any real distance, except scattering everyone from its path. The gangsters were smarter than he'd thought, posting someone at the rear of their encampment to guard against Earl's strategy. And he responded by hoisting his tommy gun in one hand and .45 Springfield in the other, blasting away with both as soon as the darkness gave him away.

The gangsters scattered, rushing in all directions, as his fire cut enough of them down to force the others away from the cover of the embankment. Earl heard the echo of fire from Sandman and the other surviving Rangers resounding to the west, followed by return fire sent wildly into the night. He thought he detected screams resounding through the air as well, but couldn't say for sure.

By the time he made it back to the creek bed, the gangsters on both flanks had all either fled or been gunned down. But at dawn's first light, three Rangers were dead with another almost certain to follow. Earl had barely gotten around to writing his report when he got word from Austin that Molly and Jim had been moved to a Ranger barracks for protection after The Outfit out of Chicago had threatened their lives.

For Earl Strong, that proved to be the tipping point, taking him to a place in his being he'd never known before. Even putting men on the chain in Sweetwater and Gladstone had been undertaken with a degree of lawfulness and respect for rights. But here in the west Texas desert, all bets were off.

Earl briefly considered heading north to Chicago to call out the men holding the strings that pulled triggers and spread opium through the country, before settling on a different strategy. He and the surviving Rangers changed their focus to the mules, their goal being to shut down the flow of drugs from Ciudad Juárez once and for all.

"It's frontier rules all over again," he told his Rangers. "You all know what that means."

"We do," Sandman Sanchez said, speaking for all of them as he leaned on his crutch.

"Any man who hasn't got the stomach for this kind of work should walk away with no harm done to his name or reputation. But I'll tell you this, and mark these words, it's gonna get ugly now."

They'd all heard the stories of the things Rangers of the past had done in the name of justice. The frontier era, and the numerous border wars that followed, came with an often-callous disregard for human rights. The lack of accountability was much to blame here, and Earl knew he had that same atmosphere on his side in the present.

But in later years he never once told the tales of the weeks that followed. Of cross-border incursions and the blood-soaked ambushes of drug mules carrying their deadly product northward. There were hangings, with the bodies left suspended from tree limbs to be driven under by the next mules. There were mass graves dug and blood plumes spit into the air when the bodies were dumped in. There were bonfires fueled by burning opium bags that lit up the night.

Earl had no stomach for such brutality, but also no choice, not after they'd threatened the lives of Jim and Molly. Still the depth of his deeds had begun to weigh on him, stealing his sleep, when the pleading eyes of a desperate mule strung up on a tree met Earl's. Recognition flashed in both their gazes.

"*El Rinche*," the Mexican muttered, Earl knowing him as the father of Juanita Rojas and grandfather to his son.

"Not you," Earl heard himself say.

"Please, spare my life. I will tell you anything if you spare my life. I will tell you where the poppies are stored now. Just let me live. This is *blood* you are talking to!"

"Where?" Earl asked him.

"Sauer and Company on Avenida Juárez, stacked in the basement. Bags and bags piled up since your raids have put everything so far behind." The Mexican swallowed hard. "Please do not hate me."

Earl didn't say whether he did or not.

"You will let me live now, *el Rinche*?"

"You can't go home, sir, least not until this is finished."

"I understand."

"They'll know you talked. They always do."

"I understand that too."

After the man disappeared into the night, Earl turned to Sandman Sanchez.

"You ever been to Juárez, Ranger?"

84

"George Sauer was a merchant specializing in groceries, wines, liquor, and cigarettes," D. W. Tepper continued. "Made himself a fortune during Prohibition by running liquor out of that very building in Juárez lined floor to ceiling with cases of bottled beer and booze. Whether he was in on the opium business, we'll never know for sure."

"What happened?" Caitlin asked him.

"Well, as I hear it told, after Earl and his boys were done there wasn't a bottle left whole by their bullets and they'd burned every bit of the opium stored in the basement in the middle of the town square. The people, they say, came out and cheered them. It became a party."

"Not for my grandfather, it didn't."

"No, it did not. Those months changed him in a way he never really recovered. Never quit rangering, of course, but his days of gunfighting were done. When Earl left Mexico, he left the past behind. Sauer and Company itself closed up immediately thereafter, but the building still stands in Juárez to this day. I once heard Coahuila governor Nazario Ortiz Garza himself was killed in the gunfight, but never confirmed it for myself."

"Nazario Ortiz Garza was Emiliato Valdez Garza's great-uncle," Caitlin told him, referring to the drug lord she and Cort Wesley Masters had faced off against in Casa del Diablo a year before, surviving thanks to the intervention of Guillermo Paz.

"Guess that explains why the Strongs never exactly been on the Garzas' Christmas card list," said Tepper.

"Thanks for filling in the gaps, Captain."

"Reason your grandfather and father didn't, I suspect, was 'cause they didn't want you to think less of Earl Strong."

"Why would I?"

"On account of the fact that Earl thought considerably less of himself afterward. By the time I met him in 1960 or so he hadn't fired his gun in a decade, the years having mellowed him a bit."

"Nice way to put it, Captain."

"Put what?"

"Why don't you tell me?"

Tepper's eyes looked dry and tired. "He wasn't the man I was expecting, Caitlin. Problem with being a legend is things freeze around the time that make a man one. You meet that man thirty years later, you expect him to be the very same from the pictures and stories. Earl Strong was past sixty when I first met him, your dad and I having joined the Rangers at the same time. Thin as a rail with eyes that took you in without really caring about what they were seeing."

"You're saying he never got it back after Juárez."

"I believe he just turned his life around to different concerns. Molly, your grandma, passed when Jim Strong was not much more than thirteen, so Earl took to fathering a lot more than might have been in his nature. Truth be told, I think he welcomed pulling it all back. I think he got his fill in Sweetwater, Clifton, the west Texas desert, and finally Juárez. You take nothing else from the rest of Earl's story, take that."

"Because you're afraid that's what's happening to me."

Tepper's eyes seemed to moisten, his gaze growing stern but warm. "I believe you've already had your fill and then some. When Earl headed down to Juárez to finish things, I don't think he ever expected to come back. Your dad showed me a letter addressed to him one day not long after Earl died. Earl had written it prior to the gunfight in Juárez, to be sent only in the event that he died. In it, he begged little Jim never to strap on a gun, never even think of becoming a Ranger."

"Because my granddad didn't feel proud of it anymore. Is that what you're saying here, Captain?"

Tepper shook his head and ran a finger along the length of a deep furrow stretching from temple to jawline. "Let's just leave things there, you don't mind."

"And what if I do?"

"You need to trust me on this, Ranger."

"On what?"

"On the fact you've heard the whole story now. It's done and gone, no more of it to tell."

"So long as it's the truth, D. W."

"Close as we can come," Tepper said, looking away so Caitlin couldn't see his eyes.

85

TUNGA COUNTY; THE PRESENT

Cort Wesley drove his truck in the middle of the Ranger convoy. He rode with the windows down, enjoying the cool of the morning air not yet marred by the windswept desert dust that could crack flesh or paint it a dull sandy brown.

He hadn't slept at all the previous night, not even after Caitlin finally nodded off in his arms just before dawn. Cort Wesley spent those long minutes feeling strangely content and secure, wondering what it would be like to do this in his own home with his boys sleeping peacefully instead of being watched over by three geriatric Texas Ranger legends.

Not that home was his favorite place in the world right now either. The hole he'd plowed had been plugged by a construction crew that used to pay "tribute" to the Brancas in return for city contracts. They'd done a decent job of patching up the mess, the smell of fresh lumber heavy in the air and sawdust residue clinging to the furniture and walls.

In prison, all he could think of was getting away from a life reduced to a six-by-eight-foot box. Once out, though, he'd realized how much more control over his life he'd had in the smaller confines, everything reduced to basic simplicity. Leroy Epps, the aging, diabetes-riddled, ex-boxer lifer who'd taken a liking to Cort Wesley from the start once told him he didn't mind not getting out anymore because the world scared him more. At least inside, Epps said, he knew where everything was.

Cort Wesley always missed Epps most in his more deeply contemplative moments, lying with his arms entwined around Caitlin Strong as the first light of dawn finally swallowed the motel's flashing marquee, being a prime example. Which was why he wasn't surprised when his imagination conjured up the smell of the talcum powder Epps used to disguise the stench from his decaying skin. Cort Wesley turned to his right and saw the old man seated on the motel room's lone chair, legs crossed to better enable him to pick at the scratchy sores dotting his exposed ankle.

Leroy Epps looked back at him and grinned.

"Just like old times, ain't it, bubba?"

Cort Wesley eased Caitlin from him and sat up on the bedside. "Not from where I'm sitting, champ."

"What you done got yourself into now?"

"You once told me a man can change himself, but not the world made him who he was."

"I did at that."

"I'm just figuring out what that meant."

"On account of your boys, no doubt."

"Complex matter."

Epps switched to his other leg and leaned forward a little. "Bubba, you seen the crap. I seen you realize it's a lot simpler than you think."

"I think my oldest boy's fixing to follow in my footsteps and that scares the hell out of me."

"Not as much as something else, though."

"Champ?"

Epps flashed his once white grin now marred by teeth gone brown on their way to rot. Long red lines had leaked across the whites of his eyes, looking like spiderwebs etched in blood. His eyes drifted to Caitlin, glistening playfully. "You and the Ranger seem to be doing just fine."

"Knew we'd be getting around to that."

"You blame me for bringing it up?"

"Not if you mind me changing the subject."

"Take your time." Epps winked. "Got nowhere else I gotta be right now."

"*What do you want me to say, champ?*"

"*That you messed things up with the mother of your children and you're doing your share of thinking on how not to repeat the same mistake with the Ranger gal.*"

Cort Wesley chuckled.

"*What's so funny, bubba?*"

Cort Wesley glanced at Caitlin sleeping peacefully. "I think I'm an idiot for thinking this has a chance to work between us."

"*Same thing you said about Maura Torres.*"

"And I was right, champ."

"*Making you feel, what, like you got license to be right again?*"

"I chased a man off who was about to kill her last night. Second time I missed killing the bastard."

"*So I heard.*"

"Figured you would've been watching."

"*Was sitting in with Robert Johnson at the time, trying my hand on the drums. Know that story about him selling his soul to the devil at the crossroads in exchange for the blues, bubba?*"

"Sure."

"*He confessed to me it wasn't true. He went there all right, but the devil never showed. Robert didn't have a car so he busied himself waiting for the bus over the next six hours strumming his guitar in rhythm with the world around him. That's how the blues was born, no help from Satan at all.*"

"There a point to that?"

"*Lots of legends ain't what they're cracked up to be, bubba, but that don't make 'em any less true. Give my best to your boys, will ya?*"

At that, Cort Wesley lurched up in bed, roused suddenly from his dream. He looked at Caitlin, who was just starting to stir, and then at the room's lone chair to find Leroy Epps was gone.

The day already seemed much hotter by the time the Ranger convoy headed into the last stretch down the freshly paved road leading to Hollis Tyree's land in Tunga County. Speaking to his boys during the drive had calmed him a bit. They both sounded good, except for the fact that the batteries in Luke's handheld video game had died and Dylan had emerged from his room the night before to find one of the old Rangers planted in a chair directly in front of the door to Maria's room.

The image made Cort Wesley smile now, surprising himself with the brief respite from the turmoil of his thoughts. Then Hollis Tyree's worksite came into view, and what he saw brought it all back and then some.

86

WASHINGTON, D.C.; THE PRESENT

Caitlin took the treadmill next to the big man jogging up a storm, thinking of how Cort Wesley told her to just go to a gym. The man wore a sleeveless workout shirt wet with sweat at the midriff that looked ironed onto his skin and glowed slightly beneath the bright lighting. This time of the morning, at the Sports Club/ LA adjoining the Ritz-Carlton Hotel, a treadmill was there for the taking while reservations would be needed later in the day.

"Hello, Mr. Smith," she said to the CIA agent she'd met in Bahrain the previous year.

"It's Jones here in Washington."

"You're kidding, right?"

"I'm a man of mystery, what can I say?"

Caitlin set her speed to the same pace as his and quickly fell into the same rhythm, as Jones frowned condescendingly. He was slightly less tall but even broader than she remembered, his hair grown out into a dark nest of waves. Only thing the same were eyes that looked more like marbles wedged into his head in their utter flatness. It was like looking at a shark through the glass of an aquarium.

"I move too fast for you, Ranger, don't bother trying to keep up."

"I've taken up boxing," Caitlin told him. "You wanna go a few rounds, let me know. Gotta warn you, though, I've got a habit of breaking noses."

"Already had enough of the shit kicked out of me. See, I helped this lady out back in Bahrain well under the radar. Turned out I helped her uncover some things she wasn't supposed to. So here I am, back in Washington."

Caitlin's lungs had started to heat up, but she wasn't about to cut her speed until Jones did. She'd welcomed the long flight earlier in the day the same way she welcomed the drives through the emptiness of Texas from one Ranger assignment to another. Time spent alone with her thoughts, sorting through the muddle of truth making up her feelings. Cort Wesley Masters had been the topic for her mind on this day. She kept nodding off on the flight, one dream of him and his boys following another, sometimes in sequence. She wondered what her seatmate made of her waking up with a smile on her face.

"And that got you sent home?" Caitlin said to Jones. "I'm truly sorry."

"Actually, I was reassigned based on need, my expertise required over here more than there."

"Care to enlighten me, Jones?"

Jones turned toward her while continuing to run. "You know I can't do that, any more than I can explain whatever it is you think you got going on."

"Come again please?"

"You look winded there, Ranger."

"Just say what you've got to say."

"Got nothing to say. Hollis Tyree's clean as they come in our book. Gives money to all the right causes, if you know what I mean."

"I asked you about his land. Anything you could find out for me that could explain how folks are getting poisoned in a town twenty miles away?"

"I look like the EPA to you?"

"This is too big for them. Tyree's people took over that town I'm talking about. I almost had to shoot it out with a few of his fake deputies."

"Lucky for them it was just almost," Jones told her with a grin.

"Add to that the fact that there's a serial killer named Macerio, who's been drawing a line of bodies across the Texas-Mexico border for fourteen years, connected somehow and I thought a call to the cavalry might be in order."

Jones hit the red emergency stop button on his

treadmill and watched the rubber grind to a halt with his hands on the support arms. "You say his name's Macerio?"

Caitlin stopped her treadmill too. "I did."

"What's your security clearance?"

"Don't believe I've got one."

Jones draped a freshly laundered towel over his broad shoulders. "You're about to."

87

TUNGA COUNTY; THE PRESENT

"What you make of this, Masters?" Captain Tepper asked Cort Wesley as they walked about the section of Hollis Tyree's fields that had been dug up the night before.

"Don't have a clue. I only know what Caitlin and I saw last night and what I'm seeing now. Just doesn't make any sense."

"I'll say."

The site, bustling with frantic activity under the spill of sodium vapor work lights just the night before, had been abandoned. No trace of any people Cort Wesley could see, the remnants of their presence visible only in the long rows of reconstituted FEMA trailers and pre-fab office spaces, the doors to many of which banged up against their frames in the wind. Discarded heavy equipment, including the loaders, excavators, and conveyors, littered the near grounds, already gathering dirt and dust as the unforgiving desert sought to consume them. Farther out, the long line of towering water drilling rigs stood empty and unmanned for as far as the eye could see.

A few hats blown free of heads had gone unretrieved. Some stray plastic water bottles rolled about as if in search of a refuse container. A family of prairie dogs scrabbled about the hard earth.

But the workmen had left without taking their belongings from the trailers and the offices looked to have been abandoned in midstream as well. Work orders, schedules, and requisition slips still hung from clipboards tacked to the walls and the phones were still functional, powered by the same underground cables that fed electricity to the camp.

Whatever Tyree had been after last night, he must have found plenty of it to boot. And now it was gone and so was everyone who'd been working these fields.

"Dump trucks, Captain," Cort Wesley said suddenly.

"Come again?"

"There were six of them, big construction-sized rigs. You find them, you find whatever's behind all this."

"You say six, son?"

Cort Wesley nodded. "Why?"

Tepper hocked up some flem and spit it on the ground. "Because the bodies of six men identified as truckers were found about fifty miles from here just before dawn. Looked like they'd been ambushed, their rigs hijacked."

"So whatever it is Caitlin and I saw being pulled out of the ground . . ."

"Long gone by now," said Tepper.

88

Caitlin sat across from Jones at a table in the Sports Club's Sidewalk Café. It wasn't crowded, but he seemed distinctly uncomfortable amid the floor-to-ceiling windows. Caitlin took a sip from a smoothie that tasted like a McDonald's shake, the flow of sweat from her pores abating at last.

"I'm not the only agent sent back stateside from a Middle East post in the past year."

"Your little private world downsizing, is it?"

"More like a change in priorities, Ranger. Men like me are sent where the bad guys are. We trail them like hound dogs, to use a metaphor you're probably more comfortable with. Your captain tell you about the trip he made to Austin recently?" Jones asked her suddenly.

"How'd you know that?"

"Because I was one of the presenters. Recall the subject?"

"Something about new domestic terrorist threats."

"From Mexico in particular, specifically a colonel named—"

"Renaldo Montoya," Caitlin finished, recalling her last phone call with Commander Fernando Lozano Sandoval from Thomason Hospital.

Jones leaned across the table as if he were going to grab her. "Seems like you know a damn bit more than you've been letting on, Ranger."

"I do my homework too, Jones."

Jones weighed her words. "How much do you know?"

"Nothing besides the fact Montoya got pissed off and disappeared after his being an Indian froze his career path. Took his hostilities out on American tourists, making him a wanted man."

"A wanted man everyone in Mexico's too afraid to catch. Montoya took with him a whole bunch of the Special Forces Zetas he commanded when he disappeared. Word is he's joined forces with the Juárez and Sinaloa drug cartels, supplying them with his Zetas to use as enforcers in what's become a forty-billion-dollar-a-year industry. Smart money says he's planning a coup he's financing in large part through the drug trade. Even smarter money says Montoya may be planning a guerrilla war inside the United States."

"What's water in Tunga County got to do with that?"

"Why don't you tell me?"

"Well, the first time I was at Tyree's development, they were drilling for water. But last night something else entirely was going on."

"Describe it."

"Looked to me like they were mining something out of the ground. Sucking up dump trucks full of earth in a suddenly cordoned-off area."

"Looked official?"

"Very. And Macerio was there to pick up some young Mexican women who'd outlived their usefulness servicing the workers." Caitlin leaned across the table to better meet Jones's stare. "You still haven't told me where he fits into all this, why mention of his name almost threw you off the treadmill."

"Because he's Colonel Montoya's brother."

PART NINE

After getting the lay of the land, so to speak, Bigfoot Wallace moved from Austin to San Antonio, which was considered the extreme edge of the frontier, to sign up as a Texas Ranger under Jack Hayes. In them days, Texas was as wild as the west could get. There was danger from the south from the Mexicans, danger to the west and north from the wild frontier filled with Indians and desperados, and to the east the settlements still had problems with the Cherokee Nation. General Sam Houston himself had appointed young Captain Hayes, a hero from the battle of Plum Creek, to raise a company of Rangers to defend San Antonio. Hayes had high standards for his men. They were the best fighters in the west, and they had to be, considerin' the fact that they were often outnumbered fifty to one. A man had to have courage, good character, good riding and shooting skills and a horse worth a hundred dollars to be considered for the job.

—"Bigfoot Wallace and El Muerto," as retold by
S. E. Schlosser, *American Folklore*

89

"What kind of gun is that?" Dylan asked Bo Dean Perry.

Perry swung his wheelchair around to face him in the noon light. "Here give it a hoist," he said, handing Dylan the funny-looking shotgun.

Dylan nearly doubled over from its weight, couldn't believe a crippled man confined to a wheelchair could wield it so effortlessly.

"It's a Remington Over-Under twelve-gauge with four screw-in chokes. That there's a walnut stock you got your hand on. Receiver's plate nickel with a blued barrel and single trigger. Takes three shells in the chamber."

"Heavy."

"Something you get used to. Your dad ever take you hunting?"

Dylan frowned, handed the old man back his gun. "Nope. Said he lost his taste for it after the Gulf War. Said after you spend enough time hunting men, hunting animals isn't something you got much call to do anymore."

"I grew out of my teen years in Korea and did a stretch in 'Nam myself."

"How'd you get hurt? Somebody shoot you when you were a Ranger?"

Bo Dean grinned. "Never stop being a Ranger, son."

"An active one I meant," Dylan said, his voice mixing between tones in search of the right one.

"Nothing so dramatic as a gunfight. Was a drunk driver crossed the median and plowed into me on the interstate. I wasn't even on duty. Told the first responders everything was fine. I was just a little stuck. Didn't know it at the time that my legs had been crushed and my spinal cord severed."

"You filling this boy's head with your crap, Bo Dean?" came the booming voice of Ranger Terrell Scuggs, a still-strapping sort who wore his .357 magnum revolver Western style in an old-fashioned holster. His boots clip-clopped across the porch and he was eating from a bowl of milk-rich cold cereal. Corn flakes, Dylan thought.

"Thing about Ranger Terrell Scuggs, son," Perry told him, "is that he ain't smart enough to know how dumb he is."

"Screw you, you old fart."

"My wife didn't pass, I wouldn't be living here on this ranch with your sorry ass."

Now it was Terrell Scuggs who swung toward Dylan. "They had two kids moved as far away from their daddy as physically possible. Damn, even our heifers and hogs know enough to keep their distance."

"Ask him about his wife, son," Bo Dean demanded, poking the air with his Remington. "Had the good sense to walk out on *his* sorry ass 'fore he could mess up her life as much as his own."

"Where's your girl?" Scuggs asked Dylan.

"Taking a shower."

"Reminds me of a story. Know the dumbest man I ever arrested?"

"Oh shit," moaned Bo Dean. "Here we go again. . . ."

"High school janitor decided to drill himself a hole into the girls' gym locker room," Scuggs continued to Dylan, paying Perry no heed at all. "Two of them, actually. One for his eye and one for . . . well, you get the idea. Anyway he sticks old Mr. Friendly into the lower hole and presses his eye against the upper one and, lo and behold, turns out the dumb son of a bitch had drilled into the boys' locker room instead of the girls'. Know what the kicker was?"

"Can I take things from there?" asked Bo Dean.

"Be my guest," Scuggs invited.

"His boner got stuck in the hole. Tough arrest, wasn't it, Terrell?"

"Was that much and more, Bo Dean. You try saw cutting through wood looking at a man's privates the whole time."

The door opened and Dylan watched ex-Ranger Clinton Samuels shuffle out, readjusting the hearing aids that protruded from both his ears.

"Phone ain't working," he said, sweeping his gaze about the expanse of grounds making up the ranch's front.

"You check your 'lectric ears there?"

"Don't even need them to know if there's a dial tone or not."

Dylan went for the cell phone in his pocket.

"Coverage is hit or miss in these parts, son," said Scuggs. "Remember?"

Bo Dean Perry started his wheelchair toward Dylan. "Wait a minute, you telling me you left that thing on?"

Dylan looked down at his cell phone. "So?"

"Oh boy . . ."

Dylan cupped his hand over his eyes, staring into the sun. "Cop car's coming. Hauling ass down the access road."

Bo Dean Perry squinted, trying to see it as best he could. "What color is it?"

"You're as blind as a goddamn bat."

"Don't need to see much of a man to hit him with my Remington, Terrell."

"Black and white," Dylan told him.

"Sheriff's cars been all white for two years now."

Dylan felt something change in the air in that instant, static jumping about as if an electrical storm was coming.

"There's an old irrigation tunnel runs out from the barn to the edge of the property," Terrell Scuggs told him. "You get your brother and your girl and hightail it outta here that way."

"Entrance is under the horses' water trough," Bo Dean added.

"Get yourselves in there and don't look back. We got your back, son."

Dylan looked from one Ranger to the other, all of them nodding.

"Now get moving," ordered Bo Dean Perry, "and let us do what Rangers do."

90

Colonel Montoya sat in the uppermost tier of seating that overlooked the ruins of the ancient ballcourt he'd unearthed here in the jungle. Down below two teams of four of his soldiers battled amid the weed-infested grounds for control of the nine-pound, solid rubber ball using only their hips. The winner would be the first team to push the ball through a stone goal barely large enough to accommodate it ten feet off the ground.

The game was as old as Mayan culture itself, played for sport as well as ritual. Montoya had personally taught it to the troops who'd accompanied him to the jungle to instill discipline in them as well as an appreciation of history. The game was also a superb conditioning tool, lest his soldiers grow slow and lazy here amid the fetid heat bred of the tropics.

Many games would end with both teams bruised and exhausted, no goal having been scored. To the uneducated and unfamiliar, the task looked impossible. But with the proper practice, discipline, and dedication, one team would emerge victorious. Montoya watched now as the rest of his soldiers cheered their counterparts' every move, much as the Mayan people had for the warriors who took to the court in centuries past. Cheering for both winners and losers, hoping for the ultimate prize to be awarded.

Montoya loved the thud of the ball striking the stone walls and ricocheting back outward. The players might not score but they would collapse in exhaustion in trying to, both then and now. His would be the last people standing when the End Times came at last. And as the last to stand they would be the first to rise to claim the new world fashioned from the remnants of the old. It was all written in the glyphs on the temple walls, along with a likeness of a man who could only be him.

As the ball smacked stone, just missing the goal, Montoya saw how his entire life and work had been building to this moment. His strange eyes and distressing appearance having toughened him up for the Special Forces while leaving him with a callous disregard for the sanctity of human life. To Montoya the many he butchered were no different from those who had shunned him as a child. He had learned to live without feelings in service to a higher power and greater cause.

Smack! banged the ball, rubber slamming against stone.

Montoya could not think of one true friend he'd ever made or one woman he'd taken without forcing himself upon her. Now he would take Mexico itself back, a new society forged in its place further fortified by bringing America to its knees. He knew his own commanders were skeptical. But they did not know what Montoya knew, did not fully comprehend the signs drawn on the walls of the temple ruins or the message they imparted.

He was what the ancient Mayans had called Cha-huku, or Bringer of Thunder. And now the leaders of the cartels he had unified had furnished the final piece he needed to succeed. That was their purpose in this, why they'd been brought to him by the same Mayan deities that had given him eyes that could see what others couldn't and a nose that could smell blood on the air long after it had been shed. Soon it would be time to head north, to Juárez, where the end would begin, and the seeds of the new world, his world, would be laid.

Smack!

Montoya knew this was all prelude, preamble to the new order that would dawn with the fall of the old. It did not mark the end, but rather a time of transition from one age to another, the close of what the ancient Mayans had called the Long Count. Those who accepted this reality would prosper from it; those who resisted would fall.

Down below on the ball court, a player launched the heavy ball airborne with a powerful thrust of his hips. It soared on line with the goal and passed straight through, much to the delight of his troops watching. Had this been olden times, they as the winners would be rewarded with the greatest prize possible. Not treasure or glory, but welcomed as gifts to the Mayan gods who valued such human sacrifices as the ultimate honor.

Even without such ritual, tonight the same gods would be happy. Smiling down upon Montoya in appreciation of his efforts to return Mexico to the Mayan people so they could serve those gods once more.

The ring of his satellite phone disturbed Montoya's reverie, jerking him back from the past. It sounded and felt all wrong for a moment better celebrated just as similar ones had been a millennium ago. But the news he was waiting for could change all that.

"Yes?" Montoya said into the phone.

"We have the trucks," said Fernando Leyva of the Juárez cartel. "The shipment will be in Juárez this afternoon."

Montoya gazed up at the sun, which in that moment looked exactly like the depictions drawn by the early Mayans as a fire in the sky.

"I'm on my way," he told Leyva.

91

PEARSALL, TEXAS; THE PRESENT

Dylan pushed himself through the tunnel's darkness, Luke's soft whimpers claiming his ear. He'd put his brother between himself and Maria so he wouldn't be able to fall behind. Maria's wet hair still smelled of the flower-scented shampoo. Every time the rancid stench of the irrigation tunnel's sour water and spoiled mud nearly overcame him, he'd catch a whiff of lilac and kept moving.

Finding the tunnel had been easy, entering it not terribly hard either. Things had gotten tough when the gunshots started just as the last of the light vanished from their path. Dylan knew dark and this wasn't dark; it was black. In the nothingness around him, every meager and minor sound was exaggerated. Meanwhile, the clack of gunfire continued to reach him as dull *whaps* to his consciousness.

"Dylan," he heard Luke whimper.

"Just keep moving," he said back to his brother.

"Dylan," came the whimper again.

"*Yo le ayudaré,*" Maria said to Luke behind him. "I'll help you."

"Dad's gonna be real pissed," Luke sobbed.

That made Dylan think of not being able to call

him without a signal, which made him think of the damn cell phone he'd left on, giving away their position to whoever had showed up in the fake cop car. He twisted onto his side in order to pull it from his pocket in the narrow confines of the irrigation tunnel. Switched it on without bothering to check for bars he knew wouldn't be there.

The glow off the phone's face was what he was after. It cast a narrow ribbon of light ahead. The tunnel was no less cramped and no less long, but it was less scary now and he could feel Luke moving more easily with Maria's help.

Dylan could no longer hear the booming reports of Bo Dean Perry's Remington shotgun. He couldn't take that as a good sign and tried to block it from his mind as best he could, focusing on the tunnel ahead and nothing else. His only world right now was the fetid muck clinging to his clothes and skin like garbage spun through a blender. He hated the smell of himself, but it told him he was alive and that it was his job to get his brother and Maria out of this.

His father didn't talk about the war he'd fought in much, and right now Dylan found himself wondering if he'd been in similar plights.

"We're almost to the end," he said suddenly, holding his cell phone out as far as he could.

"How do you know?" Maria asked him in English.

"I just do."

Problem was he didn't know what would be waiting when they got there.

92

Caitlin sat in the Reagan National departure area, waiting for a callback from Captain Tepper before her flight was called. She'd been tapping her foot so long it had started to cramp up, and she ended up pacing in front of the bank of windows overlooking the runways to pass the time.

Cort Wesley's text explaining what he'd seen in Tunga County, and the report about the ambushed truckers, had come in while she was still seated across from Jones in the gym café.

"Macerio sees what's going on in Tunga County last night," Caitlin told him, "and notifies his brother. Goddamn Hollis Tyree played right into Montoya's hands. Delivered whatever the hell's in that dirt straight to him."

"I can have a team scrambled in less than twelve hours," Jones told her before they parted. "We've been looking for an excuse to send the Eighty-second Airborne into Mexico for over a year now."

"Any of your satellites got tape feed of southern Texas?"

"What do you think?"

"Pull them, Jones, and look for a half dozen dump trucks the size of earth movers heading toward Mexico early this morning. You think you can handle that?"

Jones looked insulted. "Ranger, our birds can spot a ping-pong ball from twenty thousand feet. Six dump trucks ought to stand out like lighthouses."

• • •

It was Jones's call that came in first.

"Bad news," he told her. "Our birds had eyeballs on your dump trucks almost right up to the Mexican border. Then they flat-out disappeared."

"This anywhere in the vicinity of the Chihuahuan Mountains?"

"How the hell should I know?"

"I assume they teach you to read maps at secret agent school, or maybe you skipped that lesson. Thing is, the Chihuahuans are rich in iron ore deposits. I know 'cause they always played hell with my compass when I went camping up there with my dad. I imagine that same ore could play hell with your satellite imaging, mess it all up. If I know that, Montoya, or whoever's directing those trucks, probably does too."

"Those trucks were making a beeline to Juárez, Ranger."

"Just get the cavalry ready to travel, Jones."

Caitlin had barely hung up from that call when her phone rang again.

"D. W.?" she said before the first ring had ended.

"It's Lieutenant Jim Rollins, Ranger Strong. I got Sergeant Steve Berry next to me on speaker."

"Where's Captain Tepper?" Caitlin asked, feeling her insides starting to twist.

"His truck got shot up smack in the middle of an intersection right after you talked to him, Ranger. Mexican gunmen, near as we can tell. He's hurt pretty bad. A mess, but holding on like the tough old coot he is."

"Oh damn," Caitlin heard herself say. It felt as if

she were standing outside her body, looking down on a woman looking totally out of place here in her cowboy boots and Stetson amid the suits of Washington.

"He said you were headed to Houston."

"He was supposed to call ahead for me, arrange a sitdown with Hollis Tyree."

"It doesn't appear he had the opportunity. If you want, I could—"

"No, don't bother. I don't want to give Tyree a chance to be somewhere else when I get there now. Men like him been known to run from a fight instead of facing it. You telling me the truth about D. W. holding on, Lieutenant?"

"I am, ma'am. None of his wounds are life-threatening, but that don't mean he's out of the woods."

"Thing you gotta know now," picked up Ranger Sergeant Steve Berry, "is that we dumped that Mexican sack of shit Macerio's cell phone records and came up with a bunch of numbers that don't exist."

"Dummy exchanges," Caitlin noted.

"But we were able to get a fix on the general position of their origins from . . . What you call it, Jim?"

"Triangulation."

"Triangulation something or other. Macerio didn't place a single call himself," Rollins continued, "but every one he received came from either somewhere smack dab in the middle of the Yucatán jungle or inside Juárez."

"Juárez," Caitlin repeated, feeling a chill slide up her spine like frigid water on a hot summer day.

"Yes, ma'am."

Juárez . . .

There it was, Caitlin thought, the past and present converging, the path of her life about to collide with that of her grandfather who had fought the last great battle of his career in the same godforsaken place.

"We could dispatch a team down there," Ranger Berry was saying, "but they wouldn't know what to look for."

"Don't worry," Caitlin said. "I know someone who does."

93

SAN ANTONIO; THE PRESENT

"I've been waiting for your call," Guillermo Paz told her.

"I need your help, Colonel."

"I know."

"A Mexican colonel named Montoya's about to launch a guerrilla war on the U.S. We think he's based somewhere in Juárez. His people are likely to be hiding something they moved out across the border in dump trucks."

Caitlin heard Paz take a long deep breath on the other end of the line. "The peasant people believe this Montoya is a Mayan god reincarnated to destroy them."

"His brother's even worse. I think he's the serial killer behind Las Mujeres de Juárez."

Silence filled the line, only Paz's breathing breaking it.

"My mother was a kind of witch," he said finally.

"She used to tell me about monsters who disguised themselves with human skin to perpetuate their evil."

"That certainly sounds like Macerio." Caitlin allowed herself a deep breath. Her throat actually hurt more than it had last night and she could barely swallow water, never mind food.

"I've never seen one up close. I look forward to finding out if my mother was right."

Caitlin swallowed some air, even that painful for her. "When you told me my life was in danger . . ."

"Was this what I was talking about," Paz finished for her.

"Was it?"

"That's what brought me here, Ranger. I see that now."

"Thank you, Colonel," she said, past the dryness.

"No, thank *you*."

94

The end of the irrigation tunnel spilled out at the rear of the old Rangers' ranch, stealing the view of their house from Dylan as he helped Luke and Maria up out of the hole. The three of them were covered in muck and grime and smelled like a sewer. But to him Maria was still beautiful, especially when she finally let herself smile after letting out a deep breath.

"I forgot my Play Station," Luke said, wiping the mud from his face with an equally grimy sleeve, managing only to spread it around.

A large white-tail deer munched on saw grass at what had once been a fence line, Dylan holding his gaze upon the buck as he fished his cell phone back out of his pocket. A single bar rose, fell, and rose again, and he dialed his father's number, praying to himself he'd pick up.

"Hello."

"Dad?"

"Dylan? What's wrong, son?"

"We've had some trouble. We're okay. But we need help."

"You hear me, boy? Dylan?"

"I said we're in trouble. Can you come get us? Where are you?"

"Say that again. I thought I heard you say something about trouble. Talk to me, boy, come on."

Dylan walked forward, keeping his eyes fixed on the single bar. The white-tail buck ran off and the bar locked into place right around where it had been feeding.

"Some men came to the ranch, dressed as cops."

"Are you and your brother okay?"

"Yup. Maria too. Don't know about the old men. Heard a lot of gunshots while we were in this old irrigation tunnel. We're out now and we can't hear anything."

"Any cover you can see in the area?"

Dylan looked about. "Some."

"You wanna hide or keep moving?"

"Road's a ways off and nothing but open ground between here and there."

"Then get yourself some cover and stay put. I'll be there quick as I can."

"There's no one you can call?"

"Not right now, no. You hear everything I said, son?"

"Yeah. Dad?"

"I hear you."

"What about those old men?"

"They saved your life, boy. They did what Rangers do."

"You wanna hide or keep moving?"

Cort Wesley heard himself pose the question again in his head, as he barreled down the freeway toward Pearsall. Him asking his fifteen-year-old son what he thought was best. Cort Wesley wasn't used to providing options or deferring to another's judgment. In that moment, he believed he finally understood his son along with the depth of the trust he'd formed with him. It hadn't happened quickly or easily and he didn't realize it had happened at all. But here he was placing his faith in Dylan's judgment at a time when a wrong decision could lead to more than just those old Rangers falling to an attack.

Put that in your report and smoke it, Marianna Silvaro.

"Your boys'll be fine, Cort Wesley," Caitlin had said, trying to sound reassuring in a brief conversation a few minutes before.

"What about you, Ranger?"

"I'm headed to Houston."

"What's there?"

"Hollis Tyree III."

95

By the time Cort Wesley arrived at the ranch in Pearsall, it was swimming with local sheriff's deputies and highway patrolmen. He wasn't normally one to walk straight into a major crime scene and announce himself, but circumstances today left him no choice.

He figured on calling or text messaging Dylan upon his arrival, only his phone had no signal. So he parked his truck at the outer rim of the makeshift blockade formed by the police cars, left his guns under the seat, and walked down the lower end of the drive leading to the old-fashioned two-story log home adorned with a farmer's porch.

Cort Wesley saw the bodies when he cleared the first line of responding vehicles. Counted four of them, all dropped in the area of the lone black-and-white squad car. He glimpsed enough of two faces to know they were Mexicans.

On the porch, an ex-Ranger in a wheelchair talked hurriedly to a pair of detectives trying to keep their notetaking up with his words, while a second ex-Ranger who looked like a gunslinger took oxygen from an EMT's portable tank.

"Excuse me," a uniform said, stepping out to block Cort Wesley's path, "you got any call to be here?"

Cort Wesley calmly gestured toward the porch. "Those men up there are guarding my sons."

The uniform stepped aside. Cort Wesley started past him, then stopped and looked back. "There were three men living here."

The uniform aimed his eyes low. "One didn't make it."

Cort Wesley felt his stomach muscles tighten, still not finished with the uniform. "Take a good look a those old men on that porch, son. Take a good look at them, 'cause they are genuine heroes and that's a tough commodity to come by these days."

The uniform nodded, suddenly looking very young.

Cort Wesley mounted the steps, those on the porch going silent as he fixed only Texas Rangers Bo Dean Perry and Terrell Scuggs in his gaze, ignoring everyone else. "I'm Cort Wesley Masters. Just wanna thank you men for saving my boys' lives," he said, and retraced his steps down from the porch.

The one in the wheelchair rolled toward him. "Mr. Masters?"

Cort Wesley stopped at the bottom and looked back up at him.

"Your oldest's a heck of a boy, sir. I'd ride with him anytime."

96

HOUSTON; THE PRESENT

"I'm afraid Mr. Tyree's not in the building, Ranger," the receptionist told Caitlin over the phone.

"You have any idea where I can reach him?" Caitlin asked. Her plane had barely touched down, the tense flight from Washington leaving her stiff and cramped.

"I'm afraid not."

"Richest man in the state of Texas and you don't know where he's at?"

"I'm afraid—"

"Never mind," Caitlin told her. "I think I know." She started to lower her phone, then raised it again to continue. "Shame about what happened to those truck drivers worked for Mr. Tyree this morning."

"I don't believe I know what you're speaking of, ma'am," the receptionist said.

"No, I don't suppose you would."

SWEETWATER, TEXAS; THE PRESENT

Caitlin found Hollis Tyree III on a stretch of flatland on the outskirts of the town, standing amid a garden centered around a flowering cottonwood tree just like the kind she'd picnicked under with her dad. Tyree's knees were stained with the residue of dark mulch and a weak scent of manure hung in the air. The scene had an eerie familiarity to it, churning her mind back to the nightmares that left her under a similar tree in the dark and the rain.

Caitlin stiffened as a quartet of bodyguards, led by the man named Meeks, cut off her approach. "The men you put into Albion weren't up for taking me on and I doubt you're up to the task either, sir," she said to him. "You tell Mr. Tyree I'm here because I think I know what happened to his kids two years back."

"Let her through," Tyree called from the garden. His voice sounded soft but the wind seemed to pick it up, making it louder.

Caitlin held Meeks's stare until he finally stepped aside. A few yards past him, she stopped and turned back, finding his unblinking eyes still locked upon her.

"Assuming Sheriff Huffard and his deputies are safe, Mr. Meeks, I'm willing to give you a pass on your little charade in Albion. But if I find out you had anything to do with an attempt on the lives of some children under the Rangers' protection in Pearsall, or the gunning down of my captain, you and I are gonna meet up again. That clear enough for you?"

Caitlin started on again for the garden where Tyree was standing, careful not to disturb any of the seedlings. He looked shorter than their last meeting, his shoulders slumped, eyes drawn and tired with the crow's feet forming pale shadows around them.

"You been to Mexico, Ranger?"

"I went to see a man in Washington who told me about a lunatic colonel who's been killing American tourists. His name's Montoya and he's got a brother who makes him look like a Sunday school teacher."

She could see Tyree stiffen, his eyes starting to moisten. His expression wrinkled, as if he'd swallowed something sour or spoiled.

"You have proof?" he asked.

"That's gonna be tough to come by. But your kids weren't the only victims. Montoya's your man for sure, sir. And he's up to plenty more than that."

Tyree waited for her to continue, finally spoke again when she didn't. "I didn't tell anyone where I was."

"Didn't have to. I'm guessing you came here after you heard about those six drivers of yours whose bodies were found in the desert this morning, try to sort through the mess. That was Montoya's work too." Caitlin took a single step closer to him. "I didn't appreciate being lied to about those Mexican girls on your worksite, or about whatever's poisoning those people in Albion. But it would seem circumstances have left us with the same enemy here."

"Tell me about this Montoya."

"He's a native Indian, a Mayan who hates the world, especially Americans, for the racism that derailed his career. They tend to treat Indians down there the way our country used to treat blacks. Colonel Montoya figured he'd had enough. Decided to take out his hostilities on tourists when he failed to make general on account of his heritage. Word is he's used former commandoes called Zetas to take control of the drug cartels and may be planning to launch a guerrilla war against the United States. With your help, sir."

"*My* help?"

"Whatever was in those dump trucks is surely in Montoya's hands by now, because you delivered it to him all wrapped up in a bow. I think you better tell me once and for all what it is you dug out of the ground last night to cover up all the damage you've done."

Tyree swallowed hard and looked at her for what seemed like a long time before responding.

"Uranium," he said flatly.

97

"You did good, son," Cort Wesley said, brushing the bramble and sagebrush Dylan had used for cover off the boy's dirt-laden flesh. Some tight overgrowth and root thorns had curled into his hair and he grimaced as Cort Wesley plucked it free. "Better than good, truth be told."

"You told me to find cover, so I did."

"We'll drive with the windows open on account of the three of you smelling like cesspools," Cort Wesley said, going to work on Luke, leaving Maria's tangles to Dylan, "but right now that's the sweetest scent I ever knew."

"Ouch," Luke said, pulling away from him.

"Hold still, son."

"It hurts."

"Almost done."

Cort Wesley's gaze lifted over Luke's shoulder and saw old Leroy Epps leaning against the base of a cottonwood tree.

"*Never thought I'd see the day,*" the old man grinned. His teeth looked whiter, as if death had finally returned the pearl white color to them. "*Wouldn't happen to have one of those root beers, would you?*"

"No," Cort Wesley said out loud.

"Huh?" from Luke.

"Keep still," Cort Wesley told him, holding his gaze on Epps.

"*Fine boys, bubba. They got your heart and your ilk. Tough combination to beat.*"

"I do hope you're right, champ."

"Who's champ?"

"Oh, I'm right for sure. Where I'm at now, you see things from a whole different perspective. Seeing you this way makes me wish I had my own boys to look in on. But once you play the cards life deals you, you can't ask for new ones. Remember that, bubba. Man, I'm thirsty . . . Sure you don't got one of them root beers?"

Cort Wesley pulled the last of the brambles from Luke's hair and held his gaze on Leroy Epps.

"What're you looking at, Dad?" Luke asked him.

Leroy Epps winked.

"Nothing, son," said Cort Wesley.

98

SWEETWATER; THE PRESENT

"I figured Professor Lamb was up to something," Hollis Tyree continued, after steadying his breath, "but nothing like this."

"It was to pay off a gambling debt to the Branca crime family. Next thing you know, Brancas are looking to sell off the information to the highest bidder. That explains how Montoya and his cartel partners got hold of the report you never saw until it was too late. I'm guessing Frank Branca Jr. had already made peace with the cartels to allow him to get back in business in Texas. Rest just fell together."

Caitlin watched the red flowing in and out of Tyree's expression, as he struggled to steady his breathing. His mouth opened, but he didn't speak.

"I think I understand, sir," she said finally.

"Understand what?"

"When was the last time you weren't in control of a situation? When was the last time you couldn't buy yourself out of a scrape or send men like Meeks to clean up your mess?"

"It's not that."

The life seemed to drain out of Tyree's expression. He stood there, looking ready to keel over, then took a step away from her to balance himself. Caitlin gave Hollis Tyree a few moments before circling back in front of him again.

"This Montoya killed my children," he said finally. "And now, thanks to me, he's going to kill plenty more."

Caitlin took a step closer to him. "Sir, the first time we met you asked me what I'd do if I'd been on the case when your boy and girl went missing. Well, consider me on it now. I can't bring your kids back but I can stop Montoya from killing any more."

"Do you have any idea how many people could have been helped by the water I found in Tunga County, Ranger?" Tyree asked, as if to defend himself.

"That why you've purchased another two dozen similar tracts of land across the plains all the way to California?"

Tyree's mouth dropped slightly.

"I did some checking," Caitlin told him, "and some figuring. You're just like the guy building windmills across the state because someday it's gonna make him a fortune. You said it yourself: today it's oil, tomorrow it'll be water, and where will folks have to go to get it?" She paused to let her point sink in. "You might've thought you were doing good, Mr. Tyree, but in the end it was all about making yourself richer, come the day water gets priced by the barrel just like crude. This whole thing's about making sure it's your trademark on those barrels."

"That's not true, Ranger."

"You trying to fool me or yourself, sir?"

Hollis Tyree looked trapped between responses, his eyes seeming to peer in different directions at once. "What can I do to prove you're wrong about me?"

"Tell me about the uranium."

"How much you know on the subject?"

"Nothing 'sides the obvious."

"Well, there's a lot more than the obvious. Let's start with the fact that finding uranium in Texas is nothing new. Airborne gamma radiation surveys first found it by accident in 1954 while looking for petroleum deposits. The strikes were confined almost exclusively to the southern part of the state in areas rich in sandstone."

"Doesn't seem to describe Tunga County much, does it, Mr. Tyree?"

"I'm getting to that," he told her, as wind rustled the flowers around them. "Thing is there are various grades of uranium, and most of them, especially the strikes found in Texas, aren't worth a lick. But when we found water in Tunga County nobody knew was there, we also found uranium nobody knew was there."

"And that's what poisoned the water in Albion, turned the town's residents crazy just like drinking from that creek made those pioneers mad enough to kill each other in 1881." Caitlin blinked some dust from her eye. "Only case like that I ever came upon was an Indian Reservation where they used contaminated rocks and tailings from local uranium mines to build their homes. But that was nothing like this."

"That's because the uranium we found in Tunga County was the highly enriched kind thought to be geologically extinct for the most part, containing 99.4 percent uranium-235. Uranium is considered weapons grade if it contains as little as 85 percent."

"How many bombs is that, Mr. Tyree?"

The blood seemed to drain from Hollis Tyree's face, his complexion taking on the color of milk and look of cardboard. "Depends on how much uranium they can pull out of the soil."

"Take a guess."

"You'd need fifty-five pounds of the stuff to fashion even a single crude nuclear device, but only a fraction of that for a dirty bomb."

"How many dirty bombs in what those dump trucks were carrying?"

"It's hard to say."

"How many, sir?"

"A dozen, at least."

Caitlin let that settle in her mind for a moment. "Montoya hates Americans, Mr. Tyree, and he's got his own private army of Mexican Special Forces troops to back it up. I think he's going to use your uranium and his men to attack American cities. I think what we're looking at here now is an all-out war."

Tyree surveyed the land around him, as if seeing it for something else entirely. "This is the very site of the house my great-granddad built, where my father was born. I resolved to keep it standing forever. But a lightning storm set it ablaze twenty years back. Guess you're right about control; I couldn't stop that lightning any more than I could save my children's lives. The lightning strike happened the very same day my father passed away, and to this day I'm convinced those two things were related. Can I tell you something else?"

"Go ahead."

"I walk the streets of Sweetwater a lot to remind me where I come from and who I am. And once in a while, not often mind you, but once in a while, when I look down the street I swear I can see Earl Strong on his rounds, looking for human waste products to put on his chain."

Tyree looked as if he had more to say, but the words dissolved into a heavy sigh that escaped between trembling lips. His eyes moistened again, lids locking open as if everything had seized up solid on him. Then he sucked in a deep breath that sounded dry and crackly.

"I don't think there's a town ever been made you couldn't clean up just like your granddad, Ranger."

"Guess we'll see about that, Mr. Tyree."

99

SAN ANTONIO; THE PRESENT

D. W. Tepper awoke to the sight of the huge man standing at the foot of his bed.

"Oh, shit," he said, reflexively reaching for the pistol that, of course, wasn't there.

"We've never met, Captain," said Guillermo Paz. "I'm—"

"I know who you are, I've heard all about you." Tepper struggled to sit up, failed. "And I'm placing you under arrest."

Paz pulled a nine-millimeter pistol from his belt and laid it atop the bedcovers within Tepper's reach. "Feel free."

Tepper started to reach for the gun, then stopped. "I can't."

"No?"

"This whole thing's falling apart faster than a house in a tornado. You gotta help Caitlin Strong finish it."

"Precisely my intention, Captain."

"Then, pardon my French, but what the fuck you doing here?"

"Helping Caitlin Strong."

"Come again?"

"There's one more piece of her story I'm missing. I thought I had it all when I found out her real grandmother was Mexican. But when I saw her in the church I realized I didn't, that there was something else." Paz walked around to the side of the bed. "Am I right or wrong, Captain?"

"This is a place you don't want to go, Colonel."

"I'm almost there already."

Tepper worked the bed controls to raise himself to a sitting position. "You need to trust me on this one. It's for the girl's own good."

"That's for her to decide."

"It was already decided for her. By her dad and granddad."

Paz took a deep breath and let it out slowly, seeming to relent until his piercing gaze met Tepper's. "This has something to do with Mexico, doesn't it?"

Tepper thought about going for the gun again, but when he glanced down the bed, it was gone with him having no memory of Paz having taken it back. "I told you to leave it alone, Colonel."

"After Earl Strong came back to raise his family," Paz said, picking up his thought in midstream. "After Caitlin was already born . . ."

"I'm getting the nurse," Tepper said, feeling for the call button.

Paz didn't move. "She needs to know."

"No, sir, she doesn't. I gave my word. I promised both Jim and Earl she'd never hear it from me."

Paz leaned over the bed, his huge eyes boring down on Tepper like twin tar pits. "And she won't, Captain."

100

San Antonio; the present

Cort Wesley was waiting when Caitlin emerged from Southwest General Hospital where Captain D. W. Tepper had been taken after the ambush. The day was hot and bright, a welcome change from the overly cooled dim air of the lobby where she'd spent most of the past ninety minutes.

"How is he?" Cort Wesley asked.

"They were changing his catheter and cleaning him up when I got here. Took nearly an hour. How can something like that take an hour?"

"I never understood hospitals much. Maybe that's a good thing."

Caitlin gazed over his shoulder at the illegally parked truck with Dylan, Luke, and Maria inside.

"This is where they brought your husband too," Cort Wesley continued.

"Seems like a lifetime ago now."

"Is that why you didn't bother calling me back, Ranger?"

Caitlin glanced at his truck again. "Nope, that was something else."

Cort Wesley followed her gaze, nodding. "Fixing to finish this ride on your own?"

"The thought did cross my mind."

Cort Wesley caught the meaning in Caitlin's tone, as much as her words. "So, what, you figure I was just gonna sit the rest of it out?"

"I figured I'd take the choice out of your hands."

"What makes you think you got the right?"

"The two boys in that truck. Last time I checked you wanted to keep them."

Cort Wesley felt the sweat dripping into his eyes and sidestepped into the shade while Caitlin remained in the sun. "You wanna hear the funniest thing?"

"I could use a laugh."

"All the way driving here, I'm thinking of ways to tell you I can't push this any farther. That wondering if my kids were alive or dead was the worst hour of my life. Ended up pulling my truck over and puking my guts out 'til I reached Pearsall where those Rangers laid their lives on the line for no more than strangers."

"Not strangers to me and D. W., Cort Wesley, and that means not strangers to your boys either."

"Point being I was gonna tell you I was pulling out of this until I saw you walk out that revolving door. Look on your face told me I was a fool for even considering the possibility."

"What look is that?"

"You being glad to see me, even gladder to see my sons. That's worth more than I can say, too much to even think about letting you go the rest of this alone. I just can't do that, Ranger, sons or no sons."

"How much of that is 'cause of last night?"

"Tell you the truth, it's tonight I'm thinking about now. Tomorrow too, and the day after."

Caitlin held Cort Wesley's gaze, trying to look more confident than she actually felt. "You got social services to worry about, and I won't be alone anyway. Jones, or whatever his name is, is scrambling an army to finish things in Juárez."

Cort Wesley wiped his brow with his sleeve. His face and arms were sun dried and darkened, which made Caitlin think of the colorless, ghostlike features that had plagued him for months after getting out of prison. It was as if his skin had forgotten how to accept the sun. Or maybe the sun had wanted no part of him. But something had changed.

"Depend on others and they'll always disappoint you."

"You just make that up, Cort Wesley?"

"Comes from experience, Ranger. You go down there and don't come back, nothing else I ever do in my life will mean a thing."

"Does that include living to raise your boys?"

"If Marianna Silvaro stays true to her word, social services'll be picking them up tomorrow. 'Less I shoot the bastards, of course. And right now there's others I'd rather be shooting."

Caitlin shook her head. "This goes that way, they'll be somebody else doing the shooting."

"Since when?" Cort Wesley asked her.

PART TEN

If all the books written about the Rangers were put on top of the other, the resulting pile would be almost as tall as some of the tales that they contain. The Rangers have been pictured as a fearless, almost superhuman breed of men, capable of incredible feats. It may take a company of militia to quell a riot, but one Ranger was said to be enough for one mob. Evildoers, especially Mexican ones, were said to quail at the mere mention of the name.

—Américo Paredes, *With His Pistol in His Hand*

101

Guillermo Paz heard the door to the other side of the confessional in Mission de Guadalupe slide open and found himself staring at an older priest with jet black hair showing its true gray color at the roots.

"You're on the wrong side of the box today, Padre," Paz told him. "Because I've come to hear *your* confession."

"Do you know where you are?" the priest challenged obstinately.

"I was going to ask you the same question after you switch places with me."

"*What?* I'll do no such thing."

"Yes, you will," Paz continued, sliding out of the confessional. "One way or another."

"I don't think you know who I am."

"Yes, Padre, I do. Your name is Pena and you're a disgrace."

"Watch your tongue!"

"I don't think you know who *I* am."

"And who's that?"

"Around here, they call me Ángel de la Guarda."

Paz could see the priest's eyes widen, the man weighing his options, soon to realize he had only one.

"Let's go, Padre. Switch places."

Stiffly, the priest emerged from the other side of the confessional. He slid around the door to the adjoining cubicle, entered, and closed it behind him. He felt the heat the big man had left behind as his huge figure settled into the priest's side of the box.

"Why are you doing this, my son?"

"I'm not your son, Padre. We're not related at all, because you're a traitor to the people you're supposed to be tending. No amount of Hail Marys can get you out of the mess you're in."

"Perhaps you have the wrong man, my son."

"Call me that again and I'll cut off one of your fingers. Let's do this the right way, Father. Why don't you get things started?"

Through the screen, Paz could see the old priest cross himself.

"Bless me, Fa— . . . for I have sinned."

"Don't stop there."

"I don't know what you mean."

"Yes, you do. I'm here to hear all about those sins, Padre, and offer my own kind of absolution."

"Please, if you could just be more—"

"That statue in front of the mission."

"*Señor?*"

"The statue of this place's founder, Fray Garcia de San Francisco. Quite a man, wasn't he?"

Father Pena remained silent, his breathing the loudest of any man Paz had ever heard, like he had an amplifier built into his throat and mouth.

"He came here from Spain in 1629 and established the Mission of Our Lady of Guadalupe among the Manso Indians at the Pass of the North along El Camino Real. Not an easy task considering those Indians were very accomplished warriors themselves who had no use for outsiders. But he got his point across and baptized every single one of them out of a church made from branches and mud with a straw roof. That became the forerunner to this place, a fort as much as a mission that formed the northern-most outpost of colonial Spain. During the Pueblo Revolt in 1680 this is where the refugees came for help and Fray Garcia de San Francisco saved twenty-five hundred of them."

"Please, *señor*, I—"

"You're a disgrace to his memory, to this place he built solely with adobe. I like it here. It reminds me of home in Venezuela where a priest taught me how to read and write."

"You are a religious man, then," Father Pena said, a touch of hope creeping into his voice.

"Not for a long time, but still more than you. What would you have done with the desperate travelers who came to El Camino Real running from men who would have slaughtered them? Offered refuge and then sold them out would be my guess, just as you've done here in modern times."

Paz heard the priest steady himself with a deep chortling breath. "You should leave for your own good."

"*My* own good?"

"I am protected."

"Glad we've finally got to the point, because that's who I'm looking for: the men who are protecting you, the men who've turned the root cellars dug beneath this church to hide those who came to Fray Garcia de San Francisco for refuge into storage dumps for their heroin and weapons. The men who've turned this city into a shooting gallery, led by a man named Montoya."

"What do you want?"

"I already told you what I want, Padre: your confession."

"I have only tried to do good for my people!"

"*Estás lleno de mierda*. And when I say you're full of shit, I mean it with all due respect. You've sold your people out. Say it."

"I cannot—"

"Last chance to confess on your own before I make you."

The priest made a low, whimpering sound.

"Padre?"

"I have sold my people out," he said, barely loud enough for Paz to hear.

"You've borne silent witness to murder. You are a party to the crime that has eaten this city to the bone." Paz listened to the priest's noisy breathing. "Say it," he ordered.

"My words will change nothing."

"No, that's for me to do. Now say it anyway."

"I am a party to the crime that has eaten this city to the bone. I have borne witness to murder."

Paz felt himself starting to relax. "Back home that priest who taught me how to read and write was gunned down for standing up to the street gangs. I was just a boy then. Couldn't do a damn thing about it. That's what today's all about. The circle finally closing."

"Please," the priest whined, "I will do anything. Just tell me what I must do."

"Tell them I'm here. And something else."

In the adjoining cubicle, the priest sank to his knees, head bowed in a position of prayer. "Anything! Just spare my life, I beg you!"

"Show me where the weapons are stored," Paz told him.

102

Caitlin and Cort Wesley crossed the border into Juárez in silence, the air around them seeming instantly hotter and harder to breathe in, as if all the gun smoke and blood had sucked the oxygen out of it. Minutes later the old city center came into view with sidewalks teeming with people dodging kiosks selling water and flavored ice. Farther forward, buildings that looked a half-century older than the rest of the city proper jammed the landscape with hand-painted signs draped from their overhangs, battling for attention. Old men smoked cigarettes in the shade while the sun roasted the cracked pavement. One of the ancient cars cluttering the streets before them backfired, sending every pedestrian in view scurrying for cover.

"Well," said Cort Wesley, "here we are."

Back in San Antonio, he'd left her long enough to return to his truck and hand Dylan the keys.

"You as good a driver as you say?" Caitlin heard Cort Wesley ask his oldest son.

The boy tossed the hair from his face with a flip of his head, then combed a hand through it. "As good as you taught me."

"You think you can find your way back to Pearsall and that ranch?"

"Yup. Where you headed?"

Cort Wesley focused his next words on Luke as well. "Men who came after you today aren't about to quit unless we take the choice away. Sometimes, boys, you gotta take it to them."

Luke uttered a deep sigh, almost like a sob.

"I know you don't understand why I gotta do this now," Cort Wesley said softly, "but you will someday. I ever lie to you, son?"

Luke swiped the tears from his face and shook his head.

"And I'm not lying to you now when I say I'll be back straightaway."

"Is it gonna be like the last time?" Luke managed through trembling lips.

Cort Wesley reached into the backseat and cupped a hand around his son's hair. "I hope so, since we came out of that scrape just fine."

"Dylan's just like you," Caitlin said, her SUV approaching the center of Juárez in a series of maddening stops and starts.

"I know."

"You proud of that, Cort Wesley?"

"I'm proud he doesn't run from his true nature. That he gives into instinct and impulses, the kind that kept himself, his brother, and that girl alive."

"He got lucky."

"You don't think the same can be said for us, Ranger?"

"It runs out—that's what I'm saying."

"Did it run out for your grandfather? All those years of rangering and killing—he was, what, near ninety when he died?"

"It took its toll. Now that I've finally heard the rest of his story, I can see that. His secrets nearly ate him up, left him empty when they were finished with him."

Cort Wesley laughed.

"What's so funny?"

"You talked the same way when we were driving to Casa del Diablo."

"This is different."

"Why?"

"Because we're just spotting for Jones and his men."

Caitlin's phone rang. "It's him," she said, checking the Caller ID.

103

JUÁREZ; THE PRESENT

"We got problems," Jones said.

"I don't like your tone," Caitlin told him.

"You're gonna like what I got to say even less. Where are you?"

"Where do you think?"

"Right, stupid question," Jones said, his voice so perturbed it sounded like he was speaking through a mouthful of sand.

"Why don't you tell me what happened?"

Caitlin continued to inch forward in her SUV. The sister cities of Juárez and El Paso shared a common border and little else. Joined together by a bridge that many Texans would prefer be blown up to stop the passage of violence across the border. On bad nights, those living on the southwest side of El Paso went to sleep often enough to the staccato crackle of gunfire, sounding like firecrackers on the Fourth of July. On worse nights, some swore they could see the incandescent flare of muzzle flashes scorching the night air. A number had relocated their bedrooms on the chance a stray bullet might find a window. Others had simply up and moved.

"A new administration is what happened," Jones explained. "Us losing carte blanche to play things the way we want is what happened."

"Guess you're gonna miss waterboarding, Jones."

"That was Smith, remember? And I didn't hear you complaining when I was bringing the cavalry along for the ride."

"This is different. Hollis Tyree figures he pulled enough uranium salt out of Tunga County to set off a dozen dirty bombs in U.S. cities."

"Tell it to the president, Ranger."

"You got his number handy?"

"Even if I did, it won't change the fact that Mexico is a sovereign nation and what I was planning amounted to an invasion. People like me don't own the helicopter gunships and the boots on the ground anymore; we only rent them. You probably passed our staging ground on your drive. We were hoping to bring the rain. Now the storm's gonna have to wait."

Caitlin felt prickles of heat building beneath her

skin. "Juárez is just a way station, Jones. The contents of those dump trucks will be gone from here even if Montoya has to carry them in plastic beach pails. Then the storm won't matter a lick."

"Turn around, Ranger. Head home. Give me more time to make this happen for you and get it done right."

Caitlin gazed across the seat at Cort Wesley. "Why am I not reassured here?"

"I'm just trying to keep you alive. It's like the goddamn wild west in Juárez, Ranger, that's all I'm saying."

Caitlin thought of her grandfather leading the charge in this very place another time for another reason. "Then I should feel right at home," she told Jones.

104

JUÁREZ; THE PRESENT

"This used to be a diaper factory," Fernando Leyva told Colonel Montoya inside the warehouse on the outskirts of Juárez. "The disposable kind."

Montoya continued to walk about the sprawling confines, trailed by both Leyva and Vincente Carillo Guzman, head of the Sinaloa cartel, and their ever-present armed guards. Meanwhile, more of Leyva's people were supervising the transfer of the contents of the dump trucks into tankers for concealment as well as to better safeguard the soil layered with uranium in transit.

"The scientists who'll be assembling the dirty

bombs are already waiting for the shipment to arrive in Colombia from the port of Lazaro Cardenas," Montoya told them both. "Their most complex task will be extracting the uranium salt from the soil. From there, the creation of the bombs will be simple."

"What's your brother doing here?" Leyva asked, tilting his gaze toward a darkened corner where Macerio was currently easing a line into a fresh IV bag. He had shed his familiar toupee, his skull darkened by a fresh growth of stubble. He glanced over suddenly, as if aware they were speaking of him.

"He is capable of things others aren't."

"As are your own soldiers," Guzman picked up, shifting his gaze to the fifty men who'd accompanied the general to the warehouse; all brutal and murderous Zetas, the best trained in the Mexican army.

All but a half dozen of them were dressed in civilian clothes, looking like Mexican tourists or businessmen come to sample the wares of the United States. At present they were moving about a series of tables, selecting from an assortment of laptops, PDAs, identification papers, and light weapons—all of which would accompany them across the border as the first wave in the guerrilla war that would bring America to its knees. Montoya needed to see it all for himself, be there when the invasion began this very night.

"My brother is different," he told the cartel leaders. "I wouldn't trade any ten of my Zetas for him."

The colonel didn't bother to add how uncomfortable he felt outside the jungles of the Yucatán. Even having Macerio by his side at last couldn't totally relieve that. He thought of all his brother had done for him over the years, not the least of which was the path of blood he continued to leave along the border with Texas. No one had ever made the connection that his victims were actually sacrifices, *ch'ab'*, to the Mayan cause, a line of demarcation that someday no American would dare cross.

At that moment, a loud rapping fell on the sealed factory doors. Leyva and Guzman exchanged a nervous glance, while Montoya's Zetas readied whatever weapons they could lay their hands on.

Macerio slid forward from the corner, holding no weapon at all. He moved to the heavy sliding door and slung it open to reveal Father Juan Alejandro Pena standing there. The priest stumbled in, panting and gasping for breath. Rancid perspiration that stank like raw onions soaked through his shirt.

"*¡Está de vuelta!*" Father Pena managed finally, hands on his knees.

"Who's back?" Macerio asked him.

"*¡El gigante!*" And when that provoked no response from anyone, Pena added, "Ángel de la Guarda."

"What guardian angel?" Montoya demanded, starting forward. "What are you talking about?"

"The man who has killed many of our men in the *barrio bajos*. The man the local peasants believe was sent here by God to protect them." Pena finally managed to straighten up, more of the vile onion stench wafting off him. "He is back, *señor*."

Montoya turned to his brother. "Take charge of the tankers. Get them to Lazaro Cardenas." Then he swung back around to face the priest. "Now, tell me where we can find this Ángel de la Guarda."

105

JUÁREZ; THE PRESENT

Caitlin and Cort Wesley found Guillermo Paz seated at a corner table of El Herradero de Soto Restaurant surrounded by chips, pork skins, red salsa, and pico de gallo. The restaurant overlooked the main square on Avenue Juárez diagonally across from Mission de Guadalupe.

"I ordered extra, in case you were hungry," he told them, munching on a pork skin. "We have time."

The exterior of the V-shaped El Herradero was finished in mauve stucco, with an extended portico and hardwood door adorned by a dozen individual windowpanes. Brick-lined walls dominated the interior, the restaurant's lighting dim even in daylight over bare slate-colored tables.

"Change in plans, Colonel," Caitlin said, sliding into the booth across from him, while Cort Wesley remained standing.

"You're not hungry?" Paz asked him.

"We don't have any backup," Caitlin continued. "No gunships, no commandos sliding down from the sky to help finish this."

"No surprise."

"Doesn't seem to bother you," Cort Wesley noted.

"I expected as much. Your grandfather fought his last great battle here," Paz said to Caitlin.

"I know, at Sauer and Company."

"I'm impressed."

"Don't be, Colonel."

"It's right across the street, the Casa Sauer Building

now. Not much more than a strip mall. You can see the names of the stores on the overhang."

Caitlin gazed out the nearest window through the late afternoon's fading light. The sky had taken on an angry red color, the promise of a storm held in the dark clouds converging on the last of the day's light. With the heat having been bled from the air at last, people spilled out into the street and sidewalks, congregating in small groups amid the continual choke of traffic. Between the time the sun gave up its hold and the fall of night brought out the gangs, there were precious few moments to enjoy the outdoors. The square itself was lined with all manner of shops from electronics stores, to bodegas, to tattoo parlors, to drug dispensaries catering to an American clientele with cutrate prices and offerings not available just steps away across the border.

"Did anyone ever tell you how that battle ended?" Paz raised between bites.

"Colonel," Caitlin started, not bothering to hide her impatience, while Cort Wesley held his steel-like gaze out the windows as if expecting an attack any moment.

"I told you, we've got plenty of time." Paz swabbed the rest of his plate clean with a tortilla and dabbed the corners of his mouth with a napkin. "We were talking about your grandfather."

Caitlin fidgeted anxiously. "He won. Shot up every bottle in the place and burned all the drugs is what I heard."

"There's more," Paz told her. "He and the other Rangers gunned down the *narcotrafficante* and their mules, all right. Problem was the dynamite he laid in the basement to destroy the opium they'd stockpiled never ignited. Your grandfather would've gone back inside to finish the job, but he had three wounded Rangers and he figured their lives were more important than destroying those drugs. I bet that stayed with him for a while, leaving the job unfinished. All those drugs he didn't destroy making their way across the border."

Caitlin's gaze joined Cort Wesley's out the windows, looking for what she couldn't say.

Paz checked his watch. "Earl Strong left Juárez with a tommy gun in one hand and an unconscious Ranger over the other shoulder. I heard he carried that wounded man all the way across the border smoking a cigar the whole time." Paz leaned back, fixed on Caitlin as if Cort Wesley wasn't even there. "They still talk about Earl Strong in Juárez, the most famous *el Rinche* of them all."

"And so ends the story," Caitlin said, letting her gaze drift out the window.

"No," Paz told her, "it doesn't."

106

SAN ANTONIO; 1979

Caitlin's mother had just put her to bed when the gunmen came. Her husband, Jim Strong, was away as usual, but had warned her this day may come. He'd told her about how his father had waged war with Mexican drug runners south of the border and how they'd vowed revenge after he and the Rangers had dealt them a setback from which it would take them years to recover.

Jim Strong talked about his father spending many a night on the front porch when the weather was good, and by an inside window when it wasn't, waiting for the night he knew was coming. Jim himself had done the same often enough, never once believing the Mexicans had given up just because Earl finally retired. He'd almost quit the Rangers on numerous occasions because he hated leaving his family alone for nights at a time. But he hated the thought of not being a Ranger even more, so kept to his work and called as often as he could.

A storm had taken out the phones the night the men finally came, but a phone wouldn't have done much good anyway. The windows of the one-story house exploded in a cacophony of fire that seemed to be coming from everywhere at once. Caitlin's mother dropped to the floor and crawled into Caitlin's room, pulling her terrified daughter from under her covers and pushing her beneath the bed.

"Mommy," she protested, when her mother began to ease herself away.

"Hush, baby. I'll be right back. You just stay put. Don't move for nothing or nobody, you hear?"

Four-year-old Caitlin felt herself nod. Then her mother was gone and the house fell into an almost interminable silence until the gunfire resumed with even more fury than before.

The shattering of her own window sent Caitlin scurrying out from under the bed. First pressed against the wall and then padding softly toward the den where her father watched television with his feet propped up on an overstuffed recliner when he was home.

She had peeked around the corner, just as the front door burst open ahead of a trio of dark, ugly men who pulled her mother's hair and pushed her to the floor. Caitlin would have screamed if she'd found the breath. As it was she simply slid down the wall and sat slumped there when a brief flurry of gunfire returned, followed by nothing except the rain and cold flooding the house to mix with the bitter sulfur stench of gun smoke and rank sweat left behind by her mother's killers.

107

JUÁREZ; THE PRESENT

Caitlin sat in silence, listening to the rhythmic pounding of her own heart. She felt Cort Wesley reach over and close his hand atop hers. It was warm and strong to the touch, but hardly reassuring.

"The police found you outside in the rain under a cottonwood tree, covered in your mother's blood," Paz continued. "You were in shock and had no memory of anything. So your father and grandfather resolved never to tell you the truth of what had happened that night. They thought it would be a blessing for you to believe your mother got sick instead. Maybe they were right."

"Captain Tepper told you this."

"He thought it was time you heard the truth."

Caitlin tried to figure out what she felt, divided

between shock and understanding since Paz had explained her very nature in a few brief moments. Everything that had never made sense to her before suddenly did. But she took no solace in that.

"My grandfather moved in with us right after my mom was killed," Caitlin said, her voice drifting. "Until the day he died, I can't remember a time he wasn't around me."

"To protect you for sure," said Cort Wesley. "A man like Earl Strong would never let the same thing happen again."

Caitlin looked back toward Paz. "Was it really about vengeance, Colonel?"

"The Mexicans who did battle with your grandfather in this very square would never have forgotten the harm he did them. And neither would their sons and grandsons." Paz turned his gaze toward the window overlooking the ancient square. "Some of their descendants are probably out there now and you're going to get your chance to do battle with them, to finish what your grandfather started."

As if on cue, six cargo vans pulled into the square on Avenue Juárez and double-parked one behind the other. Caitlin and Cort Wesley watched the traffic that had been crawling along come to a complete stop, as van doors slid open allowing gunmen dressed as civilians, but armed with all manner of assault rifles, to spill out in constant streams into the square concentrating on El Herradero de Soto Restaurant. It reminded Caitlin of circus cars where the clowns just kept emerging.

"Zetas," she said just loud enough for Paz and Cort Wesley to hear.

"How did they find us?" Caitlin asked, joining Cort Wesley on his feet.

"I made sure they knew you were coming," Paz told her. "Had a coward who calls himself a priest pass the word."

Cort Wesley lowered himself over Paz, face starting to twitch, the veins in his forearms pulsing. "Are you out of your frigging mind?"

Paz grinned and reached under the table, his hand emerging with an M16 he handed up to him. "Yours to do with as you please."

Cort Wesley took the M16 and jacked it into firing position.

"The priest I told you about is from Mission de Guadalupe up the street," Paz continued. "A few of the townspeople I spoke with told me he has been bought off by the *narcotrafficante,* that they use the basement of his church to store their guns and ammunition and occasionally their drugs."

Cort Wesley posted himself against a wall so he could peer out into the street beyond.

Paz held his gaze on Caitlin. "Just like the *narcotrafficante* your grandfather chased down here used the Sauer Building."

"They're surrounding us," said Cort Wesley, ready with his M16.

"Your grandfather was no expert with dynamite," Paz said to Caitlin, removing his cell phone from his pocket and pressing out a number without raising the device to his ear. "That's why he didn't realize the fuse he set was probably damp from the journey and couldn't hold a flame. Explosives are tricky to work with."

"I think I just spotted Montoya himself," Caitlin said, still peering out the window, recalling the picture Jones had e-mailed to her BlackBerry.

As if on cue, across the square Mission de Guada-lupe exploded in an orange ball of flame that blew outward from its core. Cort Wesley twisted from the window and dove under the nearest table an instant before the blast's percussion shattered the glass lining the east side of the restaurant. The patrons still able rushed about in all directions, settling in a panicked charge for the door.

Then something like an earthquake shook the very ground. Caitlin figured another explosion must be coming until a mass scream erupted outside, loud enough to rise over the crackling flames and panic be-yond. She watched as a nonstop flood of armed men dressed shabbily in near rags poured into the square in a constant stream. They carried pistols, assault rifles, and submachine guns she recognized as absolute top-of-the-line. The kind of guns the cartels were known to import from the United States and had likely been stored in the church basement until Paz appropriated them. But the weapons looked utterly wrong in the peasants' hands, a fact further borne out when they began firing wildly into the air to accompany their bel-lows.

The last of the sun dropped behind the mountains, allowing dusk to settle over Juárez.

"Right on time," said Paz.

108

Colonel Montoya couldn't believe what he was seeing. The peasants he had long discounted and ignored in his plans for Mexico's future were converging from all angles into the square. The odds of the battle he had insisted on leading personally had changed in one explosive instant. All along he'd been certain he was Chahuku, the Bringer of Thunder from Mayan mythology. Now it seemed he'd had that all wrong. Chahuku was someone else entirely, this Ángel de la Guarda, and the thunder he brought was raging all around Montoya in the old city square.

"I warned you about him!" Fernando Leyva screamed over the cacophony of gunfire, Vincente Carillo Guzman having already fled with his men. "I warned you!"

"Just as I warned you not to come," Montoya sneered at him. "But you insisted, said men here would cower at the sight of you. Are they cowering now?" He shook his head, snarling. "Just tell me when you see this guardian angel."

"No one ever sees him until they're dead."

"Not tonight," Montoya said, as his Zetas opened fire into the crowd surging toward them.

Caitlin watched Cort Wesley lurch back to his feet, M16 tight in his grasp.

Paz handed her one as well. "They come from the

barrio bajos, the peasants the *narcotrafficante* and other vermin terrorize for sport," he told her, grasping a pair of M4A1 assault rifles, a shortened version of the M16 with a collapsible stock favored by the Special Forces. "I am quite well known to them."

"Ángel de la Guarda," Caitlin said, looking him right in the eye.

Paz held her stare. "I'm impressed, Ranger."

"You're not the only one who does their homework, Colonel."

More gunfire erupted in the square, the people of the *barrio bajos* firing wildly into the space previously ruled by the Zetas who'd emerged from the cargo vans. Their random fire blew out store windows on both sides of the street. Caitlin could see how unfamiliar the weapons were in their grasp, just as she could see the rage brimming in their eyes. These were men who'd spent their entire lifetimes in poverty, servitude, and fear, their lives too long dependent on those who would just as soon see them dead. She knew each and every one of them had lost a friend or loved one to the intractable violence that had consumed Juárez, perpetuated by the drug cartels controlled now by Colonel Montoya.

Both Caitlin and Cort Wesley had started for the door to join the battle when Paz blocked their path.

"The people of the *barrio bajos* are shooting at anyone with guns."

"That street'll look like a slaughterhouse when the Zetas are done with them."

Paz started toward the rear of the restaurant. "Come with me."

. . .

Montoya opened up with his assault rifle, spraying bullets into a throng of peasants who seemed to dance before crumpling under his fire. The Mayan tradition of leadership was defined by the great warrior kings who led their troops personally in battle. The gun jerked in his hands, the smell of sulfur and gun oil thick in his nostrils, even as gunfire deafened his ears to all other sounds.

His great battlefield sense told him his superbly trained commandoes would triumph over this ragtag group of wild men. Even now his Zetas were taking cover from which to fire, leaving Montoya leading a small group hoping to stem the raging assault long enough for the rest of his men to gain the ground needed to turn the tide. Once that happened the peasants would flee, cowards to the core with their advantage of surprise gone.

He could have used his brother Macerio now. But the tankers needed protection too. The tankers were everything.

Montoya turned left, then right, jacking another magazine into place without missing a beat as bodies continued to crumple everywhere around him.

The narrow stairwell spilled out onto the roof, providing a clear view of the people of the *barrio bajos* falling to the suddenly concentrated fire of the Zetas. Montoya's men had managed to find cover within shattered storefronts and behind buildings, easily cutting down the peasants who were lost for a response with the surprise of their attack squandered.

"Don't think we came this far just to watch," said Cort Wesley.

And he opened fire on a concentration of Zetas nestled in an alley across the street, shooting high to kick chips of brick and stone into their faces to push them to their feet before mowing them down. Caitlin added her fire, swiftly finding a rhythm to the M16 thanks to several range sessions with one over the past year just in case she'd ever need to wield one again. She heard the squelching crackle of Paz's fire and glimpsed him firing in two different directions at the same time, his arms akimbo, more of the Zetas falling to his gunfire or diving for cover to avoid it.

Through the endless barrage, Caitlin was vaguely conscious of the rapidly descending night being brightened by the glow from the flaming Mission de Guadalupe. The fire cast shadows through the square that trapped both gunmen and peasants alike in their grasp. And thick smoke had begun wafting over the square in waves that blocked the view of the warring factions from her rooftop perspective.

Cort Wesley's and Caitlin's stares met. They shared the slightest of smiles.

"Cover us, Colonel," Caitlin told Paz.

109

Montoya felt the tide turn all right, but in the wrong direction. The peasants had not fled for their lives as he'd expected, choosing to stay and fight as if this were their land to defend. Worse, his and Fernando Leyva's men were being cut down in spite of the superior positions they'd gained, as if the enemy had found the sense to claim the high ground. The angle of fire drew his eyes to a rooftop where a massive figure fired downward with twin rifles that looked like toys in his grasp.

Ángel de la Guarda . . .

He was real, after all, the Chahuku behind the trap the colonel and his men had walked straight into. Instinct and duty told Montoya to make his way toward the rooftop and confront the man who had baited him into this. But he could not, under any circumstances, risk letting his greater plans for Mexico dissolve and disappear here. Not with the means to launch his guerrilla war heading toward Lorenzo Cardenas even as the battle raged. Sometimes even the greatest commanders know that the best means to assure ultimate victory was a temporary retreat. The first wave of incursion into America's cities would be delayed, that's all, his plans reoriented as a result.

Montoya had never retreated in his life, not from any challenge, and doing it now proved surprisingly hard. But the Mayan warrior kings of the past had not ruled an empire for a millennium without facing such difficult choices and placing the needs of their people above their own.

So Montoya gnashed his teeth and pulled back deeper into the darkness and smoke, hating to leave the spill of blood and fall of bodies behind. He tore his uniform top off to reveal a plain white T-shirt beneath it. An instant later he had crossed through the jagged line of peasants still stubbornly firing wild volleys and disappeared into the night.

Caitlin felt the smoke in her lungs as soon as she and Cort Wesley emerged through the restaurant's rear door. She remembered sneaking a puff of her grandfather's cigar one day, inhaling a deep drag and gagging up the smoke while he snoozed in a chair. Her throat had felt as if she'd swallowed scalding water and her lungs burned with every breath for days afterward. Strange how she had forgotten all about that until now, until the burn returned and left her fighting back the same kind of retch.

She discarded the M16 and drew her SIG as they neared the building, the coarse smoke stinging her eyes now. Then she felt Cort Wesley throw himself into her and up against the side of the building lined with cracked windows that had managed to hold fast to their frames.

"The Zetas are moving for the vans," he whispered. "Turning tail to run."

"Any sign of Montoya?"

"It's a goddamn blur out there. Got an idea, Ranger. Just hold on here."

"Where are—" Caitlin started, but he was already gone.

. . .

Cort Wesley figured the Zetas couldn't see him any better than he could see them, or even discern whose side he was on, given all but a few were dressed in civilian clothes. He charged into the square among the former members of the Mexican Special Forces, pretending to fire at the congestion of peasants still rushing about. Then, suddenly, he turned his weapon on the nearest Zetas and mowed them down before ducking into the thick smoke for cover.

From there, he opened fire into their vans. Shooting at tires and glass, and blasting away at the engines and gas tanks. His ears bubbled from the nonstop barrage. He thought he sensed the heat of return fire sizzling past him, but it could just as easily been flaming embers fanned by the wind.

The smoke stole the world before him until a bright shaft of light sliced through it, pouring daytime brightness onto the scene while a whirring sound pushed at the periphery of his hearing.

Caitlin watched the helicopter hovering overhead, a newsman wearing a harness leaning out the open side with camera pinned to his shoulder. The chopper's rotor wash whipped the smoke about, enough breaks in it for her to recognize the call letters of an El Paso television station come to cover the battle obliterating the old center of the city.

She could no longer see Cort Wesley amid the spreading smoke, had no idea how many of the enemy he had downed or if any of the Zetas' return fire had found him. She didn't dare risk a shot at shapes and shadows out of fear they might have belonged to the peasant army stirred and armed by Guillermo Paz, or even Cort Wesley himself.

Then a trio of men she recognized as Zetas from the now disabled cargo vans stormed her way, firing wildly back into the smoke. Caitlin steadied her SIG and reeled off six shots in rapid succession, two per each, all three downed before they even saw her. Head shots in case they were wearing body armor under their shapeless civilian clothes.

She heard a staccato burst of automatic fire that sounded clearer and closer than the others, followed almost immediately by screaming. Caitlin pressed her back against the raised wood structure bracketing the nearest set of window frames. She peered inside El Herradero Restaurant to see two gunmen rounding up customers stranded there by the battle to use as hostages. Then she glimpsed the face of a third man she recognized as Fernando Leyva, head of the Juárez drug cartel.

Inside the restaurant, a man tried to intervene when one of the gunmen threw his wife against a wall and Leyva shot him in the face. He'd been shot himself as a younger man and even now Caitlin could see through the angry snarl how one side of his face drooped lower than the other. The two gunmen jerked a family of five to their feet from behind a toppled table, sticking their rifles into the children's faces to make the parents cooperate.

The hovering chopper's spotlight rotated into the restaurant, splaying fissures of broken light across the scene, enough for Caitlin to register the fear on the faces of the gathered hostages. In that moment the colored world seemed to fade to black and white, taking on the grainy texture of the old photographs picturing Earl Strong with pearl-handled Colts dangling from his waist. She felt she was back in 1934, fighting alongside her grandfather in this very square against a different enemy.

What would Earl Strong have done?

The question had barely left her thoughts when Caitlin threw herself into the side windows of the restaurant, cracked in spiderweb fashion by the percussion of the blast that had leveled Mission de Guadalupe. She hit them on a side angle, feeling splinters from the shattered wood frames pricking at her skin and conscious of glass slivers digging into her scalp when she hit the floor.

Caitlin didn't know how she found the sense or aim to fire, or what moved her to risk shots that just as easily could have claimed captives as captors. She could have sworn she heard her grandfather's voice, no longer cracking with the strain of age, directing her fire at the two gunmen, one hurled over a table and the other blown into a wall by her bullets. And when she rolled onto her stomach, for a moment, just a moment, Caitlin thought she glimpsed Earl Strong standing over her, firing with pearl-handled Colts clutched in either hand.

"Get the boss man, Ranger!"

And then she was firing anew at the shape of Fernando Leyva surging for the door just before its remnants burst inward behind a booted kick from Cort Wesley. Impossible to tell whether it was her fire or his that dropped Leyva, the hate on his face freezing under the spill of the funnel-shaped light shed by the news chopper until his features disintegrated in the hail of bullets.

The chopper hovered lower, its spotlight cast over the bodies littering the square while the congested buildings of more modern Juárez twinkled in the near distance. This part of the city had been locked in a different time, perhaps so the ghosts of the past could walk its streets with their kin from the present. The sounds of gunfire had ended, ceding Juárez to the thumping rotor wash and stubborn crackling of the flames still feasting on Mission de Guadalupe.

Caitlin and Cort Wesley emerged from the restaurant, to find Guillermo Paz waving his arms to signal the news chopper to land in an open section of the street adjoining the shotup forms of the cargo vans. Probably believing he was a *federalé* or Mexican army regular, the chopper complied.

"Looks like we're going for a ride," Cort Wesley said to Caitlin, her hair tossed about by the rotor wash.

110

Juárez; the present

The cabin made for a tight fit, as the helicopter lifted off again, the reporter promised the story of his life in return for his help. Caitlin and Cort Wesley fitted the spare sets of headphones over their ears, leaving Paz to listen and speak above the vibration and sounds that reminded Caitlin of an air hammer left to its own devices.

"Take us over Route two," Cort Wesley told the pilot. "Straightest route to the deep-water ports on the Pacific," he added to Paz and Caitlin. "That's where they'll be taking the contents of those dump trucks for sure."

"Doesn't figure they'd risk driving heavy loads across the desert," she agreed.

"No chance they were figuring on us either." Cort Wesley looked about the chopper's interior, face wrinkled in a frown. "We'd be sitting pretty for sure, if this was one of those gunships that never showed."

"It is now," said Paz, his voice slicing through the engine roar, grenade held in either hand.

Before Macerio, the lights of the convoy bracketed by armed Humvees operated by more of his brother's Zeta commandos cut a narrow ribbon from the night west down Mexico's Route 2. The entire contents of the six dump trucks had been transferred into four massive tankers labeled DANGER—HAZARDOUS WASTE to assure the convoy a smooth ride undeterred by hijackers or law enforcement personnel.

Their freighter was already docked at Lazaro Cardenas to take the tankers to Bogotá by sea. Macerio worried for the fate of his brother, the mission lost without him. But he had to have faith, faith that the blood trail he had laid across the land over so many years would satisfy the angry Mayan gods enough to keep both of them safe long enough to achieve their destiny.

Macerio had just felt a strange sense of certainty about the future, when he heard the heavy sounds of a helicopter overhead.

. . .

"There!"

Paz tapped the pilot on the shoulder and gestured down at the convoy of tankers speeding along the narrow black strip across the Mexican wilderness heading west. The lights of nearby towns dotted the distance, creating the effect of a vast tunnel carved through the center of them. Paz had grenades clipped to his belt, in addition to the pistols and spare magazines wedged into the slots of his ammo vest. A human armory was what he looked like and it seemed to suit him well, as he cracked the side door open. Cool night air rushed in, buffeting the cabin.

"Zeta gunner on the lead Humvee's swinging toward us," said Cort Wesley, maneuvering to find a fire angle for his M16.

"Not for long," said Paz, leaning farther out into the night.

Macerio could see nothing of the chopper's interior through the night, but knew Ángel de la Guarda was on board nonetheless. A coldness rooted deep in his core told him this was an enemy unlike any he'd faced before, one whose blood would not be so easy to shed, if he bled at all.

He raised the walkie-talkie linking him to the other vehicles in the convoy to his lips. "Shoot them down," he ordered the Zetas in the Humvees.

The chopper had just drawn even with the lead tanker marked as toxic waste transport when the first rounds from the M60 clanged into its fuselage, a few stray shells ricocheting about the cabin. Paz lost grasp of a grenade he'd readied just before he pulled the pin and it skittered across the cabin floor. He scrabbled for it, as Cort Wesley managed to free his harness and then moved to help Caitlin free hers. He took her down to the cabin floor, more fire whizzing over their heads.

Caitlin watched Paz grab hold of his grenade just before it rolled out the door, daring the M60 fire as he measured off his toss.

"Now, Paz!" Cort Wesley yelled. "Do it!"

Paz tossed the grenade out into the night. He knew in the next instant his toss was slightly off, swept off target by the wind, so he followed with a second immediately, as the M60 continued to spit fire their way.

Paz watched the second grenade skitter across the mount and disappear.

Then he closed his eyes.

Macerio saw the first grenade bang off the lead Humvee's hood, no time to rejoice before a second dropped straight into the gun mount. He watched the machine gunner flail desperately for it, thought he could see the terror and panic in the man's eyes.

"Slow down!" he ordered the driver of his tanker. "¡Desaceleración!"

Macerio heard the hiss of the brakes being applied, bracing for possible impact with the next closest tanker that may not have been able to respond as quickly. The big vehicle buckled slightly, listing badly from side to side, the distance growing between it and the lead Humvee in the last moment before the Humvee exploded.

• • •

Caitlin watched the blast launch the Humvee six feet into the air, before spinning it around and dropping its mangled carcass back on the highway, spewing rubber and metal. The lead tanker slammed into it, further dissolving its remnants and scattering them in all directions. She watched the tanker's tires lock up, the vehicle still moving as the cab portion angled sideways leaving the tanker to chase it into a wild jackknife.

The tanker spun around on an axis created by the cab, whipsawing toward the trailing trucks that careened into one another in desperate attempts to avoid it. The screech of metal impacting against metal came accompanied by showers of white-hot sparks that disappeared into the night as quickly as they'd flashed.

Caitlin saw the tankers spinning wildly across the road, one kicking up huge plumes of dust as it settled to a halt, only to be obliterated by another tanker whose panicked driver must have jammed the brakes instead of pumping them. A third sliced that one clean in half and rolled over atop its carcass, its wheels still turning as if to ride the air, leaving only the lead tanker still upright, though twisted across the highway.

The trailing Humvee, meanwhile, skidded off the road and flipped when its tires ground into the desert floor. But it somehow landed back upright, its M60's trigger jammed backward from the impact, a wild, churning spray of bullets fired upward.

The chopper's occupants all felt it list suddenly one way, then the other, evidence of the tail rotor catching part of the barrage. The pilot managed to angle the chopper away from the careening tankers, the desert floor beyond the freeway coming up fast.

Caitlin and Cort Wesley braced themselves for impact, while Guillermo Paz remained frozen in the open doorway, peering into the night beyond him.

Through it all, Macerio had the sense to realize that his tanker remarkably, miraculously, had remained standing. His shoulder and neck hurt from the harsh restraint of the safety harness during its spinning trip across the highway. He tried not to think of the other three tankers that had no doubt perished behind him. There was still this one, however damaged, still enough uranium to be sifted from the gravel to make several dirty bombs capable of spewing poison through Washington, New York, Los Angeles, maybe more.

"Drive!" he ordered the man behind the wheel, still trembling so hard he could barely grip the wheel. "Drive!"

"Where are you going?" the man asked, as Macerio took an assault rifle in hand and threw open the door.

"To clear the way for you."

Caitlin smelled gasoline, felt the heat of flames building around her in the cabin. The drop had rattled her insides, leaving her feeling like her teeth had been pushed back into her jaw. The chopper had landed on its side, leaving her leg pinned under a sheared strip of metal beneath the pilot's collapsed seat. He and the cameraman had been thrown from the cockpit on impact and lay barely stirring atop the rough ground surface nearby.

"Come on, Ranger," said a voice that might have been her father's.

Then a hand was tugging at her, but Caitlin resisted, the way she'd done as a little girl when her father had tried to rouse her in the predawn hours to go fishing in a pond surrounded on all sides by the prettiest flowers she'd ever seen.

"Caitlin," the voice said again.

She finally pushed herself alert, snapping her thoughts back into place and feeling disappointed that her clearing vision revealed Cort Wesley Masters in her sights instead of Jim Strong.

He coughed out some smoke, as he tried to free her. "I can't budge this damn thing."

"Let me," Guillermo Paz said, leaning back inside the chopper. His left arm hung lower than his right and his face was a patchwork of scratches and cuts. "You go after the last tanker."

Cort Wesley resisted.

"Go," Caitlin told him. "Finish this."

He touched her cheek, then pulled himself toward the door, squeezing past Paz. When he was gone, Paz leaned his upper body all the way inside, trying to wedge Caitlin free, bending the steel wedged over her foot back before her eyes. The exertion squeezed his features taut, Caitlin wiggling her foot from side to side in an attempt to shimmy it out to no avail. Flames poked through tears in the crashed chopper's carcass, licking at her one exposed boot. Twisting sideways, she caught a flash of movement outside.

"Colonel!"

Paz lurched all the way inside the toppled cabin,

pushing Caitlin low beneath a burst of bullets that clanged off steel, close enough to her to feel their gush of heat. She heard heavy footsteps, then a shadow fell over the cabin as a figure wide enough to block out the moon leaned inside the chopper.

Macerio!

Caitlin went for her pistol, couldn't find it. An assault rifle was angling toward her when Paz lashed out with a kick that sent Macerio sprawling, following him into the night as the smoke and flames continued to build around her.

III

MEXICO; THE PRESENT

Cort Wesley managed to grab hold of the smashed-up tanker's rear-mounted ladder just as the driver got the vehicle righted and started it on again down the freeway. He hoisted himself upon its top, finding handholds in the ridged depressions designating one tank compartment from another. The tanker's gears ground, balking as the driver tried to accelerate. Finally the transmission caught and the tanker began to pick up speed into the empty night ahead.

Cort Wesley felt the wind force pushing up against him and held on as best he could, willing to sacrifice purchase for pace to reach the cab before the truck's increasing speed would render the task impossible. The best he could do was keep stretching one hand before the other, pulling himself forward.

· · ·

Macerio hit the ground hard. His head smacked gravel, disorienting him and stealing away his grasp on his rifle. His knee was throbbing in pain again, the whole leg stiffening. But he found his rifle, just as a huge shape lurched toward him, silhouetted by moonlight.

Ángel de la Guarda . . .

He had to be a Mayan; no other explanation sufficed. Macerio felt they were battling for a heritage, a people. And in that moment he saw the giant as the last thing standing between him and the successful completion of the line of blood he was drawing across the border. Defeat the giant and nothing could stop him. Defeat the giant and his sacrifices would continue unabated, invincibility his at last.

Paz saw Macerio resteady his grip on his rifle and kicked it from his grasp, a harmless volley sent echoing into the night. Macerio caught his next kick out of midair, twisting and shoving the leg backward in one violent notion.

Ignoring the pain in his knee, Macerio lurched back to his feet, smoke from the burning helicopter wafting over both of them. He caught Ángel de la Guarda glancing back inside it and chose that moment to attack, his charge slowed by his stiffening leg.

Paz twisted aside at the last instant, springing his trap and adding his own force to Macerio's momentum. Macerio slammed hard against the helicopter's burning fuselage. His skull whiplashed backward, denting the steel. Paz watched his eyes go glassy and jammed a hand onto Macerio's throat, squeezing as Macerio extended an arm downward for his waist.

Caitlin was stretching her hand toward her lost SIG Sauer pistol, almost there when Macerio freed the knife from the sheath on his belt.

Cort Wesley walked the top of the tanker like a tightrope. His father had made him take a job as an offloader one summer as a boy, so riding trucks like this was nothing new for him. Except those had been parked in depots instead of speeding along a highway.

He dropped down from the tanker onto the roof of the cab, his boots clacking against metal. His knees buckled, then found balance with his arms swaying to the sides, leaving him with the feeling he was surfing the air.

Then he was on his stomach, clinging to the roof with one hand while the other snaked through the driver's side window and latched onto the driver's hair.

Paz glimpsed the knife slashing toward him. He managed to arch his midsection backward, the slash gashing him along the surface. He dug his hand tighter into Macerio's throat, heard him gurgling for breath but not seeming to weaken yet. Another swipe of the knife caught Paz on the side and a third dug into his shoulder.

Feeling the chopper's carcass ready to blow at any moment, he thrust his left hand back inside the cabin in search of Caitlin Strong's wedged foot. Her form was nearly lost to the building smoke. He was holding his breath against it now, feeling blindly for the last of the steel trapping her amid the flames.

"My gun!" she wheezed, starting to gag on the smoke.

Macerio's knife slashed across Paz's chest, shredding muscle. His already damaged arm, the one inside the cabin, went numb, but Paz's fingers managed to scrape across the Ranger's SIG and push it toward her.

Macerio started his knife forward, slowed by his dwindling breath just enough to give Caitlin the time to grab and right her pistol.

Paz felt the muscle layered around Macerio's throat finally slacken to a roaring *BANG! BANG! BANG!* that obliterated his face and skull. Macerio's blade stopped just short of its thrust's end, still somehow jabbing at Paz as what was left of him sank to the ground, his IV bag popping on impact.

The world dimming, Paz held to enough presence of mind to jam his other hand into the smoke, holding his breath and feeling the singe of flames as he grabbed hold of Caitlin Strong and hoisted her out into the night.

Cort Wesley felt his fingers close on hair wet with a combination of sweat and hair gel. He lacked the leverage to do anything but hold fast until he could lean his other hand in. One of his legs slipped off the roof, but his second hand locked on the tanker's steering wheel an instant before he would have dropped to the highway below.

His eyes met the driver's hateful gaze, glimpsed the gun in his hand and jerked the wheel hard in toward him. The tanker's sudden veer stole the driver's aim and the shot flew harmlessly into the night while the blast's echo rocked Cort Wesley's eardrums.

Cort Wesley could feel the tanker list heavily, could see the driver fighting to resteady his pistol on him, and jerked the wheel as far down as his meager leverage allowed. The tanker seemed to slip sideways, actually straddling the highway for a brief time, then crossing the median on only half its wheels, before tumbling over and throwing Cort Wesley outward into the night.

Paz dragged Caitlin free of the chopper in the last instant before it exploded. He collapsed to the ground, allowing the flames' glow to illuminate the figure of Cort Wesley Masters, framed by the toppled tankers strewn across the highway, jogging toward them.

Caitlin coughed the smoke from her lungs and climbed to her feet, staggering out to meet him.

"I believe we're finished here, Ranger," Cort Wesley said between labored breaths. "Where's Paz?"

"Right over—"

Caitlin stopped when a sweep of her eyes showed Guillermo Paz nowhere to be found.

112

JUÁREZ; THE PRESENT

The *federalés* stationed in the city of Juárez went at Caitlin and Cort Wesley together in a conference room that stank of stale coffee and strong, hand-rolled cigarettes.

"Your government can protest all it wants, but we

can keep you here as long as we like," a major who said his name was Batista threatened. "Just tell us about this big man who's been terrorizing Juárez."

"Terrorizing?" Caitlin repeated. "Is that what you call saving peasants from the drug dealers and mules your office has been protecting?"

Batista got right in her face, close enough for Caitlin to smell the peppers and onions on his breath. "If you cooperate with us now, I will forget that you said that."

"Don't bother," Cort Wesley told him.

"Was I speaking to you?"

"Look, you and I both know you're corrupt as they come. You'd sell your mother out for a dollar."

"I was thinking a peso," Caitlin added, "and his country for plenty less."

"I've shot gringos for less," Batista fumed.

"How about Texas Rangers?"

Batista ignored her and sat down across from Cort Wesley, straddling a chair. "I know you've done time in jail, but don't believe you'd fare too well in one of our Mexican prisons." His eyes moved to Caitlin. "Neither of you."

"Look, Captain," she started, trying to sound more conciliatory, "you're likely right that there's not much our government can do about our current predicament down here. But the Texas Rangers aren't a part of that government. You wanna hold us for no good reason and risk them coming down here to stage their own kind of intervention, be my guest. Times have changed, sir, but the Rangers haven't."

"I am not scared of *el Rinche*," Batista said, even though it was clear from the beads of sweat that had formed over his upper lip and sudden shifting of his eyes that he was.

"You'll be the first one they gun down, Captain. Tends to make subordinates more cooperative."

"Just tell me about the big man, Ángel de la Guarda."

"Nothing to tell."

"I hear there's a price on his head in Venezuela and three other countries," said Cort Wesley. "That's not why you're so interested in him, is it?" He stood up slowly, as if to dare Batista or the other officers to stop him. "Now, if you don't mind, the Ranger here and I gotta be getting home. I got two boys need tending to and if I leave now I can make them scrambled eggs for breakfast. I don't and we'll scramble yours instead."

Batista rose and backed away from the table, comfortable shooting distance if it came to that. "You will not return to my country again, either of you. If you do, you will find me far less hospitable the next time."

Cort Wesley waited until Caitlin pushed her chair back, then started for the door just ahead of her.

"Been nice knowing you, Major," she said. "You ever get to San Antonio, look me up. I'm not hard to find."

Epilogue

The fundamental fact is that the present-day Ranger has no frontier upon which to paint a heroic picture of daring and courage. The Ranger of the old order belonged to a primitive and highly individualistic society which offered him great opportunities. The modern, complex society has reduced his proportions, but it has not changed his nature.

—Walter Prescott Webb, *The Texas Rangers: A Century of Frontier Defense*

There was a reception at the ranch for those who'd attended the funeral of Clinton Samuels, and when these few had gone, Caitlin and Cort Wesley sat at the oak butcher-block table with Bo Dean Perry and Terrell Scuggs. Luke Torres clung to his father's shoulder while Dylan sat moping in an easy chair, sullen over Maria Lopez being taken into custody by immigration officials so she could be returned to her family in Mexico.

"Say," Bo Dean Perry said to Caitlin, angling his wheelchair toward her, "I ever tell you 'bout the time your granddad tried to teach me how to draw?"

Caitlin had called Marianna Silvaro on her way to the ranch.

"Congratulations on your promotion to supervisor," Caitlin greeted.

"Tell me something, Ranger," Silvaro said from the office she'd moved into that very morning. "Do I have you to thank for this?"

"You have no one to thank other than yourself, ma'am. You were passed over for less-qualified applicants three times. The fourth being your last shot, I'd say justice was done."

"So there's no quid pro quo?"

"Ma'am?"

"I'm talking about the sons of Cort Wesley Masters."

"I'm confident the right thing'll end up getting done," said Caitlin.

"I turned over all my cases to the woman replacing me. The Masters file wasn't included. Investigation's been closed."

"Thank you, ma'am."

"Nothing to thank me for, Ranger. Just doing my job, like you."

"Anyway," Bo Dean Perry continued, "I didn't listen much to old Earl, being a stubborn young man, 'cause who needed to quick draw even in those days. Earl said I was missing the point. Well, about a year later, I was drawing my gun during a prison riot when the damn thing went off and winged me in the foot. I was so embarrassed I told folks I'd dropped a rock on it. Didn't bother listening to your granddad saying the draw's not about the speed, it's about process and technique. Hell, my foot still hurts most times when it rains."

Caitlin smiled. "You check in on D. W. Tepper?"

Terrell Scuggs, decked out in cowboy boots and old-style western holster as always, nodded. "Says he'll be back to work in no time and the doctors can't wait to be rid of him. Told me to tell you he's sorry, and that you'd know what he was referencing."

"He's got nothing to apologize for," Caitlin insisted, her voice sounding sadder than she'd intended. She wanted desperately to remember the night her mother had been killed, because until she did, it would feel unreal no matter how much she knew it to be true. But she also knew the terrible truth would no longer haunt her sleep, the nightmares replaced by the sad reality of that night years before that had left her soaked in blood and rain under a cottonwood tree.

"Well, lemme tell you something, missie," said Bo Dean Perry, "this Colonel Montoya's boys ever come back to Texas, they're gonna be chewing on the barrel of my Remington for breakfast and gulping down their own brains."

"I don't believe we'll be facing that problem," Caitlin told him. "I told Hollis Tyree the man responsible for the deaths of his children was still out there. Told him we can't get him and the Mexican government is still too frightened to try."

"What you suppose he'll do about that?"

Colonel Renaldo Montoya stood in the ruins of the Mayan temple, using a soft brush to clear away dust and dirt from the final drawing on the temple walls. He hoped it might yield some clue as to what had gone wrong, maybe provide a reason as to why. He still believed in his destiny, although now a different path was clearly required for him to achieve it.

In the wake of the End Times, the message from his Mayan ancestors was that a single man would lead the transition back to light once darkness consumed the world. His mistake had been to forge an alliance with the drug cartels whose priorities had muddled his own. Their dirty bombs would have been counterproductive, leading to a cataclysmic response in kind that could topple him from the very power he was prepared to seize. Much better to simply send his soldiers into the cities to wreak havoc in keeping with his original plan for a guerrilla war America was ill prepared to fight. They would blame the very same drug cartels and, from the presidential palace once his coup was complete, Montoya would pretend to crush them, only to continue his murderous rampage.

Montoya stepped back from the cleared final drawing to better regard it. But his eyes seemed to deceive him, the picture revealed making no sense at all:

What looked like a giant bird of prey, blood dripping from its beak and talons, descended on the same bullheaded figure who'd been on the verge of a great triumph over the vast army to the north in the previous drawings. Though a believer in *mut,* omens, Montoya could make no sense of what the surrounding glyphs called a *pip*.

Then he heard a crackling roar overhead, realizing in that moment that he wasn't Chahuku at all, nor was the big man the peasants called Ángel de la Guarda. Montoya stepped outside the temple just as the real bringer of thunder soared overhead in the form of a steel bird of prey, lightning spit from its underside. He'd gotten the End Times wrong; they had come early, now.

Montoya followed the missiles' sizzling descent, then closed his eyes to meet his ancestors in the last moment before a surge of heat nearly knocked him off his feet and the jungle exploded around him.

Caitlin walked with Cort Wesley along the rim of the saw grass. The fields looked finely mowed and plowed, the smell of old fertilizer replaced by the fresh scents of mesquite and pear cactus the cool wind had blown in.

Caitlin stopped and brushed the hair from her face. "What'd you tell Dylan about Maria?"

"That I'd drive him to Mexico to visit myself whenever he gets it in his mind."

"Being that he'd find his own way down there otherwise."

"Yeah, he's my son, all right. And stop changing the subject."

"Didn't know this conversation had one."

Cort Wesley picked up a strand of saw grass and stuck it in the corner of his mouth. "You don't remember watching your mother get gunned down."

"I think I've seen it in those nightmares, but the only thing that sticks in them is waking up in the storm."

Cort Wesley shot her a look that was strangely warm and reassuring. "That storm broke up your marriage and damn near broke us up too. It's like you can't let yourself get too close out of fear the same thing'll happen again. Anything not to become that little girl hiding from monsters in the thunder again. But I'm here to tell you they'll have to get through me first from now on."

Caitlin felt the breeze rustling through her hair and the sun warm on her neck. "Something tells me I won't be seeing that little girl anymore, Cort Wesley."

She'd started to reach for his hand, when her eyes shifted suddenly to the old fence line.

"What you looking at, Ranger?"

Cort Wesley followed her gaze to find, of all things, old Leroy Epps leaning against a rickety post still supporting some strings of wire.

"You can see him too, can't you?" he heard himself ask her.

But it was someone else Caitlin was seeing: Earl

Strong standing against a different fence post, pearl-handled Colts and all. She watched her grandfather stoke a match off the heel of his boot and light up a cigar, while Cort Wesley watched Leroy Epps drink out of a frosty bottle of the same root beer he'd smuggled into The Walls for the old man.

They started toward the fence line only to find Earl and Leroy gone by the time they got there, the smells of tobacco and soda pop lingering until the wind brushed them away.

Read on for a preview of Jon Land's

STRONG AT THE BREAK

•

Available now from Tom Doherty Associates

I

QUEBEC; THE PRESENT

From the street the house looked like those nestled around it in the suburban neighborhood dominated by snow cover that had at last started to melt. A Mc-Mansion with gables, faux brick, and lots of fancy windows that could have been lifted up and dropped just about anywhere. The leaves had long deserted the tree branches, eliminating any privacy for each two-acre spread had the neighbors been around to notice. Problem was the neighborhood, part of a new plot of palatial-style homes, had been erected at the peak of a housing boom now gone bust, so less than a third were occupied.

Caitlin Strong and a Royal Canadian Mountie named Pierre Beauchamp were part of a six-person squad rotating shifts in teams of two inside an unsold

Copyright © 2011 by Jon Land

home diagonally across from the designated 18 Specter, the marijuana grow house they'd been eyeballing for three weeks now. She'd come up here after being selected for a joint U.S. and Canadian drug task force looking into the ever-increasing rash of drug smuggling across a fifteen-mile stretch of St. Regis Mohawk Indian Reservation land that straddled the border.

Beauchamp lowered his binoculars and made some notes on his pad, while Caitlin looked at him instead of raising hers back up.

"Something wrong, Ranger?"

"Not unless you count the fact I got no idea what we're trying to accomplish here."

"Get the lay of the land. Isn't that it?"

"Seems to me," Caitlin told the Mountie, "that the DEA got that in hand already. You boys too."

"It's task force business now. We need to build a case for a full-on strike."

"You telling me the Mounties couldn't have done that already, on their own?"

"Not without alerting parties on the other side of the border, who'd respond by dropping their game off the radar, eh? When we hit them, the effort's got to be coordinated and sudden. That doesn't mean two law enforcement bodies working in tandem, it means two *countries*. And that, Ranger Strong, is never a simple prospect."

"So we've got to tell both sides what they know already."

Beauchamp shrugged. "Put simply, yes."

"I guess I'm just not cut out for this sort of game," Caitlin said and sighed.

The thunk of car doors slamming froze Beauchamp's response before he could utter it. Both he and Caitlin had their binoculars pressed back against their eyes in the next instant, watching six big men in black tops, black fatigue pants, and army boots approach the grow house from a dark SUV lugging assault rifles and what looked like gasoline cans.

"Uh-oh," said Beauchamp.

"Hells Angels?" asked Caitlin, following a bald pair of black-garbed figures who looked like twins.

"Yup."

"What exactly are they doing here now, while there's people and drugs still inside?"

The Mountie moved his gaze back to her, his expression flatter than she'd seen in the three weeks they'd been working together. "Only one thing I can think of."

2

MOHAWK INDIAN RESERVATION;
THREE WEEKS EARLIER

The DEA's lead agent, Frank Gage, drove Caitlin out to the St. Regis Mohawk Indian Reservation first thing when she reached St. Lawrence County in upstate New York, her unpacked bags stowed in her motel room. They turned off Route 37 down a bumpy road formed of cracked pavement lost to the snow the farther they drew into the woods. March was the absolute dead of winter in these parts, and Caitlin had never seen so much snow and ice in her entire life, enough of it to make the trees sag under its weight.

"Peak of the season, this road's got more snow than you can imagine," he said, finally snailing his car to a halt in a clearing that opened into a picturesque, white-encrusted scene of a frozen river that somewhere contained the border between the United States and Canada.

Caitlin followed Gage out of the car and down a slight embankment atop snow that crunched underfoot before hardening into ice. Her boots had the wrong tread for this kind of ground and she found herself slipping, unsure exactly of where the land ended and frozen water began beneath them.

"Welcome to the source of our problems, Ranger," Gage told her.

"Where's the border exactly?"

"There isn't one. That's the problem," he said, pointing across the vast whiteness to the woods on the other side. "That's Canada over there, but it's also part of the Mohawk Reservation on their side of the border too."

Caitlin followed Gage's gaze and spotted an old Indian man cutting a hole in the ice. He had a fishing pole resting on a foldout chair behind him; if he was aware of their presence, he chose not to acknowledge it.

"Who's that?"

"Old tribal cop. A legend in these parts who hates the druggers almost as much as he hates us. Comes pretty much every day to catch his dinner. Locals say he might be as much as a hundred years old."

Caitlin watched the old man plop down in his chair and ready his pole over the perfectly circular hole he'd fashioned in the ice.

"That all makes this a virtual sovereign nation the Canadian authorities are reluctant to violate even more than we are," Gage said, picking up where he left off before Caitlin had been distracted by the old Indian. He turned toward her, breath misting in front of his face. "More drugs come into the country over this and other frozen rivers, what we call 'ice bridges,' than any other spot in the country."

"Excluding Mexico."

"No, Ranger, not excluding Mexico at all, no offense to you."

"None taken," Caitlin said, trying to make sense of what the DEA man was telling her.

"We estimate fifty-five billion dollars a year in drugs now comes in through Canada. Compare that with forty-five, maybe fifty, through Mexico."

"You telling me we been fighting the war on drugs in the wrong place?"

"I'm telling you that over the past five years or so a new front's opened up in that war and you're looking at it. Starts with the grow houses, pharma and meth labs organized throughout Quebec and parts of British Columbia by the Hells Angels."

"Same biker gang we got?"

"They operate on both sides of the border. An elaborate network of fully franchised businessmen backed up by the usual armed sons of bitches riding Harleys. Angels are responsible for manufacture and shipment across Mohawk land here with the Natives' full blessing, since plenty of them end up as major distributors of the product themselves. I'll show you the homes of some of the biggest suppliers later. Goddamn mansions sitting just down the road from shacks generally unfit for human habitation. Tribal dealers use runners to sell their product to networks loyal to Russian organized crime throughout New York, Ohio, and

Michigan. And that's just for starters since it doesn't even include the truckloads bound for other suppliers."

"You've sold me on the severity of the problem," Caitlin told him, feeling the wind sift through her hair. The air was bitingly cold, the bright sun offering a measure of respite, though not very much. "But I don't really see how the Texas Rangers can help you solve it, sir."

"Rangers can't; you can."

"Come again?"

"You've become a real authority on the subject, Ranger Strong."

"Not by choice, I'll tell you that much."

"All the same, you've been fighting your own war on drugs for more than two years now."

"Sure, back where it's smuggled in through tunnels dug out of the desert floor or old irrigation lines. Where I come from, we still got drug mules carrying product in rucksacks or on the backs of donkeys."

"While up here," picked up Gage, "it's driven by the truckload across frozen rivers by men who speak French instead of Spanish. You can see what I'm getting at."

"Not really, sir, no."

"Problem's the same; only the language and geography's different."

"I speak Spanish, not French."

Gage gave her a longer look this time. His thinning hair blew about in the stiff breeze, exposing a swatch of bald patches. He smoothed it back into place as best he could, but then a fresh thrust of wind tousled it once more.

"Only language drug people speak is money. Accents don't matter a whole hell of a lot to them. Where we're at now is the planning stage. Trying to handle this piecemeal's gotten us nowhere. What the task force is putting together is an overall strategy, kind of a master plan."

Gage had continued to kick at the gathered snow, revealing a deep symmetrical, crisscrossing pattern cut in the ice. Caitlin followed the pattern farther out onto the ice, convincing herself it ran from one side of this frozen swatch of the St. Lawrence River all the way across to the other.

"What is it?" Gage asked her.

"These trucks of yours carry enough weight to need snow chains?"

"Never thought about it."

Caitlin rose from her crouch, brushing the snow from her gloves. "You should, sir. What we got here looks to be big freight jobs running on double tires with only the outer ones chained. You're talking about some haul if it's drugs they're carrying in those cargo bays."

Gage finally looked up from the chain marks and studied Caitlin for what seemed like a long time, long enough for her to note his cheeks had gone cherry red in the cold while his nose remained milky pale, like his whole face was out of sync.

"I'm operating on a shoestring here," he told her. "Six agents, some locals and state cops out of New York, the Royal Canadian Mounted Police, a tribal policeman, and now you."

"Well, now that makes me feel a whole lot better."

"It's like this," Agent Cage explained. "The growers buy homes at foreclosure sales mostly across Quebec and British Columbia as well as outside Toronto and other venues. They pretty much gut the interiors to turn them into grow houses for an especially potent strain of marijuana known as BC Bud. The head growers get all the soil laid down, seeds planted, lighting and environment set up and turn things over to immigrants to handle the tender loving care."

"Did you say immigrants?"

"I did indeed, Ranger. Chinese mostly, totally beholden to the druggers for their very lives after being smuggled out of their home countries. A separate syndicate charges a fee to get the immigrants into Canada and then turns them over to the druggers to work off the rest with a ticket to the good old USA when the time comes. Poor bastards can see the American Dream across the border and will do pretty much anything they're told."

"My granddad arrested plenty of Mexican runners in the thirties bringing marijuana and black tar heroin across the border for pretty much the same reason."

"Hard-core druggers have certainly made a life's work out of feeding on desperation, haven't they? By the time their pigeons realize they've signed on to a sham, fear keeps them in line." Gage shook his head, thin wisps of hair shifting with it. "Not much changes."

Caitlin looked toward the vast expanse of land across the frozen river that looked postcard pretty and very small in the distance, thinking about another front opened in a war they were already losing. "In this case, it just gets worse."

3

"What do you mean?" Caitlin asked Beauchamp, watching the black-garbed figures heading up the walk to the front door, three of them lugging the gasoline cans.

"Didn't Agent Gage explain what the Angels do to the houses once they're done with them, once the mold sets in?"

"Burn them to the ground. Only this house hasn't been harvested. No mold yet, nothing like that. And there's still people inside."

"Meaning . . ."

"Jesus Christ," realized Caitlin, binoculars still glued to her eyes, "they're on to us."

"It does seem that way, eh?"

Caitlin moved closer to the window in response. "How many immigrants we got in that house?"

Beauchamp checked his notebook, flipping back a few pages. "Seven, by my count. I recognized two of the Hells Angels, the big bald ones with those arrow tattoos painted on their skulls: the LaChance brothers. They're from your side of the border in Michigan but wanted for murder in Canada too."

Caitlin lowered her binoculars and watched the Mountie fumble for his cell phone. "Then how 'bout we go arrest them?"

But Beauchamp had the phone at his ear. "We gotta call Gage first. See how he wants this handled."

Caitlin was already on her feet, pushing the blood back into her legs, taking her mind to a distant, yet familiar place. "Only one way it can be handled, Mountie."

"He's not answering." Beauchamp's eyes flared in the room's thin, ambient light. "I've heard the Rangers are the next best thing to Mounties."

"Funny," said Caitlin, "I've heard almost the same thing."

Standing now, Caitlin pressed her binoculars back against her eyes and focused on the grow house. She caught splotchy glimpses of some of the Angels spreading the gasoline about, dousing everything in their paths. There were glimpses too of the biggest ones, the American LaChance brothers, smacking a few of the Chinese around, ignoring their protestations since clearly they held no more value than the lumber and furnishings about to go up in an inferno.

"They're gonna burn those Chinese along with everything else," Caitlin said and pushed back her jacket to expose her holstered SIG Sauer nine-millimeter pistol.

"Then what are we waiting for?" Beauchamp asked her, pocketing his phone and ripping out his pistol in its place.